SHRUTHI RAMAN

Hide and Go Seek

First edition

Editing by Ashley Wyrick

This book was professionally typeset on Reedsy.
Find out more at reedsy.com

393000006448574

Contents

II   I Am Not In The Dark Anymore

Dedication

For Mom, Dad, Shreya, and Sidharth, for listening to my ridiculous, fantastical stories.

Prologue

It smelled so citrusy and good, and she remembered watching the sunset, with Peter's fingers still entwined in hers. Peter had reached into his messenger bag then, and pulled out a daisy as pure and white as a dove. His big green eyes searched her gray ones for permission, and when she smiled at him, he reached up and put it in her dark, raven-colored hair. She remembered looking at the fiery tail of sparks that the sun left behind. Peter was looking at her as if she were the sun, if he could stare at the sun directly without damaging his eyesight. In his mind, she was just like the sun, shining brightly and lighting everything around it ablaze, such as his own, young heart.

I

When I Am In The Dark

When I am in the dark
And I cannot see
When I am lost
Who will be there for me?
Like a blanket in the cold
Or a lighthouse at sea
Will someone take my hand
When I am in the dark
And I cannot see?

1

A Secret

C assandra Black was not an ordinary girl. At least, she strived not to be. Since she was five years old, she hated the idea of being like everyone else. To blend in with the crowd. To be yet another smiling face in a yearbook filled with a million other faces. To be jaded and forgotten after she was gone. So, she decided to live an extraordinary life.

She was a rather peculiar young lady. For one, she listened to a lot more music than was humanly possible. Secondly, she obsessed over Billboard's Top 100 almost as much as she listened to music. Lastly, she always dressed in black. However, Cassandra was not a goth, had never been a goth, and never would be a goth. She dressed in black to symbolize that a hundred, maybe a hundred and twenty years from now, we would all eventually fade and wither away, forgotten and faded, as flowers when removed from their bushes.

Pulvis et umbra sumus.
We are but dust and shadows.
~Horace

Cassandra's early life was rather tragic, and it was unusual for a 16-year-old to have experienced so much tragedy in their short life, but she tried to stay positive. Cassandra was five when it happened, and she barely remembered it, for which she was grateful. Remembering meant hurting, and even though the memories can fade, the hurt never does. It pierces like a knife through the heart until one fine day it gives in. She could just barely remember her parents' faces, but the details had eroded and faded away, as time wears us all away slowly. All she remembered of her parents was a beautiful face with long black hair cascading down her shoulders, beautiful gray-blue eyes shining when they looked at her, and a man with ruffled brown hair and kind hazel eyes that were framed by black glasses. She could still see the jewelry box that her mother had owned, though. She could see it as clearly as if it had been printed into her brain. The jewelry box was small and silver, and when wound up, played a beautiful, but somber, song. The interior was a soft, velvety pink, and it had a small mirror in the shape of an oval, just behind a little ballerina, dressed in pink. This ballerina twirled while music played.

She had been sleeping when it happened. It was around midnight. A fire had started in the house. Her mother woke up first, hearing the noise. She shook her husband awake and told him to exit the house immediately and call for help. She said that she would find Cassandra and bring her out. Cassandra's father protested and tried to convince her to let him do it, but her mother, strong-willed as ever, refused and forbade him from doing so. She went into her daughter's bedroom and woke her up. Quickly, they had made their way to the entrance of the home to exit when suddenly, the ceiling caved in. Her mother had pushed her out of the door just in time and saved her life for the price of her own. One month later, her father had committed suicide because of heartbreak. Cassandra then learned a very valuable lesson in life after that tragic occurrence, that love can cut through the heart like a knife, and therefore should be avoided at all costs.

After her father had died, Cassandra went to live with some distant relatives from her father's side, in hopes that they would treat her as if she were their own child.

Oh, how wrong she was.

They always acted like she didn't exist. They never spoke to her, apart from the occasional grunt. They had two children, who were around

Cassandra's age, who they loved dearly, named Helen and Rowan. Helen
and Rowan mimicked their parents and treated Cassandra no better than
their parents did. Cassandra didn't think she could handle living there if
she hadn't had Jamie.

James Carter Taylor was her best friend and had always been there for
her. Cassandra couldn't think of a time when she didn't have Jamie by her
side, for he had always been there for her, and would always be there for her.
Like a stone, she felt he would always be a familiar light in the dark, and
she felt very grateful for it. They were the best of friends and had sworn to
keep it that way.

* * *

On Saturday morning, Cassandra awoke to the sound of shouting. The
sunlight cascaded into the spare bedroom her guardians had grudgingly
given her through the window on the wall and lit the room with a bright
kind of light. Cassandra rose from the small, twin-sized bed to open her
door and peer curiously outside to see what was happening. Helen was in
another one of her rages, and this time it was because Rowan had borrowed
one of her dresses and stained it. "You're such a klutz, and you have no
respect for other people's property!" she shouted to her sister.

"It's called BLEACH!" Rowan shouted back.

Cassandra walked out of her room after she was done brushing her teeth,
and started to make her way downstairs to make breakfast. She made her
way down the staircase and pulled out a pan from the cabinet, and a few
ingredients from the pantry. Mixing together the ingredients for pancakes,
soon enough, she was piling up pancakes on the plates for her aunt, uncle,
and cousins, leaving just one for herself.

Cassandra sighed. She hated cooking. She only did it because her
guardians forced her to. Now, her aunt, uncle, and cousins just started
to come down, and she glanced up. Her aunt considered her as if she were
looking at a large black cockroach in the middle of her beautiful living room.
She did not show any emotion right now, for she was used to it. However,

when Cassandra had finished her breakfast and started to make her way back to her room, she hid her extended middle finger in the pocket of her worn-out jeans.

When she got back to her room, she started to play her acoustic guitar. It had been a gift from her other half, Jamie, and helped to get rid of the uncontrollable rage that filled her when her aunt treated her like garbage. She poured her heart out into the chords; lived and breathed the notes. Suddenly, she heard her own name being called. She recognized it as Helen's voice. Cassandra hastily put her guitar back into her hiding place beneath her bed as Helen burst into the room without knocking. She kept her guitar hidden, for if Helen knew she loved it, she would surely destroy it.

Helen cleared her throat loudly as she strutted into her room, and Cassandra looked up with an annoyed expression on her face. "Cassandra, take this dress to the dry cleaners, Jason asked me out to the movies tomorrow, and I want it washed so I can wear it there."

"Say please," Cassandra said. With her aunt, there was no pushing back, but with Helen and Rowan, she could give them all the hell that they gave her.

Helen stuck her nose in the air like the spoiled little brat that she was. "Why don't you try and make me?"

"I could, but I couldn't guarantee that Jason would still want to go out with you after that,"

Helen swore and threw the short, purple dress onto Cassandra's desk, scuttling out of the room like Cassandra was emitting some sort of poisonous odor. However, Cassandra did not much care, for her attention had been occupied by a clatter that told her that something had fallen off her desk and shattered. Cassandra fell to her knees immediately to examine what had broken. Once she saw what it was, two emotions broke free inside of her– her heart sunk with sorrow, and she almost went out of her mind with a murderous type of anger. Helen stood watching safely outside, and when she looked up, Cassandra wished not for the first time that she could wipe that smirk off of her pretty, smug little face. By the time Helen had slammed the door behind her, and Cassandra decided that she would do it, would finally kill her, would finish the job tonight. She was looking at a million small and shattered pieces of the small jewelry box her mother had given her before she had died. Cassandra grabbed her worn jacket and ran out the door.

She didn't stop until she was far into the woods behind the house. Cassandra's eyes scanned around for The Tree, not any tree, but the single most important tree out of all the trees in the vast woods. The Tree was immense with thick roots where Jamie and Cassandra always met to talk. Once she found it, she ran to it. She found Jamie sitting under it, smiling up at her. Jamie's tousled blond hair reached just above his shoulders, and some of it fell into his eyes, but he didn't care enough to push it away. Jamie had always been the one person who had been able to read her like a book. As he looked at her, he quickly realized that she was distraught.

"Cassie? Did something happen?" This was amazing, Cassandra thought, for she had practiced hiding her emotions for what seemed like her entire life and was good at it too. But all disguises fell away before Jamie's luminous green eyes. She could build up walls, and hide inside her fortress, but Jamie had always been able to pull it apart effortlessly.

"Cassie?" Jamie asked again. No one called her Cassie but Jamie. She had to admit that she liked the way it sounded on his lips. So she let him. With a sigh, Cassandra started describing the events of the morning to him.

When she finished, Jamie told her, "Cassie, I'm so sorry. You could bring it to my house later today. I have super glue. We can try to put it back together."

Cassandra shook her head sadly. "There's no use. It broke into tiny pieces. It'll never be the same." Suddenly, a hopeless rage flared inside her, lighting everything inside of her on fire. "Let's see how she likes it when I break her into very small pieces," she remarked nastily.

Jamie laughed. He looked charming when he laughed, Cassandra noticed, which was peculiar, since she had never paid much attention to looks. Jamie took her hands gently, as if they were made of glass and could shatter at any moment if he weren't careful enough, and looked directly into her gray-blue eyes. He said, "Will you come, anyway? I have something to tell you." His face turned a deep scarlet, and he looked away.

"Jamie, what is it? Why are you acting so weird? Are you okay?"

Jamie shook his head, and blond hair fell into his eyes. He impatiently pushed it aside. "Later."

Cassandra rolled her eyes at him but smiled. Jamie could always make her smile, no matter how sad she was. "Come on. Let's go to the library."

2

Pink Ballerina

When Cassandra got back from the library, the summer sun was shining weakly through her blinds, which cast shadows against the red wall. She was heavily laden with books, and she started to make her way to the other side of her room to arrange them on the bookshelf when she felt a searing pain on her foot. She scowled and looked down to see pieces of the jewelry box strewn on the floor, where she had neglected cleaning them up. After putting the books on the shelf, she attended to the mess with a broom and a dustpan. When she was done, she examined the dustpan to see if there were any large pieces that she could keep. She was disappointed to find that there were no significant pieces of porcelain when something caught her eye. It was the pink ballerina, the one that twirled when wound up. It had a small, pale face and was wrapped in a baby pink tutu. Its delicate feet were adorned with pink ballet shoes. But this was not what interested her. What interested her was that the ballerina was too made of porcelain, but it had not broken in the three feet fall from Cassandra's desk to the floor. With a funny look on her face, Cassandra picked up the small ballerina. She then used a stray piece of metal spring to clasp the small ballerina onto the locket her father had given her when she was four. She always had the locket around her neck, so a piece of her childhood would always be near her heart. She tucked the pink ballerina under her shirt, where it wouldn't be spotted by Rowan and Helen, who would likely make fun of her if they saw it.

Cassandra took Helen's dress to the dry cleaner's on her way to Jamie's house. She followed the familiar route to his house, walking because she knew her relatives wouldn't drive her there if she begged them to. The house was two stories, and the exterior was painted mahogany. No one but Jamie was home, because his mom had work and he was an only child.

He was seated in a white lounging chair at the porch with his speaker blasting a song named "Wild Love" by James Bay. He looked up at her and smiled when she arrived. "James Bay's new album is the reason for my existence," Cassandra remarked.

Jamie smiled as if to say, 'this is why we are such good friends.' "It really is pretty amazing. Would you like to come in?"

Cassandra nodded, and the pair walked inside to Jamie's room. They spent half an hour just talking about the latest rock music and the recent occurrences on Billboard's top 100. And then, Cassandra asked him what he wanted to tell her.

"So, what did you want to tell me?" Cassandra inquired.

"Um…" Blood rushed to Jamie's face as he stammered. Cassandra was shocked. She had never seen her best friend look so uncomfortable before. Cassandra took his hand and looked into his eyes. Stormy gray met sea green, and Cassandra said, "Jamie, you know you can tell me anything, right? What happened? Why are you acting so weird?"

"I have an idea. Why don't we just go back to rock music and forget I ever said I wanted to tell you something. That's a great idea, isn't it? Let's do that!"

"Jamie, just tell me what you wanted to tell me and I'll stop bugging you."

"Did you know James Bay can play electric guitar and acoustic? He's good at it too. Just listen to Pink Lemonade in his newest— "

"Jamie,"

"And Avenged Sevenfold wrote this song called 'Nightmare.' It's pretty good. I think you'll like it too. It has a few curses though, but— "

"Jamie,"

"And I heard this new song that I really like. It isn't rock, it's pop, but it's still pretty good. It's called "Bored" by Billie Eilish. She's popular but not too popular, which is why she hasn't made it onto Billboard yet, but I hope she— "

"Jamie!"

"Oh, alright, fine. What I wanted to say was that I… I just… I really… I really like you, Cassie." He bit his lip and looked up at her through his long, dark eyelashes. He had a tentative look in his eyes.

"I really like you too. You're my best friend."

"No. I mean… I love you, Cassie. I have for twelve years. I hid it from you for this long, and I can't anymore."

Cassandra's eyes were wide. "No. I can't. I mean… I don't love you. Love makes you weak, and I'm not weak." Cassandra turned away and started to get up from her seat on the floor near the window. As she turned away, she saw the hurt on Jamie's face.

Jamie got up immediately and said, "I understand. I'm sorry to have sprung that on you. I hope we can still be friends. I'd rather have you as a friend than not at all." Jamie looked up at Cassandra and saw the pained expression on her face. "Cassandra, I…" but it was too late. She had run from the room.

Cassandra raced from Jamie's house back the way she had come and into the woods. She found The Tree and sank down near its roots. She hugged her knees and rested her forehead on them. She heard her phone ring. She looked up at it for a moment. It was Jamie. Stuffing it into her pocket, she ignored the next nine phone calls. Eventually, they stopped. Jamie must have realized that Cassandra didn't want to talk. Suddenly, she thought she saw a flash of flame and a face. She assumed she was seeing things. Cassandra gazed up at the sky, and her breath was taken away. The summer sun was starting to set, leaving a beautiful outburst of color in its wake. Cassandra recalled a line from a poem she had read somewhere.

Nothing gold can stay.

~Robert Frost

She thought about how this was true about her friendship with Jamie. She couldn't get the look of hurt on Jamie's face out of her mind, as if she had stabbed him with a knife. She hated herself for snapping at him, for making him hurt the way he had. She also hated him for telling her that he loved her and making her snap at him. She wanted nothing to do with him; she only wanted to distance herself from him, make sure that there is absolutely no chance that she falls in love. Because falling in love is like falling off a cliff– there's no coming back.

3

And It All Burned Up

Sunlight. Catching the shiny, delicate glass of the ballerina's shoes and setting them aflame in an explosion of light. Sunlight, reflecting on the small, beautiful drops of dew that the leaves adorned so arrogantly like expensive jewelry. Everywhere, bringing the dark mahogany of The Tree's trunk to a warmer, coppery shade of russet, sunlight, illuminating the whole world and bringing light to the darkest of places.

But now, though the sunlight lit everything up with a gentle, warm feeling, something stronger, more powerful filled the air around her, lighting her up with manic energy. Something was undeniably not right. She could smell it in the air, and on her mind, and some little voice inside of her that had kept its sanity where the rest of her had fallen away to pieces told her to run, run away, run far away.

Everything was dark, then it all lit up.

It was dark but light. Ignorance, but knowing what was going on. Wanting to be seen but hiding in the shadows. Everything burning down until there was nothing left. And nothing did survive, but herself, her father, and the jewelry box. But what was the point of any of it when it was all gone? Everything had gone for her father immediately when her mother died, and everything had gone for Cassandra slowly, piece by piece, first when her mother had died, second when her father killed herself, lastly, when Helen had broken the jewelry box. What was left? All that was left was the shadow of a girl with the ghost of a feeling of love.

And it all burned up.

She could see the flames again now, vividly, as though it were real, really happening again, smoke and fire and ashes and tears.

And there was a boy holding a teddy bear and a rose.

She opened her eyes and started. She had heard the faintest of sounds– a leaf rustling and a twig snapping. Cassandra stood immediately and walked around to the back of The Tree. She peeked out then, curiously. She had always been curious. Curious about everything. Suddenly, she saw a flash of brown hair. Then, two girls and a boy emerged to the clearing near The Tree. Two of them looked about 16, the last about 14.

The boy with brown hair and amber eyes said to his companions, "And he set fire to everything. Luckily, I had my blessed metal blade with me, so I was able to drive the spirit away before it could do any more harm to anyone else." Cassandra blinked. She must have been hallucinating. Just then, she lost her footing and slipped. She met the ground and ducked out of sight, but it was too late, for the trio had already seen her. The blonde was the first to react. Swiftly, she moved to stand immediately in front of Cassandra, who had moved out of the way of The Tree when she saw that the group had already seen her and there was no point of hiding. She was standing so close to her that it was rude and looking at her as if she were something disgusting she had found under her shoe. Cassandra stood her ground and looked up at her with a glare that had just as much venom as the one she was giving her and some more, too. Cassandra cursed herself silently for letting her walls down in the short amount of time that she was sitting under The Tree and gazing up at the fiery sunset. But they were already up again as if they had always been there.

"What do you think you're looking at?" Cassandra spat.

"I think I'm looking at a girl who was eavesdropping on our conversation, you little sneak." The girl retorted.

"Call me that again honeybunch, and I'll shove my fist into that mess you call a face."

The girl glared at her.

The silence broke when the brown-haired boy started laughing. The girl turned around and looked at her accusingly. "What?" he asked. "You deserved that!"

She turned back to Cassandra. "Who sent you?"

"Yo mama sent me. Who do you think sent me? I came here of my own accord." Cassandra shot back.

"My mother is dead. Who are you?" she returned.

"I don't see any reason that that's any of your business." Cassandra was not in the mood to take anyone's shit today. Not that she ever was.

"Roslyn. She's not acting. She legit has no clue what you're talking about." The brown-haired girl told the girl named Roslyn.

"You don't know that, Ana." The girl told her.

"I can see it on her face." The other girl, Ana, said.

With another glare, the blonde girl turned around and walked back to her friends. Cassandra stuck her tongue out at her. They turned to leave, but then she stopped. She turned around once more. "Did you see anything suspicious around here? A spark, maybe, or a flame, that may have appeared spontaneously? We've been getting reports of a spirit in these woods." Roslyn asked, her green eyes pierced into her gray ones.

"Maybe," Cassandra said casually, raising her eyebrows and smirking mockingly. Cassandra was thinking back to the flash of flame that caught her eye. Maybe she wasn't imagining things.

"Where did it go?"

"I never said I did."

Roslyn turned to leave.

"I never said I didn't either."

Roslyn made an exasperated sound. "Look, kid, if you saw something suspicious, just tell us now." He knew by the look on her face that he had said something wrong.

"I am not a kid. I'm freaking sixteen years old. You can call me Cass." Cassandra narrowed her eyes at her.

"I'm sorry," she said reluctantly and turned, though she didn't really sound even remotely remorseful. "Atticus, you look for the fire spirit that way,

15

Ana, you go that way. I'll go forward. Call me if you find it. Let's meet near the clearing if we don't see anything."

Cassandra started to walk away. She was disappointed. The one place that she thought no one would be at was infiltrated by three delusional teenagers. She was walking on the path back to her aunt and uncle's house when she saw the flame again. This time, it was more clear, and she saw the shadow of a man in it. Puzzled, she kept walking. Then, the flame kept getting nearer and nearer. The man in the flame approached her, but she didn't back away. She remembered how Jamie had always said that her pride was both a blessing and a curse because she had often gotten herself into trouble for it. She studied the man in the flame. He looked young, about twenty, with black hair and dark brown eyes, but there were circles under his eyes as if he had seen 100 years of sorrow rather than twenty. The man smiled. When he did, he looked absolutely dreadful, and Cassandra was disgusted, but she hid it well, the way she always did with Helen and Rowan. The flame expanded. Once again, Cassandra's pride got the best of her, and she didn't back away.

"What are you, and what do you want?"

The man said nothing but just growled. The fire expanded and touched her hand, but she felt no pain. She was astonished. In one mad moment, she grinned. Even though something quite peculiar and possibly life-threatening was going on, Cassandra, obdurate as ever, did not stray even an inch from her original position.

Now, the man grinned and started to mutter something incomprehensible under his breath. He reached out for Cassandra once more, and now, she felt astounding pain. Gritting her teeth in pain, she moved closer to the man and punched him. The man let out a scream. A third-degree burn appeared on his skin where Cassandra punched him. Cassandra grinned and punched him again, this time with more force. "That'll teach you to mess with me." The man cried out and grimaced. Cassandra flung out her foot at him. Her kick landed on his stomach, and the wind was knocked out of him instantly. He fell to the ground and groaned in pain. Cassandra put her foot on the fire spirit's chest and looked down at him. "This day just gets better and better," she told him. Cassandra was outraged. First, her idiot cousin breaks her jewelry box, the last thing her mother gave her before she died. Next, her best friend tells her that he wants to be more than best friends, then a rude boy has to start saying crazy, delusional things. Lastly, she finds out that those crazy, delusional things are true. Yup, this day simply was the best day ever. Suddenly, the girl named Ana walked out into the clearing.

"Guys, that girl we met earlier found it!" she called out to her friends. Shortly later, Roslyn and the boy that she had called Atticus came into the light. Atticus grinned at her. Ana came forward and pulled a long sword out of her belt as she did. She handed it over to Cassandra.

"You do the honors," she said to her. Cassandra grinned and took the sword from her. The sword fit into her hand just right, like it had been made for her. Something inside of her flared and blazed up, and she knew exactly what to do. Slowly, she raised the sword over her head and pulled it down swiftly, into the chest of the spirit. Before his eyes closed, the man grabbed Cassandra's leg and started whispering something under his breath. Cassandra said a word she knew her mother would hate if she were still alive and kicked the man one more time, hard. The man smiled and closed his eyes. "Congratulations! You just slew your very first spirit!" Ana said.

"Are you one of us?" The question was posed by Atticus, whose laughing eyes were now curious.

"What do you mean, one of you?" Cassandra was genuinely bewildered.

"Here, hold this." Atticus handed her a blade. Cassandra took it in her right hand. "Now focus." He told her. Cassandra closed her eyes and did just that. A gust blew through her hair, and suddenly everything just felt right. Cassandra felt her mouth quirk up at the corners. Atticus stepped forward and took her hand. He shoved the blade back into his jacket and examined her hand. The place where she just held the weapon had a red imprint on it. It was a symbol. The symbol was a rose with thorns, and it was already starting to fade away. Atticus grinned. "She is."

"I'm what?"

"Heaven's Chosen," Atticus replied.

17

"I have literally no idea what you're talking about. Either this is a really bad dream, or I finally lost it."

"Trust me. You haven't lost it. Yet." Atticus said with a smile. Cassandra punched him, laughing. She was grateful. She really needed a laugh right now. Ana launched into an explanation. She seemed the type to fill people in on things that they didn't know, or anything that pertained to intelligence. "The Pol Electi are a race of humans who have the courage and bravery to
   do anything. They are fearless and strong and possess the ability to see and fight ghosts."

"So, what I just killed was a ghost?" Cassandra asked, half-joking.

"Yeah," Ana answered, as though she were as secure in the existence of ghosts as she were in the sun coming up in the morning.

"No. That did not just happen."

Ana smiled.

"So that's why that man got third-degree burns when I punched him." Cassandra reasoned.

"Actually," Atticus intervened, "That was actually not supposed to happen. Do you have blessed metal?"

Cassandra looked at him as if he had just told her that the earth was really a giant doughnut.

"Huh. That's weird. Usually, when a spirit uses its elemental power on one of us, we cannot escape it unless we have blessed metal. It reduces the effects of evil energies and spirit magic." He explained.

Cassandra looked at the ground where the spirit was laying. "Now, what do we do? Is he just gonna stay there?"

"Nah. We're gonna trap it in this Arca. " He held up a transparent tube. He crouched down and held the tube slightly above the spirit. The spirit started spinning and assumed the shape of a small black tornado, the thinnest part of it at the tube. As soon as it was fully in, Atticus took a cork and slammed it at the rim, sealing it shut and giving her a wicked grin when he saw her bewildered expression.

"When we get back to the sanctuary, we're gonna send it through the portal to hell," Ana answered her unasked question. The three friends turned around and started to walk away.

Cassandra sank down. She felt a searing pain in her leg that she had tried to ignore, but could not ignore anymore.

"Are you coming?" Atticus called out to her. Cassandra didn't answer. He turned around and saw Cassandra crouched on the ground. "Hey. Are you alright?" Now Ana and Roslyn turned around to see what was happening.

"I'm fine. And I'm not coming with you. I've had enough madness for a month." Cassandra attempted to stand up but stumbled. Too proud and arrogant to let anyone see her fall, she leaned against a tree. The pain was getting more intense.

"I think you've been cursed, Cass. You need to come with us to the Sanctuary. May is good with this stuff. She can fix you up."

"I'm fine," said Cassandra.

"You should probably have a healing elixir before it's too late. Spirit curses can lead to death if not healed properly within three hours, depending on how strong you are." Ana added helpfully.

"I'm good." Cassandra was picking up a fallen branch from the ground and using it to help her stand.

"You don't look good. You need help. Seriously. Your leg is bleeding." said Atticus. Roslyn didn't seem to care whether she lived or died, with the expression on her face.

Cassandra looked down at her leg. It was indeed bleeding, and her blood was staining her ripped jeans. Atticus came to her assistance. "I said, I'm fine!" she said, and pushed off the tree and used her makeshift walking stick to walk. She got approximately three steps away from the tree before she passed out and collapsed into Atticus' arms.

4

Constipated

She didn't have the nicest childhood. Born to a Caucasian father and an Indian mother, she was biracial and often faced teasing from other children for her being so. Neither side of the family approved of the marriage, and all three of them were shunned from the family and were no longer invited to birthday parties, weddings, or any other special events that happened in the family. It had pained her plenty of times to hear of other children enjoying their grandparents' company and speaking of visiting their homes, for her own had cut off all ties to herself and her parents.

She was born in Canada but later moved to New York. She was raised on the crowded streets of Brooklyn, and she had picked up a lot of bad habits that her mother and father reprimanded her for. She remembered getting scolded for holding up her middle finger at a man who had stepped on her foot and "forgotten" to apologize. Yes, it was wrong of him to do that, and yes, he was an idiot who deserved to fall down a cliff somewhere and die, but no, it was not alright for her to use epithets, her parents had told her. She remembered coming home drunk once. She was grounded for two weeks. Her parents were strict, but she supposed that the discipline that they raised her with was why she was such an amazing person.

Though those who were around her truly believed that she had a lot of self-confidence, it was all fake. A cover-up for the lack of confidence, the insecurities and fears that she had developed in her childhood. It was like a wall. A wall that she had built around herself, metaphorically speaking, the self-confidence was like an additional layer of paint added onto a wall to cover up the peeling paint beneath.

But he had seen through the paint. He saw past the wall and past the numerous layers of paint she had put down to hide away, and he had stripped it all away effortlessly. There was something about his voice that made her want to tell him everything, and nothing but the truth every time. She supposed that this was dangerous. Then, she had found out that it wasn't his voice, or the beating of his heart, or even his steady breathing when he was sleeping, that assured her that he was human, that he was there, and that if she broke down these walls, she'd find him hidden there. There was something about him that made her want to pour herself out to him, or even tear herself apart for him. That was when she found out that she loved him.

She had learned that love was not about beauty, or money, or race, or religion, but about a mutual feeling that you would do anything for someone else. She didn't know what he looked like, or how wealthy he was, or what his race was, or his religion, or how attractive he was, but she was ready to walk through hell for him. She used what her parents had told her about love and what she had learned from books to guess that this was love. If this wasn't love, she didn't know what was.

She loved music. She had an angel's voice. She aspired to be a singer when she grew up. She remembered singing in her cell once, a piece that spoke of sorrow, hope, and peace. She had thought no one was paying attention. He had been quiet for a while, so she had assumed that he was asleep. She probably wouldn't have sung if she had known he was awake. He didn't speak until she was finished, and he told her that she loved her voice.

"That was so beautiful. Why didn't you tell me that you had an angel's voice?"

"You heard all of that? I thought you were asleep."

"Thank goodness I wasn't. It was the most alluring sound I have ever heard."

"You thought that was good?"

"Of course." he sounded incredulous. "You have taught me the meaning of true beauty in five minutes."

"Thank you. That means a lot to me."

"Don't thank me. Just sing for me again."

And so she did.

"Your voice makes me feel like I'm flying. I get the best feeling in the world when you sing. I feel like I'm…free again. Thank you for making me feel so alive," he had thanked her, and erupted into a fit of coughing.

"Are you alright?"

The coughing stopped abruptly, and after a moment, he spoke to her. "Thank you for your concern. I am fine."

"What was that? Are you sick?"

"Yes."

"How sick?"

"Very sick. I wasn't born sick; I just got sick. They took me from my parents and my little sister. They thought that I was the blessed one. They were wrong." He laughed, but there was no humor in it. It sounded hollow and sad. "They tested me with the fireball, but I survived. But there's a catch. I caught a disease from the deepest realms of hell, where spirit magic comes from."

"Oh, why didn't you tell me? Is there a cure?"

"I don't know. And even if there is, it would probably be hard to come across, because it's a hell disease. They've kept me here because of it. They made a fake body for the Pol Electi to recover, and they're observing me."

"Oh, I'm so sorry. I'm going to get you out of here. I'm getting you out of this hellhole and back to the earth, and I'm going to find you a cure. I'm going to fix you up. I'm not going to let anything happen to you. I promise."

"Why? Why would you go to all of that trouble for me?"

"Because…well, I don't know exactly."

"There's something that scares me."

"What scares you?"

"What scares me is that I can see the same for you. What is that?"

"I think it's…love."

"Love? Do you love me?"

She swallowed. "I think so."

He took a moment before he confessed, "I think I might just love you too."

"Really?"

"Really. I've never been in love before, but I think this might be it."

She laughed. "How do you like it?"

He considered it for a moment. "A lot. I feel ecstatic, and giddy, and reckless, and young, and free, like I'm flying, and high, like I took a dozen shots, and there's this feeling in my stomach, like butterflies, and I feel…"

"How do you feel?"

"Promise not to laugh."

"I promise."

"Constipated."

She giggled. "You feel constipated?"

"You promised not to laugh!"

"I'm not laughing. I'm giggling."

"That's not fair!" but he was already laughing.

5

Feisty

When she woke up, she was in a room with four mahogany walls. She was lying on a soft bed, and there were no bandages on her leg. Her leg looked and felt as if she had never been cursed. There was a mahogany side table near her bed, and there was a cup of black liquid next to a get well card. She picked up the card, curious to see who it was from. It had a picture of a bouquet of flowers on the front. The inside was empty except for a line scrawled in messy handwriting near the bottom. It said,

Told you you weren't fine. :P
~@icus

Cassandra couldn't help but laugh. Just then, a woman walked in. She had graying brown hair and a kind face. "Are you feeling better, dear? Is your leg better?" she asked. Her face had a calming feature to it, though Cassandra couldn't quite place her finger on it, it was there. Something like a motherly look for a stranger. Cassandra already felt so much better.

"Yeah. I feel better. I'll get going now. Thank you." She pushed aside her blankets and started to get up. She was still wearing her ripped white sweater and her ripped bloodstained jeans. Thirty seconds later, she sank back down, clutching her head.

The woman rushed forward. "You'll need to drink that elixir, dear. It'll help make up for all the blood you've lost. Then, you should take some rest. You won't be absolutely better until tomorrow." Though her face was kind, her voice was firm.

Cassandra opened her mouth to protest, but her head screamed in agony, and she nodded her head reluctantly and pulled herself back under the sheets. The woman that Atticus had referred to as May took the black liquid from the side table and handed it to her. Cassandra took one sip, expecting it to taste disgusting, but she was pleasantly surprised. It tasted of black cherries and blueberries. She sipped it slowly. When she was done, she set it back on the table. A wave of relief passed through her. Just then, the door opened, and Ana walked in. She smiled at her.

"Are you feeling better now?"

"Much better," Cassandra said, and she was pleased to report that she was telling the truth. "Where are we?"

"This is the Sanctuary of New Jersey. It's called that because our kind is hunted by spirits, so we created the Sanctuary, a safe haven for Pol Electi. We use this place to hide from evil spirits, and every now and then we track and kill them for kicks. Besides, we kind of have to. They can hurt humans, and humans can't see them, and therefore can't defend against them, so we're supposed to protect them. We have a portal here, and we use it to send them where they belong. Not all spirits are evil, though. The good ones find their way to heaven." Ana said.

Cassandra was baffled. "So they just up and turn evil?"

Ana's eyes lit up as if she were hoping that she'd ask. "When someone dies with unfinished business on earth, they turn evil with grief. We are supposed to send them to hell and not heaven for the sins they have committed. Once they are punished for their sins, they are allowed to go to heaven. It's a lot to swallow, I know, but you'll get used to it."

"So, there are spirits conspiring to attack me right now?" Cassandra asked sarcastically. She saw flashes of the fire that killed her mother in the back of her mind. She was puzzled.

"Actually, yes." The door opened again, and this time, it was Atticus and

Roslyn. Roslyn looked harried as if she had tried to convince Atticus into not coming to visit Cassandra, failed, and decided to come along due to lack of anything better to do.

"Hey," Cassandra said.

"'Sup?" Atticus said. His amber eyes that so resembled Ana's were looking straight at her, his expression easy going.

"Nothing much. Just lying in bed drinking weird liquids in a weird building with weird people I've just met who are telling me weird stories after just casually killing an evil spirit and helping capture it to send it to hell. No, it was just an ordinary day."

Atticus smirked. "Someone's feisty."

"I get that a lot."

"I can tell."

"Your eyes are just like Ana's."

"I didn't know you were paying that much attention to them," he told her in a smug voice, "She's my little sister." He really did look a lot like her. They shared the same skin tone, eye color, and brown hair, though where Atticus' hair was rather unruly, falling over his shoulders in adorable curls, Ana's was neat and braided. They both had extremely curly hair.

"Did you read my card?" he asked.

"No," she replied. Cassandra wasn't about to let him have the satisfaction that he was right.

"Oh." He looked slightly crestfallen. Cassandra almost felt bad for him, though not quite.

"So, we're going to a movie. You can come too, if you like," Ana invited.

"Ooh, is it horror? I love horror."

"Actually, we haven't chosen yet. We're putting it up for a vote."

"Cool. I'd love to come."

"Absolutely not," said May with her stern voice, walking into the room. "You have to take rest in order for the elixir to take action and replenish your blood supply."

"Aw, come on. There's a chance it's going to be a horror movie. You don't know how much I love horror." Cassandra protested.

"You heard me," said May, adding a little sass into the mix before she went to a different room of the Infirmary.

"Look, if you wanna come with, you'll need to sneak out without May figuring out. Otherwise, she'll be angry at all of us for not letting you take rest." Atticus said, a frightening look in his eye. "And, trust me, you don't want to get on May's bad side." He shuddered inwardly.

"Ok," Cassandra said, intrigued. "I'll meet you outside."

"Oh, and I brought you a spare outfit," said Ana. "I figured you'd wanna change." Cassandra looked down at her blood-spattered jeans and red-stained sweater.

"Thanks," Cassandra said and caught the jeans and t-shirt that Ana threw to her.

Roslyn stayed quiet through this entire conversation, her face glossed over with an expression that implied that she had better things to do and that she wished that she were elsewhere. Cassandra wondered what her problem was.

"How're you gonna get out without May noticing?" Atticus asked curiously.

"I'll figure it out," Cassandra said, grinning. The trio walked out of the room then, and Cassandra went into the bathroom to change. When she was finished, she washed her face and looked into the mirror. The only Cassandra she ever knew stared back at her. Long, messy black hair and gray-blue eyes. Helen always said that her complexion was too pale to look nice with a shock of black hair, but she had never really cared much. There was a brush in the dresser of the vanity. *My hair is messy. Should I brush it?* She thought to herself. She looked in the mirror and smiled. *Nah. I don't give enough shit to do that.* She walked out and crossed the room to open the window. A gust of night air flew in and ruffled her hair. She pushed the side table to the window. Then, she climbed the table and stood on top of it. Slowly, she lowered herself to the ledge of the window and sat down on it. She looked down. The height was dizzying, but Cassandra was unfazed. Heights didn't frighten her. She took a deep breath. And she jumped.

6

I Like It Like That

She landed on her feet, crouched, with one arm out to steady herself. She stood then and looked up. Ana, Roslyn, and Atticus were staring at her. She grinned. "Ready to go?"

"Did you really jump down the window?" Atticus asked.

"Yes," Cassandra replied.

"You realize that that was like 50 stories," Ana informed her.

"Yup,"

"And you figured, YOLO, if I die, it was worth it for kicks?" Atticus inquired.

"Uh-huh,"

"Does gravity not apply to you or something?"

"I don't know yet. Maybe I should go up to my room and jump again to see if it does." Cassandra started to the entrance of the Sanctuary.

"No! Let's just go. You don't need to jump again," Ana said.

"Okay, then. If you say so," Cassandra grinned.

"So the options are The Happytime Murder and Crazy Rich Asians," Atticus said. "Roslyn, what say you?"

"I've heard some good reviews on Crazy Rich Asians," Roslyn said. "Imma go with that."

"Ana. You next."

"You know how I am with horror. Rom-com all the way," Ana said.

"How are you scared of horror movies?" Cassandra asked disbelievingly. "You kill ghosts for a living."

Ana shrugged. "I don't want to constantly be doing something related to them. I see ghosts, I deal with ghosts, I kill ghosts. I don't want to have my life revolve around them. Besides," Ana added, "I like to keep my work life and my home life separate, like Wemmick from Great Expectations."

"Scaredy cat." Atticus teased. "Ouch!" Ana had kicked him in the shin. "Cass? You?"

"Horror. Rom-coms make me SICK," Cassandra replied.

"Me too! I can't stand them either," Atticus agreed.

"It's a tie. What're we gonna do?" Ana inquired.

"How about this? Roslyn and I can go to that rom-com, and you and Cass can go to the horror movie. We can meet outside when we're done and walk back to the Sanctuary together," Ana said.

"I-" Roslyn said, sounding tentative. "Can't we all just go to Crazy Rich Asians?"

"It's okay, Rosie," Atticus joked. "I'll keep Cass safe."

Cassandra made a sound of outrage. "I can take care of myself!"

Roslyn scoffed, looking her up lazily, exaggeratedly examining her leg, where she was cursed. Cassandra felt her face redden in anger. "Clearly not. Besides," Roslyn shook her head, "it's not that."

Atticus tilted his head, uncomprehending. "Then, what is it?"

Roslyn looked uncomfortable, then shook her head imperceptibly. "Nothing. That's a great idea."

"Great," said Ana, eager to break up the tension. They started walking to the theater. They walked on the sidewalk, which was paved elegantly. Shortly, they were at the theater, which was a large AMC. They walked in and went to the counter. Cassandra offered to pay for all of their tickets, to pay them back for saving her life by taking her to the Sanctuary for treatment after she got cursed, but they didn't let her. When they were done purchasing tickets, she and Atticus walked into screen six.

They chose seats at the back, where the best view was. There were the usual ads, and then the screen went blank for a bit, as the movie only started at 7:30. Atticus went to get popcorn.

Cassandra was bored, so she looked through her phone. She had twelve messages and eight voicemails, all from Jamie. She was curious, so she looked through them. Unfortunately for Jamie, she had no intention of answering to even one of them.

Cassie, are you okay?

Cassie, I'm so, so sorry.

Can we put this all behind us?

Please?

We don't ever have to talk about that again.

Can we please be friends again?

I promise I won't ever bring it up again.

Cassie, please.

I can't think of my life without you in it.

Cassie?

Are you there?

I'm sorry. :(

She was reading the last one as Atticus came back. He had a large bucket of popcorn in his hand as he sat down.

"Want some?" he asked.

"Nah. I'm good. Thank you, though."

"No problem." They then began to watch the movie, which had just started.

Halfway in, Cassandra said, "So how'd you like the movie so far? Is it good, or are you too scared?"

Atticus laughed. "'Scared' isn't in my dictionary. Are you?"

"Honey, horror movies are never in my nightmares, but rather in my dreams."

"Are you sure that's good for you? You could be mentally unstable." Atticus proposed, cracking her that usual puckish grin. It kind of infuriated her.

"There's nothing wrong with being a savage. If I didn't know any better, I'd say you were jealous," Cassandra told him, putting her nose in the air.

"Hardly. I can be pretty savage too," Atticus told her casually.

"I seriously doubt that." The movie started then. Cassandra smirked. She loved having the last word. When the movie ended, they waited outside. Unfortunately, they had to wait for half an hour, because Crazy Rich Asians was half an hour longer than The Happytime Murder. Cassandra decided to amuse herself by kicking pebbles she found on the sidewalk. Shortly, Atticus joined her. They had a kicking pebble competition, in which Atticus won. This occupied ten minutes, so Cassandra challenged him to a race. The track started and ended near the entrance of the theater. They would run 300 meters to a large tree, circle around it, and race back. Cassandra called the starting time. She won by a long shot.

"God, how do you run that fast?" Atticus asked her when the race had ended, panting.

"I was diagnosed with a genetic disease called 'Betterthaneveryoneelseiosis' when I was born. I take medication for it every day, but I still seem to be better than everyone."

"Very funny," Atticus replied.

"So, did you know that I Like It by Cardi B, Bad Bunny, and J Balvin still holds number three on Billboard? I think it's well deserved. I even memorized it. Check it." She started to rap.

"I like dollars I like diamonds, I like—" She broke off as she saw the confused look on Atticus' face.

"I don't speak Billboard," Atticus said.

"I can tell." She hoped that Atticus would understand, but she kind of expected it. Jamie was practically the only other person in the world who spoke fluent Billboard.

She got a bit quiet, thinking about him. They had never been apart for so long. Since she met him, they hadn't had a fight this bad. She still remembered the day she met him. Her mother had just died, and the house was on fire. He was her neighbor, but they hadn't really known each other that well. She was crying, saying, "Mommy, Mommy, come back." Her father looked shocked, he had gone very pale and had sunk to his knees, and everything stopped and moved very slowly for some time. Then, a slight, skinny boy came up to her and held out his hand to her. She still remembered the words he said to her on that dreadful day.

"Please don't cry. I have something to make you feel better." She had looked down at his hand, where he held a flower. A rose. He gave it to her, fixing it in her hair. Then, he took her hand and took her to his room and stood on top of his bed in order to reach the top rack of a shelf, from where he pulled a soft brown bear. "My daddy gave this to me before he died. I used to hold it and cry when I missed him. It helped me feel better. But you need it more than me." She had clutched the teddy bear to her aching heart like it was a lifeline and let the tears fall. She still had that teddy bear; it was in her room. She hated to admit it, but she missed her best friend a lot. She did her best to remove him from her mind.

"I do speak Spanish though," Atticus said, abruptly pulling her from her mind. "And Greek. My dad had Greek origins, and my mom was from Barcelona. My dad named me a Greek name, and my mom chose a Spanish name for my sister."

"That's really cool," Cassandra said, perking up a bit. She was rather practiced at hiding her emotions. "I can say a line or two in Spanish, too. 'Como te llamas' means count your llamas. And 'Buenos tardes' means peanut butter jelly time." Atticus cracked up.

"My dad was from New York, and my mom was from New Jersey," Cassandra informed him. "So, I'm totally awesome and foreign, too. Also, I like your name. A lot."

Atticus turned a bit red. "Thank you." Just then, Roslyn and Ana walked out of the theater.

"How'd you like the movie?" Atticus inquired.

"It was great," Ana said with a smile.

"Yeah," Roslyn agreed. "How was The Happytime Murder?"

"It was...interesting," Atticus replied.

Ana shivered. "I don't know how you guys watch that stuff." Cassandra gave her an evil grin, and they started walking back to the Sanctuary. As they passed by, a woman with brown hair put up in a bun smiled at them. It wasn't a very pleasant smile. Ana looked sideways at her brother. Roslyn drew out a tube and sword. Cassandra noticed that it had a picture of a rose with thorns in black on the hilt.

Roslyn stepped forward. "I got this."

"I don't understand. This is a normal woman." Cassandra said.

"No, she isn't. Look at her eyes. She's possessed." Atticus pointed out helpfully. Cassandra looked into the woman's eyes. They were black, with live, moving fire in them. Cassandra made a face.

"Just give me the girl, and I'll spare your lives." The woman growled. She looked directly at Cassandra. Everyone turned to look at her.

"I'm not going anywhere. If you wanna fight, I'll take you. Unless of course, you're too scared." Cassandra said fiercely.

The woman cackled. "If you wish." Roslyn reluctantly gave her the soul blade.

The soul blade was used especially for possessed people. It cut only through the soul, and left the body entirely intact. Possessed humans still had their own souls, which had been controlled by the stronger spirit.

Unfortunately for Cassandra, this spirit was way stronger than the other one she faced. Fire was protruding from her hands, and she raised them, facing her palms toward her opponent. Cassandra reflexively put her hands up to cover her face, but no harm came. When the fire reached her, it caressed her upheld hands and vanished. The woman growled. Cassandra stepped forward, and now she was close enough to touch her face. The woman raised her hand and struck out, but Cassandra had raised an arm to block her. The blow connected with Cassandra's arm and the woman looked surprised for a moment. Another moment later, the expression disappeared from the woman's face. Cassandra reached out to touch her, but she retreated. Then, she did a type of kick that a sensei would've called a badly executed inner-crescent kick. Cassandra had not expected this, so the woman's kick hit her off guard. Cassandra dropped to the ground, the wind blown out of her. The woman moved towards her, leering when suddenly, a flash of silver and the woman's face fell forward. With a sickening thud, her whole body fell forward, and Roslyn stood there, wielding another long silver blade, looking murderous. Cassandra stood up, brushed the dust off of her jeans and grinned.

"Thanks, man."

"Don't mention it," Roslyn said, her mood grim and her voice dull as always. The moon was a shining beacon in the sky, the wispy clouds like downy feathers in the sky, and the young woman, who had a terrifying expression on her face less than five minutes ago, now looked peaceful and young in her sleep, lying upon the sidewalk. Ana stepped up to her and took her shoulder, and a moment later, her eyes sprang open.

The look of shock and disbelief was enough to make Cassandra laugh, though she thought it would be insensitive and bit her lip.

"Where am I?"

Atticus spoke up. "M'am, you're at the AMC at Monmouth. You passed out, and we shook you awake. Would you like us to call an ambulance?"

The woman looked so frightened that Cassandra felt bad for almost laughing at her. "But I don't remember coming here," she murmured softly.

"Can we call someone to come pick you up?" Ana asked her.

After being silent for a long time and looking distractedly at the floor, the woman abruptly nodded. "I'd like that." She distractedly gave Ana a string of numbers and babbled something about her husband. Atticus rushed back into the theater and bought her a bottle of water, which seemed to help get the color back into her face. The group waited for fifteen minutes with the lady, and her husband came in a green Chevrolet, hurriedly and haphazardly parking the car, its sides jutting out the sidelines. The man ran out to her, where he hugged her shaking body to himself, crying, and they turned away politely.

"Thanks for finding her," the man managed when he had finally stopped crying. "I don't know what I'd do without her,"

"It's quite alright," Ana responded for them all. "Have a good night, and take care."

The man nodded. "I will." He carried her back to the car, put her seat belt on, and draped a blanket over her dutifully before carefully backing out of the parking lot.

"I want someone like that," Ana said dreamily.

"You want a thirty year old married man?" Atticus asked suspiciously.

"No." Ana wrinkled her nose. "I want someone to love me like that."

They all started the walk back to the Sanctuary, and crept to the shadows when they reached it.

When they entered the Sanctuary and went to the library, where Ana told her the portal was, Roslyn stuck her head through the moving colors for a moment to check if the destination was right, then tossed in an Arca from earlier carelessly.

They were quiet for a while, or at least until Roslyn broke the silence with a snarky remark in the direction of Cassandra. "Why did she want you?" she asked. "You're untrained, unarmed, useless. You didn't even know you were Pol Electi until earlier today." The way she spoke made her feel unimportant, as though, though she barely knew who Cassandra was, she knew just enough to know that Cassandra was beneath her, and treated her like trash. Cassandra loathed being treated like trash. Surely anyone would, but it affected her in a different way than it did others, thanks to her lovely family back home.

"I don't know, do I?" she shot back. "Why don't you go to hell and ask her?"

Roslyn's lips had thinned then, and her forest green eyes lit on flame dangerously, as though she had something quite horrid on her mind, but thought better than to say it. It seemed better this way, Cassandra thought, or the group would have had to witness three fights today instead of two.

"Girls, please," Atticus said with his irritating smile, "I'm sure there's a reasonable explanation. Maybe she got the wrong girl."

"Or maybe," Roslyn proposed, "she got the right person. And whoever wanted her dead knew just how annoying she is."

"What do you have against me?" Cassandra asked, growingly more irritated by the moment.

Roslyn didn't even give her the respect of answering her. Instead, she turned to Atticus as though she did not speak at all. "Why is she even here again?"

Cassandra crossed her arms over her chest and huffed. "Oh, I don't know. Because I saved your lucky ass by killing that spirit and nearly died, and so you kidnapped me and took me to this place?"

Roslyn smiled coolly. "I voted against saving your life, actually."

Cassandra made a very rude gesture, and Ana gasped.

"That's quite enough. Both of you can shut up or meet my beating stick!" Ana reprimanded.

Cassandra turned to Atticus inquisitively. "She has a beating stick?"

Atticus stared solemnly at the ground. "I see her every day."

Cassandra almost laughed at the stare the little brown-haired girl was giving her- it was almost way too stern and mom-like that it seemed uncanny, especially considering her small stature. Cassandra wondered how much control and discipline were contained in such a small frame.

"You know," Atticus said, breaking from his sad look to one of silent amusement, "you should probably get back to your bed before May comes in to check on you again. I wonder if she's already noticed."

Cassandra turned back to Ana, and even she looked scared now. She mouthed but one word, "Run."

Cassandra had to take very good care in sneaking back up the stairs without May noticing. It proved to be very hard indeed, but she had succeeded in the end by having Atticus walk into the Infirmary and talk her off about different types of race cars until she finally lost patience and told him that she had to use the restroom. When she did, Cassandra had snuck into the Infirmary and lain down on her bed.

Shortly after, after making sure that Atticus was nowhere in sight, May had come back in and found Cassandra tucked obediently under the covers. She had checked her vitals and discharged her then, and Cassandra had gone back home.

The next morning, Cassandra went to such efforts to avoid Jamie like the plague. It hurt her to do so, but she knew that in the end, she was only saving herself. It was time to start thinking about other things.

For instance, Pol Electi. She could see in her mind's eye, how Roslyn had slashed down with her sword like there was no tomorrow. Whatever her attitude, Cassandra had admired her for that.

She was Pol Electi, too. Though it had taken her so long to realize it finally, she was, and she wanted to take advantage of it.

She wanted to fight. To be beautiful and dangerous like all the Pol Electi, to be strong and courageous and brave.

She wanted to be like them, and she knew exactly what to do.

7

Marks On Her Skin

It was six in the morning, and Cassandra was at her martial arts studio. To be fair, Cassandra hadn't even known that they opened at six, but apparently, they did. She had been restless for quite some time now, knowing that she was Pol Electi and wasn't with the others, training and fighting. She wanted to be like them, all fierce and strong and beautiful, but she simply wasn't much experienced. Coming into battle with them would only mean that she would be a liability, for they would have to protect her while they fought. Cassandra did not like being seen as dead weight. It made her remember the way her aunt and uncle treated her.

So, she was here to train. And she did, hard. She had purchased a membership with the money she had earned hard at work at Sam's Club, for they were the only place that hired broke sixteen-year-olds.

Sweat ran down her neck and back in lines, calluses from previous training sessions lining her careful, musician's fingers. She didn't remember when she had started to go here exactly, but she supposed that it was sometime after the incident in the forest when she had met Atticus, Roslyn, and Ana.

She remembered how they moved, graceful and lithe, like a jaguar slinking through long grass. There was something that set them apart from the others- something that she couldn't quite put her finger on, but it was there. And ever since she had seen the mark on her skin, she had wanted it too.

I am strong.

Her fist hit the sparring bag with a thud.

I am graceful.

She turned around and threw the side of her foot into the bag.

I am Pol Electi.

She screamed out in pain as she threw her fist forward again, harder than ever. She was immediately rewarded by the violent swinging of the sparring bag and the popping of several knuckles in her fist.

"Hey," A voice sounded. Cassandra did not respond at first and had probably dismissed it as one of the pitiful sounds that the unfortunate sparring bag had made.

"Hey," The voice said again, placing a hand on her shoulder. Cassandra swung around and caught the arm of the figure with the voice, sweeping her foot down and making her victim lose their footing as she had been taught in her martial arts class. She caught a flash of curly brown hair as the figure, a lanky young man, leaped from the floor and did what Cassandra identified as a butterfly kick, bringing Cassandra to the floor. However, before she fell to the ground, she instinctively grabbed the man's shoulder to keep herself from falling. This action did not prove to be of very much use, however, for she ended up going down anyway, with the young man tumbling on top of her.

"Hey, again," the lad said, comically grinning for a humorous effect.

Slowly, Cassandra's vision readjusted, and she found that the young man lying atop her was Atticus.

"Get off of me."

"Right," said Atticus hastily, pushing off of the ground and leaping as gracefully as he always did. He dusted himself off even though none had accumulated on his clothing.

"What are you doing here?" asked Cassandra, turning back to her sparring bag.

"I'm here to see you, of course," Atticus told her.

"You're stalking me?"

"Yes. I mean, no," Atticus said, tucking away a golden pen into his jean pocket.

Cassandra paid no attention to him and kept abusing her punching bag. "I will call the police on you."

Atticus flipped his hair. "The police don't arrest people like me," he said, sidling up to her. "I'm way too irresistible to arrest."

"You're right," Cassandra agreed. "They'd hang you instead."

Atticus chuckled. "There's no need to be defensive, my sweet. I'm merely checking on your well being."

"Why?"

Atticus pondered the question. "I don't know. It might be because you're so small and inexperienced that I feel like I have to protect you from the dangers of the world."

Cassandra had him in a headlock against the wall before he could say another word. Atticus said nothing, but rather looked impressed.

"You've been training," he noticed.

"Yes," Cassandra agreed, and with a final glare, went back to her punching bag.

"Why?"

"Because I'm going to join up," Cassandra said, as though she were teaching a small kid that two plus two equaled four.

"No, you're not," Atticus countered. "You don't have too much practice yet."

"And who are you to judge that?" Cassandra asked.

"Atticus James Brooks, head of the Training Centers at the New Jersey Sanctuary for Pol Electi."

Now, Cassandra stopped punching her bag. She took a moment to breathe, then turned around to look him in the eye.

"But I can fix that."

8

Candy

She couldn't sleep. Jamie kept calling her, and she didn't want to answer. She didn't want to be flooded with the emotions that accompanied being separated from him for so long.

Lying down in bed, she closed her eyes. Her body was broken from practice when Atticus had dutifully trained her day and night because she had insisted. He had told her to take a break multiple times, but she hadn't stopped, staying that she wanted to be as fast and strong as them.

She had blacked out at some point, pondering over things on her mind, and she would have thought it was a dream if not for the glowing pendant at her chest.

They were sitting on the grass outside the house, He put his hands out for her, and she giggled as she placed them in. Her short black hair was ruffled slightly, and her cheeks flushed from the effort of playing. She watched as he flipped his hands and giggled when she pulled her small, chubby hands from his, just in the nick time before his own, slightly more developed hands came down.

"Aw, come on," the young boy said in mock anger. "I really thought I'd win that time."

The girl with short black hair giggled infectiously, and the boy couldn't help but smile in spite of his loss. "Let's play again," she urged, but the boy shook his head gravely. "We need to pack."

The little girl frowned. "Again?"

41

The boy nodded sadly.

The girl crossed her arms over her chest defiantly. "I'm not going. I'm going to miss all of my bestest friends."

The hazel-eyed boy sighed as though a million pounds had been placed on his thin, twig-like shoulders. "You have to, Lana. It's not safe for you."

The girl did not budge. "I'm not going."

"Come on, Lana. Please."

She did not say a word.

"What if I gave you candy?"

The younger child considered it for a moment. "Hmm. Okay."

The boy sighed in relief. The girl started to go into the house but then turned back around. "Do you promise to give me candy?"

The boy nodded and placed a hand over his heart solemnly. "I promise."

The girl smiled. "Okay."

Cassandra sat up in bed with a start. Her head was throbbing, and she had to massage her temples to keep from crying aloud.

Hmm, she thought, *must've been a bad dream.*

9

Ten Bucks

"So, tell me a bit more about your world," Cassandra prompted. They were at the room connected to the training room in the Sanctuary, where they kept bandages, towels, refreshments, and extra equipment. Atticus had gone off to get more Gatorade for the fridge. Cassandra had just had a long training period with Atticus and Ana and was tired as hell.

"Everything you previously believed is a lie," Ana began.

"Okay?" Cassandra said, smiling.

"You see, the universe is kind of like a triangle. On each side of the triangle, there is a dimension. Hell, Heaven, and Earth. Demons live in Hell, Angels live in Heaven, and we live on Earth, along with normals, Figura Mutante, the shapeshifters, and Veneficae."

"What's that?" Cassandra asked, curious and intrigued.

"The Veneficae are beings that can shift dimensions at will," Ana explained. "They also possess very, very powerful magic, but they don't live too long."

"Why?"

"Because magic takes a price. Just like we give up some of our energy when we perform magic, it takes its toll on their bodies. Except, they can't get it back with rest and food," Ana told her. "They're very rare. There's only one way you can tell,"

"What's that?"

"Their eyes. Their eyes turn colors. One moment they're blue, the next, they're violet. It's very hard to notice. They, like the Figura Mutante, are a tricky sort. Anyway, there's one last type of being."

"What's that?"

"The In-Betweeners," Ana said.

Atticus walked into the room, hauling a large cardboard carton full of Gatorade. He set it near the fridge and started to stock it up, pausing to tell Cassandra, "And no, they are nothing like the British sitcom." He seemed to be incapable of saying anything serious- he always made Cassandra laugh.

"Tell me about them." Cassandra pushed.

"The In-Betweeners are the people who live in the middle of the triangle," Ana said.

"What's there?"

"Nothing. Just vast emptiness. They only see white. Living in the space between, they can't feel anything. Some are like guardians, and others are tricksters. It all depends on how old they are. They're immortal, and to feel nothing for so long, you get kind of bitter and numb after a while."

"And us? Can we move through dimensions?" Cassandra asked eagerly.

"Nah," Atticus said, finishing his task and breaking the box down to throw into the trash. "Only Veneficae can do that. The only chance we have at seeing the other dimensions is through a portal. And we can only see through it. We can't actually go through."

"Why?"

"Living things can't go through the portal. If they do, they get lost in the vast In Between," Ana told her helpfully.

"If we can't shift dimensions, where do we go when we die?" Cassandra asked.

"Nowhere. We're reincarnated into a different body, at a different place on Earth. We never go anywhere. The only ones who truly die are the Veneficae. Demons, Angels, and In-Betweeners are immortal. Pol Electi, normals, and Figura Mutante are resurrected," Ana filled her in.

"Then, what are spirits?"

"Spirits are formed when someone dies without their wish fulfilled. Their grief turns their will into an uncontrollable rage until all of the goodness of their souls are stripped away, and they turn evil."

"How do you deal with them?" Now, Roslyn came into the room, a look of slow anger over her face. Cassandra wondered if this was what she looked like on her birthday. She sighed loudly and angrily, as though she had been searching for the three of them for hours.

"We can't. No one can, except for the demons. That's why we send them through the portal to hell."

"Should we really be telling her all this?" Roslyn asked Atticus, as though Cassandra were not there.

Atticus shrugged. "Why not?"

Roslyn looked at him the way one might look at a person while attempting to teach them why one plus one equals two. "Because she's a normie."

"I'm not," Cassandra said, eager. "I'm one of you. You saw me. You saw my mark in the forest, remember?"

Roslyn looked at her as though she had just remembered that she was there. "You might as well be. You haven't been trained, haven't even had a single battle before. You're deadweight."

"I've been training," Cassandra told her proudly. "I can fight. And that I haven't been in a battle can be changed."

Roslyn scoffed. "Training? You've probably just taken a ten-dollar membership at some stupid, broken down normie martial arts dojo close to your house."

Despite her pride, Cassandra blushed, for that was exactly what she had done before Atticus had agreed to train her. Angrily, she got into Roslyn's face. She was done with this nonsense.

"Actually, I can really fight. Atticus has been training me."

Something in the air between them popped loudly, and Cassandra saw Roslyn glower at Atticus and heard him shout something before Roslyn's hand made contact with Cassandra's cheek.

She had slapped her so hard that Cassandra actually staggered back a few steps. Roslyn stormed away so quickly and so viciously that when Atticus called after her, she had already put fifty feet between them. Ana rushed to her side and examined her cheek.

Cassandra's cheek was bright red, her skin screaming in agony. She kept her head down to hide the surprised tears that had somehow found their way to the corners of her eyes.

"I'm so sorry about Roslyn," Atticus said. "She's just like that. Jealous."

"Of what?" asked Cassandra, incredulous. "Of not having parents? Of being treated like garbage at home? Of not having much experience in battles?"

"Of course not," Ana said, sounding reasonable as always. "She's worried that we're going to leave her for you."

Cassandra was appalled. "Why on earth would she think that?"

Atticus shrugged. "That's just how she is. She'll warm up to you soon, don't worry."

"I'm not worried about that at all," Cassandra said. "You should go follow her and tell her that she's still your bestest friend."

Atticus grimaced. "I should probably go talk to her."

Cassandra nodded, still looking down. "I'm going home. Don't wait up."

10

Heartbeat

J amie put his phone down. He knew there was no use calling. She wasn't going to pick up. *Great job, Jamie. You screwed it up for real. Your best friend, who you haven't had a fight with for longer than you can remember, won't talk to you.* Jamie waited for the voicemail option, but somehow, it didn't come. His heart leaped as he picked up the phone. "Cassie?"

"Hey."

"Hey."

"Wanna go to the library tomorrow, at five?"

"Yeah. Cassie, I'm so, so sorry. I promise I won't ever talk about it. We can talk about books and Billboard, and we can go to the park and race, and you can beat me, and I'll fail miserably. And you can play your guitar, and I can sing, and we can pretend it never happened." He sounded breathless.

"Hey. Chill. It's cool. We can talk at the library."

"Okay."

"Bye."

"Wait. Cassie?"

"What's up?"

"Am I dreaming?" Cassandra burst into laughter.

"Dude, I don't know. My life is so awesome that I can't tell dreams from reality."

When they hung up, Jamie was smiling. It was normal for Cassandra to have a lot more self-confidence than everyone else, and her saying what she did assured Jamie that she wasn't angry anymore. Jamie collapsed backward onto his bed and stared at the bed. Did she know that his heart sped when she walked into the room? Did she know that her name rang in his head like a heartbeat, never failing, repeating, and inevitable? Did she know that he yearned to listen to her play her guitar, listen to the beautiful and soulful sound of it? Did she know how much she meant to him, and how he breathed his every breath to see her smile light up his world again? He stared up at the ceiling, unseeing. *Stop wanting what you can't have.* Jamie shook his head to clear her off his mind. He had done this countless times before, and it never helped, so he didn't know why he was doing it now. She stood out in his mind like the big shining moon in the night sky.

* * *

Cassandra was sitting at their usual table at the library the next day, a small table with two plush chairs near a large window. Cassandra and Jamie used to come to this place during spring, choose a bunch of books, and read them to the calming sound of the rain. Cassandra was staring wistfully out the window at the beautiful summer view outside when Jamie entered the library and sat down across from her. His emerald eyes had lit up as soon as he saw her, and she wondered if this was the first time she had noticed. He was looking at Cassandra as if she were pure gold as he sat down across from her.

"I missed you," Cassandra said.

"It's been a while," Jamie agreed. It had been close to three months. He was disappointed that she hadn't called him back earlier.

"So, did you know that Meant To Be by Bebe Rexha featuring Georgia Florida Line is still on the charts? It's at twenty-six." Cassandra started chattering excitedly.

"Yeah," Jamie said. He looked down.

"And I have a new book recommendation for you. It's called Clockwork

Angel. I really enjoyed it. It's fantasy, and I think you'll like it too."

"That's nice." Jamie's eyes didn't move away from the floor.

"Jamie? Is everything alright?"

"What? Yeah. Everything's fine."

"You sure? Your face is turning scarlet." Cassandra reached out to hold his hand, but he tensed. Cassandra looked hurt. Jamie's expression was pained.

"I'm fine. Excuse me." Jamie got up from the chair and ran to the restroom.

Jamie felt as if someone had pulled his heart from his chest and cut it with a knife. He slammed the bathroom door shut and sank to the floor. He sat there for several long moments, his lanky legs spread out in front of him, his head in his hands. There was hesitant knocking on the door.

"Um, Jamie? Are you alright?"

"Yeah," Jamie said in a hoarse voice. "You go on without me. I'll be fine."

"Okay." He tensed for a moment, or at least until he heard footsteps walking away. He looked down at his hands. How was he going to get her out of his head? Like a song on repeat, playing in his head all day, every day, she seemed to have snuck her way into his heart, and he didn't know how to get her out. *Please leave, Cassandra, and leave me be. Leave my heart alone. Stop hurting me.* He buried his face in his hands.

* * *

On the way home, Cassandra was so full of her thoughts that she almost walked into someone, who avoided her by dodging to the left at the last minute. Cassandra didn't remember the last time she was so distracted. She felt as if Jamie had punched her in the stomach and left her there, with the wind blown out of her to sit there and contemplate what she had done to receive the blow. When she got to her room, she immediately collapsed into bed and fell asleep.

She is in a corridor. She walks forward, and the overwhelming darkness seems to swallow her. She reaches out and feels desperately around for something to hold on to. Her hands find something soft. As she moves closer, squinting, she can see a figure. It's Jamie, holding his brown teddy bear in his hands. He offers it to her smiling, but Cassandra pulls it from his hand, rips it apart, and stomps on it. Jamie looks astonished now, as if she had just stabbed him in the gut. He holds out his hand. Cassandra crouches to the ground, retrieves a shard of broken glass from the mirror on the inside of her mother's jewelry box. She turns it around in her hands, examining. Then, she puts the edge to the tender skin on the inside of Jamie's hand and slowly draws it across. A cut appears on Jamie's hand, where blood wells up and stains his pale skin, dripping to the white floor. Jamie reaches up to the collar of his shirt and draws it down slowly, and Cassandra can see that a scar identical to the one on his hand has now appeared on his chest, just above his heart.

Cassandra awoke with a start. Morning sunlight was pouring through the window, drenching everything in brightness. It was only a nightmare. Cassandra knew it was only a dream, but she still couldn't get the picture of Jamie's pained face out of her mind. So she decided to text him.

Hey

Hey

Are you alright?

I'm fine.

So…do you want to go to Starbucks with me? We can walk together. On me.

I'm busy today

Busy doing what?

Busy getting you out of my head.

Jamie,

But he had already switched off. Cassandra felt dreadful. Her Jamie, her best friend, was hurting, and it was because of her. What had he done to deserve that pain? She only did what she had to do to save herself and him from pain if anything happened to him. But what could possibly happen to him? Cassandra thought. *Nothing. Absolutely nothing at all. Cassandra contemplated the possibilities. The house can go up in flames. There could be a car accident. He could spontaneously combust. A wild rhino can chase and kill him. He could be killed by a spirit.* Cassandra frowned as she noticed something. Cassandra, confident, strong, and fearless, was afraid of love.

* * *

Cassandra made her way to The Tree. She trudged her way through the leaves and twigs on the ground. When she reached the tree, she sank down under it and let her head fall back against the tree. She gazed into the morning sky. It was an interesting shade of blue today. *What have I done?* She pulled out her phone and subconsciously called Jamie, which was a reflex for when she was sad. It went straight to voicemail. She called again, and three more times after that. Voicemail. So she sent one.

"Hey. Jamie. It's me, Cassie. I'm sorry. I know you're hurting, and it's my fault. I'd never want you to feel that way, and I can't stand to know that it's because of me. The truth is, I'm scared of love. Ever since my…" The voicemail beeped and signaled it's ending. Cassandra dropped the phone and stared ahead, unseeing. She just wanted to hear his voice again.

* * *

As Atticus crept into the woods, the sun illuminated his soft brown curls and brought a sheen to them. There was mud staining his black Nike sneakers, but his khaki shorts and white shirt were spotless. He wondered if she was even here, and on the off chance that she was, if she'd even want to hang out. She seemed nice. When he reached the place where he met her, he was pleased to see that she was there, but she looked like she was deeply in thought, lost in her own mind. Atticus wondered what she was thinking about. "Hey, Cass."

Cassandra was pulled from her thoughts with a start. She looked up to see Atticus staring down at her. "What are you doing here?" she inquired.

"Oh. Um. First of all, I'd like to apologize on Roslyn's behalf. She's like that sometimes. Second, Roslyn, Ana, and I were going to go to the park to hang out, and we were wondering if you'd like to come with."

"Fine," Cassandra agreed, surprising even herself. The truth was, without Jamie, she felt rather lonely. And after her parents had passed, feeling lonely was often a pass time for her. So, she decided that since she was bored,

51

miserable, and needed some distraction, why not? Atticus offered her a crooked smile, and then his hand. Cassandra ignored his hand and got up on her own, dusting herself off.

They started strolling through the woods. There was a slight drizzle, and it threw water on the leaves on the trees, looking like early morning dew. "Which one?" Cassandra asked.

"Holmdel."

"I had a cross country meet there once."

"You run?"

"Yeah."

"I should have known. Only someone with a whole lot of practice can beat me in a race."

"I could've beaten you without practice."

"Could not."

"That sounds interesting. So, what are we doing?"

"We're going to meet Ana and Roslyn to play basketball. They're waiting for us."

"Do you guys live at the Sanctuary or something?"

"Ana and I do. Since we lost our parents. We've got no living relatives, so we live at the Sanctuary. Roslyn doesn't though."

"Oh. I lost my parents too. I was five."

"I'm sorry."

"I'm sorry for your loss too."

"Thank you." Just about then, they were passing a graveyard. A stooped old lady was staring at them. She raised one hand and beckoned Cassandra forward. Puzzled, Cassandra stepped forward. She looked at her eyes, and she saw that no fire dwelled in them, just pure brown. She also noticed that the woman was not standing, but rather floating one inch above the ground.

"Heaven's chosen. Tell me. How do I find heaven?" she asked Cassandra.

"Oh, that's easy. Just take a right at the first exit you see on Garden State Parkway. How am I supposed to know?" Cassandra answered. Ironically, the woman smiled.

"You're sarcastic. My daughter is sarcastic, too. I love my daughter." She smiled and closed her eyes. Promptly after, she vanished. Cassandra turned around to see Atticus. He shook his head, and curly brown locks fell into his eyes.

"Honestly, Cassandra. 'Just take a right at the first exit you see on Garden State Parkway.' You're crazy." Cassandra smiled.

"I know that." They started walking again. When they reached the park, they found Ana and Roslyn leaning against a large white van, waiting for them. Roslyn had a basketball under her arm.

"Hey, guys," Cassandra said.

"Hey, Cass," Roslyn said, looking down. She seemed ashamed, in spite of herself.

"Hello," Ana said. Roslyn pushed off the van with her elbows and started to walk, dribbling the ball as she did and gesturing for the others to follow. Her companions shortly fell into step with her. They walked until they got to a road, bordered by trees. They started to walk into the woods. Cassandra had always found the woods calming. She found something reassuring about the quietness, the smell of pine trees, and the beautiful and delicate design of sunlight and shadows that fell around the trees.

"So, I was talking to a woodland nymph earlier, and she said that she felt a commotion of angry souls close. They are forming groups to hunt us down. It's getting more and more dangerous for us to dwell past the borders of the Sanctuary." Ana told them.

"Why do they hate us so much?" Cassandra asked.

"To take the life of one of heaven's chosen gives spirits more power. And with power comes greed. Great greed for still more power." Ana filled in. They reached a clearing in the woods. They walked further, or at least until the woods ended. Walking past a parking lot, they found themselves standing in front of a basketball court. They chose teams, Ana and Atticus on one, and Roslyn and Cassandra on the other, so that they might have time to make up, though Roslyn didn't seem like she was about to apologize for her behavior any time soon. Ana started at half court, and she and Cassandra passed the ball to each other. She then passed the ball to her brother, who threw the ball and got it through. Ana caught it as it fell and threw it to Roslyn, who dribbled and ran towards the court. Atticus was in front of her, blocking her. Roslyn faked toward the hoop and threw it to Cassandra. Ana was blocking her, but Cassandra jumped and caught the ball, dodging around Ana. She then aimed at the hoop, and it went through. Roslyn grinned at her. She genuinely seemed to be trying to be nice to Cassandra, though her expression conveyed that it was quite hard for her. Atticus caught the ball as it fell and passed it to Ana, who backed up, eyes squinting in concentration, and threw the ball. The ball soared through the air towards the hoop and was intercepted by Cassandra.

"That was a good interception," Atticus complimented her.

"She's on the other team!" Ana said accusingly.

"But it was," Atticus said. Cassandra threw the ball to Roslyn, who caught the ball and threw it but missed the hoop. Ana caught it as it bounced off the hoop. She passed the ball to Atticus who missed the ball because Cassandra had intercepted him. She leaped and threw the ball into the hoop. The ball slammed into the court below with a satisfying thud. Atticus caught it. The light drizzle had just turned to heavy rain, falling down in sheets, making splattering sounds on the court. Ana put her hands up to shield her head.

"Ugh. I wish I brought an umbrella. My hair frizzes up when water touches it. I wish my hair was like yours," she said to Atticus. His luscious brown curls had gone damp from the rainwater but had retained their curliness. They hadn't frizzed up; the rain had only added more shine to his dark curls. Atticus grinned. Cassandra noticed that when he smiled, he looked like a devil in an angel's body. Cassandra liked his smile.

"With great hair comes great bragging rights," Atticus said importantly.

"It's 'With great power comes great responsibility,' you ignorant moron," Ana retorted. "Once again, I wonder if I am actually related to you, or if you've only fooled everyone to gain fame and glory."

"And you call me the ignorant moron," Atticus muttered. "Ouch!" Ana had elbowed him in the rib cage. "That hurts!"

"You deserved that," she replied. Atticus scowled. Ana, Atticus, and Roslyn ran over to the domed picnic area for shelter from the rain. Cassandra, however, stayed where she was. She looked up and saw the rain fall in sheets from the sky, which had gone an interesting shade of gray-blue. Cassandra never understood why people associated rain with gloom. Cassandra absolutely loved rain. She loved when the sun shines after long and heavy rains, the rays of sunlight falling into puddles of water and making them shine with luster, and it never failed to bring a smile to her face. She jumped in puddles, splattering her black lace-up boots and ripped jeans with mud and rainwater, and her mouth twisted into a crooked smile. The mud brought back childhood memories of herself and Jamie jumping in puddles, making structures out of the mud and staining their hands and clothes, and they had sometimes managed to get mud on their faces as well. They would run through the rain, water sloshing in their boots, wild, happy, and free. Cassandra ran around the field next to the basketball court, boots slipping and sliding in the wet, rain-soaked grass.

"Are you coming?" Ana called.

"No. I like the rain."

"Are you mental?" Atticus asked. His tone was not unbelieving, but rather amused.

"I think so, yes," Cassandra said. She grinned. For the first time since she broke Jamie's heart, she felt truly happy because she was alive, and in this moment.

11

Call Me Back

Cassandra lay in bed, staring at the white ceiling. It was plain, except for a few of the glow in the dark star stickers she had stuck up when she was seven. She couldn't sleep. She had gotten back from the park about two hours ago, and it was about ten o'clock. Cassandra missed her best friend so much. They hadn't had a fight this bad in her memory. That was, if this was even a fight. Cassandra thought that this wasn't a fight and that rather, Jamie was just heartbroken. She was desperate and would do anything to hear Jamie's voice again, to see his crooked smile and his beautiful, knowing green eyes reading her like a book. Cassandra sat up in bed and picked up her phone from the bedside table. She looked for the multiple voicemails that Jamie had sent her that she had never read.

Voicemail #1

"Hi, Cassie, it's Jamie. Are you alright? Has this come as a shock to you? I'm sorry to have sprung this on you as I have. Can you please call me back so we can talk?"

Voicemail #2

"Cassie? I'm sorry. I won't talk about it again. I promise. Do you want to go to the library? We can recommend books to each other. Or you can come over to my house. We can obsessively check Billboard's Top 100 for any updates. Or go to a movie? Or the park? You can beat me in a race like you usually do?"

Voicemail #3

"Cassie. Call me back, please. Please don't be mad at me. I didn't think you'd be so angry."

Voicemail #4

"Cassie, please."

Voicemail #5

"Did I do something that hurt your feelings in any way? If so, tell me. I will fix it. I won't hurt you again, I promise, and I never meant to in the first place."

Voicemail #6

"Will I ever hear your voice again?"

Voicemail #7

"Did someone break your heart? Is that why you pushed me away? If so, tell me. I will personally track them down and kill them slowly and painfully. And you should know, I'd never break your heart."

Voicemail #8

"Cassie, I understand if you don't feel the same way as I do, but can we still be friends? Please?"

The last one struck Cassandra with an instant realization. Jamie wasn't not talking to Cassandra because he was disappointed that she wasn't interested in him; he wasn't talking to her because she showed no value to their friendship. Jamie had always been there for her, always had her back, always stood beside her whether what she was doing was right or wrong. And he wouldn't push her away because she didn't love him. He was upset that Cassandra hadn't listened to his voicemails, replied to a single one of his text messages, or called him back even once. He had never pried, never asked her why she did what she did, never asked why she was feeling a certain way. He had expected her to open up to him in time, trust him with her secrets, and was always there, steady and reliable to hold them for her. And she had just taken it with stride, never apologizing for making him hurt, never explained why she was acting the way she was acting and expected him to spill everything out to her in return. *Oh. I'm a terrible friend.*

* * *

As Atticus trudged back to the Sanctuary with Ana, his little sister talked him off about some research she had done on a certain type of spirit magic. Usually, Atticus would be interested in this, but today he couldn't focus. He kept seeing her in his mind's eye as if she was all he looked at for days together. She was printed in his mind. He loved her recklessness, how she sometimes acted extremely immature and childish, and how she was fearless. He had memorized the waviness of her dark hair, the curve of her lips when she smiled, the quirk of her eyebrows when she was amused. *I think she's cool. I think she's nice. But I don't love her. I won't fall in love. I will never fall in love.* He tried to ignore it, but it kept coming back. Her smile was embedded in his mind, and her name was on his lips. *Cassandra.* "Attitude, are you paying attention to a single word that is coming out of my mouth?" Atticus scowled. He hated it when Ana called him that.

"To answer your question, no, I wasn't paying attention to a single word you uttered."

"What a lummox," Ana muttered under her breath.

"The hell does that mean?" Atticus asked curiously.

"It means you're a moron, you blockhead."

"Oof. Someone's in a bad mood."

"I'm not. I just get annoyed when I'm ignored. So tell me. What's on your mind?"

"Wha– there's nothing on my mind. What makes you think anything's on my mind? My mind is clear. There is nothing on my mind. There has never been anything on my mind. When I was born, the doctor didn't say 'It's a boy!' he said 'this kid has a crystal clear mind.'" Ana smirked.

"Sure."

"How do you do that?"

"Do what?"

"Always know what I'm thinking."

"It's actually pretty easy." Atticus made a disbelieving noise.

"I am not predictable."

"Um, you are soooo predictable. Stop that."

"Stop what?"

"Stop trying to change the topic of this conversation." Ana raised her brown eyebrows and looked at her big brother with a quizzical expression.

"I'm not telling."

"You'll have to eventually, you know I'll keep bugging you if you don't." Atticus sighed.

"I'm gonna say it once, and you have to promise not to bug me after that."

"I promise."

"Okay." Atticus took a sweeping look at his surroundings to make sure that no one was stalking them and conspiring to hear his secret. Finally satisfied, he took a deep breath and whispered a breathless cluster of words into his sister's ear.

"She's stuck in my head, like a good song." Ana's eyes lit up like fireflies on a summer night. She loved this stuff. She immediately launched into guesses.

"Who? Tell me, tell me, tell me!" She gushed. Atticus shook his head firmly.

"You promised," he reminded her. Ana smiled a sweet smile, and at that moment, she looked like an angel.

"I lied." She brought out the hand she had tucked in her pocket and indicated her fingers, which had been crossed. Atticus rolled his eyes, and Ana grinned up at him. Atticus trudged forward on the forest floor, leaves under his black sneakers. His eyes were on the floor, and he was willing someone out of his mind. He could not fall in love. He would absolutely not allow it. But fighting it seemed like attempting to swim against a water current. Cassandra. His lips shaped the name; it gave him life, like a heart; it was his every breath, his every heartbeat. He bit his lip, hoping that the pain would clear his mind. Blood, hot and sticky trickled down his lip. Atticus looked up, and the setting sun glinted in his amber eyes.

"Roslyn."

"No."

"Harley."

"No."

"That ugly possessed woman that Roslyn and Cassandra slew."

59

"Ew. No." Ana opened her mouth to say something else, but Atticus held a hand up to stop her. "You know, I'm going to say no to everyone you say. You might as well just stop trying."

"How about...nah," Ana said.

"Chloe."

"No." Ana paused for a moment, during which she assumed a thoughtful expression. Suddenly her eyes lit up like a firefly on a summer night.

"Jessi–"

"No." Ana looked disappointed. Then, she gave her brother a sly look.

"I know who it is."

"What? No, you don't. You don't know. You can never find out. It is impossible to guess. And besides, I'll never tell her. She's in my head, and I'll get her out. That's it."

"Cassandra." Atticus sucked in his breath. How was she able to pinpoint everything so easily?

A look of shock passed through his face and was concealed as quickly as it came. "No. No. No, I don't like Cassandra. I mean, she's so childish, so immature, and she can be really savage sometimes. Frankly, it's unflattering. And her eyes, they're a mix of gray and blue. They would look nicer if they were one solid color. And her hair is too dark and wavy for my taste. And she likes music, but she's a bit obsessed. It's annoying." Atticus had an interesting expression on his face. He wanted to smile because he was thinking of her, and thinking of her made him smile and filled him with a sort of giddiness that he didn't quite understand. But he would not let himself betray his secret. So he had an expression that was a mixture of elatedness and contempt. It made him look constipated. Ana smiled.

"Okay. So you like Cassandra. What are you going to do?"

"Wha– I just told you, I don't like her. When she smiles, the ends of her lips turn in a weird angle, and I find it very distracting and rather amusing."

"That settles it," Ana said, looking serious now. "You don't like Cassandra." Atticus exhaled a breath of relief, and it was evident by the look on his face that he really was relieved.

"Thank you."

"You REALLY like Cassandra."

"Do not! What makes you think that?"

"Well, for one, if you noticed all of those things, you've obviously been paying a lot of attention to her."

"But–"

"And you hesitated when I said her name,"

"No, I didn–"

"And you assumed a very interesting expression when you started talking about her."

"Damn it. Why you gotta be so smart?" Atticus inquired. He looked firmly downward, determined not to let Ana see the deep scarlet that had crept slowly to his face. "It doesn't matter anyway. I'm not going to tell her."

"What? Why not?"

"I can't let myself fall in love."

Why not?" Atticus shook his head. Then, he started to run. He heard his name called out by his sister in the distance, but he didn't care. Where he was running, he did not know. If he'd stop running, he wasn't sure. Why he was running was also unknown to him. But he didn't stop until he got there.

12

I Don't Know

When she woke up, it was with a burning sort of pain in her head. In fact, it was so extreme that she felt as though her head might burst. "Ow," she moaned and rubbed her head.

"Are you alright? Are you hurt?" came the voice almost immediately.

"Oh, it's nothing," she answered. "It's just a headache," she told him, flattered by his worry.

"I wish I could take care of you," he confessed. "I wish I could hold you and take care of you."

She gasped. She hadn't felt care like that in so long. "Why?" she asked. "Why do you care about me when you should be taking care of yourself? You're sick. You need more care than I do."

He paused for a moment, thinking about it. It seemed he didn't know the right answer himself. "I don't know."

Her heart ached. She had been here for so long. But something about his voice made it all be somehow better. Something about his voice made it all seem like less on her shoulders.

13

Fireworks

C assandra chose a book off the shelf and slid it into her brown messenger bag. She threw her phone in, too and walked out. The rain had stopped an hour ago, so it was safe to go out without an umbrella. She started running, hoping that the pain that she gets in her throat after running too much would help her forget. When she got there, she was surprised to see that someone was already sitting under The Tree's shade. "Jamie?" She called out to the figure. It was dark, so she couldn't see the figure's face.

"Actually, it's me, Atticus."

"Atticus? Why are you here?"

"I...um...well...I don't know."

"Perfect! I come here when I don't know what to do, too!" Atticus smiled. A warm summer breeze blew through and pushed some of Cassandra's long wavy hair into her eyes. She didn't care to push it away. She walked up to Atticus and sank down under The Tree's shade.

"Oh, dude, I just remembered, it's Independence Day! There are going to be fireworks! Aw, man, I love fireworks." Cassandra grinned.

"Me too," Atticus said. Cassandra looked up at the night sky and smiled. Atticus stared at her, taking in her gray-blue eyes, the shape of her lip when she smiled, and her scent of the sea breeze and lemon. Cassandra abruptly got up. She started walking away. "Where are you going?" Atticus inquired.

He got up and started to follow her.

"You'll see." Cassandra kept walking until she reached a clearing in the woods. She sat down on the ground, not caring that dirt and mud were staining her clothes. Then, she lay down on the forest floor, her hair going askew, her large gray eyes observing and taking everything in curiously. "Jamie and I come here every year to look at the fireworks. There are fireworks at the town square too, but it's usually crowded there. But, there's an excellent view of the fireworks from here, and it isn't crowded, so we come here every year." Atticus sat down.

"Who's Jamie?"

"My best friend."

"Oh. Why isn't he here?"

"He's mad at me."

"Why?"

"It's nothing."

"Sorry, I don't mean to intrude."

"Don't be sorry. I always intrude. I just don't feel like talking about it right now."

"Okay."

"Hey, did you know that–"

"Shhh. It's starting."

Atticus looked up. It had started. Fireworks of all colors, red, blue, gold, purple, and green had started to burst into the air and make the sky colorful. Cassandra paid attention to each and everyone, fully submerged in the colorful lights. They reflected on her eyes. Atticus saw that as she had said, the view was really great from here. Atticus started to say something. "Your eyes are the exact color of the sea right now." But Cassandra showed no signs of hearing him. "Cass? Can you hear me? Earth to Cassandra." The fireworks stopped, and Cassandra snapped back to attention.

"Did you say something?"

"No. I didn't say anything."

"Okay." Cassandra stayed just where she was, though the fireworks display had ended.

"What are you looking at?"

"The stars," she replied. She started pointing to each star and naming them. But Atticus had already left. That is, his mind had left. He was not mentally there, his mind was wandering again, and when he was pulled back to reality, he realized that his hand was right next to hers. With horror, he jerked his hand away from hers. Cassandra didn't seem to notice. She kept going on about the stars when abruptly, the topic was changed to Billboard. "Wait a second. How'd we get to Billboard? You were talking about the stars a minute ago."

Cassandra looked puzzled. "Yeah. How did we get to talking about Billboard?" She shrugged. "It's an interesting topic."

"So you've heard 'I'm A Mess' by Bebe Rexha, right?" She continued.

"Yeah,"

"Guess where it is on Billboard."

"Um, 165?"

"No, silly. I mean Billboard's Top 100."

"65?"

"It's at 43, actually." A look of disbelief had come over Atticus' features now.

"I know, right? It's such a good song! It deserves to be at the top 20, at least!"

Atticus chuckled. Cassandra frowned. "What?"

"I didn't think someone could possibly like music that much."

"Everyone says that."

"You know what? I don't think you like music all that much. I think you are somehow mentally obsessed with music. I think that you have a type of mental problem called Billboard Syndrome." Cassandra rolled her eyes but smiled. "Can I maybe change the topic, so I actually know what's going on?" He went on.

"Sure."

"What's your favorite color?"

"Blue. It reminds me of the ocean."

"Who's your favorite singer?"

65

"Lorde. Lorde always. She's amazing. Did you hear Buzzcut Season? After I heard it for the first time, I thought I died, because I was in heaven. It was so freaking good."

"Whoa. You're talking about her as if she's a goddess."

"She might be. We may never know. She is our Lorde and savior. Get it?" Atticus rolled his eyes.

"Alright. That was a bad pun." Atticus smiled at her devotion to music.

"Bad is an understatement," Atticus muttered. "Ow!" She had punched him.

"What's your favorite TV show?" He asked her.

"I don't watch television too much. I'd rather read or listen to music. Besides, there are a lot of stereotypes that piss me off."

"I know, right? I hate that there's always a mean girl and that the mean girl likes the nice girl's crush, and the mean girl is always blonde. The nice girl always has brown hair, too. And anyone who's smart has to wear glasses."

"Yeah. I totally agree with you."

"And don't even get me started on how the girl has to be a cheerleader and the boy has to play football in high school romance movies."

"I know, right?"

"So, what's your favorite color?" Cassandra inquired. Atticus was caught off guard.

"I like the color of your eyes. They remind me of a storm at sea." He blurted out.

"What?"

"Nothing. I didn't say anything. What makes you think I said anything? I have never said anything in my entire life. In fact, I'm mute." Atticus silently cursed himself. *What is going on with me today? You really are a lummox, just like Ana said.* Cassandra smiled and closed her eyes.

"Okay," Cassandra said in an amused voice.

"Why are you smiling?" Atticus asked curiously.

"I like that sound."

"What sound?"

"The sound of silence. It's peaceful."

"I like that sound too, but I like another sound more."

"What's that?"

"I like the sound of your voice."

"Cool. I like the sound of my voice, too." Did Cassandra know he was flirting with her? Because she did not make a single move that implied that she had any clue about that. Atticus did not want her to know; he didn't even know what he was about to say before he blurted it out. He was horrified that he was saying all of these things but didn't seem to be able to stop. Cassandra didn't seem to mind, though, to his relief.

"Cass?"

"What?"

He clapped a hand onto his mouth before his incontinent lips started to pour everything out as if someone had removed the cork from a bottle of wine. *I love you, I love you, I love you, get out of my head, get out of my head, get out of my head right now.*

"So, have you read any good books recently?"

"Yes. I recently added the Dark Artifices series to my collection. As you can see, I love a good fantasy novel." Now it was her turn to ask him a question.

"Atticus?" Her large gray eyes pierced into his amber ones, and for a moment, Atticus was afraid that she could read him like a book.

"Yes?"

"Why are you holding my hand?"

Damn it. He looked down and saw his fingers entwined with hers. When did that happen? His face turned crimson. He pulled his hand back quickly. "Scared of the dark?" Cassandra teased.

"No, I'm not. I just…I gotta go." He stood up to leave. "Bye."

"Bye."

Atticus took off in a run. Cassandra was puzzled. She shrugged and closed her eyes and listened to the sound of silence.

A tall woman with long black hair and gray-blue eyes and a man with brown hair and hazel eyes are standing at a park. A child, looking about the age of three, is on a swing set. A boy is pushing her. He has brown hair and hazel eyes. The child on the swingset is laughing. The woman smiles and looks at her husband, who smiles back.

"They're saying that the legend is about her. They're saying she's the Blessed One." The woman stopped smiling.

"It's not her. The legend says that the stars are in a specific order, a lunar eclipse on the moment the Blessed is born. And it wasn't with her."

"They're going to come for her anyway. They aren't going to believe us. We'll have to hide her."

"How long are we going to do this? I'm tired of running and hiding. I want to fight."

"Ella, you know we'll be outnumbered if we try to do that." The man said.

The woman sank down to the ground and lay on the grass. She wore a defiant expression.

"They are taking so many of Heaven's Chosen's lives, sure that each time it's the real one from the legend. And we're just going to sit back and watch?"

"If we do something about it, they'll know our location."

The woman sighed. "I guess you're right."

"I'm sorry, Ella."

Then, the girl ran to her father. "Daddy!" Her father lifted her into his arms with a smile.

Cassandra started and looked around, wondering where she was. She was startled by the sight of brown tree trunks and dark green made just visible by the pale moonlight. At her chest, something was glowing.

Maybe I'm going insane, Cassandra thought dimly, as she pushed herself to her feet and walked back home.

* * *

The inhabitants of the vast Sanctuary were assembled neatly around the dining table. Near the head of the table, where Alana sat, Atticus sat across from Ana and beside Roslyn. Alana was in a loud conversation with Peter, ravenously digging into her usual pasta with vodka sauce. Alana didn't like to eat anything but pasta and vodka sauce. Atticus respected it. He had never been all that fond of vegetables, either. Atticus supposed that Alana would be in danger of dying due to her lack of vitamins if Peter didn't force her to eat at least a bit of salad with her lunch.

Beside him, Roslyn sat, turning her lasagna around and around in her plate.

"Are you okay?" Atticus inquired. This had been going on for a while now, and Atticus had noticed. However, he did not wish to pry and knew that she would tell him when she believed that it was time.

"Yeah," Roslyn agreed, and forced a large piece of her dinner into her mouth rather abruptly. Perhaps she was only lost in her thoughts. Atticus could relate. It was probably her parents. His own seemed to take up his mind more than ever these days.

Across from him, Ana inconspicuously snuck glances below the table while she sipped her soup every now and then. Atticus looked under the table and saw that a thick book was propped open on her lap.

Obviously, he thought, *why hadn't I guessed?* Ana was very into books.

A loud screeching issued across the room, perhaps louder to Atticus than it actually was in the loud room, because it came from right beside him. Roslyn got up from her seat and hurried away. Atticus called after her, but she was already long gone.

14

Cherry

Roslyn hurried up the stairs and to her room, slamming the door behind her, rushing to the other end of the room where her bathroom was located. She threw herself into the room, vomiting into the toilet. She knew she shouldn't have eaten that lasagna, but she couldn't have resisted it. Lasagna was her favorite, in all its tomato and melted cheesy goodness. Besides, Atticus was getting suspicious.

Sick. She was sick. She had been for a while now, and she didn't think she would get better any time soon.

Helpless. She looked down at herself, and she could see it. Her bones, she could see them clearly through her translucent skin. She could count her ribs. Her fingers went around her wrist, with some left over.

Stupid. She had wanted so much for it to be true that she had almost believed it. At the side table where the box of pills, half empty. She had been taking more and more in order to be good enough for him.

Weak. She had known it when they had sparred; she was getting weaker and weaker. When she had hit Atticus with the side of her fist, her hand had been in the right form. She was just getting more sick.

She peered at her small, slim figure in the mirror. A scared little girl stared back at her. Hooking her finger under her oversized sweatshirt, she pulled it up slightly to expose her stomach. She paled infinitesimally if that were even possible in her already colorless features.

She sighed, letting her sweatshirt drop back down. She always wore clothes like this to hide how small she really had become, but she didn't think it helped. They had probably noticed but were waiting for her to come out and say it herself.

Pale. Her lips were pale. How was that even possible?

Pulling open a drawer in the bathroom cabinet, she grabbed her blonde hair dye and started to work on her hair. The dye stood out starkly against her albino skin, but she liked to pretend that she was normal like everyone else.

Roslyn held back a laugh. *Normal.* She wondered what that felt like.

Stepping onto the bathroom scale, she prayed and prayed before she looked down. Nobody knew but her parents, and her dear parents, sweet as they were, had always kept it a secret from everyone that they knew.

Look.

But she was too afraid to.

This was how she was. She wasn't afraid of ghosts. She wasn't afraid of possessed people. She wasn't even afraid of her own death.

She looked down at the scale and nearly fainted.

Stepping off and taking deep breaths, she willed herself to calm down. It would all be over soon, she told herself. One day the laxatives would suddenly start working, and she would gain weight, and she could eat again, oh how happy she would be! How happy she would be to be normal, like everyone else, to not have to hope to fade into the background like faded flower wallpaper.

The albinism didn't have much of a cure. But she could always get a spray tan and dye her hair.

A knocking on the door came, breaking her abruptly from her thoughts and making her open her eyes to her unfortunate reality once again. Hurriedly splashing water onto her face and toweling off with a small white towel, she pulled her sweatshirt back down and wrenched open the bathroom door.

There was Atticus, sitting on her bed. He had let himself in as always, for there was nothing weird about it, nothing weird about letting himself into a girl's bedroom and sitting on her bed, not this girl anyway. Roslyn wondered if it was because he thought of her as a sister. She grimaced. She didn't want him to think of her like that.

"Rosie, are you okay?" Atticus asked, his concerned amber eyes boring into hers, and she wondered if all of her thoughts flew out of her mind and rearranged themselves on her face, where he could see them clearly. She wondered if he could read her like a book as she always feared he could.

"Rosie?"

"I'm fine."

"Okay," Atticus said, looking unconvinced. But as usual, he didn't pry. She could see in his eyes that he knew that something was wrong, but that he trusted her to tell him in time. Roslyn felt a pang at the base of her heart. She'd have to tell him at some point.

Atticus looked out the window, out at the garden below, where she had planted her seeds. In April, the seeds had collected enough water to grow large and elegant in May, but now in July, the sun had gotten too hot for the beautiful creatures to grow. Instead, they withered away. Roslyn wondered is that would happen to her if she didn't get cured soon. She thought of death as a prospect in her future that would happen at some point, like marriage or children. She didn't shy away from it, but rather accepted it. She also had at times, wondered if it would just come already. Sometimes she just wanted to go and have over with it.

Atticus had something in his hands. She hadn't noticed it when he had greeted her, but it was there, and it visible. Small and cube-like, it hid easily in his long, artful hands. She loved to create, make new life, beautiful creatures that reached for the sun. She'd always known Atticus was something else, a different type of beauty, something unknown to the world and too pure for it. She had to protect him from the world. She had to protect him from herself.

Atticus looked her up, studying her. "Are you sure you're alright? Whatever it is, we'll fix it. Is someone bothering you? I'll rip them limb from limb. I'll-"

"It's okay, Attie. I'm alright," Roslyn lied.

"Are you sure?"

Roslyn nodded. "Of course."

Atticus nodded, his Adam's apple bobbing. "I believe you."

There it was again, that horrible feeling at the bottom of her stomach.

"On a brighter note, I've brought you something," Atticus said, handing her the small box.

Roslyn smiled. "And what is that?"

Atticus put his finger to his lip. "It's a secret. You've got to open it to find out."

Roslyn giggled and shook her head. Only Atticus could do that, make her laugh when she felt like the biggest mess on planet Earth. "Why?"

Atticus looked at her incredulously. "Because it's your birthday, of course. July twelfth. Everybody deserves a little something on their birthday."

"Thanks, Attie," she told him, genuinely taken aback by his small act of kindness. So much had happened. It was the week of his parents' decease, so she was sure that all of the remaining space in his mind that was not devoted to wondering where Ana was, strayed to them. So much had happened, but of course, Atticus remembered her birthday and brought her a present. In the end, she felt like kissing him more than ever before.

"Shut up and open it," Atticus urged.

Giggling, Roslyn tore open the red wrapping paper to find a few chocolates.

"They've got cherry filling," Atticus said. "Happy birthday, Roslyn Lydia Barnes,"

Roslyn felt the blood rush up to her face and flood from it at the same time. Atticus was watching her, waiting for her to try one, but she couldn't. If she didn't have one, it would look rude, as though she didn't like his present. If she did, she'd throw up. She couldn't have Atticus see her when she was like this, helpless, weak, sick.

"I'm actually really full right now," Roslyn told him. "I'll have one tomorrow. Thank you for the chocolate, Atticus."

Atticus' face fell slightly, but he kept his voice cheerful. "Of course." He stood up to leave but stopped at the door.

"Oh, one more thing, Rosie. Do you want to go out?"

Roslyn's breath caught. This was the moment she had been waiting for her entire life, it seemed. Whenever she fought spirits, she felt that she might not guard her life if it weren't for him. She didn't even much want it anymore. The only thing that kept her caring was the fact that she had wanted this so badly before she died. One kiss, just one time, to be able to hold his hand so tight for once like a lover, and not a best friend. She did not want to be Atticus' best friend anymore.

"Go out?" Roslyn asked, breathlessly. Her heart was racing; it was so hard to breathe, Roslyn thought it good luck that she was sitting atop her bed, for she felt she might pass out. Her mind was running through the endless possibilities, her heart bursting into flames and burning her up from the inside. She was dead, she was sure, for things like this didn't happen to people like her, people at all. She had to be dead, in paradise. That was the only thing that she was sure of. *Say it*, her mind said what her lips wouldn't, *tell me you love me the way I have always loved you.*

"Of course," Atticus said. "Ana and Cass could come too. We could go to Sundaes to get a scoop of icecream. It'll be fun."

Roslyn felt as though she were a flying bird and had landed face-first on the windshield of a car. *Of course*, she thought. *Of course, he couldn't have been asking me out. I should have known better. Boys like him don't ever want girls like me. You just believed it because you want to believe it.*

"I think I'll pass," Roslyn said, "I feel a little under the weather today."

"Oh," Atticus said, worried. "Do you want me to stay with you?"

Staying with each other through the night wasn't peculiar for the pair of them. It had started happening when she was nine, when she had been coming to the Sanctuary so often that Alana decided that it was time to cut the crap and just give her a room. Sometimes she stayed at the Sanctuary when she trained late into the night it was far too late for her to call up her parents and ask them to pick her up. It had always been soothing to know that if they haunted her in his sleep like they haunted her waking moments, he would be there, right beside her, waiting to pull her out.

It had always haunted her, the knowing, that she had real, living, blood

74

parents, who loved her so much, and that she would never get to know them. She supposed it was even harder for Atticus, who had known his parents, had seen their death and known that there was nothing he could do to stop it even as it happened. He always tried to act cool and uncaring about the past in front of Ana to keep her from worrying, but Roslyn knew well that even Atticus had a breaking point. He never truly let go in front of anyone but her. He had often waited until he was with her and they were alone to lash out and break things and fall to the floor crying. Roslyn was the only one who could calm him down, stop him from banging himself against the walls of the training room until his body finally gave in and broke.

"I'll be fine," Roslyn said. "I just need some rest."

Atticus' eyes widened, concerned. "Are you sure? I don't mind."

Roslyn knew the unspoken question in his eyes. He had been getting bad dreams, as well. He needed someone to be beside him tonight.

Roslyn turned around and placed her present on her bedside table along with the pills. She knew Atticus could see them, but she had told him that they were vitamin D tablets for her deficiency. They were definitely not laxatives.

"Okay," Atticus said carefully. "Take care of yourself. Call me if you need me. Is your dad picking you up?"

"No, I think I'll stay here."

Atticus nodded. "Alright. I'm right across the hall, okay?"

"Okay."

Atticus walked across the small space between them and placed a kiss on her cheek. Though it was soft and affectionate, Roslyn knew it was just a friendly, knowing gesture. He had never meant anything more. And she hated herself for it.

Why aren't I good enough?

Atticus left the room, leaving her alone with her forbidden feelings. Roslyn moaned and tossed Atticus' chocolate into the trash can.

15

Haiku Time

The next morning, Cassandra called Jamie on the phone. To her astonishment, he answered.

"What's up, Cassandra?" Cassandra flinched at the sound of her own full name.

"Hey, Jamie. Can we talk?"

"Sure. When do you want to talk?"

"Later today. At the park. We could have a picnic."

"Okay. See you then."

"Jamie?"

"Yes?"

"I'm sorry."

"Sorry for what?"

"Sorry for everything." She hung up. Cassandra didn't know what she was going to say to him that would express that she really felt sorry for what she did and that she really cares about his friendship. Cassandra was still reaching out in the dark when 12:00 came. She waited at Holmdel Park for Jamie, who arrived soon after she did. They spread out a blanket on the grass and had sandwiches and dark chocolate. Dark chocolate was Cassandra and Jamie's favorite type of chocolate. They loved how it's not too sweet and not too bitter, just in the middle.

"So what did you want to tell me?"

"Well, I know why you were upset. It was because I'm not a good friend. And I'm sorry, I can be clueless sometimes, but I never wanted to hurt you. You're the last person I want to hurt. Your friendship means a lot to me, and I need you to know that."

"I forgive you, but I'm not upset at you. I'm just annoyed at myself. I shouldn't have sprung something that big on you, that wasn't cool. I almost lost you, and I never want to do that again. I'm sorry."

"Don't be sorry. Thank you for always being by my side. You're like a guardian angel."

"No problem. And I'm never going to leave your side." Cassandra gave him a hug and rested her head on his shoulder, the way she always did when she was sad.

"So," Jamie said. "Wanna have a race?"

Cassandra frowned. "You hate running."

"I know. But I'll race you to cheer you up."

"You know me so well." She smiled, and they took off in the summer sunshine.

When the race was over, Jamie was panting. Cassandra had won again. She started to walk into the woods. She gestured for Jamie to follow. His face was red when he followed Cassandra under the shade of the trees. "What...is...it?" Cassandra motioned for him to come closer. When he did, Cassandra noticed with a start the way he was looking at her, as if she were made of gold, like she was the one thing in the world that was good and clean when everything else is contaminated. He was gazing at her as if she was the best thing in the world, like she was precious and fragile, and she could break at any moment.

"Why are you looking at me like that?"

"Looking at you like what?"

He doesn't even know.

"Never mind. I want to tell you something crazy, and I don't think you're going to believe me."

"Even if you told me that a giant doughnut ate the Eiffel Tower, I'd still believe you."

"Thanks." She told him all about her weird encounter with Heaven's Chosen. When she was done, his eyes were wide.

"Whoa." was all he said. His eyes were wide, the luminous green staring at her. "I believe you, but it's going to take me some time to process that information." Cassandra grinned. Suddenly, her phone rang, a sharp noise cutting into the beautiful calmness of the quiet, Jamie's beautiful voice, and their breaths, soft. She picked it up to see that it was Atticus.

"Cass?"

"Hey, Atticus. 'Sup?"

"Ana's been kidnapped."

"Cool. Wait, what?"

"We think it was that rebellious gang of spirits we've been hearing about a lot these days, but now we have no clue where she could have gone." He sounded as though he had been crying.

"When did you last see her?"

"Last night, when I got back to the Sanctuary."

"Hang on. I'm on my way."

"Cass?"

"Yeah?"

"Thank you so much."

"Don't mention it."

Cassandra turned to Jamie. "Who was that?"

"Atticus. His sister was kidnapped. I'm going over to check it out. Wanna come with?"

"Sure."

* * *

When they arrived at the Sanctuary, Jamie was gaping at its architecture. "Dude, this place is lit!" Cassandra rolled her eyes. She pointed to a window.

"I jumped out that window once," she said casually.

"Cassie, may I ask you a question?" he asked calmly.

"Sure. Shoot."

"Are you mental?"

Cassandra grinned mischievously. "I'm a daredevil, and I don't think things through, and yes, sometimes I can be totally mental. I need intense therapy for 48 hours." She grinned at him. Cassandra walked up the stairs and rung the doorbell. Atticus opened the door immediately and let them in.

"Cass. Thank you so much for coming on such short notice. You don't know how much this means to me." Atticus' sharp and elegant features looked distraught. "My parents were killed by lightning spirits, and Ana's the only family I have left." He looked at Jamie. "Who dis?"

"I'm Jamie. I'm Cassandra's best friend."

"Oh, she told me about you. I suppose you're talking to her now?"

"Yup."

"That's nice." An awkward silence passed.

"Anyway," Cassandra said hastily to break up the silence. One could always count on her to be *that* person. That person who fills in the blank with a word everyone else is trying to avoid, that person who talks when there is an awkward silence, that person who can sometimes be so clueless as to what is going on that they say something totally random and unrelated. Jamie had always said that she could never figure out if someone is implying something without just saying it out loud. There was once a boy who asked her out in 8th grade. He had given her a box of chocolates and asked her if she would go to formal with him, and she refused saying that she hated dancing, hated makeup, and absolutely detested dresses. She also told him that she didn't like milk chocolate and that she only liked dark chocolate. She had waved goodbye and kept walking as if she hadn't just ripped out his heart and run it over with a Mack truck. Jamie had to admit that he was pleased, but didn't know why he had. Now he did.

"Do you have any leads?"

"Not really, no but we've already sent a group of Pol Electi to search for her." Jamie though Atticus seemed nice, but he didn't like the way he was looking at Cassandra, as if he were longing for her, like she was something he always needed but knew he could never have. Stop it.

"Let me show you the map room." He ushered the pair into a room with a warm and cozy look and mahogany bookshelves. There was a long table in the middle of the room, with chairs lined up all around it. There were large maps spread out on top, mapping out everything.

"So, we have been finding reports of a group of rebellious supernatural beings around here," He pointed to an area on the map. "but the Sanctuary is over here. So, they must have kidnapped Ana and brought her back to their headquarters. This group is named "Infernum." They are the suspects. We need to collect information about where the headquarters are because that might be where they're keeping her." Footsteps sounded on the mahogany wood flooring, and Roslyn entered the room.

"Hey, Cass," Roslyn greeted her in a manner that seemed force. Cassandra didn't mind.

"Hey, Roslyn," She walked to the other side of the room and started polishing large blades.

"Dude. Those knives are large."

"I know. We use them to help send bad spirits back to hell." Atticus said, helpfully. Then, rather spontaneously, he added, "Wanna hear a haiku I made?" If one were to use five words to describe him, they would come up with funny, innocent, pure, strong, and spontaneous.

"No," Cassandra said. "I do not."

"Ok. Thank you for your enthusiasm and support," he replied.

"I sat on the couch
It smells like a diseased goat
I hate my life"

"That last one was only four syllables," Jamie pointed out helpfully.

"I never said I was good at writing haikus," Atticus said, rebelliously. "Do you want to hear another one?"

"No," Roslyn and Cassandra said at the same time.

"Okay. Here goes."

"I went to ShopRite
I bought my Cheese-Its today
I–"

"Shut up, Elsa!" Cassandra said.

Roslyn laughed so hard that tears came out of her eyes. "That's your new nickname."

"Elsa? Why are you calling me–ohhh. Because my sister's Ana," a dawning realization came upon Atticus' face. "That's not funny."

What was ironic was that he had always been the type to laugh along. Even though the joke was made against him, in a normal situation, Atticus might have at least chuckled, if only for the first time. However, not even the trace of a smile came to his lips.

It didn't even seem funny. Nothing ever seemed funny anymore.

It might have occurred to the others that most people didn't make jokes when their sisters had been kidnapped. That was true, but he was not like most people.

When their parents had died, Atticus had been five, and Ana had been two. Even though it was a very young age, he still could understand what was going on. That's the thing adults never got about children. They're not quite as stupid as you think they are.

Even though Atticus had wanted to pretend that everything was alright, he knew that it wasn't, and his little sister was crying. He had to think of a way to calm her down, quickly.

And that was when he had got his nervous habit that when he was miserable, he always cracked jokes. They were considerably bad jokes, however, never even slightly good, and that could never compete with his other jokes. He was trying to make his sister laugh, while silently tricking himself that everything was alright, and that his parents would be home shortly. He couldn't allow himself to be sad in front of Ana, who would surely catch on and start crying again. Instead, he would act as though nothing has happened, and if Ana thought that something had, she was surely wrong. He had to be her lifeline, for if he broke down, there was nothing left for Ana to hold onto.

And now, she was gone.

He should have taken better care of her. He would already be punishing himself like Dobby from Harry Potter if he hadn't had to go look for her.

"It is so funny," Cassandra told him.

"Is not."

"Is too."

Atticus scowled at Cassandra.

"So, have you told the search party about where you think Ana might be?" Jamie inquired, breaking up Cassandra's teasing, though Atticus knew what she was doing. She was trying to bring his mind away from his sister. She had been hurting for a while now, and she knew the signs.

"Yeah, and they will be searching there." Atticus told him. *Goddamn it, Atticus, keep your head.* "What we need to do is go around to popular haunts near the Sanctuary and see if we can torture any information out of them that will help find Ana."

Roslyn stood up. She opened up her black leather jacket to display a number of very dangerous-looking weapons on the inside. Their blades shone in the dim light of the fire in the lantern that hung above the table. Roslyn grinned. Cassandra grinned back. Atticus stood up and gestured for Cassandra to follow him.

"If you like that, you're going to love this," he told her.

She followed him out of the room. They walked through a narrow hallway lined with expensive-looking oiled paintings and walked up a spiral staircase. They reached a corridor. Atticus walked to the third door and opened it. It was a normal bedroom, and there were large bookshelves lining the walls. They were filled with books. At the side of the room stood a bed. It had not been made. There was a dresser across from it with a mirror. Atticus walked over to a bookshelf. He counted the books and stopped at the ninth book. His slim fingers lingered on the book titled "Chinese Cuisine." He pushed the book, and there was a clicking sound. However, the clicking sound came from somewhere else in the room. He walked over to the side of his bed and pushed it until it met the bookshelf. A door was revealed. Atticus walked over to it and pulled it open. A ladder led down into the opening in the ground. Atticus motioned for Cassandra to join him. She turned on the flashlight on her cellphone and started to descend the ladder. When they reached the bottom, they found it was very dark. Atticus lit a candle because there were no lights down here. He placed the candle in a lantern hanging from the ceiling. The room was instantly illuminated. Cassandra saw that there was an enormous and impressive display of weapons, ranging from wooden poles with sharp metal edges, knives, blades, daggers, nunchucks, sais, which were smaller wooden poles attached to sharp metal triangles, and rifles. They hung on the walls, were on shelves, and on tables.

"Epic," Cassandra said.

"I know, right?" Atticus walked toward one of the shelves and chose a few blades. He put them in the pockets on the inside of his jacket, where they would be hidden. Then he turned around. Cassandra was examining a long sword with absolute awe, and she was looking at it like it was a god.

"Well, are you going to take one?"

"Oh. Yeah. Where do I put this?" She was holding a large and heavy sword as if it weighed no more than a feather.

"You can borrow one of my jackets when we go back up."

After they were done making their selections, they went back up, Atticus pushed his bed back, and they locked the secret door by tugging the book back. Atticus went into a walk-in closet and emerged with a black jacket.

"Thank you," Cassandra said to him.

"Don't mention it." Cassandra shrugged the jacket on. She found pockets on the inside, where she shoved a few of her weapons.

"Ready?"

"Uh-huh." They made their way back downstairs and back the way they came to find Roslyn and Jamie talking animatedly about the history of the Sanctuary.

"Is he one of the Chosen?" Roslyn asked Atticus.

"I don't know, actually. Let's check." Atticus answered.

He held out a sword to Jamie, who raised his eyebrows and took it. Its weight was not supported by Jamie, and it immediately sunk, hilt in his hand, the blade on the ground.

"Ouch. This doesn't feel right." Jamie said, trying to carry the sword and look like a badass. It wasn't working. Roslyn looked disgusted.

"Nope," Atticus said as he took the sword back. "He's normal and boring."

"Thanks," Jamie told her sarcastically. Then, he turned to Cassandra. "Did you get a tattoo? I didn't notice that until now." Jamie said to Cassandra. Cassandra followed his gaze down to her arm where a red outline of a rose with thorns was fading.

"No. That's the mark that we get on our arm when we hold blessed weapons."

"Ohhh."

"Okay, then," Roslyn said, standing up from her place near the fireplace. "Let's bounce."

The group made their way outside the Sanctuary and was immediately greeted by the warmth of the summer sun. Roslyn led the way. They were going to an old broken down house south from the Sanctuary, where a cluster of spirits wandered. When they got there, Cassandra noticed that the house looked like it had an immense amount of water damage. They picked their way into the house, the lock giving in after Cassandra had kicked it. They walked in quietly, the floorboards creaking and threatening to give in. Suddenly, a sharp voice greeted them.

"Who dares disturb my slumber?" a voice intoned. Jamie put his hand over Cassandra's mouth before she opened her mouth and said something that would have angered the spirit because he knew how her pride and temper always got the best of her. They kept walking until they reached a living room with an old sofa that used to be florally patterned but was now stained a dark red that gradually turned to brown and sunk down with age. Roslyn frowned with distaste. They walked on and found themselves in a room. It had a broken down dresser in it, and a splintering cot. At a corner of the room, there was an emaciated looking man. There were shadows under his eyes. He looked up as the group entered. He started to laugh, a hoarse, choking sound that raised the hairs on the back of Cassandra's neck. Atticus stepped forward. "I'm going to give you two choices. Answer truthfully or be slain."

He laughed again. "Well, you're going to send me to hell anyway, so what's the point of telling?" he said.

"I won't if you tell me the truth. You have my word."

"What is your word to me? You could be lying." Atticus exhaled hard in exasperation. Cassandra stepped forward and put a sword to his neck.

"Where is Ana?" He looked afraid now. She dug it in further, about a third of an inch. "Or do you want to die for a second time?" he gulped.

"She's with the Infernum."

"I knew it," Atticus said.

"Where exactly?" Cassandra went on as if he hadn't spoken.

"At the headquarters," he told her, looking frightened. Cassandra lowered the blade. They made their way out of the house. Atticus sent a message to the search group, and they started to walk back to the Sanctuary.

"He could have been lying." Roslyn proposed.

"I don't think he was, though. People don't think when they're afraid, and he probably spilled out the truth."

It was about 6:00 when they got back. Atticus was worried, and his usual swagger wasn't about him today. Roslyn put a reassuring hand on his arm.

"They'll find her, don't worry."

"But what if she's harmed by the time they find her?"

"Then I will personally track them down, tie them to chairs, and kill them in the slowest and most painful way," Cassandra said.

"Thank you." Despite Cassandra's rather bloodthirsty statement, Atticus looked reassured. "The search party told me that they'd get back to me tomorrow. I can't stand the waiting, though. I would have gone with the search party, but I'm apparently underage and too young to go investigating." Atticus made a face. "They don't know that we interrogated a spirit. So keep it to yourself." Cassandra and Jamie waved goodbye and started to walk back home. They walked in the summer sunset, and the trees looked black under the colorful burst. When they reached Jamie's house, Cassandra felt a pang in her heart that he had to leave. *Don't be ridiculous. You'll see him tomorrow.* Her mind full of thoughts, she walked back home.

16

Symbol

Cassandra awoke to the sharp sound of her phone ringing. She opened her eyes sleepily and took her phone from the mahogany nightstand. It was Atticus.

"Why?"

"Why what?" Atticus asked.

"Why'd you wake me up?"

"I just got information from the search group. They captured a few members of Infernum. They brought them to the interrogation chamber. They're going to start the interrogation in an hour. Wanna watch?"

"Sure. Can I bring Jamie, too?"

Atticus hesitated for a moment. "Sure."

* * *

Half an hour later, Jamie and Cassandra were standing at the large mahogany doors of the Sanctuary. Roslyn opened it this time.

"Hey, guys." She greeted them. "Atticus is already there." She led the way. They walked into a kind of screening room.

"This is the interrogation room?" Jamie asked, incredulously.

"No, silly. We can't actually be inside the interrogation room. We're underage. So I installed cameras inside the interrogation room when no one

was watching. We're going to watch the interrogation without permission."
She smiled a crooked grin.

"Hi." Atticus greeted the trio. He was seated in a set near the back of the room. Cassandra sat next to him, Jamie next to her. Roslyn was messing around on a laptop, and she connected a cord to it. A room showed up on the large screen. Roslyn left the computer open and walked over to sit on Atticus' other side. Cassandra found herself peering into a large, dimly lit room. The only light filtered through a grimy lantern hanging from the ceiling and added to the eerie feel of it. There was a restless looking man seated in a chair, with cuffs on his hands, binding him to his spot.

"Those cuffs are made of blessed metal," Roslyn pointed out helpfully. "It burns spirits." There were gray shadows under the man's eyes, which seemed to be a trademark symbol for spirits. He kept looking around, moving his feet occasionally, and he grinned at a young woman seated in a chair opposite him. Her face was elegant and composed. She looked young but experienced as if she had seen and experienced many horrors that people her age usually do not face. Her pale skin was starkly contrasted with her glossy ink colored hair, which brought out dark parts in her gray-blue eyes. She looked rather gothic and donned a spiked black choker, spiked earrings, a ring on her nose and two on her lip. Her frame was lanky and slim, and dark lipstick highlighted her thick lips in her pale face, and black eyeliner brought out her hair.

She looked at him calmly and said, "You have taken one of ours. Tell me where she is, and I will let you go."

"I told you already. The Infernum hasn't taken her."

"We have reason to believe that you have. What evidence do you have to disprove that?"

"We haven't taken her, you idiot!" he said in a raised voice.

"Oh, am I an idiot now?" She said, in a silky voice that thinly concealed daggers. "So if you haven't taken her, who has?"

"I don't know. Your whole Sanctuary is being brought down by you, Alana. I don't even like Heaven's Chosen too much, but they were doing well until that cursed day when they chose you to be their leader. I don't know what they were thinking when they figured a woman could lead."

Alana's gray eyes flashed, and she stood up from her seat. She moved with a sort of grace and agility, that made all that observed her know that she was someone to respect and not one to cross. "What did you say?"

"You are a hopeless idiot." At this point, Cassandra couldn't stand it anymore. She stood up and glared at the screen.

"I'm going to find this person and teach him a lesson. He thinks girls can't lead? He can freakin' burn in hell. If I were to call him a disgusting, slimy creature, it'd be an upgrade from whatever he is. Imma mess him up. Let me at him. Let me at him." Cassandra snarled. Jamie did his best to hold her back, but she was struggling against his grip.

"Cassie, they don't know we're watching them. Besides, she looks like she's going to harm him physically all by herself." Grudgingly, Cassandra sat down.

Alana spoke. "Vincent, you don't think that women are tough, do you?" Her voice was calm, but her eyes betrayed her flaring anger. She drew out a dagger from her belt. "Blessed metal." She answered his unanswered question. "It was dipped in the holy river and gifted to my great-great-great-grandmother by an angel. Drives spirits away. Do you know what this will do once it passes through the thin barriers of your skin? Her voice was still silky, her eyes flashing with a fire that Cassandra admired. The spirit gulped. His eyes held concealed fear. Alana stepped forward, grinning crookedly, exposing white teeth. She was a very attractive woman, and the smile would have looked nice if it hadn't have been for her eyes. She was staring her opponent down with a look that was like death. She stepped closer to him, unafraid. She looked down at her dagger. It glinted in the dim light. She put it against the cheek of the man. He shrunk back. "What was that you said about women, Vincent, dear? Say it again?" She traced the dagger down in a line, and blood dripped from his cheek to the ground in drops. The man winced.

"I said," he retorted through gritted teeth, "that women aren't smart enough to lead."

"I see," Alana said. Her voice was smooth and silky. Her dark hair reached her shoulders, and her lips were red. Her eyes held a terrifying sort of danger. Cassandra really liked her. "And would you know 150 different ways to kill a spirit?" The man gulped. Alana grinned. She took the dagger and placed it on his collarbone. Slowly, she drew it down. The man cried out in pain and grimaced. Blood started to soak the front of his shirt rapidly, and the man gasped. "Relax. I haven't cut you too deep. Yet." Alana called out to a man with red hair and emerald eyes. She towered above him as she was very tall. "Peter. I'd appreciate it if you could send this spirit to the dungeons for crimes against Pol Electi, but he has made it very clear that his group hasn't taken Ana. I can hear it in his tone."

"Of course, Alana." The red-headed man with the rather worn looking messenger bag rushed over to the spirit and shoved him through a door which Cassandra figured led to the dungeons.

"He thinks that women aren't smart. He can go to hell. And he will, too. Sexist freak." She then executed a swear that would have killed Jamie's mother if she had heard him say it. Then, she looked right up at the camera and grinned. "And Roslyn, I know this was you, cuz' Atticus can never figure out tech." Atticus grinned in a way that seemed to say, 'that's me.' "I like your curiosity and your skill, and I like how you can sneak around like that. It will help you when you're older, investigating cases. But I told you not to eavesdrop. And if I find you disobeying my orders again, I will personally find you two and bang your heads in. Have a nice day." She kicked the camera, and the screen went blank.

Atticus smiled. "I absolutely love that woman."

"Me too," Cassandra said. Roslyn looked thoughtful.

"There are a few spirit groups. And if Infernum isn't it, who is it?"

"I really thought it was Infernum, though. They are pretty infamous and have been known for a bunch of Pol Electi killings during the Dark Ages." Atticus remarked.

"Well there's Viri Sanguinum, and they're the second most infamous after Infernum. There's also Caedes, Inferna Electi, Venator, and Diabolus." After a quizzical look from Cassandra, she explained saying that these were Latin names. "Ana would know all of their names in English. I miss her."

"So what do we do now?" Cassandra inquired.

"We track the other groups and interrogate them for Ana's location," Atticus replied. "There are groups tracking the first three groups, and Alana gave us permission to track the fourth because they're one of the smaller groups and do little harm." He pouted. "Unfortunately we don't get to have too much fun."

"At least she let us do that," Roslyn said.

"Yeah. If it were anyone else, they wouldn't have even let us out of the Sanctuary." Atticus agreed.

"So where are they?" Jamie asked.

"Diabolus? They're at the broken-down house we saw yesterday." Roslyn told him.

"What are we waiting for?" Cassandra asked, getting up. "Let's go."

* * *

When they reached the house again, Cassandra was the first to go in, Roslyn closely following her, then Atticus, and then Jamie. When they got inside the house, they found themselves staring at the sunken sofa again. They walked into the room where they found the spirit the last time that they had been there, but found no one waiting for them. After Roslyn and Cassandra searched the house, they confirmed that the house had been cleared out of all spirits.

"You know what this means, right?" Jamie asked.

"No," Atticus said. He was looking at his feet while they walked around the house to see if anyone was there. No one was.

"It means that we know who kidnapped Ana."

Atticus looked up. "How do you know?"

"Well," Jamie said, "We came here yesterday, and the man said that he knew that Infernum did it. If they were sure that they were innocent, why did they leave?"

"That makes a lot of sense. You're clever," Roslyn said. Atticus' eyes had lit up.

"That does," he agreed. "We need to pass on this information to Alana. We can tell her when we get back to the Sanctuary."

As they neared the Sanctuary, they smelled smoke. Cassandra wrinkled her nose. When they arrived at the front door of the Sanctuary, the smell only got stronger. Cassandra had a premonition that something terrible happened when they were gone. They rung the doorbell, but the door was unlocked, so they just entered. The Sanctuary looked as it always did. The group followed the smell. They were led to the hall, in which there were fire spirits. They were roaming around. Fire danced on their fingertips, and smoke rose in tendrils from it. The members of the search party and everyone left in the Sanctuary were tied to poles with a type of thick rope. There, in the middle, of the room was Alana, struggling against the rope. The man named Vincent was cackling softly.

"How did they find us?" Alana demanded.

"I attached a tracking device to my ring." He extended his fingers to show her, the way someone might examine their nails. "They tracked me and found you." He smiled, a nasty look on his scarred face.

"I will escape. And when I do, I will find you and end you for a second time." She snarled. Alana's eyes looked dangerous. Then, she looked surprised because she had spotted the group. Vincent followed her line of gaze and saw them. A smile, even larger than the first one played upon his face.

"Oh, good. We have more guests. Feel free to join the party. The more, the merrier." A pair of fire spirits stepped up to them. The first one reached out for Jamie, the second for Roslyn. Roslyn reached for a weapon in her jacket and started fighting him. Jamie, who had never held a weapon before kicked out. The kick did not connect, however. The spirit had dodged him and caught his shoulder. His other hand was open, palm up, and a fire was in it. Cassandra realized with a start that the spirit was going to try to burn Jamie. Cassandra drew her long sword from Atticus' jacket, crept behind the spirit, and sliced its head clean off. Atticus pulled out a tube and captured his soul. He stored it on his belt. Roslyn was finishing up with her own and had expertly trapped him in a tube. Vincent growled. He sent more spirits after them, about thirty. Atticus and Roslyn gestured to

Cassandra and Jamie to run. There was no way that they could fight that many spirits at a time.

When they got out of range of the enemy, Cassandra told Atticus, "We need to go back and save them! They're going to kill them!"

To her surprise, Jamie shook his head. "No. If we do, they're going to kill us. What we need to do is wait."

Cassandra looked at him incredulously. "Wait? Why should we wait?"

"Because they know that we won't leave them behind and that we'll come back for them. So they're going to use them as bait to get us. They won't kill them, now that they've seen us. They're going to try to lure us here and then kill us altogether." Roslyn answered. Cassandra considered this.

"That does make sense. But we have to get away from here to throw them off our scent." Cassandra said. Jamie smiled. "Just stop your crying, it's a sign up of the times. We gotta get away from here. We gotta get away." he sang. Cassandra laughed.

"Any chance that Harry Styles and his girlfriend were chased by an army of angry dead people?" Cassandra asked. Jamie laughed.

"Guys, keep it down. We don't know if we're being followed." Roslyn warned. Cassandra nodded and followed as Atticus led the way through the woods they had escaped to. They walked back to the broken-down house that Diabolus used to haunt. It was the only place they could go that wouldn't have been easy to spot by the spirits. Cassandra was bored, so she decided to go exploring. She was at the edge of a room when she found a coat closet near it. She opened it curiously and found it stuffed with old coats. The coats were ripped up and had a dark red powdery residue on them.

"Cassie?" Jamie called to her.

"I'm over here," she called back. She heard footsteps, and Jamie, blond hair ruffled, shirt sleeve torn, and jeans ripped and muddy in the sunlight filtering through the broken window appeared in front of her. His eyes were wide, and he was looking at her. He looked rather vulnerable, like a child, and Cassandra felt a sudden and strong urge to protect him from any harm that might come his way.

"What are you doing here?" he asked curiously. He eyed the coat closet.

"Exploring."

"Why didn't I guess?" he asked. Jamie stepped forward. Cassandra turned around again to examine the coats. She pulled them from their hangers and threw them on the ground. She turned on her phone flashlight and peered into the closet. There were shoes on the floor. She pushed them out of the way to reveal a door. Jamie crouched down and tried the knob. It didn't budge. Cassandra raised one knee-high and brought her foot down with force on the door. It gave in and showed a set of stairs, narrow and dark. She grinned and looked up at him. He grinned back. They slowly made their way down to the dark room, Cassandra holding up her phone with the flashlight on, illuminating the way. When they reached the bottom of the staircase, they found that the floor was a little damp. There were chains protruding from a blood-encrusted pole, and dried blood powdered the floor. There were dark rags on the ground. Cassandra walked over to it and pushed it to the side with her boot. Her breath caught when she saw a dark pattern. She crouched next to it, and Jamie followed her lead. She peered at the symbol.

"That's the symbol of Pol Electi," Jamie said. "Do you think…" He let his question hang in the air between them, afraid to get her hopes up.

"No, I think you're right. Ana's been here." Cassandra called out to Atticus and Roslyn. When they got down, they made the same assumption. Atticus was kneeling near the symbol. It was traced in blood, so it was dark red.

Atticus was rendered speechless. His head down in his hands, his dark curls were falling forward. He looked as vulnerable as he had on the day of the fireworks. Cassandra couldn't help but sympathize, for she knew what losing someone felt like. She walked over to him and sank down on the damp floor, putting her hand on his shoulder. She felt him tense under her touch. She spoke in a soft but strong voice.

"It's going to be okay, Atticus. We'll find her. And when we do, I promise to find every single spirit involved in her kidnapping and end them in the most painful way known to this world."

He nodded as if in a dream. Then he put his head on her shoulder, the way she did to Jamie when she was sad. They stayed that way for a few minutes, and then they got up. "I'm going to go exploring some more," Cassandra said.

"I'll come with you," Jamie said.

"I'm going to check this room for more clues, then the surroundings for footprints or anything that can hint to Ana's location," Atticus said.

"I'll help," Roslyn told him.

As Roslyn and Atticus walked around the room examining the walls for a sign, Atticus couldn't focus. His face was red, but he hoped that Roslyn would think this was because he was sad. And he was, very. When he thought of his little sister, he remembered how she used to run through fields of sunflowers and dandelions when she was five, laughing and giggling with dandelion seeds caught up in her braids. *Catch me if you can, Atticus! Catch me if you can!* She used to say. But this was not why his face was red. He still could not believe that he had put his head on Cassandra's shoulder. She had smelt like smoke, blood, and the sea. He could still feel her hand on his shoulder like it had always been there, like they had known each other all their life. Roslyn was saying something, but he could not hear her now. *It's going to be okay, Atticus. We'll find her.*

17

Don't Stop Driving

Cassandra and Jamie trudged through the debris of the broken-down house, Cassandra stumbled against a long piece of wood and fell forward. She felt intense pain as a shard of glass from a broken window pierced through her jeans and cut through the soft skin of her thigh. She bit her lip to keep herself from crying out. Jamie, who was hurrying toward her, called out to her. "Cassie, don't move. I'm coming."

"I'm fine." She tried to get up, but her foot slipped on something, and she fell backward.

"Even you need help sometimes. And it's alright to admit it. Just like all of us, you're only human, and you can't face everything on your own. So please, let me help you, and we can face the world together." Jamie reached her and crouched down. He leaned forward, and a lock of his golden hair fell into his eyes. He seemed not to notice.

He looked worried. He was biting his lip, and his eyes were wide, two things he did when he was in pain. The sight of him wearing that expression sparked a memory of when they were twelve, and he had scraped his knees playing basketball with her. Down he had gone, basketball falling and rolling to the side, abandoned and forgotten, and he fell to his knees. Blood, sickly hot and red like love, dripped from it, staining his pants, his little face scrunched up in pain. Cassandra had run to him, told him it would be alright, and put his arm over her shoulder so he could lean on her and they walked home. She remembered how he looked then. His eyes were large, he was biting his lip, and he looked vulnerable. He looked just like that now, she thought, his eyes held a mix of vulnerability and hurt. Cassandra was confused. *Why does he look hurt?*

"Cassie, this is going to hurt, but if I don't get that glass shard out of your leg, it's going to get infected." He said, his eyes wide. Cassandra bit her lip and nodded. "I'm going to do this as fast as I can," he reassured her. His slim fingers came down to her leg and caught the glass shard. He looked up at her, two eyes of pure emerald green staring into gray-green that seemed to go on forever. "Ready?"

"Yeah," Cassandra said. He nodded and pulled the shard. More intense pain filled Cassandra, and she wanted to cry out, but she tried to avoid showing pain when she could. *Showing pain was a weakness*, she told herself. *And I am not weak.* So she bit her lip even harder. She tasted blood. Blood was welling up on her thigh, and Jamie was ripping his shirt sleeve to tie up her wound. He tied it tight enough to stop the bleeding and put her arm across his shoulder. He slowly helped her up, and she leaned on the wall. He still looked hurt.

"Why do you look like that?" She asked him.

"Look like what?"

"Look like you're hurt."

"I don't think you would want to know."

"I do. Tell me." He looked up, hesitantly, and she stared back. He nodded.

"You've become such a big part of me, that when you're hurting, I can feel the pain too. When you break, I'm breaking with you. I don't know how it happens, but it does, and I can't seem to stop." He looked down at his shoes, blond hair tumbling forward. His shoelaces were untied, his shirt sleeve ripped, and his jeans ripped. The sight of him filled her with affection for him, and she walked over to him, ignoring the throbbing pain in her leg and hugged him. She hugged him so fiercely that she could feel his heartbeat. He put his arms around her tentatively and hugged her back. When she finally let go, Jamie looked at her incredulously. "So you're not mad at me?"

She smiled. "I'm not mad at you." Relief flooded his gorgeous face.

"Oh, thank god." He smiled back at her. Jamie supported Cassandra by letting her lean on him and walk. "Explain to me again why we can't go back home?"

"Atticus said that we have to stay hidden, or the spirits that captured the members of the Sanctuary will be able to pinpoint and abduct us easily."

"Oh."

"But you can go. You're not Pol Electi, so they have no use for abducting and torturing you."

"And leave you here? Where you could possibly be captured and killed? No way. I mean, not to say that you aren't strong or anything, but I'd feel so much better if I stayed here with you and faced whatever you faced with you."

"No. Jamie, you should go. I don't want to put you in danger for my sake." Cassandra protested. Jamie shook his head.

"No way. I'll never leave your side." His voice was gentle but firm, and Cassandra knew that there was no point in trying to convince him otherwise. She reached out and took his hand, squeezing it, and smiling at him. He smiled back.

* * *

The scorching afternoon summer sun blazed, and turned Atticus' curly brown hair a beautiful hue of chestnut and brought a sheen to it. A summer gust blew and pushed Atticus' hair into his eyes. He impatiently pushed it away and stared straight ahead. He and Roslyn were walking around the house to look for any sign of Ana's location. They were disappointed that they didn't see any so far. His gait was graceful and fluidlike, and he looked like he was gliding rather than walking. Suddenly, Roslyn stopped walking. Atticus stopped quickly beside her, looking at her with a quizzical expression. "Look," she said, pointing towards the ground. There were leaves on the ground, lightly spattered with blood. There was another splotch of the dark liquid in front of it, but that was it. Atticus and Roslyn shared a worried look, then started walking in the direction of the second blood splotch.

18

Stealing Cars

It was dark when they got there. She didn't know where they were, only that she had passed out and was taken to a new location. She glanced around, taking in her surroundings. She was in a dark room, and the floor was gray and hard, with splotches of a dark substance that she could only hope was paint. She looked up and saw that the ceiling was a dirty white, with streaks of gray in intervals. The paint was peeling off the walls, and she looked down. She saw that her feet and arms were in manacles that were chained to a pole. Her curly brown, usually arranged in two neat braids were tangled and messy. Her lips were chapped and bleeding, and a long cut was on her right cheek, blood dark and encrusted on the side of her face. The door opened, letting in a little light, and a dark figure appeared. She knew by his slightly transparent skin that he was dead. He entered the room and sat in a chair in front of her.

"You know the deal. Tell us the location of the Sanctuary, and we'll let you go. It's that simple."

She looked up and gave him a nasty look. The man grinned, showing her an unpleasant array of teeth. "What have they done for you anyway? Just tell us the location, and we'll let you and your brother free." She glared but kept her mouth closed. The man scowled. "Tell me right now, you imbecile! Right now, do you hear me? I will tear you apart, flesh from bone, right now! Tell me!"

She looked straight into his eyes. She was a good strategist, and she knew that quite obviously he wouldn't dare touch her. She smiled a sweet smile, and for a moment, she looked like an angel after a long fight, and she said, "You wouldn't dare. If I were hurt, I wouldn't be in any good shape to tell you the location." The spirit's eyes widened in anger, and she could see the rage in them. He stood up and drew a blade from his belt. He grinned, she showed her the knife.

"It's very pretty, isn't it?" He held the blade closer to her face. "Now, would you like to tell me the location of the Sanctuary? I can't kill you, but I can make you bleed."

Ana was cut up, bruised, bleeding, and sweating. She had cried the first day, the warm tears running down her cheeks and making tracks on her grimy face. She had never cried again. She laughed now and then said a word that only Alana would have dared to say. She had never cursed before. She had tried to avoid even the most minor of curses, frowning at people who said rude words, thinking them disgusting for having such a revolting vocabulary. Her unruly brown hair had come out of its hairbands a while ago, and it was on her shoulders. She threw her head back and spat at the spirit. The man's eyes narrowed, and he stood up. He drew the knife across her arm, and there was a scar there now, blood seeping slowly from it. She grinned at the man. He walked out of the room, shutting the door behind him. Ana was left alone in the dark She heard the lock click into places and push any hopes of escape from her mind. She leaned her head against the wall and closed her eyes. She wondered where Atticus was now. Was Roslyn with him, looking for her? Would Cassandra search too? Would they find her at all? *Stop it.* She willed her mind to stop thinking about the unpleasant but possible possibilities. She remembered that day at the broken-down house, when Atticus, Roslyn, Cassandra, and an unfamiliar voice had come so close to finding her. They had been upstairs, she could hear them, but they couldn't hear her. She had screamed until her throat had become scratchy, and her voice hoarse. The leader of Diabolus, a woman with graying hair a nasty smile had laughed at her attempts to draw their attention.

101

"They'll never find you. And you won't ever see them again if you don't tell us the location of the Sanctuary," she had said. But Ana hadn't budged. Now she looked up. She wondered if Atticus had any clue where she was. She wondered if he was coming here, to find her, and to bring her back home. *Of course, he is. He's your brother. He loves you, and he won't rest until he finds you.* She felt so helpless and miserable. She had left a sign, the Pol Electi symbol drawn from her own blood, then hid it to make sure that the spirits don't erase it. She didn't even know if Atticus, Roslyn, and Cassandra would find the secret underground room that they hid her in, let alone find the hidden symbol. She tried to leave a clue to where they were hiding her next, but they hadn't told her. They had just knocked her out, threw her in a truck, and brought her to a new destination. This one, she concluded, was far from the first one, because she didn't remember seeing it around.

Atticus called Cassandra up and told her to come over, grudgingly allowing Jamie as well. When they arrived, it was about 6:00, the sun lighting up the sky so that it looked about noon. Cassandra and Jamie came into the sunlight, and a lock of Cassandra's dark hair fell into her eyes, but she didn't care enough to push it away. She was smiling, and at that moment, Atticus thought she looked like a dark angel. His fingers itched to push the lock of hair away from her face, but he restrained himself. And then he saw her hand. She was holding Jamie's hand, and Atticus was suddenly annoyed. What did he think, holding her hand like that? What made him think he had the right to hold her hand? There was only one person who was allowed to hold her hand, and that was him. He wanted to tear Jamie apart, limb by limb, till he was on the ground. Then he was puzzled as to why he thought this. *Jamie is nice. He's here trying to help me save my sister, and he doesn't even know me. I shouldn't want to push him off a cliff. Besides, there is a possibility that they are just holding hands because they have been best friends for so long. Right?*

"Atticus? Atticus? Earth to Atticus. Why are you staring at me? Atticus!" Cassandra exclaimed, bringing Atticus back to earth. He tore his eyes from her hand that was clasped with Jamie's and up to her face.

"Dude. I thought you became deaf for a minute there." Cassandra told him. Atticus smiled, hoping she couldn't read his mind. *I want you; I need you, I just want to hold your hand.*

"Yeah. I was just. Um. Thinking." She gave him a funny look.

"Okayyyy." He was not fully convinced that she didn't know what was on his mind, but he hoped Roslyn didn't. He turned to look at her and was quite relieved to see that she didn't suspect anything. She just kept smiling at him.

"Alright. What's going on? Did I step in dog shit or something? Is that why you're acting so weird?" Cassandra asked, cluelessly. She looked down and inspected her black lace-up boots. Convinced that she didn't have any droppings on her boots, she looked up. "So. Did you find anything of importance?"

"Um. Yeah. He looked down at the wrong spot, then started searching the ground for the blood-stained leaf. "It's somewhere here."

"It's over here," Roslyn said, pointing down at a spot next to her feet, nowhere near where Atticus thought it had been. Cassandra unclasped her hand from Jamie's and started walking over to where Roslyn was pointing to examine the spot. She got down on her knees and touched it. Some of it came onto her long and slim fingers. She looked up.

"It's wet. Ana's been here recently," Cassandra told them. Atticus looked worried.

Roslyn looked up. "Atticus, do you know where the closest haunted house is from here?"

He met her gaze. "I do."

* * *

A half an hour later, Cassandra found herself in the driver's seat of a black car. Atticus was sitting in the front passenger seat next to her, Roslyn and Jamie in the back. Atticus turned to look at Cassandra. "Tell me again how you got this car?"

Cassandra smiled mischievously. "I stole it."

"You what?!" Jamie exclaimed.

"Relax. It's Rowan's." She smirked.

"How'd you get it from her?"

"She thinks I'm getting it serviced."

"Cassie," he protested and put his face in his hands.

"Your mother raised you too well," she said, shaking her head sadly. "You pure, innocent child."

"I'm six months older than you!" Jamie exclaimed.

Atticus laughed. Then he was confused. No one had been able to make him laugh like that except for Roslyn, and he felt as if Cassandra made him laugh all the time, effortlessly. He felt an urge to hold her hand and pour his heart out to her. Stop it. Get out of my mind. Get out of my mind. But he couldn't help it. His head was swimming with her grin, and his fingers itched to reach out and stroke her hair. Atticus was pulled from his daydreams when Roslyn told Cassandra the way to another one of Diabolus' headquarters.

"Turn here," Roslyn told Cassandra, who jerked at the steering wheel and narrowly avoided a head-on collision. Everyone in the vehicle was shoved to the side of the car including Atticus, who had grabbed his opposite armrest to keep himself from slamming into the window.

"Cass?" Atticus called over the rising commotion of honking horns.

"Yes?"

"Did you ever learn to drive?"

"Do you want me to tell you the truth or make you feel nice?"

"The truth."

"I failed my driving test three times."

"You what?!"

"You heard me."

"Cassie," Jamie said calmly, "If you failed the driving test three times, maybe there's a reason you shouldn't be driving a car."

"Meh." Cassandra shrugged and kept driving.

"Ok. Take a left at that stop sign," Roslyn said, pointing. Jamie braced himself by holding onto the headrest of the chair in front of him. Atticus, however, did not, and instantly regretted it when Cassandra yanked the steering wheel sideways fiercely. Atticus fell into Cassandra's lap. He immediately got up.

"Sorry."

"It's cool," Cassandra said easily. She was an easygoing, happy go lucky type of girl. Atticus caught something red out of the corner of his eye, in the rearview mirror. He turned to see what it was and realized that it was his own face, burning up. He hastily looked down and started acting like he was texting someone on his phone, lest anyone see him blushing.

19

Days

She looked up and was immediately greeted with the pleasant scene of a blood-stained and dusty prison cell. She didn't know what she expected, anyway. She'd been here for what felt like an eternity, and she had gone accustomed to the quirks of the prison cell. She hadn't had any connections to the outside world in two years, other than the blank-eyed young woman who pushed a meager supply of food through the slot twice a day. Those were the only two times in the day that she ever saw the light.

She spent most of her days remembering. She remembered a lot. Her parents, her home, her friends, and of course, her music. It was all that got her through each excruciatingly painful day she had lived in the prison.

Well, that and him.

She didn't know what she would have done without him. He was what kept her human, what kept her grounded, what kept her from flying away into the darkness and uncertainty above. One of her heart's darkest and most secret desires was to see his face. Just once. Just for a moment. She didn't know what it was about him, but his beautiful, and very human voice soothed her and held her close. He was all that kept her from going insane.

She still remembered Day 1. It was the most terrible of all the Days. They had found her, and she had used all of her power to attempt to get away, but it was useless because they had numbers. Here, the walls were thin but strong. She knew that because she had thrown herself against it over and over again until she had collapsed to the ground, silently allowing the tears to fall from her caramel eyes.

And then, she had heard his voice.

"Hello? Is someone there?"

She wiped the tears from her eyes, cleared her throat, and answered. "Yes." Then, after a moment, she added, "How long have you been here?"

"I've been here for sixteen years. But I haven't given up hope that someone will find me and bring me home, and neither should you."

She sighed. "I'm so sorry. And it was sweet of you to reassure me. Thank you."

"If you don't mind me asking, what's your name?"

"Ariana. Ariana Rose Reeve."

She heard him blow air out of his mouth quickly. She didn't hear anything for a moment, so she assumed he wasn't going to reply when he said, "That's a very pretty name."

"Thank you."

"You're welcome. Remember, you aren't alone. I know that you don't know me and that I don't know you, but I want you to know that I'm here for you. Whatever Fiona has in store for us, we'll face it together. We'll get out of here someday."

"Okay."

He was so very kind. She had poured out her heart to him, and he had been patient, sweet, and strong, and he held it all for her. She, in turn, listened to him recount memories of his ever fading and distancing childhood. She held his heart for him, and she wondered if he felt the same way she did. She wondered if it was childish, or unattainable for love to be returned from him.

20

Welcome To Chilli's

When they finally got to the next of Diabolus' headquarters, Jamie was extremely dizzy. Cassandra had jerked the steering wheel like crazy, and the occupants of the car had all given each other looks that clearly stated, *I don't think we should let Cassandra drive next time.* Honestly, Jamie was just glad that there was a next time. He was so sure that Cassandra was going to get into a head-on collision and they would all die. They almost did, too, and it was Cassandra's fault, but of course she had to roll down the window and hurl a rude and extensive vocabulary at the innocent driver whose life she had put into peril with her atrocious driving. Cassandra was the first to enter the building. Her high ponytail had trapped back most of her long dark hair, but one lock had escaped and fell into her eyes. Jamie's fingers ached to reach up and push it back, but he restrained himself. When they all entered the room, they were overwhelmed with the pungent smell of smoke. They found a large living room that was entirely empty as if someone had recently moved out. It had dark brown wood flooring, which was streaked with red in intervals.

The group made its way to another room. Cassandra walked across. She found that when she walked at the corner of the room, her boots made a different sound than when she walked in the middle of the room. She concluded that the ground beneath the middle of the floor was hollow. Kneeling down, she felt with her hands on the ground. She found a ridge and tugged. Then, she found herself looking at a set of stairs that led to a room with light. Smoke escaped from the room when the door opened, causing Roslyn and Cassandra, who were the closest to the door, to collapse into a fit of coughing. Atticus smiled. "You have a thing for hidden doors, don't you?" he asked her. Cassandra smiled. They started to make their way downstairs. Cassandra found that the source of the light was not a lightbulb, but rather fire. There, chained to a pole, face grimy with blood, sweat and tears was Ana. A woman— a spirit rather, was grinning at her diabolically and held up a flaming hand in front of a near unconscious Ana's face.

"Tell me where the Sanctuary is you little freak!" The woman screeched at Ana. Ana shook her head, her eyes closed, and her small face pinched with terror. Atticus stepped forward immediately and drew out a long sword.

"Get the hell away from my sister, you bitch!" He hurled at the spirit. The woman's head turned, and her eyes focused on Atticus. Ana's eyes flew open. The spirit started to get up from her seat on a rickety old stool.

"What did you call me?" the woman snarled. Her eyes were wide, and Cassandra could see little flames in them.

"Oh, so you're an idiot, and you're deaf," Atticus retorted. "I called you a bitch, you imbecile."

"Mind your tongue, little boy, or you'll pay the price in blood," warned the ghost. Atticus did not listen, and he hurled yet another swear at the spirit. This flared her anger even more. She kicked out at Atticus, who doubled over, the wind knocked out of him. Then, she raised her other hand, and flames started to sprout from them. Roslyn stepped forward and raised her sword, but the woman was too fast for her. She slapped her hard across the face, and a large burn appeared on her cheek. It looked swollen, about first-degree. However, the force of the blow was very strong, and made Roslyn collapse to her knees. Blood trickled from where her hand had struck her, and she squirmed a bit, and then was still.

"Roslyn!" Ana screamed, and her voice was like a cold shard of ice through Cassandra's heart. She pulled out a dagger from the jacket Atticus had loaned her and stepped closer to the spirit. Atticus had straightened up and stepped forward, pulling out a knife from his jacket as she did.

"When you hurt my friends, you get a piece of my mind. It's buy one, get one free." Atticus said. He moved forward with great speed and agility and shoved his knife into the spirit's stomach. Blood did not spill from the cut, but rather a part of her stomach dissolved at the knife's touch. Blessed metal, Cassandra guessed. The spirit cried out and cursed. Atticus smiled with grim pleasure. The woman held up her hands again, which were now holding two twin flames and aimed to burn Atticus, but was intercepted by Cassandra, who had thrown herself between the two. Jamie's eyes widened, and he called out Cassandra's name. He did not know what he would do if Cassandra died. He would simply forget how to live life. However, Cassandra didn't die. In fact, she looked as if she were glowing. The look of understanding on the spirit's face was enough to make Cassandra frown in confusion. The woman quickly regained her composure.

"The Blessed One. Surrender yourself to us, and we will let your little friends go."

"Cassandra, get out of here," Roslyn muttered quietly.

Cassandra did nothing as the woman stepped closer to her, frozen in her stance in surprise.

"Cassandra, get out, out, out!" Roslyn shouted.

The lady pounced at Cassandra the way a tiger might pounce at a little bunny. She fell on top of her, Cassandra struggling wildly beneath while she struck out at her. Above her, a loud commotion sounded, and the lady succumbed, Atticus slashing down at the spirit wildly. The spirit shouted one last curse before she left.

"Diabolus will come back for you, and we will make you wish you were never born. Until I see you again," the woman retorted and vanished.

"Where'd she go?" Jamie asked.

"Um, she's a ghost. She can vanish and go wherever she wants. Obviously." Atticus said.

"Oh," Jamie said. "Duh."

"I'm joking," Atticus said. He looked worried about Roslyn and Ana, but seemed to know that they had both fared far worse and would be quite alright within a short period of time. "Spirits with higher powers can vanish at will. This one must've killed quite a few of us," he said quietly, as he walked over to and unconscious Ana, touching her cheek gently and undoing her binds. He shortly hoisted her over his shoulder and turned back around as though saving damsels (or damoiseaou; Atticus catered to both genders) in distress were what he did for a living. Jamie supposed, in some ways, it was. He wasn't really in the conversation, however. He was busy looking at the way Atticus was looking at Cassandra. She didn't seem to be paying attention, though. She was kneeling on the ground with her hand in Roslyn's, feeling for a pulse.

"She's alive," Cassandra exclaimed.

"Oh, thank goodness. We can find healing salve for her burn at a pharmacy," Atticus said, and tore of a bit of his shirt to staunch the blood that ran across a long scar on Ana's right cheek, single-handedly. She was small and thin, and her curly brown hair fell a little below her shoulders. Jamie and Cassandra put Roslyn's arms around their shoulders and carried her. They got them into the car, and headed back to the broken-down house; with driving, obedient to each sign and signal. They drove through the night, the moon and the stars illuminating a path in the darkness.

* * *

When they got back to the broken-down house that Cassandra had named 'Bobert,' they found a letter on the faded floral chair. It was from Alana. Cassandra was the first to see it, so she picked it up and started to read it.

Atticus and Roslyn,

The Infernum plans to go to the Cheesequake forest and perform a spirit ceremony for their leader tomorrow at around 6. They have us all locked in a room and are torturing us for information on the destinations of other Sanctuaries. You know what to do.

~Alana

Cassandra read this aloud to Jamie and Atticus and saw Atticus smiling. Ana was still unconscious, and Atticus had lowered her onto an old cot. Roslyn was also unconscious; they had gone to CVS on the way and bought her some healing salve, as well as bandages for Ana. It was amazing, the things you could get at CVS. Jamie set Roslyn into another room, and now he and Atticus were facing Cassandra in the living room, and she was looking back at them.

"Wait. What if this is a trap?" Cassandra asked. Atticus stepped forward and took the letter from Cassandra's hand.

"That's Alana's handwriting."

"But how did she write this letter if she's being imprisoned?"

"She's probably not chained, only locked in a room."

"But she would have been able to escape if she was only locked in a room."

"Not if they put barriers around it."

"They can do that?"

"They're supernatural beings."

"Well if she could write a letter, how did she send it to us?"

"She must've used the Transporter," Roslyn answered from behind her.

Cassandra, Jamie, and Atticus whirled around so fast, they were a blur. Atticus went to hug her, and she blushed, which Cassandra thought was weird. They had apparently been best friends since they were five, so why was she blushing?

"Rosie, how are you doing?"

"I'm alright. How are you guys?"

"We're fine," Cassandra said. "What's the the Transporter?"

"It's a type of pen with a special type of ink that can send things or people to different places. You have to write the name of someone who is near the place you want to go, rather than where you want it to go. That's probably how she got it here without knowing where we actually were," Roslyn answered patiently. She reached up to touch her healing burn, then dropped her hand with a grimace.

"Who's saying they're going to leave them unguarded?" Jamie inquired.

"No one's saying that," Atticus said. "They're probably not going to leave them unguarded. They will probably leave someone to stay with Alana and everyone, but most of them will probably leave to perform the ceremony. So there will be a lot fewer people than before. It should be easier to free everyone."

"You're right. We'll have to bring our daggers." Atticus agreed.

"Ok. That makes sense." Jamie said, feeling more and more out of place by the minute.

"So what do we do till then?" Cassandra asked.

"We could hang out if you like," Atticus said.

"That would be great." agreed Jamie. *Shit.* Atticus thought. *I wanted it to be just Cass and me, but I can't very well tell Jamie that to his face.* Cassandra was smiling.

"Cool! Where are we going?"

"I was thinking we could go to Chilli's for dinner."

"Okay. Can I drive?"

"NO," Jamie and Atticus said at the same time.

"Hey, I suck at driving, but I don't suck that badly." Cassandra protested. Jamie put a hand on her shoulder.

"You don't suck; we just believe that if we make the grave mistake of putting you behind a steering wheel, you will become a danger to yourself and those around you."

"That's just fancy language for 'you suck at driving'" Cassandra said.

"Hey. There's nothing wrong with the truth. Ow! That hurt!" Atticus said; Cassandra had punched him.

"I'll drive this time. Rosie, you in?"

Roslyn shook her head. "You guys go ahead, I'll stay with Ana."

Atticus nodded. "We'll get your and Ana's dinner's packed for you." They started out towards the car.

"Will they be alright?" asked Jamie skeptically.

"'Course they will. They're Pol Electi. They've suffered through worse."

Jamie's lips parted slightly. "That's terrible."

Atticus shrugged. "It's life."

When they arrived at Chilli's, they were all intact, because Cassandra had grudgingly allowed Atticus to drive the car. They entered and chose a table with benches. Atticus sat on one side, Cassandra and Jamie on the other. Cassandra started talking rapidly, and Atticus caught 'Drake,' 'New album,' '#1, replaced by this song called Egypt Station' and 'replaced again by Cry Pretty by Carrie Underwood.' Atticus had no idea what she was talking about, but Jamie seemed to understand everything she said. He was nodding, commenting on music that he liked, and debating which songs deserved #1 and which songs didn't. Atticus was no longer there, however. He was lost in his mind again. He looked up suddenly and saw that the place where Cassandra was sitting was empty. Startled, he looked around, his eyes searching. Suddenly, Cassandra popped up from below the table, her wavy dark locks going askew in the process. She smiled at Atticus and assumed a corny voice imitation of someone Atticus didn't know.

"Hi. Welcome to Chilli's." She said and plastered a cheesy grin onto her face. Jamie's golden hair fell into his eyes when he dropped his head onto the surface of the table and shook with laughter. Atticus doubled over with laughter, and Cassandra grinned and catapulted herself over the table and back into her seat on the inside side of the bench next to Jamie. Then, a woman in a black dress came up to their table. She was severe-looking, and her hair was held back in a tight bun. She looked about 50. She was holding a notepad and a pen, and she looked at them and spoke in a rather monotonous voice.

"Hi. Welcome to Chilli's. May I take your order?" She looked at them expectantly. Jamie slammed his hand onto the table and shook with laughter. Atticus started laughing so hard that tears came out of his eyes. Cassandra was laughing out loud too. She didn't even bother to try to hide it from the woman. The woman looked insulted. She glared at the three of them. "May I take your order?" she asked again.

"Yeah. I'd like grapes on the vine. Get it?" Cassandra said. This only made the boys laugh even harder.

"We don't serve grapes on the vine. We only serve grapes in a bowl. Would you like anything else?" Cassandra held her hand up to let her know that she needed a minute. When the laughter had subsided, her face was red.

"I'd like a bowl of pasta please."

"What type? We have rigatoni, ziti, seashells–"

"Sorry. I don't speak Korean." The woman looked deeply unimpressed.

"Rigatoni then. What about the sauce? We have marinara, meat, five cheese–"

"I'd like pasta sauce on my pasta, please," Cassandra said. The woman rolled her eyes and chose a sauce out of random. When she was done, she looked up at Jamie expectantly. He ordered the same. Atticus settled for some tomato soup. They ordered spaghetti for Roslyn and Ana and requested that it be packed to go. When the woman walked away, the group cracked up again.

"Grapes on the vine? Seriously? And she had no clue what you were talking about!" Atticus exclaimed.

Cassandra laughed and smiled a crooked smile. "I am the master of dumb puns," she said in a dignified voice. When the food arrived, they started to eat, and Jamie noticed that Atticus' amber eyes didn't stray from Cassandra's gray-blue ones. Jamie was pretty sure that Atticus liked her. It was written all over his face. She hadn't noticed; obviously, she never noticed when a guy liked her unless they actually said it to her face, and he hadn't. Jamie felt bad for him. He decided that he'd better tell him to give her space before she threw his heart on the ground like glass and stomped on it.

"Hey," Atticus said over his tomato soup. His curly brown locks were falling into his eyes now. "Thank you for saving my life."

"No problem." Cassandra gave him a lopsided grin.

"No really, if you hadn't stepped in front of me at the last moment, I would've died. And you didn't even know that you were capable of withstanding spirit flames. If you hadn't been, you would've given up your life for me." he said.

"It's cool. That's what friends do for each other."

"We're friends?"

"Yeah."

"Oh. Cool." His face looked remarkably less bright then it did a minute ago. Cassandra frowned.

"You don't want to be my friend?" She asked.

"No, no, it isn't that."

"Then why do you look so dull all of a sudden?"

"I want to be more than that," he muttered under his breath.

"Sorry, I didn't catch that," Cassandra said. Atticus was glad as hell that she didn't. Jamie, however, did hear him. He stood up.

"Atticus and I need to use the restroom," he announced.

"We do?" Atticus inquired curiously.

"Yes. We do. Come on." He gestured for Atticus to follow him, and he did. Cassandra shrugged and turned back to her pasta.

Jamie led Atticus outside the diner, and to the rear of the building. Jamie leaned against the wall, and the moonlight illuminated his pale skin and delicate features. He brought his emerald eyes up to meet Atticus' amber ones, and he looked back at him expectantly. Finally opened his mouth to speak, but Atticus held his finger up for him to stop.

"I know why you told me to come here."

"I...you do?"

"Of course I do. You brought me here to ask me how I look as great as I do. And I'm sorry, but it's not something you can learn. It runs in the family." He flipped his hair dramatically.

"No, I didn't."

"Then you've brought me here to reveal your great love for me in the form of a song. You've written a song for me about my handsomeness and how every time you see me you want to–"

"I'm straight!"

"Dude, chill, I was just messing with you."

Suddenly, Atticus looked awkward, hesitant, and rather preoccupied for a moment. He shuffled around for a moment, his head down and staring at his white canvas sneakers as if he were binge-watching an interesting anime show.

"Do you know if Cassandra's with anyone?" he blurted out abruptly.

"What? Yes. I mean, no. I mean, you can't ask her out."

"Why? Do you like her?"

"Yes. I mean, that's not why."

"Then, why?"

"Because she's broken." Atticus' eyes widened. This wasn't what he had expected.

"She's broken, like broken glass on the ground, and when I tried to pick the pieces up, she pierced me with the shards. I don't blame her; I just understand that she wants space and that she isn't ready for a relationship yet. I don't want you to hand over your heart too, because she might drop it, and it might shatter on the ground."

"Oh. Okay. Thank you for letting me know." Now, he really looked awkward. The boys didn't exchange another word as they reentered the diner and found their seats. When they sat down, Cassandra looked up at them and gave them a crooked smile.

"What took so long?"

"Oh. Um… Jamie had diarrhea." Atticus said.

"No, I didn't!" Jamie protested. Jamie's face turned a shade of red.

"Yes, you did."

"If he did have diarrhea, how did you find out?"

Atticus shrugged. Cassandra looked up at Jamie. He looked as he always did. Steady and reliable, like a heartbeat, he was always there when she needed him. She wondered if he felt the same way about her. He caught her looking at him and smiled at her, and she felt as if the room had lit up. *What's happening to me?* She shook her head, and her dark waves whipped across her shoulders. *I need to get more sleep.*

On the ride back home, Atticus was unusually quiet. "Soooo. Have you read any good books lately?" Cassandra said hastily to break up the silence.

"Yeah," Jamie said. "It's called Clockwork Princess. It's the third book of the trilogy, and you'll have to read Clockwork Angel and Clockwork Prince first to understand it. It's a fantasy."

"Cool." A brief period of silence passed, and Cassandra hastily broke the silence again.

"How about you, Atticus? Have you read any good books recently?"

"Not really."

"Oh." Another moment of silence passed.

"Alright, what's going on? Did I do something to piss you off?"

"No, no, it's nothing," Atticus said.

"Did something happen? Are you upset?"

"No." They pulled up to the driveway, and the trio exited the vehicle. It was well into nine now, and the brightness of the sun reflecting on the moon brought a wonderful kind of light to the earth. Cassandra trudged away from the house.

"Where are you going?" Jamie asked, curiously.

"The Tree."

"Do you mind if I join you?" Jamie asked. He was almost certain that she would say yes, so he was surprised when she agreed to let him accompany. Together they trudged into the darkness.

21

Light In The Darkness

As Atticus walked into the house, he heard laughter. He followed the voices and found Roslyn and Ana talking to each other. "...and then she called me over and asked me for Atticus' phone number."

"Did she really?"

"Yeah!"

Atticus came into the light. "Who asked for my phone number?" Atticus asked and shook his tousled hair out of his eyes. Ana looked up at him and grinned.

"This girl at the mall. Remember how we went there two weeks ago?"

"Yeah?"

"So, when you were picking out new shoes, this girl that I've never seen before came up to me and asked if you were my brother."

"Isn't it obvious that I'm your brother? We look a lot alike. You should thank god every day that you look like me. I am magnificently gorgeous."

"The girl at the mall thought so too. She asked me for your phone number."

"You didn't give it to her, though, did you?" Roslyn asked.

"Oh, I gave her a phone number. I gave her the phone number for pizza hut." Ana said. Roslyn laughed out loud. Atticus grinned and walked across the room to ruffle his sister's hair.

"I have never been so proud of you in my entire life," he said and handed her a bag containing her and Roslyn's dinner. She grinned up at him.

Five minutes later, Atticus found himself in a different room. He was leaning against the wall, his head down, staring at his white sneakers. Could Jamie be lying? He didn't look guilty, though. He just looked sad.

* * *

As Cassandra made her way through the woods, the only things that she could hear were the warm summer breeze, twigs under her and Jamie's feet, and Jamie's soft breath. Cassandra looked up and saw the moon, steady, shining, and beautiful. It lit up a pathway worn into the woods, and Jamie and Cassandra followed it for sometime before they started to stray from it. When they reached their destination, Cassandra sunk against the tree and leaned her head against palms. Jamie sat next to her under the shade of the tree.

"What's up?" Jamie asked. Of course, Jamie knew that something was up. He knew her like the back of his hand. In fact, he probably knew her better than that.

"What did that woman mean when she called me 'The Blessed One'?" Jamie looked far away.

"I don't know. We can research it if you like, at the library at the Sanctuary. They might have something on the topic."

"Alright." Cassandra agreed. Jamie put his soft, warm hand under Cassandra's chin and lifted her face up.

"If it's bothering you, I'll make it a big priority." Jamie's beautiful green eyes were wide, and he searched her face as if he wanted to paint it into his mind, as if he would never see her again and never wanted to forget her. Cassandra smiled. This smile wasn't like most of her smiles; it had no arrogance, no sarcasm, and no amusement. It was just pure happiness. Happiness because she was glad to be alive, glad to be here. She was glad to have Jamie always be there for her, to be her light in the darkness, to be her comfort in a foreign place, to be her lifeline when she was drowning. He was always there to pick her up when she fell, always there to reassure her when she was uncertain, and he always stood at her side when everyone else turned their backs on her. He never wavered, even for a moment. She found that she was so grateful for him, so blessed to have him in her life. She needed him more than she liked to admit it, and she relied on him to always be there, even if he did nothing at all but be there, for she found that that was enough for her to be content. Jamie's soft voice broke her out of her thoughts.

"Cass. Cassie. Are you alright? You're staring at me."

"Oh." Cassandra felt blood rush to her face. It was an odd sensation; she didn't think she'd ever blushed before. "Yeah. I just got lost in my own mind, I guess." Jamie smiled at her, and it was a beautiful smile.

"You have a nice smile," Cassandra thought aloud.

"Oh. Thanks." Jamie's face was also red now.

"So," Cassandra said hastily to break up this awkwardness, "Is there anything on your mind?"

There were a lot of things on Jamie's mind. Jamie was thinking about Cassandra's beautiful smile, how she was funny and talkative, carefree, and lovable. She was also loyal, fierce, strong, brave, and fearless. He never felt as alive as he did when he was with her. But he tried to push it back, tried it push it down. He tried to forget that her smile made his heart beat faster. He tried to forget that her laughter brought a smile to his face and that when she smiled, he was content. He tried to forget that he wanted to hold her hand.

Then, like a lighthouse shining its light and helping sailors find their way through the darkness of the night, she took his hand. Her hand was warm on his, and she smiled at him when he looked up at her. "You've always been there for me. You've always had my back. I just wanted to tell you that you can count on me too."

Jamie smiled. "I already know that."

"Just like the jewelry box, my whole world seems to have fallen and shattered into pieces. Everything that I believed to be true has proven not to be, and it's like the ground has vanished from beneath my feet. The only thing that's been constant is you. Stay with me."

"You know I'll never leave you."

Cassandra nodded her head.

"Don't ever doubt it, okay?"

"Okay." Then, she leaned her head on his shoulder where she could hear his heartbeat, and they stayed that way for a long time.

* * *

The next morning, when the group set out to the Sanctuary, they made sure to bring all of the weapons that they brought with them. "There are definitely going to be spirits who were left in charge of keeping an eye on the Sanctuary members. They wouldn't have left them alone. Prepare to fight." Roslyn said.

"Well, now that Infernum knows the location of the Sanctuary's location, what's preventing them from infiltrating it again?" Cassandra pointed out.

"That's a good point. There's only one other way to keep spirits out, and that's by building a sacred circle." Atticus said.

"What's that?"

"A sacred circle is a type of barrier that wards off spirits and other types of supernatural creatures." Ana filled in.

"Cool. How is it built?" Jamie asked, curiously.

"First, we have to locate the holy arrow that was given to us by an angel and recite a certain incantation in front of an open fire. Then, we need to use the arrow to draw a circle in the dirt around the Sanctuary. That line will then be the barrier that prevents spirits from entering the Sanctuary." Ana replied.

"You have more knowledge than everyone else put together," Atticus commented.

"Thank you," Ana replied.

"So where might the arrow be?" Cassandra asked.

"Somewhere in the Sanctuary. Probably in the Artifacts room." Atticus answered.

"Oh." Cassandra was rather disappointed; she had hoped that it was somewhere more exciting, such as at a spirit group's headquarters, or under the sea, or on another planet, so that they might have an adventurous escapade. Perhaps the only adventurous escapade they were going to have was a journey through a hallway and a possibly steep staircase.

When everyone was finished packing their weapons, (Roslyn gave Jamie a dagger too) everyone headed outside. The sun was shining weakly, and the sky was painted an interesting shade of blue. They all got in the car, and Roslyn started the engine. Cassandra did not want to admit that Roslyn's driving was a lot safer and had a smaller chance of being fatal than hers.

When they got to the front step of the Sanctuary, Cassandra used a hairpin to get the front door open, and they entered. Roslyn led them to Alana's room, which was being guarded by two fire demons. Roslyn made short work of them; she had the element of surprise and two long swords on her side. The spirits slumped over and collapsed, and the group made their way into the room. They found all of the members of the Sanctuary in the room, with Alana sitting at her desk. She had burns on her shoulder and left cheek. Her hair was in a messy bun, but she and the others were not tied down. There was a very shiny pen on her desk, next to a stack of printer paper. In fact, if Cassandra looked close enough, she saw that it actually looked like it was glowing.

"The Transporter," Atticus whispered into her ear and answering her unasked question. Alana saw them and grinned. She looked beautiful and fierce. The look in her eyes made her look reckless, young, wild, and free. Cassandra liked her immediately.

"I see you got my letter. And well done with the spirits outside the door. You must have an amazing teacher," she said and smiled. Cassandra guessed that Alana was their teacher.

"Actually, our teacher was mediocre. Ouch!" Atticus said. Alana had kicked him in the shin. "That hurts!" Alana grinned. Then, she looked at Cassandra and Jamie. "Who are you two?"

"I'm Cassandra, and this is my best friend, Jamie."

Alana held her hand out Cassandra, who shook it, and then Jamie, who did the same.

"I'm Alana, the leader of the Pol Electi of New Jersey. Are you guys Heaven's Chosen too?"

"Cassie is, but I'm not," Jamie said.

"That's cool. It's nice to meet you both," said Alana.

"Alright. We don't have too much time. We need to put up the barriers. We need to locate the arrow." Roslyn said.

"You're right." Alana agreed. "Lead the way."

Ten minutes, two long hallways, and three steep staircases later, the group found themselves in the Artifacts room. The walls, which were painted brown, were hung with a lot of expensive-looking paintings and portraits. There were long teakwood tables with intricately carved legs. These were lined with glass boxes. Each glass box contained a souvenir of some important event that happened in the past. Cassandra stared at them in wonder, marveling at the objects. There were golden goblets, jewelry, expensive-looking cutlery encrusted with precious gems, currency from different countries, and time periods. There was also a wide range of weapons, such as swords, knives, daggers, nunchucks, sais, staffs, spiked balls, shields, and blessed metal spears.

But Cassandra wasn't paying attention to any of it. What had caught her eye was a small silver jewelry box with a wind-up latch at the back which could be wound up like a music box to play music. She flipped it open to see that it featured a ballerina too, like the one her mother had, but this one was dressed in white. Cassandra had gone wide-eyed and started to examine it.

"How'd you get that open?"

Cassandra turned around to look into Atticus' amber eyes. "What?"

"How'd you get that open? Only one of the owners of the box can get it open." Atticus shrugged. "Maybe it's just a hoax. It's a Black family heirloom. It was made in the 1400s by Anastasia Black, as a gift to her fiancé. It has a pair. Her fiancé made one for her too, and it's startlingly identical, except for the fact that the one her fiancé made for her has a ballerina in pink. They have the magical property of showing the owner the past that might be significant to them." Atticus said. He was leaning against the wall, his tousled brown hair in his eyes, and he was smiling. Cassandra hadn't heard him come up to her. She guessed that she was so fascinated that she hadn't paid much attention to her surroundings. She silently cursed herself.

"Do you know who donated this to the Sanctuary?"

"I don't, actually. We could ask Alana, she might know. You seem really interested. Is there any specific reason you want to know?"

"Yes, actually. I'll tell you in private later."

"Okay."

"Hey, guys, I found it!" Roslyn called out from the other side of the room. She was pointing at a golden arrow that had an inscription on the side.

All that is good shall be saved.

Cassandra and the others had made their way to the other side of the room. Alana pressed her thumb to a white circle on the glass box. There was a clicking sound, and the lid of the glass box popped open. Atticus picked up the arrow from its box with startling care. "This thing's like a million years old," Ana said, answering her unasked question. "And it's fragile."

They made their way to the living room, which featured large and plush brown faux leather sofas and a large mahogany fireplace. Jamie got onto his knees and started up the fire, and Alana rushed up to the library to get a spellbook. When she returned, she had a book in her arms that looked about fifteen million years old and was in the process of falling apart. The spine was worn, and the binding was coming apart. It looked very heavy.

"Dude, that book is thick!" Cassandra exclaimed. Atticus stepped forward and placed the arrow in front of the fire.

"Hell, yeah it is!" Alana agreed. She walked in front of the now roaring fire, thanks to Jamie, and sat across from the golden arrow. She turned to Jamie. "Thank you."

"You're welcome," Jamie said. Alana flipped the book open to a page. On the page to the left, there were instructions on how to swap souls with a person of your choice. On the page to the right, there were instructions on how to build a protection spell around your house. She looked up at them then.

"Ready?" They nodded. She looked back at the book and started reciting an old incantation. Her voice rose and fell, and she said each word with perfect pronunciation. Cassandra couldn't exactly pinpoint which language it was, but she knew it wasn't one she'd ever heard before. She saw that that as she kept chanting the words, her voice grew louder and louder and the fire grew stronger, brighter, and hotter. When she finished, her voice was raised to a shout, and Cassandra could feel the warmth of the fire on her face though she was a good five feet away from it. Alana stopped chanting and paused for a moment. Then, invisible energy seemed to be sucked out of her, and she doubled over. The fire seems to glow brighter than it had a moment before. Alana panted a bit and then stood up. This was when Cassandra noticed that the arrow was glowing.

"Should I shut the fire off now?" Jamie asked.

"No. The fire is the power source of the arrow. Switch it off, and the arrow doesn't do anything. We have to douse the fire after we draw the line and put the protection spell in place."

Cassandra stepped forward and crouched down in front of the fire. She picked up the arrow. It was not hot, as Cassandra had expected it to be, but rather cool to the touch. She stood up and started walking out the door. Roslyn held the door open for her, and they stepped out into the colorful summer sunset.

"Draw the circle about ten feet away from the Sanctuary," Alana instructed her.

"Okay. She walked ten feet away from the Sanctuary, touched the tip of the arrow to the ground, and started to draw. Gold seemed to flow from it, and it went wherever Cassandra traced the arrow. Jamie's eyes were wide, and his jaw had dropped.

"Awesome!" he exclaimed. Cassandra was almost done with the circle now, but her eyes caught something none of the others hadn't seen, and she froze in surprise. Spirits were running through the woods, toward the Sanctuary and had spotted them. Their hands were raised, and a fire was sparking in their palms. Atticus drew out his dagger.

Jamie couldn't see the spirits, however. All he saw were two balls of fire hovering in mid-air. Jamie figured that it had something to do with the fact that he was not one of the Pol Electi. He took a wild guess and decided

126

they were spirits. Roslyn, Atticus, and Alana rushed forward to defend Cassandra while she finished the circle, but they were outnumbered. The members of the Sanctuary were still inside. They knew that a protection spell was being put in place, but they apparently had no clue what was going on outside. Cassandra called out to them, but she couldn't move to help her friends, because she was still drawing the circle. Alana stepped forward now, and expertly wielded her knives. She cleanly beheaded a spirit, and a few people who Cassandra did not know poured out of the Sanctuary holding a variety of weapons, ranging from crossbows to deadly daggers. Fiery balls of liquid magic had taken to flying across the space between them at Cassandra, who tried hard to focus on drawing the golden circle but was ultimately distracted from reaching this goal by plenty of spirits who had taken to throwing fireballs at her like darts at a dartboard. What was even more perplexing what that they didn't seem to affect her in any way other than bringing the destruction of her carefully gathered attention.

Cassandra saw plenty of souls and Pol Electi sprinting around in her peripheral vision, making it hard for Cassandra to keep her arrow to the floor. Now, Jamie, as always, seemed to read her mind and came to stand loyally by her side as he always did, Roslyn's sword in his hand. Slashing his glowing metal at anything that came even remotely close to Cassandra, he followed Cassandra round the Sanctuary. A ball of electric blue flew through the air, and Jamie lunged to deflect it but failed. It hit Cassandra, but now that she had Jamie covering her, her attention was intact, and she made no move that said that she actually noticed. The spirit who threw it noticed, however, and pointed at her. However, someone else seemed to.

In what was only a blur of movement in her peripheral vision, a group of spirits all lost interest in battling the other Pol Electi and became intent on capturing Cassandra and Cassandra alone, congregating just outside the circle. Loud whispers got louder and louder inside of her head, and fireballs became more and more ferociously thrown. Jamie blocked each ball to the best of his ability, doing quite well because of his practice in the sport of baseball. A shimmering knife hurtled past the other spirits poised perfectly at Cassandra.

In a moment, he saw it all. He was thinking of that time she had stepped in front of Atticus to take the blow instead of letting him die at Diabolus Headquarters. He had thought he was going to lose her forever, and it had been the most horrible feeling he'd ever had in his life. Before he even knew what he was doing, he had done it.

Down he fell, but he had passed out before he met the ground.

22

The Blessed One

Cassandra finally finished the circle. The line she drew in the ground glowed brightly, and the spirits growled in frustration. It was a terrible sound. The spirits could no longer see the Sanctuary, as it had now gone invisible to those who meant harm to the people inside. The Pol Electi outside of the circle rushed into it, and they started to hurry into the Sanctuary to treat their wounded. However, none of it was real. None of it felt like it was actually happening, because Cassandra had collapsed to the ground and was shaking Jamie frantically. Everything was hazy and far away, shadows moved in the dark, and Cassandra felt as though she were living in a hologram.

"Jamie! Jamie! Jamie, please wake up, please wake up, stay with me!" Cassandra started to tear the sleeve of her shirt off to bind Jamie's wound and to staunch the rapid blood loss, but it didn't help. She was then hit with something she just realized. *How could this possibly be happening? Jamie can't die; I can't imagine a life without him. If Jamie stops living, I'll forget how to live.*

She remembered a day, which seemed a million years ago and a part of someone else's life, not her own. She remembered a bright summer day; she remembered running to his house. She remembered talking about Billboard and news about the latest music. She remembered the three words that had changed everything. I love you.

The next few moments were a blur. People rushed over to her aid, and

129

Jamie was carried into the infirmary. Jamie was an ordinary human, so the effects that the enchanted knife had on ordinary humans was near-fatal. Therefore, May had said, it was a miracle that Jamie survived. She said that though he would survive, he would have a permanent scar. Cassandra had sat at a chair near his bed for as long as she could. As soon as he was in a fit condition to speak, Cassandra spoke to him.

"Jamie, oh Jamie, thank god you're okay. Jamie, how dare you risk your life for me? How dare you?" She punched him in the arm.

"Ow. Of course, I risked my life for you."

Cassandra looked Jamie in the eye, and he could see the concern she had for him in her beautiful gray eyes. "Why, Jamie? Why did you do that?"

Jamie sucked in a breath as if readying himself for a blow. He lowered his luminous green eyes and looked down, as Cassandra knew he always did when he felt sheepish.

"Because you're my world. And I don't want to lose you. Because if I lost you, it would be like cutting myself in half and giving one half away." Now he looked up, and his eyes were hesitant, he looked as if he expected all hell to break loose in a minute. "Please don't kick me into next week."

Cassandra looked lost. She didn't look sad or annoyed, or even angry; she just looked as if she were debating something in her mind.

"On a scale from one to ten, how pissed off at me are you?" Jamie asked, meekly. Now she did look at him.

"Negative twenty-two." Then she leaned in and kissed his cheek.

Jamie's eyes went very wide and his face very red. Cassandra looked down to try to hide the fact that she was blushing furiously. It didn't work too well. Jamie was speechless. He didn't think he had ever seen Cassandra blush before. It was strictly un-Cassandra like, along with crying, whining, being serious, responsible, mature, or obedient. Of course, Cassandra had to be the one to break the awkward silence.

"So…they're saying you're going to have a permanent scar."

"I don't mind. I can remember you by it."

She was looking down and wouldn't look up now. Then she looked into his eyes.

"Jamie, I didn't know it before, but now I do. I'd walk through fire for you. Or swim across an entire ocean, or hike up Mount Everest, or travel to Mars if it meant that I'd find you there."

Jamie's face was still bright red. "Cassie, that means a lot to me."

"Jamie?"

"Yes?"

"James Carter Taylor, if you dare risk your life for mine again, I will hunt you down and inflict a near-fatal injury on you. Do I make myself clear?"

Jamie was grinning now. "Yes, ma'am."

"That's what I thought." But Cassandra was grinning now, too. The room seemed brighter now, everything seemed so much better, and even the wound on his shoulder seemed to hurt less than it had a moment ago. However, Jamie felt very dizzy, like he had just gone on the Joker ride at Six Flags. He could feel the blood that had rushed to his face warm and burning, and he looked down. Cassandra declared that she was going to go play Monopoly with Ana and Roslyn, and hurriedly left the room.

When Jamie walked out of the infirmary, Atticus saw him and raised an eyebrow.

"What's up, man?"

"Nothing."

"You sure? You look high."

"Maybe I am," muttered Jamie.

"What?"

"Nothing."

Atticus shrugged and walked away. Then, Jamie went exploring. He went down a dim hallway and found a restroom, a common room, and a dead end. He walked down another hallway and found that it was filled with spare bedrooms. Finally, he found what he was looking for.

When he entered, the first thing he noticed was that the room seemed as vast as Holmdel Park. Bookshelves lined the wall in a deep cherry color. There were more books here than Jamie had seen at various libraries together in his lifetime, and his curious eyes took everything in. This, Jamie supposed, was what heaven looked like. He located a book titled "History of The Pol Electi" and plopped it down on a table. He seated himself, chose a relevant section, and started to read.

One such legend states that a child, born during a lunar eclipse, when the moon passes into the shadow of the Earth, will have the power to withstand the magic of the spirits, and can inflict burns on them through touch. This is because of the alignment of the stars during the time in which the child is born, which decides the horoscope of the child. This child would later go on to lead all of the Pol Electi and will be the savior of our kind. A leader of Infernum, a spirit group, later heard about this prophecy and decided to look for the child. This later became a sort of obsession. He and his spirit clan then went on to kidnap many children and put them to the test. Many unfortunate deaths occurred, until a month later in the year of 2008, in which The Pol Electi of the Sanctuary of Massachusetts discovered that they were the cause of such an atrocity, and they captured and imprisoned the entire spirit clan. Some, however, fled the country and hid from the Pol Electi. They swore to reform Infernum and come back for the imprisoned spirits.

Jamie looked up. There was a fireplace at the opposite end of the room, with a burning fire in it. Jamie supposed that someone else was here. His assumption was correct, and he found the head of the Sanctuary sitting behind a large desk, fully immersed in a book. Jamie made his way to the desk.

"Alana?"

She looked up at him. "Yes?"

"I was wondering, do you think the legend of The Blessed One is real?" She looked normal, but her eyes looked pained.

"I don't, actually. I believe that it's a hoax. I don't think anyone can have that power." Alana said. "Do you need anything else?

"No. Thank you." He started to make his way out of the library.

Cassandra was so distracted that she pushed her money bag icon past three boxes instead of five. Her head hurt like hell, and she felt a pang in her chest.

"Cassandra, what's wrong? You seem…distracted." Ana said. Cassandra was pulled back into reality with a start.

"Nothing." Cassandra lied, taking deep breaths to soothe the throbbing ache in her head. Something was wrong, though Cassandra could not exactly pinpoint it. It was like the moment before a storm, the premonition that something bad was about to happen, and the knowledge that she would have to contend with it, not knowing in advance what was going to happen or when it would.

Then, the door opened, abruptly pulling her from the thoughts, and Jamie burst into the room.

"Cassandra, we need to talk," said Jamie. Cassandra raised an eyebrow. "It's important."

Roslyn and Ana exchanged glances, and Cassandra shrugged and stood up. She followed Jamie out of the room. They walked to a dark corner, and she looked into Jamie's bright green eyes. She thought they were the most beautiful things she had ever seen in her life. But she wouldn't admit it.

"Jamie? Is something wrong?"

"No. I just did some research at the library. I got the information you asked for." Jamie burst into an extensive explanation of all that he had found out about The Blessed One at the library. By the end of it, she had gone very pale.

"Cassie? Are you alright?"

"Jamie. I don't feel good."

Jamie looked stricken. "Do you want me to get you a glass of water? Here, let's find someplace for you to sit down."

Cassandra shook her head. "I'm fine. Really."

Jamie took her hand and started walking her to the library. Halfway up, Cassandra gasped and clutched Jamie's hand hard. They stopped.

"Cassie, are you okay? Do you want to go to the infirmary?"

Cassandra shook her head. "I just need to sit down," she managed.

Jamie looked unconvinced but nodded all the same. They made it up the last of the stairs when Cassandra stopped again in the middle of the hallway. She clutched her head.

"Cassie?" Jamie asked.

"I'm okay," she said quietly, sounding more as if she were trying to convince herself rather than him. "I'm okay." Shortly after, she collapsed into Jamie's strong arms.

"Jacob."

"Yes, darling?"

"I need to talk to you."

"I'm coming right away." A man with tousled brown hair and hazel eyes ran up the staircase and made his way to the roof. The ceiling was a skylight, and it was dark outside. The woman with black hair and gray eyes that so looked like Cassandra's was standing there, looking through a telescope at the stars. She was wearing a long blue dress that brought out the blue flecks in her eyes, and her hair was up in a messy bun, with hair falling loosely into her eyes. In her hands, she clutched star charts. When she heard his footsteps, she turned around. Her pretty face was pinched, and she looked troubled. The man rushed forward.

"What happened Ella?"

"Jacob, I think…I think Cassie is the Blessed One."

"What?"

She looked lost. Her eyes wandered to the beautiful and sparkling night sky behind them, and she said, "I checked the charts. She pointed to a star chart on a piece of paper she was holding. This was the star chart for last Wednesday. Look at the stars today." She gestured to the telescope. Hesitantly, the man walked toward the telescope and peered through. When he looked up, he looked unbelieving.

"No. This can't be right."

She shook her head sadly. If these are the star positions for today and these are the star positions for last Wednesday, that can only mean that…"

"Cassie is The Blessed One." The woman's eyes were wide with disbelief and sorrow. The man looked at his wife and put out his arms. She fell into them gratefully and rested her head on her shoulder.

"They've taken Alana and Julian. We won't let them take Cassandra, too. I promise we won't let them take her too." he soothed.

Cassandra's eyes moved behind their lids, her breathing catching. She twisted her hands distractedly. Her lips moved over and over, forming incoherent words feverishly.

"Cassie?"

"It's me. They're going to come for me."

"What are you talking about?"

"I'm the Blessed One. They're going to come for me."

Jamie frowned, not disbelieving. "It was all made up. The Blessed One isn't a thing."

Cassandra sighed. "I'm so lonely. Soooo lonely."

Jamie sat at the foot of her infirmary bed. "You're not alone. I'm here."

Cassandra shuddered, apparently not hearing him. "So lonely. Soooooo lonely."

"Cassie?" Jamie called.

Cassandra shuddered again, and then her eyes flickered open slowly. "Jamie?"

Jamie nodded and stood to examine her more closely. He searched her eyes thoroughly and placed a hand on her chin. "How do you feel?"

"I'm alright."

"Are you sure? You said that before you passed out into my arms."

Cassandra rolled her eyes at his worry. "I'm fine."

Jamie swallowed, and his lips thinned. "I don't believe you."

Cassandra sighed. "Jamie,"

Jamie sat down beside her on the bed and traced her lips with his fingertips. "I was so scared."

Cassandra tilted her head slightly, not understanding. She hadn't felt affection from anyone other than Jamie for so long, that sometimes she did not comprehend it. "But I'm alright. There's no reason to worry."

Jamie nodded, his eyes stubborn, his expression giving away that he didn't believe her in the slightest.

"We had a little conversation, you and I," Jamie said.

Cassandra furrowed her eyebrows. "Did we? What did I say?"

Jamie smiled mischievously. "Lots of things," he hedged.

For once in her life, Cassandra looked worried. "What did I say?"

Jamie smiled crookedly. "Do you have something to hide, Cassandra?"

Cassandra pondered the question. "Does killing someone count?"

Jamie could not hide how startled he was at that. "Cassie, are you the Blessed One?"

Cassandra paled. "I think so," she said after a while. "Jamie, I can withstand spirit magic. Remember that night at Diabolus headquarters? I wasn't harmed by that fireball that was thrown at me."

Jamie shook his head, not wanting to believe it. "But…Alana said it was a hoax." His eyes widened for a moment. "But they saw that it didn't hurt you. They know it's you. They're going to try to come for you. We need to speak to Alana about this. Can you walk?"

Cassandra took a breath and nodded. "Okay. Lead the way."

Jamie helped her up the stairs and down a hallway to the library to find Alana sitting near the fire, sharpening her long sword. It glinted in the firelight.

"Alana. Can we talk?" Cassandra asked. Alana looked up. Her hair was done up in a messy bun, and she was wearing a shirt that said, 'don't try my patience' in black print at the bottom, near the hem, and gray sweatpants.

"Sure. What's up?"

"Cassie is The Blessed One." Jamie blurted out.

"Nah, man. That can't be true."

"It is," Cassandra said. "I was able to withstand spirit magic at Diabolus headquarters and when I was fighting one in the woods."

"Are you sure, though? The legend states that The Blessed One will descend from one of the oldest families of the Pol Electi. From what I gather, you didn't even know you were one of us until a few months ago. What's your last name?"

"Black. My full name is Cassandra Chloe Black." There was a clang as Alana dropped her sword on the teakwood floor of the library.

"No. It can't be true. Are you sure that that's your last name? Did you change your name, or is that your original?"

"That's my real name," Cassandra told her, puzzled as to why this invoked so much attention. Alana was still facing the fire. A lock of her hair fell from her bun and hung from the side of her head as she shook her head frantically.

"Though that would explain a lot. I can't believe it."

"You can't believe what, Alana?" Jamie asked, curiously. Alana raised her hand and pointed over to her desk where a name placard was placed. It was written in gold.

Alana Brooke Black

"Cassandra, I think you're my sister."

23

You're Not Alone

Now that he thought about it, he wondered why he hadn't noticed it before. Cassandra and Alana shared the same wavy black hair, though where Cassandra wore it long, Alana had cut it short. They even had the same eyes, a mixture of gray and blue. They had both inherited their button noses from their father, and high cheekbones from their mother. Their differences were little and did not often appeal to those who didn't look very closely– a light dusting of freckles lay upon Cassandra's face, whereas Alana's were concealed by a thin layer of foundation. Cassandra was shaking her dark head slowly now, too. "No. That can't be possible. If you are my sister, why didn't you live with us?"

"They took me. Infernum took me."

"What?"

"The Infernum. The leader of the group, Vincent's grandfather, had an obsession, to find The Blessed One. He kept taking Pol Electi children and putting them to the test. I was six." She looked into the fire, and her eyes glinted in the light.

"Alana, I'm so sorry. That's terrible." Jamie said. Cassandra couldn't say anything. She was speechless.

"I escaped before they could test a fireball on me, though."

Cassandra remembered the look in Alana's eyes when she was interrogating Vincent. She looked vicious, angry, and murderous. At the time,

Cassandra had guessed that that was how she looked at all spirits, but she seemed to have a special death stare reserved for Vincent and his spirits.

"Why didn't they just check your star charts for when you were born?" Jamie inquired.

"Only Pol Electi can read them correctly. We have long perfected the art of star readings."

"Oh."

"My parents looked for me, for so long, but by the time I had escaped, they had lost hope in my survival. My Mom had given birth to another child, you, and they fled to keep you safe." Now she did look up. "That was you. So all this time, I've had to stay here, wondering where my parents were, and hoping they hadn't given up on me."

Cassandra looked up now. She was heartbroken for this girl that she had met two days ago. "But it's alright now. You can take me to them. We can be happy again." Her eyes were wide; she looked as if frozen in the middle of a hallucination, seeing something she knew wasn't real, but wished so badly for. Cassandra looked down and shook her head slowly, tears running down her face.

"No. No, no, no, this can't be happening." Alana was shaking her head rapidly, more hair coming out of her bun in the process.

"I'm so sorry, Alana," Cassandra said softly. Tears were streaming down Alana's face, now too. "They found us and set fire to our house. It killed Mom, and Dad killed himself out of grief.

"But that doesn't make sense. Why didn't they take you? That's the reason that they attacked you." Alana said.

"Actually, this happened after the attacks were stopped. The people who murdered my mother might not have been Infernum. It could've been…"

"Diabolus," Jamie finished. His eyes were wide.

"But why would they have wanted to kill us?"

"Our Mom held a resistance group. She refused to play this morbid game of hide and seek, which is our lives. Our father was in it, too. Together they led a bunch of attacks on the spirits who took Julian and me." She stopped for a moment, her eyes wide as if she had said something she hadn't meant to say.

"Julian?" Cassandra echoed. "Who's Julian?"

"No one. Don't worry about him." Alana answered.

"Who's Julian? Tell me, Alana! I deserve to know! My parents raised me for five years and let me think I was an only child. Stop leaving me in the dark."

Alana sighed. "I guess you're right. I didn't want to tell you before, because I didn't want you to feel bad, but we had a brother, too."

"Had?"

"He died. The Infernum took him and tested a fireball on him."

"How do you know he's dead? He could've escaped, too."

"They found his body near Infernum headquarters."

"Oh." Cassandra's eyes shed tears for a boy she didn't even know.

"I'm so sorry, both of you," Jamie said. He stepped forward and put out his arms. Cassandra sunk into them gratefully and rested her head on his shoulder, the way she had always done when she was sad. Jamie wrapped his arms around her tightly in a warm embrace. They stayed that way for some time.

* * *

She was lying on the ground and staring up at the ceiling, her hair fanned out around her. She hadn't taken any time to arrange it, just tied it into a ponytail and walked out of the room. Now she was staring at the wall, wondering how in a matter of three months, her whole life had come apart like the little jewelry box that her mother had owned. The door opened slowly now, and a figure walked in. The room was dim, but Cassandra knew who it was.

"Atticus?"

"Hey, Cass. What are you doing here?" Atticus responded.

"I don't know."

"That's fun." Atticus walked over to her and sat down next to her. His amber eyes looked down into her gray ones. He found her eyes beautiful, like the sea before a storm.

"Do you want to talk?" He continued.

"Sure. I need a distraction." Cassandra allowed.

"What grade are you going to next year?" Atticus asked though he was pretty sure that he knew the answer.

"I'm going to be a senior in September."

"Me too." A moment of silence passed. "So, what's your favorite subject in school?" Atticus urged, hoping to continue the conversation.

"Probably math."

"Mine's History."

Cassandra didn't know how she felt, precisely. She supposed her feeling was like that of the one associated with being numb; she could not feel at all and did not quite know why. She knew she ought to be crying for a boy she never knew, but she didn't feel sad at all. Her stomach just felt a little funny.

"Dude, there was this time in freshman year, when my teacher pointed to an angle and asked me what it was called," Cassandra told him, laughing at the memory.

"What did you say?" Atticus inquired, intrigued.

"I told her it was gay," Cassandra said matter of factly, as though this were a completely normal statement.

"What?" Atticus was thoroughly confused.

"It looked less than a hundred and eighty degrees, so I mean, it couldn't have been straight, could it?"

Atticus laughed so hard that tears came out of his eyes. No one was able to make him laugh like she was. And she did it so easily.

"And when I learned about postulates for the first time, I didn't know that the reason that postulates existed was to prove statements. So I figured that postulates were dumb statements written by dumb people so that they could gain fame and glory," Cassandra continued, "So I wrote a book of dumb postulates. It's in google docs. Wanna check it out?"

"Yeah. I wanna see this." Atticus said, curious to see what she had come up with.

She turned on her phone and went to the Google Docs app.

Postulate #1

The earth is flat.

Postulate #2

I'm always right.

Postulate #3

Don't make me angry. If you do, all hell will break

loose.

Postulate #4

If someone lives in a house next to you, it means that they are your neighbor.

Postulate #5

Beavers have feelings too.

Postulate #6

If someone has the same teacher as you at the same period as you, it means that

they are in your class.

Postulate #7

One often hears that muffins are just ugly cupcakes. This is not true. In fact, true
beauty comes from the inside. Therefore, as blueberry muffins have blueberries in
them, and other varieties of muffins, at least in most cases, have sweet things
inside, whereas, cupcakes do not. Therefore, muffins have real beauty, and
cupcakes are just wannabes that dress up to act beautiful, though they really
aren't, and will never be.

Postulate #8

Most people eat lunch at 1:00 A.M.

Postulate #9

Never drink poison. If you drink poison, you will die.

Postulate #10

The sky is sometimes green.

Atticus had doubled up in laughter. He was laughing so hard that tears were falling from his eyes. "Oh…my…god…that…was…hilarious." He panted.

"There's more, too. I wrote like, fifty."

Atticus was wiping tears from his eyes now. "Honestly, the earth is flat. You're crazy."

"Thank you. I get that a lot. Postulate #56. doughnuts can be used as an alternative for shoes at desperate times." Atticus doubled over again, and his face was red with laughter.

"What's going to make you desperate enough to wear doughnuts on your feet?"

"On my feet? Why would I wear doughnuts on my feet? I would wear them on my hands! That's where shoes are worn by sane people."

Atticus collapsed to the ground in laughter. Cassandra smiled. She liked making people laugh.

Atticus was suddenly very aware of his surroundings. He was within a 3 feet radius of Cassandra, and he wondered if she was disgusted by him. He felt very self-conscious when he was around Cassandra, somehow. So, he sat up immediately and backed away. Cassandra frowned.

"Do I smell?" She raised her armpit to her face and smelled herself. This only made Atticus laugh more.

"No, no, you don't smell."

"Are you sure? I don't think I've taken a shower in like, a week."

"No, you don't smell."

"Then why did you back away? Do you not like me?"

What? How could she possibly think I don't like her?

"Of course not. I really like you. I just feel really self-conscious around you, and I feel like every move I make is being judged by you." He blurted out before he could stop himself.

"What? Why would you think that? I wouldn't judge you. Besides, it's not like you did anything dumb."

I'm afraid I'm going to take your hand again and betray my secret. But he couldn't actually say that to her.

"If you don't want me to be here, you could've just told me so." She stood up to leave.

"What? No, don't leave. I wasn't lying when I said I felt self-conscious around you." She had walked across the room to the door behind which was a staircase, and she had paused with her hand on the doorknob. Then she turned to face him.

"Why would you feel self-conscious around me, though? I'm like the most imperfect person in the entire world. I don't believe you." She turned back to the door and started to turn the doorknob.

"No! I feel that way because I love you, Cassandra." Now she froze, and stood right where she was, her hand half turning the doorknob, very still, and there was a pin drop silence. Atticus clapped both hands over his mouth, his eyes were very wide, and he had gone very pale.

"I'm so sorry. I didn't mean to tell you like that. I know you're broken." Cassandra turned around. Her eyes were also very wide, and she had also gone very pale. Then, she looked up at a staff distractedly.

"Who told you that?"

Atticus swallowed. "Jamie," *You, Atticus, are the dumbest creature this earth has ever seen. You were supposed to keep the fact that you love her a secret.* "He told me so that I wouldn't do anything dumb that would hurt you or myself."

"I'm not broken. I just don't want to fall in love, because my Dad killed himself after my Mom died. Love makes us weak." Cassandra told him in a rather hollow voice. Atticus was speechless, and his eyes were still wide. He felt terrible for Cassandra, and he knew this was entirely his fault. Jamie wasn't lying when he said that Cassandra was capable of hurting him. She had just taken a glass shard and pierced him in his heart. Now, she watched him while he bled. But he knew that the reason he felt this way was his own fault. Jamie had warned him of the fire he had been playing with, and he hadn't listened, so he got burned.

"Now, I really am leaving. I've had enough of this." Atticus opened his mouth, then closed it at Cassandra's expression. She looked murderous. "Don't follow me or apologize. Don't waste any more of my time." She turned around, wrenched open the door, and walked through, slamming it so hard that white powder from the ceiling started to fall through the air slowly. Atticus backed up slowly until his back was against the wall, and a staff that was hung up on the wall was digging into his spinal cord. He put his head back against the wall, and the curly brown locks tumbled into his closed eyes. He slowly sunk to the ground and put his face in his hands. Jamie hadn't been lying. *Great job, Elsa. You screwed it up real well.*

Atticus felt a loss at Cassandra's departure, but something weird stirred up his stomach. He started to think about all of the things that made him love her. He sat there, for what seemed like a long time, swimming through a sea of his own sorrow.

She's beautiful. He thought of her long, silky black hair, and imagined putting his fingers through it.

She's funny. He remembered how easy the smile had come onto his face when she was around.

She's crazy. He watched her through his mind's eye and saw the way she ran, wild and free through the rain in Holmdel Park.

But when? When had his friendship with her turned into love? When had he stopped liking her as a friend and started liking her as a lover? And beneath it all was the question that had haunted him the most. Had he ever loved her at all? Could one love in such a short amount of time?

He imagined kissing her. What would kissing Cassandra be like?

He imagined a fiery hot feeling, with his lips on hers, his fingers in her hair. What did that beautiful hair feel like?

Instead, he felt the blood rise to his cheeks. He felt that he would much rather hold her hand and watch her from the sidelines than kiss her and touch her like that.

Perhaps it was only an infatuation.

Atticus did not know what love felt like. Perhaps he was only guessing.

* * *

Cassandra stormed up the stairs and ripped off Atticus' oversized jacket from herself. She threw it on the floor after she chose a certain dagger she had grown fond of. She stuffed it into the pocket of her ripped jeans and started to make her way out of the Sanctuary.

When she got to the front door, she saw the golden line that she had made with the arrow. She walked past it and into the woods. She pulled out her long sword and began to carve a path for herself through the weeds and the creepers.

Something was certainly bugging her, and it wasn't just that Atticus told her that he loved her. In fact, she wasn't all that mad at him. Atticus was kind and stuck up for her when Roslyn had bullied her, even though he had barely even known her. Atticus deserved the world. He deserved way better than her. She was only mad at herself.

She had vowed that she would never fall in love the day her father had died. He had been such a happy, positive person, and Cassandra couldn't understand why he would throw it away, throw everything away for love. Love was stupid, and she wanted nothing to do with it. Now, she was here, thinking about Jamie's lips.

Stupid. That's what she was. Stupid, dumb, nincompoop, numbskull, idiot. She knew it come and bite her in the ass someday, but she couldn't stop.

And now she was going off like a bomb and hurting other people by making them love her.

She brought her knife down hard on a sapling and shouted her frustration. Then, she thought about what Jamie would say if he saw her cutting down trees to suffice her angry mind. It made her laugh a bit.

What was wrong with her? Why couldn't she stop thinking about him?

She was sick. That was the only plausible reason. She was sick, with Jamieitis, a disorder that one is not born with, but that one develops when in close proximity to the harmful rays of Jamie.

She had to stop. It was getting worse; she was going to lose her mind.

But then again, hadn't she already lost it?

* * *

When Jamie came downstairs for dinner, he was surprised to find that Cassandra and Atticus were missing. The only people at the dinner table were Ana, Roslyn, Alana, and a few people Jamie didn't know. So, he went searching for his best friend. He guessed that she was in the weapons room, since she seemed to really like them, and showed a certain type of fascination towards them. He didn't find her there, though. What he did find was a heartbroken boy with his head in his hands.

Jamie entered the room soundlessly, and Atticus didn't notice that he had come in.

"Atticus? Is Cassandra here?" Atticus looked up with a start. Quickly, he attempted to strip all expression from his face. It didn't work. He looked like he died inside a bit.

"Atticus? Are you alright?"

"I'm fine. And Cassandra isn't here."

"What do you mean, she isn't here?"

"I mean, she isn't here. She left."

"Why did she leave? Wouldn't she have told me? Oh. She was probably angry, wasn't she? She has these rages sometimes. She has a very bad temper."

"Wow, you know her very well. Are you her shrink or something?"

"Yeah. I'm her shrink/best friend/punching bag when she's pissed." he sighed. "Guess I'd better find her." he started to the door. "Do you know why she was angry?"

Atticus swallowed and nodded his head.

"Wait. Don't tell me."

"You were right."

"Atticus,"

"I didn't mean to. It just…slipped out."

"You realize she's gonna be pretty pissed at you."

"Yup."

Jamie walked over to him and crouched down to look him in the eye. "Atticus, you want to be very careful. Knowing Cassandra, she may very well be making plans on how to end your life in the most painful and excruciating way possible. Be careful."

Now, Atticus laughed, though it didn't have much humor in it. "Wow. She really hates love."

"Yeah. But I don't blame her." Now, he stood up to leave.

"Jamie."

He turned around. "Yes?"

"You were wrong."

"What?"

"You were wrong. She isn't broken. She just doesn't like it when people tell her they love her because she thinks it makes her weak. Her Dad killed himself after her Mom died, and she thinks it's because love makes you weak."

Jamie's eyes were wide. He remembered a different day, at a different time, at a different place. No. I can't. I mean... I don't love you. Love makes you weak, and I'm not weak.

"Oh. Okay. By the way, do you know which room Cassandra went to throw knives at a picture of your face?"

"Actually," Atticus swallowed, "I think she left as in the left the building."

"What?!" Jamie said. His eyes were wide now.

"Relax. She's 16. She can take care of herself."

"Cassandra is the Blessed One. There are literally clans of spirits that would kill to get her powers! She's strong, but the spirits have numbers!" Jamie started pacing, lacing his fingers through his hair worriedly as he did, so that he looked as though he might pull out every last stitch of smooth gold that inhabited the top of his head. "Where could she have gone?"

"Hold up. You're saying that Cassandra is The Blessed One, the one from the prophecy made like, literally, 3,000 years ago. You're joking."

Jamie shook his head slowly. "How do you think she escaped that fireball that was meant for you without getting a single burn?"

Dawning horror showed on Atticus' face. He turned very pale. "We need to tell Alana."

"Alana knows."

"She does?"

"Yeah. I need to go." He sprinted to the door.

"Wait. I want to help. After all, this is all my fault."

For an absurd moment, Jamie laughed. Atticus frowned. "What's so funny?"

Jamie shook his head. "You don't know Cassandra like I do. And she despises the idea of people falling in love with her. If I let you come with me, she will literally kill you, chop you up into bacon-like strips, and then feed on the remains. She's cool, but she can be pretty bloodthirsty." Atticus paled remarkably. The thought of being cut into strips was not a pleasurable one. But secretly, he adored Cassandra for her fierceness.

"Alright, then. Can you tell her I'm sorry when you find her?"

"Sure." Now, Jamie did leave, and Atticus was left to listen to the calm, soothing sound of silence.

* * *

Cassandra stormed through the woods and unleashed her wrath on a pair of innocent saplings. Severing the plants with her knife, she ran to a place heavily sheltered and hidden from the outside world, where she found a dead tree on the forest floor. She sat down on it and started a fire. Then, she put her hand near it, touching the flame. It wasn't spirit magic; she could feel the pain, and yet she did not cry out. She felt she deserved it, for breaking Atticus as she did, leaving him to pick up the shards of his heart and attempt to put it back together. She thought of the jewelry box. There's no point. It'll never be the same. She remembered the day that Jamie had broken. He had taken such good care of her. She was the one who always made reckless decisions, and he was always the one who talked her out of them. It was always that way. She remembered the look on his face when he broke. She had never wanted to hurt him like that.

And yet, it felt necessary. She put her head in her hands and fell apart.

Twenty minutes later, Jamie found himself creeping through the woods. He knew that he would find Cassandra here, and he looked for clues that might hint to her location. Anything. A footprint, broken twigs, a sign. A moment later, he found it. A spark, between the darkness of the trees. He followed it, and he felt like he was seeing a different person other than himself walking towards the spark. It seemed involuntary to walk to Cassandra, normal, to find her and comfort her. In a way, Jamie really was her shrink. Then he saw her there, pale face illuminated by the beautiful moon, which floated above them in the dark and starry sky above them. It was a beautiful sight. *Like her eyes. Jamie shook his head. She doesn't want to be anything more than friends. I need to respect that.*

Cassandra didn't notice when Jamie approached her. Jamie wasn't surprised. This had happened before. Cassandra would get lost in her own mind, and sometimes she wouldn't be able to find her way out until Jamie called her name. He did that now.

"Cassie?"

Cassandra looked up now, her eyes large and dark, and reflecting in the blazing fire in front of her. Jamie wanted to take her into his arms and hold her tight so badly, at that moment.

"Jamie?"

"Say it again."

"What?"

"Say it again. When you say my name, it sounds brand new and beautiful. I love the way my name sounds on your lips."

Cassandra's breath caught. "Jamie."

Now Jamie's breath caught, too. Then he shook his head. "I'm sorry."

"It's okay." Cassandra smiled at him.

"Cassandra, come back. It's not safe for you here. There are spirits who want to kidnap you and are probably searching for you this very moment."

Cassandra's expression hardened. "No." She said defiantly and turned her head. Jamie sighed. They'd been through this before. He set himself next to her on the fallen tree.

"Cassandra,"

"I like that."

"What?"

"I like your voice, too."

Jamie was confused. Was she flirting? But that couldn't be. There was no possible way, not in this world, and not in any world, or even a parallel universe that Cassandra Chloe Black was flirting with him. Jamie was disappointed. He would have liked it if she was. *No, I wouldn't. I wouldn't*

150

like it if she was. I'm over her. I'm over her. Jamie didn't know why he even bothered. He knew he was lying to himself.

"Cassie, Atticus told me to tell you he was sorry."

"Jamie,"

"Cassie, just come back, please. Take my hand, and we can go back."

"Jamie, I need to talk to you."

He raised his luminous green eyes to her gray ones and looked at her with curiosity.

"Anything, Cassie. You can tell me anything. You know that."

Cassandra swallowed and nodded. Jamie was appalled. He didn't think he had ever seen his best friend look so uncomfortable. She was just Cassie, and Cassie was never uncomfortable, or sorry, or frightened, or intimidated. All of these words just seemed not to have an entry in her dictionary.

"Jamie, I don't know what I'm doing. One moment I hear the words 'I love you,' and the next moment I'm flaring with rage. You've given me a delicate porcelain vase, and I've broken it on the ground. And I see this blood on my hands, and it feels like I'm waking from a terrible dream in which I cannot control what I do." She spread her arms wide, the way she had done since she was five. Jamie came into them, and let her rest her head on her shoulder. His soft and gentle hands hesitantly patted the small of her back, and he started to murmur in her ear.

You'll be alright. It's okay. We can figure this out together. You're not alone.

"Jamie, I feel weird."

"What is it? Do you feel sick? We can walk to CVS. There's one around here. We can get you a Tylenol and–"

Cassandra shook her head. "Jamie, I'm so sorry. I'm so sorry that I broke you. You've always been there when I was hurt, and I hurt you. I shouldn't have done that."

Jamie blinked. "Cassandra, you don't have to be sorry. I understand if you don't feel the same way as me. I shouldn't have sprung that on you in the first place." Cassandra was looking down, and she looked distracted. She shook her head, as in a dream.

"No. You didn't know. Jamie, I'm not broken."

"I know. I know that you believe that love makes you weak because of what your father did, and I respect that. I don't need this. I don't even deserve you. I don't know what made me think I did." His voice was bitter.

"Jamie!" Cassandra was appalled that he was saying these things.

"And I'm sorry, I won't ever talk about it again, and I understand if you don't want to be my friend anymore. I just don't want to make you sad."

"Jamie! Don't you ever say you'll stop being my friend. If you ever stopped being my friend, I'd pitch myself off a cliff. I need you. Your friendship means a lot to me, and I value it a lot more than I show."

Jamie's eyes were wide. "Cassandra, I–"

Cassandra held a finger up to his lips. "Shh. I love you, I need you, and I can't bear to be without you. I wouldn't be able to bear it if you left me. And you're right. You don't deserve me. You deserve someone better, someone who has enough sense not to break you apart when you come close. And I hope you find her, Jamie, because you deserve so much better than me." Her voice was also bitter now.

How could she say that? How could she possibly believe that? Did she think it was easy to get her out of his head? Because he had tried, and he couldn't manage it. He never could. He knew then that he had fallen into a hole that went on forever. A choice that couldn't be changed. A mistake that couldn't be fixed. A wound that would never heal. Cassandra was in his head, and she would be there forever.

"Is that what you want?" Jamie asked.

"That's what's weird. I don't know what's going on. I should want that, as a friend, and I should try to be a good friend and want for you what's best, but I don't want that."

Now it Jamie's turn to be appalled by what he was hearing. He looked distracted, and his eyes wandered up at the tree when he asked Cassandra, "Why?"

Cassandra shook her head frustratedly. "I don't know. What is happening to me? Maybe I haven't gotten enough sleep recently. Maybe I've caught the fever, and I'm hallucinating. Maybe I've gone mad. But one thing is certain in my mind– and that is that I can't stand the thought of your arms around someone else." She swallowed. "What's happening to me?"

Jamie shook his head. "That can't be. That can't possibly be."

Cassandra looked up now and looked Jamie right in the eye. "Why can't it be?"

"Because that's how I feel about you." Cassandra's breath caught now. She took Jamie's hand and held it between two of her own.

"What does that mean?" Cassandra was genuinely curious.

"You wouldn't want to know."

"I do."

"Maybe, just maybe, you're in love."

"If this is what love feels like, I can imagine why you want it so badly. I think I might just want it, too."

"Cassandra," Jamie looked into her large and dark eyes. She looked back at him, and at that moment, he saw everything that he had always needed. He shook his head and was silent for a moment. Then he looked up. "If love makes you weak, then I'm weak."

Cassandra shook her head. "I think I had it wrong all along. Love doesn't make you weak; it makes you stronger. Look at when you took that knife for me. That was out of love. And you were brave and courageous, and incredibly kind. If that's weak, then I don't know what strong means."

Jamie shook his head. "No. Cassandra, don't convince yourself that you're in love for me. I don't want to give you what you don't want. I will wait here, with my heart, which I have put back together with your help, and I will keep it until you are ready to hold it."

Cassandra took Jamie then, into her arms, and held him fiercely. She kissed his forehead, his cheek, and his soft, fine hair, his hands in hers, and then smiled up at him. "Thank you."

A look of contentedness and satisfaction had found its way onto Jamie's handsome, chiseled features. He firmly believed that he looked extremely unattractive and that everyone thought that he looked ugly, but this couldn't have been more wrong. He looked gorgeous with his blond hair that fell to his shoulders and in his eyes and curled near the nape of his neck. His eyes were emerald green, and when he smiled, dimples appeared on his chiseled face. He had high cheekbones and pale gold skin. He looked like a cover model for Seventeen, the kind of guy who would carry a guitar around and be a sort of chick magnet. But this was her Jamie. Not just any guy. This was her Jamie, who was one cut above all the others, always there, steady like a heartbeat, and always sweet. This was her Jamie, who would never admit that he looked pretty hot, not even a little. Her Jamie, who held her back when she tried to physically harm a boy who followed him around and called him names when they were seven. Her Jamie, who had held her hand when the doctor gave her stitches after a basketball injury. Her Jamie who had held her when she had cried, for the first and last time, and offered her his teddy bear when her mother died in the fire. Her Jamie, who she could not live without, who she could not live apart from. Then, he spoke.

"I will wait for you. I will wait here, with the pieces of my heart, and I will wait for you. And when you are ready, you can find me, and tell me that you are ready to pick up the pieces from my bleeding hands and put my heart back together."

He was looking up at her now, with wide eyes, he looked at her as if she was the one thing in the world that mattered the most. She had taken him for granted for all these years, and he had never really cared.

"What happens now?" Cassandra asked him.

"Now, we keep reading the book and find out." Jamie smiled, and they held each other and just stayed there.

II

I Am Not In The Dark Anymore

Suddenly, I see a light
And feel the warmth of your gentle hands
You reach out
And pull me through
And then I am not in the dark anymore

24

A Few of My Favorite Things

I t was quiet and dreary, and she yearned to hear his beautiful voice. It seemed it made even the darkest things light.

"I want to go to the playground."

"What?" She was bewildered, intrigued, hungry to hear his honey-sweet voice again.

"I want to go to the playground. I want to go on the swings, and I want to swing you. I want to slide on a slide."

"Is that your favorite thing?"

He took a moment to consider it. "No."

"What is your favorite thing?"

"You."

25

And She Didn't Even Smoke

As Alana walked down the hallway, she looked around to check her surroundings. Satisfied, she crept into the room. It was familiar, the firelight coming from the fireplace and the lantern above the long tables. She walked past the artifacts. Her legs took her where she wanted to go without her having to think about it much. As if in a dream, one of her long figured hands traced the lines on the box. The other crept to the back and wound it up, and she flipped it open. The white ballerina spun around and around, and a sweet tune started to fill her head, to put her in a sort of trance. It only opened to her touch or the touch of another Black.

She was puzzled at why Atticus had asked about it. She knew what she was going to do. She knew why she had to. If they found out that she was the original Alana Black, not just someone named after the one kidnapped at five, they would feel bad for her. And she didn't want anyone's pity. So, she had run from her old self, turned herself into a different person, tore the pieces of her old identity into shreds. She had burned that old identity. And as she had tried to keep the wall from breaking, there were chips in it, where some parts of her old self showed through. Her rage was all hers, and she had always been this fierce, but she had let the people who care for her think that she was into music. And she was, though not as much as they thought. She was into books. She could get lost in them, the way one might get lost in the woods. She let the words fall over her and then carry her away like the waves of the sea. When no one else could help pacify her, the words held her rage for her, if only for a few minutes.

And then there was him. When he was there, he seemed to break down her walls with just one look. She didn't know what it was about him that made her feel that way, but she tried to ignore it. She hadn't meant to tell him; it had simply slipped out. But he didn't show her pity. He acted the same way towards her as he would to her if she didn't have all of her scars. When she had asked him why, he had given her a simple, true answer.

"I love you," he had said.

Alana had blinked in surprise.

"Why?"

Then, he had looked surprised. "Why wouldn't I?"

Then, she had removed her ripped jean jacket, and she was wearing a black tank top under it with "fight me" across it in white. Her long arms were large and had a lot of muscle in them. She had been up in the training room, lifting weights until she collapsed in exhaustion to help her forget the family she had lost. A precious amount of minutes, it had felt like. Now, her arms were corded in muscle, a large tattoo of a flame showed on her shoulder, another of a pair of angel wings on the side of her neck, and there were scars on her arms, from various battles. Burn scars, cuts, scratches, scrapes, and bruises lined her arms like souvenirs of occurrences with spirits. She had looked up at him then.

"Look at me. Look at all of these scars. These will never go away, or heal over, or vanish. They are a permanent record of battles. I am scarred. Don't you want someone else, someone who isn't scarred? Someone who doesn't have all of these marks on her body? Don't you want someone else who doesn't remind you of terrible events, someone who has a more pleasant past? Someone who doesn't bring sadness to you when you look into her eyes?" she had asked with him wide gray eyes.

He had shaken his head then, and soft, straight black hair had tumbled into his ocean eyes. His blue eyes seemed to pierce through her walls and carefully, effortlessly tear them away until he got to the real her. The real

Alana, who was scarred, who was hurt, who had a troubled past, who had held herself together just barely, had built up her walls, only to break and fall apart like the pages of a very old book in his arms. "Everyone has a breaking point," he had said. "Even you."

"No. Of course not. I don't see any scars. I see talent, bravery, courage, fierceness, and kindness. Alana," he shook his head, "Don't you understand? Your scars are what I love you for."

Alana had had plenty of boyfriends before. She seemed to go through boys like she went through toilet paper. But something about Charlie made her keep him for a while.

Now she stood here, tracing her fingers along the lines of the box. He snuck up behind her and held her other hand. She turned to him now, gazing into his storm blue eyes. He was wearing a maroon sweatshirt and sweatpants. Her eyes grew dark, and she mirrored his smile. She didn't know how he made her feel that way, but he did.

"Alana."

Alana took a deep breath. "Charlie. You shouldn't be here."

"I know. But I had to see you."

"Charlie," she sighed. "You know how the others feel about you."

"I know. But they don't know I'm here."

"Charlie," but she was already grinning. "How'd you get here without anyone noticing, anyway?"

He raised a slim fingered hand and indicated the fireplace. An infectious grin spread across his handsome features.

"Charlie, you did not climb down the chimney! Who are you, Santa Claus?"

Charlie's eyes widened, and his jaw dropped in mock surprise. "How'd you find out my secret identity?"

"Charlie," she laughed and elbowed him on the rib cage.

"What? I am! In fact, I've even brought you a present."

"Charlie, you didn't have to," Alana started.

"Yes, I did. It's our dativersary."

"Our what now?"

"Our dativersary. It's been one year since I finally gathered up the courage to ask you out. Remember?"

"Oh! Yeah! It has been one year. I'm so sorry, Charlie, but I don't have a gift for you."

"Love, your heart is the greatest gift you could ever give me." At this, Alana smiled.

"Thank you. That was sweet."

He leaned in and kissed her cheek. "Like you." Then he reached into his pocket and pulled out a single rose. Though it wasn't much, Alana smiled. It was worth everything to her, for it had sparked the memory of one of the happiest days of her life, one that had taken place on a different day, a different year, and a different time.

It had so far been an ordinary day. Killed a couple hundred spirits, interrogated a few dead people, and then captured the souls of a few spirits and sent them through the portal to hell. Just another usual day as the head of the Sanctuary. That was, until the note.

Until then, he had lived there for about a year. He had slid a piece of paper under the door of her bedroom, with two words on it.

The roof.

She hadn't known who it was, or why he was calling her there, but she ascended the stairs and came to the roof. She hadn't noticed him until he made himself visible and forced himself out from behind the rose bush. She was bored and was sitting on the edge of the terrace with one foot placed on the roof and the other on the railing. She was gazing up at the stars.

"Hello?" she had called. No one answered, so she had figured it was a prank. She was about to go back to her bedroom when he forced himself out from his hiding place behind the rose bush. He looked stunning, and his cheeks were scarlet. He was wearing a brand new, neatly pressed suit and held a single rose in his hand. Alana had raised an eyebrow, and looked around, wondering if the rose was for a young woman who might be behind her. But there was no one there but him and her. Her mouth had quirked up in an amused manner, and he pushed himself forward. Alana looked up.

Dawning realization played across her elegant features. She smiled in an amused manner. "You're going to ask me out, aren't you?"

Charlie looked at her as though she had just suggested that the sun was green and comprised entirely of celery sticks.

"Well, here's my answer. Sure. Now if you'll excuse me, I have a very interesting book I want to read." She made for the door, but he had reached out and grabbed her hand. Alana raised an eyebrow, but the amused expression didn't leave her face. In contrast to her sister, love did not disgust her, but rather amused her. She found it hilarious. She had never really imagined that she would ever actually fall in love.

"Were you kidding?" he had asked her. His eyes had widened, and he shook his head rapidly, as though he were trying to shake a dream from his head.

Alana had shrugged. "I don't know. Was I?"

"No. You're not. Please don't." He stepped forward, and it was evident that he was forcing himself. He looked stiff, all of a sudden, his cheeks flamed, and his eyes were wide, as if he still couldn't believe he had talked himself into this.

"Charlie? What's going on? Oh."

She had turned then, and looked from his hand to his burning face. He hastily removed his hand from hers and looked down. "Sorry. Just don't go."

He opened his mouth and muttered something quickly and cleanly in Polish. When he and his sister had moved here after their parents had been killed by a spirit group, they hadn't found much trouble understanding the people around them, for they had adopted their ability to speak British English from London. They had, however, found it rather comical to hear the way American people spoke as opposed to themselves, as Americans seemed to stress things that they didn't and not stress things that they did. It was as though they were trying so hard to be different just for the sake of being different.

Charlie had been living in Poland with his parents for a few short years before they decided to move their family to London, looking for jobs. As a result of this, he also had the ability to speak Polish, which he achieved by hearing his parents before his sister was born. There was a good part and a bad part to this, Charlie had always thought. The good part was that when people mocked him in a different language to keep him from finding out, there was a chance he could find out and get right back at them. The bad news was that whenever he was nervous, his lips retreated back to his childhood days and he started to blabber in fast and fluent Polish.

"Sorry. I didn't catch that." Alana had told him apologetically. Charlie sighed and looked at something far away. In his hand, he held the drooping rose so tightly that his hands were turning white. His eyes were wide when he uttered the words, "Alana, will you go out with me?"

Alana's jaw dropped and the book she was holding slid from her grip and onto the ground with a thump. "I understand if you don't want to. I didn't expect you to be into me anyway," he muttered quietly, but she didn't answer. She just stood there, shell shocked, and unable to react. One who might have observed the peculiar scene might have been inclined to believe that she was indeed comatose and that Charlie was dying of hypothermia, based on how pale he was.

"I mean it," she had said. "Seriously. It's cool. Why not?"

Then, she had taken the rose, nodded, and agreed to go out with him. She remembered the way he had looked after she agreed. The way his eyes had widened as if he couldn't believe what he was hearing, the way his face twisted into a crooked smile, and how he had jumped up and down and run down the stairs two at a time shouting, "She said yes! She said yes!" and exclaiming spontaneously in Polish to members of the Sanctuary who had no remote clue of what he was talking about.

She had kept that rose, and put it in a glass vase, and had it enchanted. She still kept it in her room. So, when people came to her room to speak to her, and they saw the rose in the vase, they assumed that she was really into Beauty and the Beast, but this was not the case. Honestly, she hated that movie. She had always wondered why Belle had put up with the Beast anyway.

If it had been her, she would have come banging on the Beast's door, held a knife to his throat and demand that he release her father lest she use him as a knife sharpener. If he disagreed, she would have built a fire on a broken branch with a cigarette lighter she could have purchased at the nearby convenience store (she didn't smoke) and threatened to burn his castle down if he tried to harm her father. Problem solved. She had been separated from her own parents for way too long that when people had even the slightest chance to be with theirs and didn't take it, it made her frustrated.

Anyway, Alana took the rose now and held it close to her heart. Then, she embraced Charlie. She could hear his heartbeat, slow, and steady.

"Alana, it's been a year, but you still take my breath away."

Alana laughed. "How are you smooth AF all the time?"

"I just speak from my heart."

"Are you sure you don't practice in the mirror?"

Charlie laughed. "No. I did for the first week, but it didn't help much, because I still stammered when I saw you, but not anymore. Do you want to go somewhere?"

Alana shut the jewelry box with a snap. She smiled at Charlie. "You know, I do."

Charlie smiled back. "Shall I keep it a secret?"

"Yes. I like suspense."

"Okay." Dimples showed on his cheeks, and he was flushed. He leaned down, wrapped his arms around her in a warm, close, embrace, and whispered in her ear.

I don't know what I did to deserve a blessing like you in my life.

Then, he slipped a knife out of his sleeve and held it against her throat.

26

Sick

Though he moved with a sort of grace and agility that hinted to years of training and practice, Alana was simply way too quick for him. She slid from his grip like a glass cup from buttery hands and removed a knife from her boot, which was earlier concealed. She spun around then and held the knife to the back of his neck. Slowly, she urged him to the wall. She had him cornered to the wall with a knife at his throat. She grinned, and her smile was like daggers.

"Mitchell. Long time no see."

Charlie's handsome face twisted into a grimace, and then slowly, his features melted away to reveal a man in his mid 20's, with brown hair and yellow eyes, like a cat's. His kind always had peculiar eyes.

"Alana. How did you know it was me?"

"Oh, it was quite easy. First of all, your kind loves hot conditions. And it's pretty cold for you here. No one else would wear a sweatshirt and sweatpants in summer. Secondly, you said you came in through the chimney. Charlie comes in through the back door. It's usually deserted. Lastly, you were smooth. Charlie is never smooth. Ever." Then, she pressed the edge of the knife closer to his throat. "Now, it's your turn to speak. How'd you get in?" He had looked hopeful for a moment until Alana drew out another sword from her jacket and held it at his arm.

Alana started to trace the knife downward, releasing a little bit of red from his neck. This seemed to be a trademark move for Alana. She would make her enemy feel the pain little by little, and then all at once. Mitchell grimaced. "You'll have to kill me to get it out of me."

"Oh, but that's tempting. Trust me. You can give the answer to me in two ways– the easy way or the hard way. And you don't want to know what the hard way is." She smiled pleasantly, and her blood-red lipstick outlined her perfectly white teeth. "I will tie your limbs to a pole, slowly rip your skin from your flesh, impale you on a long sword, let the blood drip slowly from the top of your head, and–"

"Stop! Stop! I'll tell you all I know." Mitchell squeaked.

Alana smiled silkily. "For once in your life, Mitch, you're doing something smart."

Mitchell gulped. "I have the Gem."

Alana's looked unbelievingly. "That's ridiculous." The Gem of Incantations hadn't been found in over a million years. It possessed the power of removing enchantments. It was very useful for healing magic-induced wounds. It was highly unlikely that Mitchell was telling the truth.

Mitchell's eyes widened, and he fished an object out of his pocket. It had immensely lustrous and blue as a sapphire. It glinted in the dim light, and Alana's expression looked disbelieving but was concealed as soon as it had come. "Where did you find it?"

Mitchell's eyes drifted down to the knife at his throat. Then he looked up at Alana's eyes. They held thinly concealed rage.

"It was being worn as a chain by Fiona." Fiona was the second in lead of Infernum, and Vincent's wife. "My clan killed her."

Alana wasn't surprised. However, since the Figura Mutante did not know how to capture the souls of spirits and send them to hell after their material bodies were disposed of, Fiona would regenerate and return. She would look for the Gem. Alana had to make sure that no one else could infiltrate the Sanctuary. She was in charge of all of these people, and they trusted and loved her. She would not let them down.

Alana put out her hand, then, and Mitchell obediently placed the Gem in it. Alana slipped it into her leather jacket's pocket and smiled.

"Now, where have you kept Charlie?" Mitchell gulped but said nothing. Alana smiled, and her eyes held a very frightening fire in them. She looked down at his throat, where she started to trace another line, blood seeping through his gray sweatshirt and making it warm and dark.

"Oh, dear. You know what that means," she said in a mock worried tone, though her face looked anything but sympathetic. Alana turned over her shoulder. "Peter! It's interrogation time!" About a minute later, a red-headed man with freckles barreled in through the door, and shortly doubled over, panting. He wore an expression of awe and extreme admiration when he spoke to her.

"Shall I take him down to the interrogation room then, Alana?"

"Yes, Peter. That would be great." He nodded frantically, his eyes wide, and ran over to Alana's aid. He clasped pure gold handcuffs on his hands, for pure gold burns the Figura Mutante, and pulled the neck of his sweatshirt so that he was dragged across the floor and underground into the interrogation room.

"If anything happens to Charlie, boy, I promise, I will make you wish you were never born." She hissed into his ear before he was carried away into the darkness.

* * *

As Cassandra ran through the dark, she could hear Jamie panting at her side. They had only gone a mile, and thanks to six years of cross country practice and training, and hardcore workouts that had left her tired and exhausted but feeling alive, she was able to run it without breaking a sweat. Jamie, however, had refused to join the cross country team with her, saying that he was more interested in chess. Jamie was a good strategist. Or rather, pretty damn amazing at strategizing. He could've been an army general, directed his soldiers on how to fight and when to fight, and have won every battle. Though Jamie wouldn't have lasted for a single day at cross country practice, he was probably the smartest and most cunning person in the entire room. Cassandra admired him for that. Not that it would help them in the current situation.

After Cassandra and Jamie had held each other for five minutes, her eyes had perceived a flash of something bright.

Something between the sun and shadows, between light and dark, they glimmered in the dark green reminiscence of the slightly damp forest. They were a play on words, an oxymoron, contradicting terms, for they were as beautiful as they were evil. Their eyes enticed them and pulled them closer, while their claws were a reminder of the harm that they could inflict on them. Still, Cassandra couldn't help it when her subconscious assumed a giddy state and attempted to goad her into dancing with them.

These must be fire spirits, she told herself, before forcing herself to face forward and run as fast as she could.

They chased them through the woods. Jamie had proposed that they should go to the Sanctuary, but they had no clue which way that was.

So now they were running through the woods like two lunatics that had escaped from an asylum.

They had lost the spirits a while ago, but Jamie said that they should put more distance between themselves and the spirits. When the spirits appeared, Jamie had to hold Cassandra back. She wanted to rush forward and end them, but Jamie wouldn't allow her. He had held her hand and started to run, knowing that they, two people wouldn't be able to defeat a group of ten spirits, who had numbers.

Then, a large building loomed ahead of them. They paused for a moment. Cassandra opened her mouth to speak, but before she could utter a single word, she heard a deafening clang, and everything went black.

* * *

The interrogation room was as dim as ever, and Mitchell was chained to a chair. His filthy brown hair had grown below his shoulder, and his yellow eyes looked drowsy. Alana emerged from the shadows with a single dagger in her hand. When he looked up at her, she smiled evilly.

"Mitchell," she said in a quiet but sneaky voice, "did you want to tell me where Charlie is?"

Mitchell took a deep breath and shook his head. Alana smiled. Then she pulled her fist back and struck out at his face, and darkness greeted him once again.

When he came to, Alana was still smiling. His face felt wet and sticky with the sickly brackish taste of blood. It felt numb, too. Mitchell concluded that it was swollen. Though he hated Alana, even her greatest enemies had to admit that she was very strong and talented. "Now, Mitchell," she intoned, "did you want to tell me where Charlie is?"

* * *

Atticus sighed and got up. His legs took him to the roof, without him even having to think about it. It was a quiet and private retreat for when he felt dead inside. Usually, the only time he ever felt dead inside was when he missed his parents. His insides would feel hollow like someone cut him open with a knife and scooped his guts out. He had never been in love before. He had never felt this feeling before. There were plenty of girls who had fallen for him, fallen for his good looks and his charming demeanor, and had asked him out, but he hadn't really much paid attention to them. He remembered one of his 'relationships.' It was with a blonde girl named Emily Peterson. She was everything the other guys had wanted in a girl— tall, thin, very pretty, and a cheerleader. He was everything a girl could ever want in a guy— tall, lean, strong, and extremely hot. Not even slightly hot. He was so hot he boiled. And his brown hair was really curly. It went down to slightly above his shoulders, and he had a single mole on his cheekbone. He had been on the football team, back in freshman year. He had quit the next year, deciding to dedicate more of his time to training and vanquishing spirits from this universe. But, of course, his coach didn't think it was a very good idea. He was one of the best on the team, but he simply wasn't very interested in football. He had decided that it is a way that normals try to injure themselves without doing anything that helps save another's life. He didn't even know why he had tried out for the football team; it was because his coach had seen him play at the gym and had determined that he had a lot of talent. That was the end of that.

Anyway, Emily had asked him out to the movies, and he had agreed, not because he was interested in her, but because he had heard some good reviews on the movie. When Atticus arrived, he was surprised to see that no one else he knew was there— he had thought that this was a group activity. The movie turned out to be a rom-com. Atticus had retched halfway through and had to excuse himself to go to the bathroom and throw up. When he came back, Emily had acted very giddy and excited, and had reached out to hold his hand. He didn't want to be rude, so he let her. It made him feel weird as if she were treating him like a child whose hand you might hold when you cross the street.

And then he had almost died.

At approximately 8:33 p.m. Eastern time, the main character of the movie had leaned in and kissed her crush, and Emily squealed in delight. Atticus had pulled his hand from hers and cupped them both over his mouth as he waited for nausea to pass over him. He had gagged, and doubled over, his face turning red in the process. When he had uprighted himself, taking deep breaths to steady himself, and that was when it had happened.

It still showed up in his nightmares.

Emily turned to him then and looked at him in the same way that Alana might look at a new shipment of obsidian handled daggers. Atticus had raised an eyebrow and turned back to the movie when she had leaned in. She had cupped her hands around his face, turned his head, and leaned in to kiss him...

And then, Atticus stood up suddenly, the same way a jack in a box pops up when you open the lid, and ran. He ran as if the devil were behind him, chasing him to pull him into the evil claws of hell. And sure enough, someone was following him.

Emily, confused, perplexed, and annoyed was chasing him. Atticus kept running, curly brown locks flying behind him, and he ran to the woods and found a tree. He climbed the tree and refused to come down. Emily had shouted for him to come down.

"Atticus! Get down here! Why are you afraid of me?"

But Atticus had held on to that tree like it was a lifeline, saving him from a vicious, uncaring ocean. He kept shaking his head and refused to come down.

"If you don't like me, why'd you agree to go out on a date with me?" She had asked.

Hold on. That was a date?

Thirty minutes later, Alana had to come to the tree, and sweet talk him into coming down, which Atticus only did once Alana had promised to guard him against Emily with her life.

As you can see, Atticus was extremely inexperienced in matters of the heart.

When he finally made it back to the Sanctuary, and he explained his "date" with Emily to Ana, she laughed. Atticus was frustrated.

"How do you find my traumatic love life humorous?"

"I find it funny because you're older than me but soooo much more oblivious."

"I am not oblivious."

"Um, you are sooooo oblivious."

"Oblivious to what?"

"Oblivious to matters of the heart."

"Are you saying I should have noticed that Emily was into me? Because she just kept telling me that I had a fever. I don't think anyone could have guessed."

Ana giggled. "Oblivious," she reminisced.

Atticus rolled his eyes. "They were not crushing on me."

"Um, they were soooo crushing on you."

"Why me, though? Why not anyone else?"

"Because you may not know it, but you are really hot."

Atticus stormed up the stairs and into his room, yelling as he did, "I'm not sick!".

27

No Homo

R oslyn was very different from the other girls who had fallen
hopelessly for his love.

Because she could see clearer.

All those other girls, they all wanted Atticus, only because he was beautiful.
They only wanted him because he had the most luscious, reddest, fullest
lips, and the curliest, softest, most luxurious hair, and the cutest mole on his
cheek. They liked him because he had the most beautiful, most mischievous
amber eyes. They only saw the obscenely large muscles that lined his arms
and flat stomach. All that caught their eyes were the long, artistic, dark
lashes, and the soft indentation of the single dimple that played across his
right cheek when he smiled.

But they didn't see anything else.

No, they didn't see his adorable tendency to be stubborn and determined
to make what he wanted to happen, happen. They didn't see the intelligence
behind the brilliant fire of his amber eyes. They didn't see the scars and
bruises that lined his arms along with the muscles. They didn't see the
braveness, courage, and kindness in his young heart, how he put his life
on the line every time to protect the ones that he loved. They didn't see
the mischief in the quirk of his lips when he smiled, how it made you want
to check your shirt for a 'kick me' sign. They didn't see the laughter in his
eyes and the crookedness in his white-toothed grin. They never saw the

beautiful purity and innocence in his eyes. They didn't see the young, hurt, scared little boy who still struggled to stay adrift in his broken canoe. They didn't see his scars.

But Roslyn saw it all. She saw everything and all of his being through her piercing green eyes. And she saw something familiar in the way he spoke, the way he walked, the way he stood up for what he believed in. She saw her own reflection in this little boy's pure, innocent, amber eyes.

And she wanted it all.

But she had learned to keep it all in, never show her true intentions, lest she scare the poor boy even further. So when Roslyn went up to the roof to get some fresh air and saw Atticus staring at her, she struggled to keep her face from giving away her secret.

"What?" She asked, in an irritated voice, though she was not irritated in the slightest. Having Atticus' eyes on her as though he saw everything in this one place made her feel special, beautiful, different from the ugly creature she saw in the mirror every day. She wished that they could stay here forever.

"Nothing. I just wanted to see your green eyes again."

"Why my eyes?" Roslyn was startled.

"Because they're pretty, and they remind me of lush green hills, and that calms me when I'm sad."

Roslyn's lips quirked up slightly at the ends. "I hope you feel better."

Now, Atticus smiled, too. Slowly, he stood and folded himself into Roslyn's arms. "I don't know what I'd do without you." He muttered to her in the darkness of the night.

"I know what I'd do without you," Roslyn told him.

Atticus smiled. "What would you do without me?"

"I'd find a cliff," Roslyn began, smiling, "and I'd jump." Roslyn could feel him laughing against her.

"I love you," he told her. Roslyn tensed. Did he mean like a sister, like a friend, or like something else?

"I love you too," she told him, holding him close and wishing.

"I love you more than you love me."

"Nope. I'm pretty sure I love you the most."

"Nah. I love you more."

Roslyn sighed, and Atticus let go of her for a moment and looked at her through his dark hair, waiting for her to tell him what was wrong. It was then that she knew that she couldn't do it anymore. She had to know.

"Atticus?" She said in a gentle voice.

"Yes?" Atticus said, inquisitively.

"I need to talk to you."

"Okay. Shoot," he told her, looking down. Roslyn was glad as hell that he was looking down so that he couldn't see that she was turning 16 different shades of red.

"Okay." She took a moment to compose herself and another deep breath. Then she spoke. "I like someone."

"That's nice, I guess. Everyone likes someone," he said neutrally.

"No. I mean…I really like someone. Like love someone. Possibly." Roslyn pushed, waiting for him to ask who she liked.

* * *

"Oh. Cool." Atticus couldn't fathom why Roslyn was having this conversation with him, of all people. It would make much more sense to talk about matters of the heart with Ana rather than Atticus, who in this subject, was rather a clueless idiot.

"Don't you want to know who it is?" Roslyn asked him, voice coloring with disbelief.

Atticus shook his head slowly. The process pushed curly brown locks into the pure amber of his eyes. He didn't bother to push it away. "No, not really."

"I'll give you a hint," Roslyn said, as though he hadn't spoken at all. "He goes to our school. He's also in our grade."

"I dunno. Dylan?"

"Nope. He's Pol Electi."

"Jack?"

"Guess again. He has brown hair."

He failed to notice how uncomfortable Roslyn looked when she regarded him as he guessed, "Will?"

Roslyn shook her head, and a strand of long, blonde hair that had strayed from her elaborate braid fell into her eye. She shook it out of her eye and said, "Curly hair. Really, really curly hair."

Atticus frowned. Then, a look of understanding and recognition found its way onto his chiseled features. Roslyn looked reassured for a moment, sure that he knew whom she was talking about. He spoke with a tone that suggested that he wondered why he hadn't guessed it before. "Of course. Are you lesbian?"

Roslyn stared at him for a moment, a look of extreme incredulity on her face.

"No homo. Wow. Just wow. And I thought it was obvious."

"I'm sorry."

"No, that's alright. I'll give you a few more hints. I think you'll get it eventually."

"Okay."

"He has amber eyes."

Atticus considered it and shook his head.

"He's sweet, cute, funny, talented, innocent, and really, really hot."

"How do you know he's having a fever?" Atticus asked.

"Ugh. Come on, Atticus. Think about it. Figure out my crush. You can do it."

"Why do you want me to know who you're crushing on so badly anyway?"

Roslyn ignored this. "Come on. He lives at the Sanctuary. He's tall. And attractive. Very attractive."

"I don't know what you mean when you say attractive. I find some girls attractive, like yourself, and Cassandra, but I don't find any boys attractive, as I am heterosexual. Therefore, your saying 'he's hot and attractive' doesn't get me any closer to finding out who you are attracted to," he stated matter of factly, though Roslyn wasn't paying much attention to it.

"You find me attractive?" she asked, blushing furiously.

Atticus considered it for a moment. "I think so, yes. I like the color of your eyes; it's somewhere in the middle of blue and emerald. And you have a nice smile." He didn't look even slightly embarrassed. Or rather, he didn't look like he should look embarrassed or even slightly shy when telling a girl that she looked attractive. He looked like he was just telling her something that was true, nothing unusual or interesting.

"Can you guess who it is?" she asked eagerly.

Atticus shook his head gravely. "Sorry Roslyn, but I have no clue who you're talking about."

Roslyn looked even more uncomfortable now. "Let me make it plain. His name starts with an A and ends with an S. He's been my best friend for twelve years. I met him when I was five. He lives here. He's in my math class, and he's really funny. He's seventeen. He has a cute mole on his cheek. He's awesome at spirit slaying. Every time I see him, I want to kiss him."

Atticus considered for a few long moments. Then, he opened his mouth to speak. "No clue."

Roslyn scoffed. "Okay. This is so not funny. I know you know who it is. Making me think you don't know who it is is so not funny. Stop messing with me."

Atticus' eyes widened. "I'm really sorry, Roslyn. I'm not messing with you. I legit have no clue about who you're talking about. But he must be someone with a very nice personality, for an amazing and talented girl such as yourself to like him," he added in kindly.

Roslyn's eyes widened. "You're not joking." Suddenly, she started to laugh.

"What's so funny?" he asked.

"You. You're so funny."

"Thanks," he said sarcastically.

"I'll give you one more hint. He's sitting right next to me."

Atticus looked around, expecting to see a boy with curly brown hair sitting next to Roslyn, who he hadn't noticed before. When he saw that there was no one there but him and her, he was a bit confused.

"Oh," he said after a little while, finally piecing everything together. "You mean me." He looked down at his shoes, and an awkward silence ensued, which was shortly broken by Roslyn.

"No kidding."

Atticus looked up then and flashed her a grin that made butterflies flutter around in her stomach and lit up her world. "But there must be a mistake. You can't possibly like me. I'm so…unattractive. And weird. And imperfect. You deserve better than me."

"That's ridiculous. First of all, if you think you're unattractive, you clearly have never looked in a mirror before. Boy, you are so hot, I could use you to cook me an omelet. Secondly, yes, you are weird. But that's good. If you weren't, you'd be a clone. I'm glad that you're different. I love your differences. Lastly, you're right. You're not perfect. But you're everything I could possibly ask for. And I feel like if I could have you all to myself, then I'd be complete. You're the missing piece to my puzzle. I need you. Don't you understand?" she took his hands. "I can't be without you."

"Really?"

"Really."

"But…"

"But what?" she asked him.

"But I'm scared."

"Is this scaring you?"

He swallowed, then nodded.

"That's alright. I'm scared too."

"You are?"

"Yes. It's always scary when you explore the unknown. But we'll never know if we'll like it or not until we try it."

Atticus stared down at his shoes and nodded.

"We can take it slow. We don't have to rush. We have all the time in the world. We can get a little taste of it before we see if we want it all." Then, she brought his hands up and rested his arms on her shoulders, and his hands clasped together behind her neck. She leaned her forehead against his and said seven words she had wanted to say for ten years. "Atticus, I have loved every moment spent with you. I want to be your lover."

His wide amber eyes met her green ones, and she could hear his heartbeat racing. Never had he been so close to a girl who wasn't his sister before. He was frightened, scared, and felt as if he had let go of the rope tying him to what was old and familiar as if he had been pitched through a large dark ditch at the end of which he knew not what lurked.

"It's alright if you don't want to go. I've liked you for so long, but I never had the courage to ask you. And now I have. Say yes or no now. I don't have my hopes high much anyway."

For once in his life, Atticus was at a loss for words. Roslyn shook her head sadly and started to the door. "It's cool. We can still be friends."

"Wait." Atticus jumped to his feet and walked over to Roslyn, blocking her from the door. "I'd love to go out with you."

A small and mischievous smile played its way on Roslyn's beautiful face. "Really?"

"Really." Roslyn hugged him.

"Great! We can go to the movies! I have tickets!" She pulled out two tickets from her jacket.

Atticus raised an eyebrow. "I thought you said you didn't have your hopes high."

Roslyn put her hands on her hips. "I lied. I've been waiting for ten years to say those words. I had my hopes up higher than the Chrysler building."

"Oh. When are we going?"

"We're going right now." Roslyn grabbed Atticus' hand and yanked it down a flight of stairs leading down from the roof.

"By the way, do you know where Cassandra and Jamie are?"

Atticus gulped. "Um."

Roslyn paused for a moment. "Atticus," she said, "do you know where Cassandra and Jamie are?"

"Well, technically, I don't, but–"

"Atticus! They could be captured by spirits this very moment! We need to go after them right now!"

"Can we maybe do that after the movie?" Atticus took one look at Roslyn's face and shook his head. "No. I guess not."

Roslyn stormed off. "I can't believe you let them go off like that! I'm getting my weapons. You get Ana, and meet me at the front door."

"Okay."

28

Angel Tears

When Cassandra came back into consciousness, she was tied to a pillar with a thick and rough rope. Jamie was tied right next to her, and they were uncomfortably close together. She had been resting her head on his shoulder, and he had been stroking her hair back with his careful hands. They had left his hands untied, which seemed weird at first, but then he noticed that the pole was much too thick for either of them to reach behind towards the knot at the back side of the pole.

Suddenly, Cassandra's eyes had widened, and her expression illustrated extreme and hopeless rage for the first few moments. She got rope burns where she had helplessly struggled against the rope. Her voice got hoarse the more and more that she screamed out in anguish, while Jamie had held her hand, stroked her hair, and murmured to her in the dark. Then, she felt something else. This something else was something she hadn't felt since she was very little, when her parents had died. It bit deep down into her chest, making her feel heavy and weak. It came in waves, spreading itself in her chest like a violent, lethal disease. She felt sick, sick, sick.

Slowly and faintly, memories started to flood back into her head, slightly dulled by the pain. In her mind, she watched herself run out of the Sanctuary like a child, lettering her temper get the best of her once again. Then, as always, Jamie, her savior, had run out to calm her down. She didn't like this feeling, knowing that she was the reason that Jamie could possibly be hurt. It didn't even matter that she might be harmed, but knowing that Jamie might be hurt and that she couldn't do anything about it made her more scared and angry than she had ever been before. She wanted to watch things crash and burn, break and ruin, knowing that Jamie, her Jamie, could potentially be harmed.

Jamie had a long cut on his collarbone, and blood dripped from it and stained his white shirt scarlet. And the worst part was that Jamie wasn't even angry at her. When she asked him how angry he was at her, he said, "I'm not mad at you. I recognize that you're human, and that like everyone else, you aren't always going to make the best choices. And that's alright. We're going to be alright. We'll make it out of here. And when we do, I will say, 'I told you so.' Don't fret. It's going to be okay."

"But Jamie, how can you possibly not be even slightly mad at me?"

"It's simple. I love you. I love you so simply and dearly that no matter what you do, you can't make me stop loving you. Not even the angels in heaven can make me stop loving you."

"Jamie, you're hurt."

Jamie glanced down at his collarbone and saw the long cut that looked as if it had been cut by a knife. Jamie shrugged. "I don't remember getting that." he lied.

He remembered the entire thing. Cassandra had passed out after a deafening clang when a spirit who had hidden in the shadows swung a large metal stick at her leg. Her leg had broken, and she had passed out in pain. She crumpled forward, and Jamie reached forward to catch her in his arms. Then, he saw the enchanted knife. The knife came closer and closer, and with a start, Jamie realized that it was coming in Cassandra's direction. He leaped in front of Cassandra just as it flew towards her, and felt the savage burn on his skin. Nothing, he had thought, not even the cursed dagger he had taken the other day, had made him feel such pain. It grazed across his collarbone, and blood spilled behind his shirt. "Cassie, Cassie, wake up, please, we have to get away from here. Cassie please."

But she hadn't woken up.

They had offered him freedom, under the condition that he allow them to

181

enchant him with a concealment spell that would prevent him from telling anyone about the location of the large building at the edge of the woods, and that he agreed to leave Cassandra here with them. Of course, he didn't agree. Nothing, not even all of the riches in the world could have made him leave anywhere that Cassandra was.

They had dragged him down the hall, down a hall of prison cells. He remembered seeing a man with blood splattered on his arms and pure, hazel eyes through a small opening in the door, through which a possessed woman was pushing a cup of unpleasant looking gruel. Jamie winced.

James Carter Taylor, if you dare risk your life for mine again, I will hunt you down and inflict a near fatal injury on you. Do I make myself clear?

He looked sheepish when he said this. Cassandra knew well after 12 years of knowing him that he couldn't lie. James Carter Taylor was an extremely bad liar. But Cassandra, who had been his best friend since they were five would've been able to tell when he was lying and when he was telling the truth even if he wasn't a terrible liar.

"Jamie,"

Jamie swallowed and braced himself.

"Jamie! You're lying."

Jamie shook his head frantically. Cassandra rolled her eyes. "Jamie, you took another knife for me, didn't you?"

Jamie looked down. "How'd you know it was a knife?" he said weakly.

"Jamie! You could've died! How dare you risk your life for me?"

"Cassandra, there's no use yelling at me. Because I'd do it again for you. You can yell at me and hit me and kick me, but I'd do it again. I don't regret a thing."

Cassandra sighed. "Jamie," she said. When had this happened? When had she started reprimanding Jamie for making poor decisions? Wasn't it supposed to be the other way around?

Jamie reached out then and pushed a lock of dark hair that had fallen into her eyes when she had struggled against the rope that had bound her torso to the pole. Her arms and legs were bound, because she was Pol Electi, and might have fighting talent that might lead to her and Jamie's escape. They had assumed that since Jamie was only human, he hadn't been trained, and hadn't bothered tying his hands back. Only his legs were bound to the pole. Suddenly, Cassandra's eyes lit up like the sun, and a mischievous smile and spread across her face.

"Jamie. In my jeans," she whispered.

Jamie was bewildered. "What?"

"In the back pocket of my jeans. I stuffed it in there before we started running. My knife. It might still be there. Can you reach?"

Jamie nodded. He reached his hand out to the pocket of Cassandra's ripped jeans. He put his hand under the tough material of the rope and inside of her pocket. Then, he fished out the knife. A grin that exposed her white teeth had come onto Cassandra's face. Slowly, Jamie used the knife to cut through the rope that bound him to the pillar. Then, he freed Cassandra. She found that her leg was no longer broken. Maybe the spirits fixed it. She wondered why they would even bother. She leaped up and looked around for a mode of escape. The only mode of escape was a latched door. Cassandra backed up against the opposite wall and braced herself for impact.

"Cassandra, I don't think this is a very good idea–" he began as the door opened and a possessed man entered the room. Jamie was frozen with shock as the man yelled.

"Where do you think you're going?"

Cassandra moved in the shadows of the dim prison cell and took the knife from Jamie. Before the spirit could even blink, she had flung the knife at him. The man collapsed backward, and black blood started spreading on the floor around his throat. Cassandra crept up to him and pulled the knife out of his throat with a sickening sound, wiped the blood on her jeans, stuck it into her back pocket, and walked out of the room. Momentarily, she entered the room again, walked over to where Jamie was still standing, and reached out and grabbed his hand, and dragged him out of the room.

Jamie had never seen so much blood in his life. He was still in shock when Cassandra yanked his arm up seven flights of stairs and into another room, which was empty. Cassandra raced around, peering around each corner desperately searching for a door, Jamie at her heels. The raising of all of the hairs on her back notified her that two spirits had started chasing them. She willed her feet to be faster, quicker, lighter.

They hurried around a corner, the spirits left looking around, wondering where they had gone in their wake. Cassandra exhaled in relief when she finally found a door. Putting all of her strength into it, she wrenched the doorknob and but it did not give way. They pounded their fists against it, sending a clear sign as to where in the building they were, and the spirits, two women started laughing nastily and building fireballs in their palms. Then, three more women emerged from a different room and started to pull Cassandra away. Screaming and kicking, she struggled away, but their grip was iron. Jamie, who had finally recovered from the shock, pulled the knife out from Cassandra's back pocket and struck out at one of the hovering fireballs holding Cassandra back. A sound, like nails on a chalkboard, screeching and deafening, sounded, and a tornado of black energy floated upward, a pleasant surprise for Jamie– he hadn't expected to be able to maim any spirit severely.

Now, the attention shifted to Jamie. The spirits didn't let go of Cassandra but rather started to throw fireballs at Jamie. Cassandra pulled away savagely from the spirits' grasp and stood in front of Jamie, three black fireballs flying and sinking into her body, but failing to elicit even a single reaction from their victim. Jamie, who had flinched back and put his hands up to shield himself, shouted in surprise to see the fireballs hit Cassandra and burn a hole through the back of her black tank top, though she didn't even wince. It was evident that she was unharmed by it, and Jamie exhaled a breath that he didn't even know he was holding. A harsh snarling from behind them made them turn in time to see a woman built a new fireball in her palm when the door burst open.

They felt flames scorch their mortal bodies, and coughed on smoke, tripping over splintered wood, and blinking in blind darkness. And from the darkness of the night emerged three figures.

"I told you so."

Atticus, Roslyn, and Ana. Roslyn unsheathed the longest sword Jamie had ever seen. Atticus was holding a long staff with a spear end. Ana wielded a type of blade in the shape of a circle. Her thumb was skillfully placed on the top of the wheel, and her middle finger placed on the bottom, and she threw it at the throat of one of the spirits, neatly beheading it. Like a boomerang, the wheel spun around and found its way back to Ana's hand. Her small face was contorted in rage, an expression that he had never thought he would ever see on her delicate features.

Roslyn was fighting fiercely, her teeth bared in anger. Her long blonde hair whipped across her shoulders as she shredded spirits into strips with her sword. Her eyes flashed with anger, and she spun around, stabbing one in the chest. The spirit sunk down and its soul flew up, which was captured by Roslyn in a tube. Atticus swung his long staff and leaped up doing a kick in mid-air. He landed on the ground, sitting on top of the chest of a spirit, and struck the spirit in the heart with his spear. Then, he threw a tube to Jamie, who promptly caught it, and captured its soul. Though Jamie could not see spirits in their mortal forms, he could see their souls. He threw the tub back to Atticus, who grinned and stuck it through his belt. Cassandra was free now. There was a spirit in front of her. Atticus stepped in front of her with his staff, but Cassandra shook her head.

"Atticus, fam, I'm feeling a bit bloodthirsty at the moment. You don't mind, do you?"

Atticus shook his head and moved out of her way, clearing her path toward the spirit. He grinned at her in a cute way. "Be my guest."

Cassandra grinned at Jamie, who slid her knife out of his pocket and threw it to her. She caught it, and the hilt touched her skin, and a red mark of a rose with thorns showed up on her arm. Cassandra grinned and started forward toward the spirit. The spirit had realized that its magic could not harm her and that she didn't have any enchanted swords on her, so she started to back away. Cassandra showed no mercy, and while her entire experience and training in the art of knife throwing added up to a grand total of zero, something inside of her clicked, and she threw the knife the way she had watched Ana throw it, eyeing the exact place she wanted it to land and flicking her wrist. She was rewarded when the knife lodged itself

185

in the spirit's gut. She was aiming for its chest, but she supposed this would do. It cried out, and Ana stepped forward and offered Cassandra a tube. She took it and captured its soul.

Ana smiled. "You, Cass, are a true born Pol Electi."

Cassandra smiled back and took a deep and sweeping bow. "Thank you, Ana." Then she turned around to the open door. "Now, let's get the hell out of here."

They started out into the woods, in the direction of the Sanctuary, with Roslyn's compass. Jamie was still puzzled about how they had gotten there.

"How did you find us, anyway?" Cassandra asked.

Atticus answered. "Well, after Jamie went after you, I told Roslyn, who promptly yelled at me and I got Ana, and we started to look for you in the woods. We couldn't find you there, and we saw burn marks on the trees, so we guessed what had happened."

"And then we followed your footprints in the muddy ground. We've been trained for this sort of thing, you know." Ana filled in helpfully.

"Well, thank you for assuming that we would die in the woods on our own. You really helped us back there." Jamie had to be the one to say it. Cassandra, prideful as ever, would never admit that she needed help sometimes. 'Sorry, my bad' and 'thank you' didn't appear to be in her dictionary. The only time she ever used those two words were when she was around Jamie.

"You're welcome," Roslyn said. The summer breeze was blowing through her straight blonde hair, and it fell into her eyes. Roslyn pushed it away impatiently and led the way. A branch blocked their way, and Atticus took one long sweep with his staff and cut it down. When they made their way to the front steps of the Sanctuary, they found two of the Pol Electi standing at the front door. Atticus and Roslyn exchanged a glance as the guards let them in.

"Something must have happened," Roslyn said.

Atticus nodded, and they walked to Alana's desk at the library. She was there, studying a map. She feverishly circled areas on the map and kept writing Latin names near each circle. She was whispering to herself and didn't look up as they walked in. She hadn't noticed them.

186

"Alana? Has something happened?" Ana asked.

Alana looked up. She shook her head and looked down again, continuing to mutter under her breath while she circled areas on the map.

"Alana, you know you can tell us anything. We want to help."

Alana didn't look up. "Nothing's happened."

"Alana, you stationed guards at the door!" Roslyn exclaimed exasperatedly. Alana took a deep breath and looked up.

"Mitchell found the Gem of Incantations, and came in here disguised as Charlie."

Atticus looked perplexed. "Why would be disguise himself as Charlie though? Charlie is a backstabber!"

"He's a double agent! He's been working for us the entire time! He's been transferring classified information to me in secret. I didn't want to tell you because I was afraid he'd get caught. And you know what they do spies."

Atticus' eyes widened.

Alana started again. "And now, Mitchell's got him trapped somewhere. How else could he have transformed into him?"

It was true. *The Figura Mutante* could only transform into those from which they had something. A fingernail, or a lock of hair, or a vial of blood, something to identify who they were transforming into.

"I've interrogated him. He's hard-shelled, but he cracks under pressure. I've got the location, but he could be lying. I have him trapped in the dungeons. We need to make sure we aren't walking into a trap."

Cassandra's eyes widened. Then she smiled mischievously. "I've got an idea."

Ten minutes later, Atticus, Ana, Roslyn, Cassandra, Jamie, and Alana were standing in the library, and Alana held a thick book in her hands. She kept flipping until she got to where Cassandra had requested her to turn to. When she did, she handed it back to her little sister. Cassandra's long and slim hands that seemed to be made for playing the guitar traced delicate lines on the brittle pages, and read aloud the title.

"Soul Swapping Spell. Chant the following words and add the following ingredients into an open fire or a raging sea. This spell apparently lets you swap souls with someone. Lasts for hours depending on how many ounces of angel tears you add."

"How do you choose who you're swapping souls with?"

Cassandra's gray eyes scanned the page before she read out the answer. "The person who you are swapping souls with can be indicated in the bit of them that you add to the spell." Then, she found the ingredients list and read them out loud.

"We need a page of a loved book, possessed blood, angel tears, and something of the person you're transforming into. We can get all of these ingredients, transform into someone Mitchell trusts, and get the truth out of him."

"That's brilliant." Alana's eyes had lit up, and she was grinning. Cassandra grinned back. Jamie loved her smile. He loved that she looked mischievous when she smiled. It was a smile that made you wonder if she did something devious when your back was turned, like she knew something that you didn't.

"If we're doing this, the person who's transforming has to transform into Mitchell's brother, Michael. They trust each other with their lives. We have a page from a loved book and spirit blood, but we don't have angel tears or something of Michael, like a lock of his hair or something."

"Where do we find angel tears?" Cassandra asked.

"The black market. And someone will have to track down Michael and get a lock of his hair." Atticus replied.

"How about this-

Atticus and I can go to track down Michael, and Jamie, Cassandra, and Ana can go to the black market." Roslyn proposed.

"We can do that," Cassandra said.

They set off. Ana was holding a piece of paper with instructions on how to get to the black market, Jamie was holding a velvet bag of precious gems, and Cassandra had stuffed her jacket with as many weapons as it could hold. Alana had told them that it sometimes gets rough at the black market. The trio decided to take the car because it was too far from the Sanctuary to walk. Jamie drove because Ana didn't have a license yet, and Cassandra's driving was often fatal. Ana read out instructions, and they drove for an hour and found themselves in Iselin. They parked at a deserted parking lot and started walking down the street lined with shops selling everything from sparring gear to hoop earrings. Ana stopped abruptly in front of a dark shop that looked semi-corporeal.

"I think this is it," Ana said.

Jamie looked at Cassandra. "Are you ready?"

Cassandra looked at him seriously for a moment. "Aye aye, captain!"

Jamie doubled over and shook with laughter. When he finally stopped laughing, his face turned red. "I can't hear you!" he said.

Ana looked confused. "But she's right there." She indicated Cassandra with her thumb. "Why is this funny?"

Cassandra laughed. "Spongebob," she said, by way of answering her question.

"Oh. I hated that show. Atticus loved it though. I was more into anime," Ana answered. Cassandra exchanged a serious glace with Jamie.

"We must educate her on the traditions of our cult."

"The Spongebob cult," Jamie said, with a dignified look.

"You've got to be kidding me. You can't seriously still watch that!"

Cassandra looked back at Jamie. "She knows too much," she said in a dangerous voice.

They laughed so hard that their faces turned red. When they stopped laughing, Jamie said, "Alright, seriously, though, are you ready?"

"Yeah. Let's do this." Cassandra said. Ana nodded in agreement, and they entered the black market.

The first thing that Cassandra noticed about the black market was that it was called black for a reason. The walls, the floor, the table cloths, the bottles were all black, or dark themed. The room was very dimly lit, and lanterns hung from the ceiling. Cassandra supposed it was because they were too cheap to pay for electricity. The room was lined with tables, each holding plenty of dangerous-looking weapons and elixirs, powders, and jars suspended with plenty of unpleasant-looking things. It looked like an opioid den. Loud and hoarse voices could be heard, advertising their products and prices. Cassandra moved forward to the front of the store and cleared her throat. An ancient woman looked up at her as if daring her to speak. "Pol Electi. I don't sell to your kind."

Jamie exaggeratedly pulled the immense velvet bag from his jacket and dropped it on the table. The spirit looked eager now. She let her wrinkled hands wander to the bag, and she was about to open it, but Jamie took his other hand and laid it atop the hilt of his dagger. Cassandra smirked. "What was that about not selling to my kind again?"

The woman swallowed and gave her the most unpleasant smile she had ever seen. "What do you want?"

"Angel tears," Ana said. "Three ounces."

The woman reached under the table and pulled out a jar, which contained a shimmering liquid. It did not look one definite color, and Cassandra saw a million different colors all at once. It made her slightly dizzy. The woman caught her eye and smiled. "125."

Jamie and Cassandra turned to Ana, who shook her head. "No. That's exorbitant."

"No, it's not!" The woman shrieked. The group turned away, and she called after them. "Wait, come back! How about 100? 75? I'm not going any lower than that. Ana looked up.

"Wait, 75 is actually a fair price." They walked back to the table and gave the woman what looked roughly around 75 small gemstones. The exchange was made, and Cassandra put the jar in her jacket. They turned to leave and found themselves surrounded by a bunch of hungry-looking spirits.

29

So Lonely

He was laughing. She didn't know why, but he was.

"Hello?"

No answer. Just more hysterical laughing.

"Are you okay?"

He stopped. She could feel her heart stopping. *Please be okay*, she prayed. *Please be okay. If you're not okay, I won't be.*

Something broke inside of her head. She could hear him again.

Unbound, uncontrolled crying.

"Please,"

"Don't go," he said. "If you go, I'll be so lonely."

"I'm not going anywhere."

He seemed not to hear her. He was crying so quietly that she wouldn't have heard it if she didn't always pay such close attention to him.

Why did she pay such close attention to him? She did not know. But she did know that she wasn't about to stop anytime soon.

30

Sharing Is Caring

"The Figura Mutantc hcadquarters is in New York. Train?" Atticus asked.

Alana shook her head. "Why bother when you have the Transporter?" Alana, Roslyn, and Atticus made their way to Alana's desk. Alana pulled out a small, golden contraption from one of the drawers and handed it to Atticus. Roslyn stepped forward. Atticus placed the tip of the pen to her arm and wrote 'Michael Reed' on her arm. Then, he removed his own jacket and gave the pen to Roslyn, who wrote the same on his hand. Then, they held hands, and the air shimmered and rippled for a moment. Then, Roslyn and Atticus vanished from sight.

Roslyn felt extreme happiness, and ecstasy for a moment, and then extreme loss and tragedy, and then, she felt sick. Very, very sick. Roslyn got there first, and she landed face first on the front lawn. Atticus arrived second and fell right beside her. He uprighted himself and sat beside her on the lawn, with his knees pulled in and his hands propped up behind him. He was smiling. Roslyn was very pale. She got up and took deep breaths, but she still felt nauseous. She doubled over then, and clutched her stomach.

"Roslyn? Are you okay?" She could hear Atticus' concerned voice over her pain and struggled to nod.

"It's the Transporter. Some people are allergic to its effects. Are you cold?" Atticus asked.

Roslyn was shivering, though she hadn't noticed until he had pointed it out. Though it was the middle of summer, Figura Mutante had the tendency to inhabit warm places and emit coldness. For a fifty feet radius around the large building, it was below 50° F. And yet, Atticus removed his jacket. He was wearing a black sleeveless shirt underneath, and he started to shiver. Goosebumps started to show up on his arms when he reached over and draped his jacket over Roslyn's shoulders.

"But Atticus, aren't you cold?"

Atticus lied and shook his head. "I've been told that I'm very hot." Atticus shrugged and smiled. Roslyn laughed and tugged the jacket closer around herself, and they stood up.

* * *

"That's a lot of gems you've got there. Did your teacher ever tell you that sharing is caring?" A man with gray hair and red eyes said.

"Yes. Sharing is caring. But I don't care. I don't give a shit what happens to you." Cassandra replied sneakily. Cassandra reached into her jacket and let her hands run over the hilt of a longsword. She pulled it out with one smooth movement and neatly beheaded two spirits at once. She turned to see that Ana was spinning her metal disk and killing many spirits methodically. Jamie had removed an arrow from his sheath, fastened it onto his bow, and let it fly. It wasn't blessed metal, just ordinary material, so it didn't feel weird on his skin when he touched it.

In five minutes, they had cleared a path to the door, but more spirits kept coming over and blocking their way. Cassandra stepped forward and warded them off with her longsword. Spirits started to throw fireballs, and their eyebrows rose when Cassandra wasn't hurt by them. Using their moment of surprise as a distraction, Cassandra grabbed Jamie's hand and ran. Ana followed them, and they made their way out into the summer sunset. Spirits started to speak in loud voices and started to flood out of the black market. They ran into the car. Jamie started the car, and they sped off.

Jamie was driving through Garden State Parkway on the way back to the Sanctuary. He was dutifully obeying all of the road rules and driving at a speed way below the limit. The cars in all the other lanes were speeding away, but the cars in the lane that Jamie was driving in was slow and careful. Jamie had passed his driver's test the first time he had taken it, Cassandra had failed hers three times. It was practically illegal for her to get behind the wheel. There was once a time when she got pulled over for driving a car at 70 miles per hour and had nearly run over fifteen innocent pedestrians. Jamie was in the passenger seat on that cursed day, because she had told him that she was good at driving and poor Jamie, innocent and trusting as ever had believed her.

She was lying.

The police pulled her over and demanded that she take a breathalyzer test. She still remembered the incident and considered it one of the best days of her life. Jamie sat in one seat, his head in his hands, silently praying that he and Cassandra don't get arrested because he was sure that if he did, once he got out, his mother would skin him alive, and then deep fry him. Cassandra, on the other hand, was taking selfies of herself in the driver's seat of her car with the police car in the background and posting it on her Instagram, with the subtitle, "Pulled over for the first time! :P". She was praying that she would get into jail. One of her life's ambitions was to get put into jail and make friends with people with terrifying names, such as Lucy 'Angel of Death' Smith. She also aspired to lift gigantic weights in order to get ripped abs and biceps. She dreamed of having an overall intimidating air about her, and she planned to make this happen by getting plenty of unappealing and rather scary looking tattoos over all over her lanky body, as well as multiple piercings on her nose and ears, and possibly on her lips and eyebrows. She wanted to look like what she called 'a gangster' (pronounced gang-STAH) and what Jamie called a thug who was likely to be put into prison for four hundred and fifty years after the discovery of $3.5 billion worth of cocaine, $4.5 billion worth in marijuana, $2 million worth in heroin, $1.5 million in fancy exported liquor, $2 million more in vodka, and three dead bodies, all hidden in various different locations at various clubs internationally.

When the test was over, and they found that Cassandra was not drunk, she showed them the fake driver's license she made earlier, because oddly enough, she got a bad vibe from Jamie, and she figured he probably didn't want to go to jail. They let her go with a $200 fine. Jamie offered to pay it, but Cassandra didn't let him.

"This is a milestone in my life. My first ticket for speeding!" Cassandra had said delightedly.

"How are you possibly happy that you got a ticket for $200?"

Cassandra smiled mischievously.

"Cassandra,"

"Alright, fine, I'll tell you. But only because you're my best friend. I'm happy that I got away with only a $200 fine."

"Because," Jamie continued.

Cassandra smiled at him. "Because I stole that car."

"Cassandra! You told me that it was Rowan's car!"

Cassandra snorted. "As if Rowan would let me borrow her car. Besides— Rowan's car is white. This one's blue."

Cassandra was certainly an outlier. She had an angel's face and a demon's heart, which was exactly what Jamie loved most about her.

After two minutes of quietness, Cassandra decided that there was way too much silence in the car to be healthy. So she decided to make Jamie and Ana laugh. She began to think about something that they would find funny. She figured that they would find funny what she found funny. So she thought about what she found funny.

Most people liked to read books in which two characters fall in love and get together.

Cassandra wasn't like most people.

She loved books that had characters that went through love failure, heartbreak, rejection, tragedy, bloodshed, and death. Cassandra didn't understand why. It seemed rather comical and hilarious to read or hear about unrequited matters of the heart. So, she decided that she would break the oppressing silence by making people laugh.

"Hey, Jamie, remember Noah Sanders?"

Jamie made a face. "I hated that guy. Coming up to you and asking you out like that. I wanted to tear him limb from limb. What did he think he was? An asker-outer?" The words spilled out of his lips before he could clap a hand over them.

Cassandra had an amused expression on her face. "An asker-outer?"

Jamie turned red. "Is that what you heard? Because I didn't say that. You must not have heard me properly."

Cassandra's raised an eyebrow, and she twisted her lips like she was chewing gum.

"Okay. So there was this guy called Dylan. Dylan Shaw."

"Oh my god. You're going to tell her about how you rejected him, aren't you?" Jamie said. A smile spread across Cassandra's face.

"Yes."

"Rejection? Aww, I feel bad for him already," Ana whined.

"Don't feel bad for him. He was a dumbass."

"Cassandra!"

"What? Was I not supposed to say that?"

"Yes! That's a swear!"

"Oh." She shrugged. "Oops. Sorry, Mommy."

Jamie spluttered. "I'm not your–"

"Anyway," Cassandra interrupted, "Dylan was the most annoying guy you could possibly meet. And he was frankly freaky. He used to follow me around everywhere. Until."

"Until what?" Ana asked, intrigued.

"Until I broke his nose."

"Cassandra!"

She shrugged. "He deserved it."

Ana shook her head. "Poor Dylan."

"So," Cassandra said as if she hadn't said anything, "I didn't mind for the first month. He was like an entourage. I thought he was just a fan, but no, he liked me."

Ana rolled her eyes. "He was following you around for a whole month, and you didn't guess that by a single, minuscule chance, he might actually like you."

Cassandra looked unfazed. "Nope."

Ana sighed. She was so oblivious, it was sad.

"So, he found me at the cafeteria once, roasting innocent bystanders, and he decided to announce his great love for me."

Ana sighed inwardly. "Oh, no."

"He was a total nerd. He was like, a walking dictionary. He used to interrupt everyone and correct them, and they'd just ignore him and forget that he exists. I did too, after the first day he started following me around. He used to pick up everything I dropped, offer to quiz me on things we were going to be assessed on, and hold my binders. Anyway, one day, he stood up on top of a cafeteria table. He was wearing the ugliest suit I've ever seen. He said, 'Cassandra, will you go out with me?'" Cassandra frowned at the memory. "And here's the craziest part– people awwwed! And then, I walked toward the table, and he pulled out a rose,"

Ana looked in the rearview mirror and saw that Jamie looked sick. He soooo liked Cassandra. Ana thought it was the most adorable thing she had ever seen.

"And he handed it to me, and,"

"And then what?" Ana asked.

"I think people expected me to accept the rose and say yes." Cassandra looked as if it were the craziest thing ever. "Nah, man. I punched him."

Jamie no longer looked sick. He looked more alive than ever. A smile spread across his face, and he was laughing.

"And that's why Dylan Shaw's nose is crooked." Cassandra finished.

Ana felt slightly bad for Dylan but overall happy for Jamie. She could only guess how heartbroken he would have felt if she had said yes.

Ana took her right hand and slapped her forehead. She shook her head. "You're just like Atticus."

"How do you say that?"

"He can't figure out when someone likes him either. Both of you are total idiots when it comes to love." Ana commented.

Cassandra shrugged. "Can't disagree with that."

"He was a nice guy. But I'm nicer. You should go out with me instead." Jamie said. He surprised even himself when he said that. He knew he wasn't that confident.

Cassandra looked amused again. "Okay."

Jamie almost drove into a head-on collision and kicked at the brakes at the last moment.

"Wait, really?!"

"Sure." Cassandra looked amused.

Jamie's face turned bright red. "Cool." He said, trying to hide the fact that he was freaking out, and that he felt extreme ecstasy and like a total idiot at the same time. He didn't feel like he took a shot of whiskey. No, he felt like he swam in the whiskey, he felt so high and happy and elated, like walking on a cloud, like it wasn't possible, and any moment now he would fall from the sky. He felt like nothing else in the world mattered other than the fact that he, James Carter Taylor, was going on a date with Cassandra Chloe Black, the one most important person in the world to him. He didn't even care if he wasn't breathing as long as Cassandra was.

Ana felt weird. She felt as if she were intruding on a private moment. She also let so happy for Jamie. This was so cute.

Jamie, however, felt like a total idiot for letting those words fall out of his mind and through his incontinent lips. But he was glad he said them because now he could go out with her. He had hoped she would take it as a joke because if she did, and laughed, he wouldn't be feeling so awkward right now.

"So," Cassandra said, hastily breaking the silence again, "who wants to listen to Drake's 'In My Feelings?'"

"Oh, dear god, Jee-Jee in heaven, please do not let her play that song. I really do not care if Kiki loves you, Drake. Please do us all a favor and leave us alone." Jamie did not like rap. Rap, however, was Cassandra's entire reason for existing. Jamie's reason for existing was Cassandra.

"Fight me," Cassandra said.

"Rip," said Ana.

31

'Lil Mikey

A tticus and Roslyn made their way to the entrance and Roslyn reached out and pulled the brass knocker and then released it. It made a loud sound on the wooden door, and in two minutes, the door was opened by a kind looking woman with graying brown hair and green eyes.

"Hello. How may I help you?"

"Oh, we just came by to hang out and see some tourist attractions, but we were wondering, this place looks ancient. Is it a museum?" Roslyn asked in a sweet voice she assumed when she was trying to get what she wanted.

"It's not a museum, but we do have some artifacts. Would you like to see them?" The Figura Mutante asked. She clearly didn't know that they were Pol Electi; she probably thought that they were just friendly normie tourists.

Atticus grinned. "Yes, we would. Thank you for letting us see them."

The woman smiled. "You're very welcome." She pushed the door open wider and walked in. With a quick glance at Atticus, Roslyn stepped into the building.

The building was brightly lit, and the entire place smelled pleasantly of pumpkin spice and nutmeg. The hardwood floor was a deep brown, and the walls were lined with oil paintings, some depicting landscapes, others portraits of previous leaders. The woman led the way to the museum. They walked down a long hallway and entered a room. It looked just like the artifacts room back at the Sanctuary. The woman told them to take as long as they liked and shut the door as she walked out. Atticus ran his hand along the side of a glass box which contained a collection of sparkling gemstones. "Atticus. Focus. We need to find Lil' Mikey and leave. We need to wait for

a few minutes for that woman to go back to her office so that we can leave this room first." She walked over to the door and slipped it open, just a little.

Atticus laughed. "Lil' Mikey. We should start calling him that."

"Okay, Elsa."

"Roslyn! You know I hate that nickname."

"Exactly. That's why I called you that."

Atticus frowned, then reached up to brushed a bead of sweat away that had appeared near his hairline. Roslyn had removed Atticus' jacket. It was very warm in here, like a sauna. This was because the Figura Mutante could only survive in warm conditions. They also liked to live clustered together in groups, like a wolf pack. Roslyn focused and found that she no longer heard footsteps in the hallway. She gestured for Atticus to follow her into the hallway.

They stepped into the hallway, which was lined with elegant paintings, and kept walking until they found a staircase. They crept up it, and found a bunch of doors with name cards over each doorway, stating the last names of Figura Mutante families. They read Stewart, Scott, Williams, Rogers, Reed, and Howard. Then, Atticus abruptly stopped and looked at Roslyn. She nodded. He rung the doorbell. A man opened the door. "Hello–" he said, and then was unceremoniously cut off by Roslyn, who had punched him in the face and instantly knocked him out. He slumped to the floor.

Atticus turned around and looked at Roslyn pointedly. "What?"

"Nothing." Atticus was smiling. Roslyn stepped over the man's body into his apartment, and Atticus followed her. Then, he pulled the man back into the room and locked the door. Once Roslyn pulled a few brown hairs from Lil' Mikey's head, (it was comical because Michael was rather well-nourished) and placed them inside a ziplock bag, Atticus and Roslyn held onto Lil' Mikey and used the Transporter to get back to the Sanctuary.

* * *

When Jamie, Ana, and Cassandra arrived back at the Sanctuary, Jamie felt rather awkward. He didn't know why, Cassandra was still the same Cassandra she was 12 years ago when he met her, and he didn't feel awkward then, so he shouldn't feel so awkward now. But he did.

And his stomach felt weird. Others would have called it 'butterflies in the stomach,' but no, there was an angry mob of rogue butterflies protesting against his stomach and ripping him apart alive from the inside. He felt as though the butterflies carried him up, and there was a skip in his step that hadn't been there before for one second, and in the other second, he felt as though his stomach had decided to take gymnastics classes and learned to execute a somersault and a flip. His heart was beating so quickly and so fast, he had never felt this self-conscious or nervous around anyone.

They had decided on next Friday for the date. Cassandra had suggested going to the arcade to hit a few Fortnite dubs and then kill a few Roblox characters just to hear them say "oof" as they died, but Jamie decided that it "wasn't romantic enough." Eventually, they had both agreed on the Museum of Modern Art in New York, since they both enjoyed art, though Jamie had a different idea, one that he would tell her of soon.

They would take the car that Cassandra "borrowed" from Rowan. "Nothing more romantic than running from the law," Cassandra had said.

Now they were here. Standing in front of the Sanctuary, Jamie stopped. Cassandra was about to make her way to the door, and Ana had purposefully gone into the Sanctuary quickly. Jamie reached out then and took Cassandra's hand. Cassandra looked down then, at their entwined hands. He half expected her to gag, as she had once done when a guy had asked her out in middle school.

"Are you ready for this?"

"Yes," she said. The stars were out now, but to Jamie, she was the brightest star he had ever seen.

"Are you sure? If you don't want this, I don't either."

"I'm sure." She smiled, and for a moment, Jamie could have sworn that she shined like the sun in the morning sky. He smiled back.

They found the others in the library. Alana was talking to Roslyn and Atticus, who was holding a glinting object in his hand. He extended his hand and gave it to Alana, who walked over to her desk and put it away.

Roslyn and Atticus were standing in front of the fireplace, in which a fire was on, but ironically was cooling the room rather than heating it up. The flames were blue. Peter was there too, dragging an unconscious man across the room to the dungeons. In her right hand, Roslyn held a ziplock bag which contained a lock of brown hair, and in her other hand she held Atticus', and they were smiling.

Roslyn handed the plastic bag to Alana, who put it on her desk. Then, they walked away. Ana stepped forward then and started to recount the story of their battle to Alana. Jamie drew the velvet bag from his pocket and gave it back to Alana, who thanked him. Cassandra gave her the jar of angel tears.

"Very good job. You are all on your way to becoming great warriors, like myself."

"When do we start the enchantment?" Cassandra asked.

"Tomorrow. Get some rest today. You did a lot today."

"But–"

"Go. All five of you. Great job again."

"Okay."

Alana gave Jamie and Cassandra rooms at the Sanctuary, saying that they were welcome here at any time, and they started to them. Their rooms were right next to each other, and Jamie was about to turn the doorknob to go in when he saw that Cassandra had other plans. She walked right past him and started up the staircase that led to the roof. Intrigued, Jamie followed her.

"Where are we going?" he inquired curiously.

"The moon. Get it? Sicko Mode?" She saw Jamie looking confused with one eyebrow cocked. "Never mind. I'm going to the roof," she answered. When they reached their destination, Cassandra sat on the ledge. Jamie's eyes widened.

"Don't–" he began, but Cassandra had already picked both feet up off of the ground. Now, there was only one thing that was keeping her from falling down a whopping fifty feet to the road below, and that was her impeccable sense of balance. A mischievous smile played on her lips, and the moonlight danced in her beautiful gray eyes.

Jamie walked toward her and leaned on the railing beside her. "Talk to me."

"Okay. You should know that I have successfully learned to play "Stealing Cars" by James Bay on my acoustic guitar."

"Honestly, what can't you play on the acoustic guitar?"

Cassandra considered it for a moment. "No, I guess there isn't much I can't play on the acoustic guitar."

Now, Jamie assumed an inquisitive but knowing expression. "Have you ever cursed without knowing that it's a curse and regretted it later?" Jamie asked Cassandra.

"Yes. Only, I did know it was a curse." Cassandra smiled wickedly.

Jamie sighed. Then, the door opened, and a young lady of around their age came to the roof. She looked faintly Asian, with shoulder-length, straight brown hair and a short white dress on. She looked very pretty with her smokey eye and long eyelashes, her hair was out, and she was wearing six-inch heels. Jamie thought she looked as if she were getting ready to go to a nightclub. However, this was how she always dressed.

"Hey. Jamie, Cassandra. Harley told me to tell you guys to come down for dinner."

"Who's Harley?" Jamie asked.

"Harley's my best friend. She's also really into cooking. She offered to make dinner today. Usually, Teresa makes it. She's the cook."

"Who are you?" Cassandra asked.

"Oh! I forgot to introduce myself! I'm Jessica Ranger."

"It's nice to meet you. I'm Cassandra, and this is my best friend, Jamie." Cassandra told her. Jamie winced at the words 'best friend'. Cassandra didn't notice, but Jessica did. She got an amused look on her face.

Jessica squinted at him. "Nice to meet you. You're human." she noticed.

"How'd you know?" Jamie asked.

"You don't have the mark." She lifted her arm and indicated a rose on her inner arm. It looked as if had been carved in blood. Then, she turned to Cassandra. "And you're The Blessed One." Her eyes were wide as if she were observing a work of art that dated back a million years ago. Then, she abruptly spun on her heel and walked away. Jamie and Cassandra exchanged a glance and then followed her into the dining room.

When they arrived, the table was already set, and there was a variety of delicious-looking foods. Jamie and Cassandra chose seats next to each other. The table was very long, and it seated sixty people. Others got seated as well, but Alana didn't show up. Atticus and Roslyn entered the dining room, their eyes lit, their hands clasped, and their smiles wide.

After they got seated in chairs across from Jamie and Cassandra, Jamie asked, "You know that the legal drinking age is 21, right?"

Atticus looked up. "Yes. Why?"

Jamie shrugged. "You look high."

Atticus looked down immediately, but Jamie had already seen his cheeks burn.

"Oh, he's high, alright. He's high on Roslyn," Ana piped up.

Roslyn became very interested in her shoes. Atticus looked up at his little sister and shot her a venomous glare. "Shut up–" he began.

"Well, it's true." Ana said, unfazed and resumed eating her lasagna.

"Yeah, well, you stare at Carter so much, you might as well just skip the middleman and install a security camera in his room," Atticus retorted. Ana turned beet red.

"How dare you?" she asked.

"Exactly. So stop," Atticus said.

"Fine," she spat and started to stab her lasagna with her fork while looking into the distance at a dirty blond-haired boy who had a charismatic and infectious smile. Carter was gesturing animatedly with his hands saying something to a group of boys that looked about his age, while they slammed their hands on the table, laughing so hard that tears were coming out of their eyes.

"He's so funny, though. And sweet," she said dreamily.

"You should talk to him about how you feel," Roslyn said.

"But what if he doesn't like me?" Ana protested.

"But what if he does? What if he does, but he's too shy to say anything about it?"

Ana shook her head. "I don't think so. We're friends, and I'm sure he wants to keep it that way." At that very moment, Ana heard her own name called.

"Hey, Ana, want to hear something funny?" She turned to her left to see who had called her, then turned a deep shade of red.

Carter.

"Or maybe he doesn't," Roslyn said with a smirk.

"Okay. That was oddly coincidental." Jamie noticed.

"Yes. I'd love to hear something funny." Ana responded, ignoring them.

"All right. So I was walking to the public library, right?"

"Yeah?"

"And I chose a book from the shelf and sat down to read it."

"Uh-huh?"

"And my phone rings. I declined the phone call because I'm supposed to be quiet in the library. And then, my phone rings again, because I can't help it, I'm so popular, and this ancient librarian comes up to me and says, put your phone on vibrate, or I will evict you from the premises."

"That's so rude!"

"Right? And then I said, 'Why don't you put your mouth on vibrate?'"

Ana couldn't hide the smile that spread across her face. She doubled over with laughter, as did Cassandra, Jamie, Atticus, Roslyn, and a few kids around their age who had overheard. Cassandra stood up, took an imaginary card from her pocket, and handed it to Carter, who mimed taking it and reading it. Roslyn quietly excused herself from the table and hurried away, looking slightly green.

"I am very impressed. You have the potential to be a future roast master, such as myself, though you probably can't be as good as me. No one can. I can teach you."

Carter's eyes widened. "Really?"

"Yes." She responded.

Carter pushed a fist into the air. "Thank you so much!"

"If you agree to go out with Ana."

"Wait. WHAT?" Ana said. She had gone even redder now if that was even possible.

"You heard me." Cassandra was smirking.

Carter shrugged. "Okay."

Ana's eyes widened, and she fainted.

Carter raised an eyebrow and then smiled. "When's our first lesson?" He asked Cassandra eagerly.

"When do you want your first lesson?"

"Right now, please."

Cassandra shrugged. "Okay."

Carter's eyes widened, and grinning, he grabbed Cassandra's hand and pulled her away from the dining room. Jamie smiled.

"She's going to ruin him with her savage roasts," he said.

Atticus grinned. "I know." He was currently in the process of sprinkling water on Ana's face to wake her up. Then, he went out of the room, Cassandra assumed to get more water.

Carter tugged Cassandra's hand down three hallways and four flights of stairs, and they reached the entrance library. Alana didn't look up as they entered. She was fully submerged in maps. Cassandra felt bad for her. She must be hurting so much that Charlie was stolen. She wished she could do something to ease the pain. It had only been a few months, and yet all of these people felt like the family she never had.

Carter let go of her hand once they were near the peculiar cold radiating fire. They settled down on armchair and Carter observed her as if she were something he would never get the pleasure to see again.

"Wow. You're really into roasts."

"Yeah."

"Just like me! Okay. So first, you never roast when unprovoked. Because that's not a roast– that's just mean."

"Got it. What's next?"

"Always have a roast in mind. Easy to bust out when someone ticks you off."

"That's good advice."

"Thank you. Now, I shall demonstrate how to construct and execute the most savage." She stood up and assumed a cool and uncaring expression. "Expression is important. The more you smirk, the more pissed off your enemy gets. Try it."

Carter nodded attentively. Then, he smirked.

Cassandra was impressed. She hadn't expected him to catch on too quickly. "Great job."

Carter took a bow. "Thank you."

32

Stay Alive

When they came in, it was like a storm.

They broke her again and again, never killing her because they knew well that she was the only thing that kept him alive. She was their very own experiment. She wasn't Pol Electi, so they didn't care much about whether she lived or died. It worked out perfectly.

The little that she knew about Pol Electi came from what he had told her about them.

Once she was lashed, the other time held on top of a quivering flame. They practiced curses on her. Each time they tortured her only until she passed out, with him banging on the wall as hard as he could, calling out to her and hurling insults at them, though they both knew it didn't much help.

Once she had pretended that she had passed out, but that hadn't worked. They had only tortured her more that day.

She had asked them to kill her once, and they had merely laughed. "If we do that, nothing will keep the other one alive," they had sneered.

It was the only reason that she hadn't already killed herself. Hit herself in the head repeatedly against the wall. Hold her own throat. Fall asleep.

"Is it true?" She had asked. "Or are they lying?"

"It's true," he had said shamefully. "I'm so sorry."

"No," she had said. "It's okay. You're the only thing that's keeping me alive, too."

"Hmm," he had said thoughtfully. "I'd better stay alive then."
Despite her pain, she giggled at that.

33

Vodka Sauce

When Ana awoke from her slumber, the bright lights of the dining room and a million concerned faces greeted her. She yawned. "Atticus, I had the craziest dream. Carter said he'd–"

"Yeah, that's not a dream."

Ana's eyes widened. Then she shook her head "That's crazy. Stop pulling my leg."

"Oh, we're not. That all actually happened." Harley replied. She had black hair and sparkling blue eyes. She also had a faint British accent. Ana's eyes grew wider if that was even possible. Then she turned red. She abruptly rose from the seat, so quickly that it tipped over and ran from the room. Atticus grinned. Harley elbowed him. "Is she alright?"

"Of course she is. She's been drooling over that kid for 15 million years."

Harley rolled her eyes. "She hasn't even been alive for 15 million years."

"I was exaggerating."

"I know." She looked in the direction that Ana had vanished. "Are you sure I shouldn't go check if she's alright?" Harley asked.

"I'm sure."

Ana was sitting near the flames in her room. Her face was still bright red, but she was smiling. She stood up, then, and scavenged through her wardrobe for something pretty to wear on her first-ever date. She didn't even know when she figured out that she liked Carter, but she did know that she'd loved him for a very, very long time. She hadn't told anyone, not even her best friend/brother. She and Atticus were very close. So, obviously, he had figured out that she liked Carter. She was confused at first; then she saw how obvious it was. She looked up every time he entered the room, didn't pay attention to the conversation she was in because she was following Carter with her eyes, and started talking about him at rather random times.

Now, she pulled a black tank top and a pair of jeans out of her closet and threw it across the room. She pulled out a white dress and threw it onto her bed. Then, she grabbed three other dresses, the nicest in her closet, and threw them on top of the white one. She examined each one, then sunk to the floor in exasperation. Her head was in her hands.

How did we get here?

Then, there was a knock on the door. Ana sighed and stayed where she was for a moment. Then, she stood up and padded across the room to the door and opened it. On the other side was a certain someone.

Carter.

"Hey," Carter said. He looked very relaxed and not even slightly embarrassed or shy. "So, I came to see when you wanted to hang out?"

"Oh. Um. Friday's fine, I guess." Ana muttered.

"Great! We can meet up at the rooftop and figure out where we want to hang out from there." Carter smiled at her and walked away, and Ana felt like every step he took away from her was a tug on the noose around her throat, suffocating her and threatening to choke her.

Wait. Don't go. Don't leave me here, all alone.

* * *

She looked into the flames. They burned blue, like ice, and coldness seeped from the fireplace to the room. She watched as the maps curled in on themselves and turned black. The effects of Hell's Fire on nonliving were the same as Heaven's Fire. She put her head in her hands then, the heels of her palms digging into her face. She felt an explosion of emotion right then, a colorful blast of sadness, rage, fury, hopelessness, and longing. She felt

211

temporarily disconnected from her material body, and she felt as though her actions were being carried out by someone else. She was so lost in the endless labyrinth of her own emotion that she was unaware that another being had walked into the room when Peter entered the library.

She cursed herself for letting down her walls for a short amount of time when she finally noticed that Peter was here. She wouldn't have noticed if he hadn't called her name.

She was sitting on the floor, although there were plush armchairs and cushions on which she could have propped herself onto. She heard her name being called as if he had come to wake her from a dream.

"Alana."

She looked up. She wondered why he thought she was sitting here in front of the Hell's Fire, and if he knew that she was just worried that she would never get to see Charlie again. He probably thought she was stressed out about a spirit group that was causing trouble. He couldn't possibly know about Charlie.

Sure, he would know about him, but he would probably think that he was a stupid, disgusting spy, just like the others did.

Because the others didn't know.

Charlie had acted rather peculiar those last few days. She had begun to notice it and had asked him about it in private. At first, he had been reluctant to tell her, because she might accidentally let it slip, but in the end, he told her because he trusted her and because he knew that she was strong enough to keep the information in the right hands.

Charlie had been a spy.

But rather, a double agent. He spied on Infernum, for he had suspected that they were up to something that would disbenefit the Pol Electi. He had been going out at night and feeding the spirits false information. At first, Alana had been angry at him for not telling her that he was doing that, but she eventually accepted that he had to do so to keep the secrecy that was required for the job.

And then they had found out.

She remembered it, and it was as fresh in her memory as if it had just happened minutes ago.

He had been banished from the Sanctuary. Alana couldn't do anything about it, because she couldn't very well tell everyone in the Sanctuary that he was spying on Infernum and not the other way around. That information would put him in danger. And though his absence would break her heart, nothing could hurt her more than losing him forever.

So now they were here. Peter set down a plate of dinner on her desk and inched closer to Alana when she didn't respond. "Alana? May I speak to you?" he asked.

Alana sighed. "Yes, Peter. How may I help you?" She said in her usual commanding leader's voice.

"Actually, if you don't mind, I'd like to help you," Peter said in a quiet voice.

"And how will you do that?" she asked, curiously.

"By talking to you. I find that words have the power to heal at even the darkest of times."

Alana looked up. "Thank you, Peter." Her gaze was intense, and her sharp gray eyes pierced through Peter's grass green ones. He smiled and crouched down to looked Alana in the eye, level with hers. Did she know how he made her feel? Would she ever know? Did she know that in his eyes, she was the brightest star, the longest flame, bluest ocean? He took a deep breath and spoke.

"I've noticed that you are rather overwhelmed with shielding and protecting the Sanctuary and all those in it. You are a great leader, Alana, and we, as the members of the Sanctuary know that we are blessed to get such a great leader. We don't show it too much, but we love you. We'd like to help you too. You don't have to do this all on your own."

Alana looked away from the fire and at Peter. His copper hair gleamed in the firelight, and the light of hell's fire reflected in his eyes. He looked younger in the semi-darkness, and she remembered when they were just fifteen. It was only five years ago, but they had both grown and changed so much. She was then overcome by gratitude– gratitude for how Peter was so kind and sweet to her all the time. He had never once given her a reason to doubt him, and he was always there, ready to walk through hell if she wished it of him. He trusted her blindly, and so did she, and she needed him more than she liked to admit.

"Thank you, Peter. That was very kind of you."

Peter turned red. "Of course. I've brought you down something to eat. I brought you the pasta with vodka sauce. I know you love that stuff. Let me know if you'd like to talk some more."

He noticed that? Alana thought to herself. She nodded. "I will. Thank you, Peter."

Peter nodded. "You're very welcome." He made his way to the door and quietly slipped out of the library. Alana was left in the darkness, with the only light radiating from fire, catching the metal of her Black family ring and making it gleam.

34

Finesse

Cassandra's eyes moved behind their lids, and her pink ballerina shimmered ever so slightly in the morning sun that cascaded through the slightly parted curtains. Shadows danced across her eyes, teasing her and beckoning her forward.

She looked at the wall. It was white. She saw a girl looking back at her. She had black hair, short and wavy and pulled up into a bun, and piercing gray eyes. This girl looked about three. There was a young boy standing next to her. She watched as the little girl dipped her pale, clean, and soft fingertips into a small bottle of ink that looked like it was something that might have been used in the 1600s. *It was an antique. Mom collected them. She was very interested in the past,* she thought, as though it were obvious. Black ink-stained her fingers now, and she drew.

Black lines spiraled out from under the fingertips and onto the white wall. She watched as the little girl ran her fingers across the wall as the picture came together. She realized what it was now.

A star.

But not the type that you would expect a five-year-old to be able to draw– a five-pointer drawing with crooked angles– no, this star looked professionally drawn. Cassandra watched the girl in awe as she drew the star in the night sky. By now, the child's hair started to fall out of her bun and into her eyes, and she pushed it away with her ink-stained hand, smearing black onto her face in the process.

Is this me when I was younger? Then, she heard the sound of a door opening. She turned to see who it was and saw that a young woman with the same dark and flowing hair and gray eyes as her daughter had walked in and looked at her daughter's mural on the wall. Cassandra thought her mother was going to yell at her for drawing on the wall, but what happened was quite the opposite.

"Alana, what are you doing?" The woman asked.

The little girl turned around quickly, smiled as if hiding a secret, and hid her hands behind her back.

The little boy stepped in front of the girl now. "Mommy, it was my fault. I did it," he said in a soft voice.

Her mother stepped closer to her children. She then examined the boy's hands. They weren't stained, which quite obviously gave away the fact that he was lying to protect his sister from scolding.

"Julian, that's sweet, but I'm not angry." Now, the young woman looked over at her daughter. "Drawing aren't you? With my ink on the wall?" Alana looked down and nodded as if ashamed.

"It looks very beautiful. Like the amazing, smart, and talented young woman you'll someday grow to be. You know, it's easier to come right out and tell me the truth than to hide it." Her mother went on. "You'll be a great artist someday, just like your dad. Now come on. It's time for dinner." Alana smiled and said, "Okay.". Then, she and her big brother followed her mother out of the room. Cassandra smiled, and then everything went black.

Cassandra awoke to the calming scene of summer sunlight pouring through the window and dancing across the floor, as the trees swayed in the summer breeze. She sat up in bed then and looked at the wall.

Ten minutes later, she had pulled on a pair of ripped Hollister shorts and a black tank top. She didn't bother to brush her hair, just pulled it up into a messy bun, which she stuck two hair chopsticks into. She wore her white converse sneakers and walked across the room to the door. She turned the doorknob then and found herself looking into a pair of luminous emerald eyes.

Jamie.

"How long have you been here?" she asked curiously.

Jamie looked like a deer in headlights. His blond hair was slightly tousled, and his hands were behind his back like he was hiding something. Jamie considered her question for a minute. There was a slight pause.

"A half an hour," he answered truthfully.

"Why?" Cassandra asked.

"I wanted to give you this." He pulled a wrapped present from behind his back and held it out to her. Cassandra smiled and took it.

"Jamie, you didn't have to," she started, but Jamie was already shaking his head.

"I know. But you deserve it for being the best best friend anyone could ever have. This is to celebrate another year of your existence. Seventeen years have passed since you entered this world and made the world a better place." he said. *Of course,* she thought, and looked to the calendar, which was hanging on the wall above the desk. *It's my birthday. I forgot my own birthday, but Jamie remembered.* She looked up and smiled at him, and it was a beautiful and sly grin, like she was telling him something that was forbidden. She grabbed his wrist rather abruptly, pulled him into the room, then kicked the door shut.

She tugged him to the middle of the room and sat him down on the rug in front of the fireplace, in which blue flames were bursting. Her long, slim fingers traveled across the wrapping paper and tore it open carefully, revealing a box. Cassandra opened the box and found another box. Inside that box was yet another box. She laughed and opened that one too, to reveal two pieces of paper.

Concert tickets.

They were going to see Lorde, for her new album, Melodrama, at the Beacon Theater. Cassandra's face lit up with the brightest smile Jamie had ever seen, and here eyes went very wide.

"We're going to see Lorde in concert! We're going to see Lorde in concert! We're freaking going to see Lorde in concert! Ahhhhhhh!" she yelled. Jamie smiled.

"So you like it?" he asked. "I was worried it wasn't enough, but—" Jamie was cut off by Cassandra, who had pressed her lips to his.

It was the best feeling that Jamie had ever had. It was like going on a roller coaster, like spinning in the darkness. Like going on a sugar high, or hanging upside down from the ceiling. It was like ice cream when it's hot, and like sunshine on a rainy day. It was everything and nothing, a strange kind of happiness and content, a feeling of ecstasy and elatedness and joy. He felt like everything could disappear, and that all of his favorite possessions could vanish, and nothing would stay, but him and Cassandra, here in the beautiful darkness of the morning, that quietness and comfort. And he would be happy with just that.

Thirty minutes later, there was a knock on the door. "Come in," Cassandra said. Harley opened the door and entered. Jamie was sitting on the windowsill with a book in his hand, and there was loud rock music by the Darling Buds was playing from a small purple speaker in the shape of a devil emoji. Jamie loved books. In fact, there was rarely a time at which he could be found without a book. He collected them, and he had 63 so far. Cassandra was dancing to the music. Harley smiled.

"When you're done listening to your emo music, Alana said you two should come down to have breakfast."

All three laughed. "Okay. Thank you, Harley," Jamie said.

"No problem," Harley said and left.

"Why were you waiting for half an hour outside my door to give me my birthday present, anyway?" she asked him.

"Because," Jamie said, promptly turned red, and didn't elaborate.

"Because of what?"

"I don't know. I just...I guess I was kind of shy."

"Shy? But it's only me. You've known me for eleven years."

"I know, but for eleven years you were only my best friend."

"Oh," Cassandra said in a mock understanding tone. "And now I'm an extraterrestrial creature with three horns protruding from my head."

"No. I mean now, you're my girlfriend." He averted his eyes, as if he had seen something he shouldn't have seen, and turned even redder if that was even possible. Then he winced. "Too much? Do you not like it?" Jamie asked.

"No, I do. It's perfect."

Jamie looked up now. His eyes were wide, and he looked rather adorable. "Really?"

"Really."

"Okay."

They started to make their way downstairs to the dining room for breakfast. Teresa had made them waffles and a tropical fruit salad with pineapple, kiwi, and watermelon. It was delicious. Cassandra and Jamie joined the 50 other members of the Sanctuary and sat in the same seats as yesterday, facing Roslyn and Atticus. Alana joined them this time. Her eyes looked red, like she had stayed up all night. She probably had. Jamie couldn't help but notice the way that Peter was looking at Alana, like she was the most amazing and fascinating thing in the world. Cassandra was, as usual, making a lot of people laugh.

"So, she was like, 'can you like, not talk? Because your voice is irritating.'" She mimicked the rude girl's voice. "Yeah! She legit said that to my face! She was just jealous that I'm this awesome. Anyway, I was like, 'sweetheart, I think you got lost. The circus is that way.' And she was like, 'How dare you? You're such a freak!', and I was like, 'Here, I have a riddle for you. What is very large but has nothing in it?'. She didn't know. Do you know what I said?"

"What did you say?" Carter asked.

"I said, 'your head.'"

"Oh, snap! Someone's in a mood!" Atticus said, and the whole table laughed, including Alana.

Cassandra smirked, and at that moment, Jamie stole a kiwi from Cassandra's salad and popped it into his mouth. Cassandra acted astonished and very angry. Harley passed her the salad bowl so that she could have another kiwi, but she wasn't actually angry. She instead passed the bowl to Atticus, who took some and gave it to Roslyn, who politely refused.

"How dare you? How dare you finesse my kiwi?" she said and elbowed him while he laughed and snuck a kiss on her cheek. She looked up at her sister. "Alana! Jamie finessed my kiwi! Punish him."

Alana smiled. "James Taylor. You are condemned with the act of performing black magic and finessing Cassandra's kiwi. You shall be burned at stake for witchcraft and heresy. Do you wish to plead innocent?"

Jamie shook his head, gravely. "No, ma'am. I confess that I am guilty."

"Very well. Your burning shall take place immediately, by Cassandra Chloe Black, head burner and roaster, who shall roast you to death for committing the federal and personal offense of finessing her kiwi," Alana said. "Cass. Roast him."

"As you wish, sister," Cassandra said. Then, she turned to Jamie. "The only thing I like about you is your earrings."

Jamie was puzzled. "But I'm not wearing any– ohhh! That's mean!" he said, as everyone at the table burst into laughter. Atticus reached across the table to give her a high five.

"Dude. You are a low-key savage. I am proud to call you my sister." Alana praised her.

"I know. I'd be proud to call me my sister too." Cassandra said. Alana gave her a withering look, and Cassandra smirked.

"Roast him again," Carter said.

"Yeah!" A bunch of guys at the other side of the table yelled.

"Okay, okay," Cassandra said in an annoyed voice, but Jamie knew she was loving the attention. Jamie flinched and put his hands up as if to block a knife to his face.

"Please go easy on me."

"I make no promises," she said. "Your mom's got to be the bravest person in the world."

"Why?"

"Because she looks at your face every day."

"Ohhhh! Cassandra is a queen!" The boys chanted. Cassandra stood on her chair and bowed down.

"Thank you to all my fans and my fan club, but please, no autographs," she said. Jamie rolled his eyes, but he was smiling. Then, she sat down and whispered something in his ear that made him smile.

"That was a joke. I actually love your face."

Jamie flipped his blonde hair, which fell to his shoulders exaggeratedly. "I know you do. Who couldn't love this?" He joked.

"No one," Cassandra said in that special voice she had reserved for him. Now, she snuck a kiss onto his cheek.

Twenty minutes later, Jamie was pinned against the wall, with Alana's palms placed on the wall on either side of his face, and her own face inches from Jamie's. She was blowing a bubble in her bubblegum, and she popped it before she spoke.

"Did I see you kiss my sister?" she asked in a low and rather threatening tone.

Jamie gulped. "Yes, ma'am." He didn't see the point in trying to lie his way out of this.

"Alright. Let me make this clear." She removed her hands from the wall and pulled a knife from her hair, which she had previously used as a hair chopstick to fasten it. Her hair fell down, and Alana removed the knife from its sheath and started to file her nails in a rather exaggerated and threatening way. This made Jamie want to put as much distance between himself and her. "If you break my sister's heart, I will break you into little itsy bitsy pieces." She looked up, and her gray eyes pierced Jamie's green ones. "Got it?"

"Yes, ma'am."

"Kay." Alana looked back down at her nails and resumed filing them with her knife.

"She actually broke my heart first for your information."

"Oh." She was smirking. "Did you cry?" She asked teasingly.

"No. But I did step in front of a car and get stitches," Jamie said, just to see her reaction.

"Did you really?"

"No."

"That's a shame. Things would have been more interesting if you did." She looked at him, and a dangerous fire danced in her eyes. Then, she smiled, rather unexpectedly. "Nah, man, I was just messing with you. I like you. You're alright. But seriously, though. Don't hurt my sister's feelings."

"I won't," Jamie promised.

"Alright. Now, Imma start getting that spell ready. You guys can join later if you like." She smiled and walked away.

Jamie started to make his way upstairs to Cassandra's room when he heard loud rapping. He knocked twice on her door, and Atticus opened it. Atticus, Carter, Jessica, and a bunch of guys he didn't know were flooded in the room, some standing and nodding, while others sat on the bookshelf and window sills, shouting "ayy" every now and then as Cassandra rapped Post Malone.

Jamie made his way to the back of the room and stood at a corner near the speaker, which at the moment was blasting rap background music. Where Cassandra had learned to rap like that he didn't know, but he was sure that she was very capable. She was very into rap. When she finished, everyone yelled "ayy!" again, and punched their fists into the air. Cassandra took another exaggerated bow. Then, she started to rap Sicko Mode by Travis Scott.

Although Jamie hated rap and preferred soul, R&B, rock, and indie, he clapped loudly when she finished. Then, the other boys exited the room, leaving Carter and Atticus, who both gave her high fives and left. Jamie was left alone with Cassandra. She walked over to her speaker and turned it off.

"Alana said she's getting the spell ready. We can go check it out when she's done. Want to go somewhere while we wait?" he asked.

"Sure. Where do you want to go?"

"The woods. I want to see the individual leaves, and watch as the sunlight filters through the trees. I want to pretend that it's like the old times. We might need to bring blessed metal to ward off spirits, though. Just a precaution."

"Yeah." She walked over to the bookshelf and pulled a book named 600 Easy Vegetarian Dinners, which acted like a lever and opened a secret compartment in the wall. Cassandra walked over to it and removed a piece of blessed metal. She stuck the knife into the back pocket of her jeans and shrugged on her jacket.

35

Beautiful Darkness

Ten minutes later, the pair found themselves trudging in the woods. Cassandra held her knife out in front of her like a shield, and her messenger bag hung across her neck at her side. Her hair was falling forward into her eyes, and it was knot-free but rather messy, just the way she liked it. Jamie was behind her, guarding their back. When they found that all was clear, they found a large tree and sat down under it. Jamie didn't know why this was calming, but it was. He supposed it reminded him of old times.

He remembered when they were very small. They were still kids, still young, but they had started to come to the woods for peace and quiet since they were five. It had started when Cassandra's mother had died. Her father became very depressed. He seemed to have lost hope in the world. It made Cassandra very sad. He would go up to the roof of their new house sometimes and stay there for hours. When she had asked her father where her mother was and when she'd be back, he'd tell her, "She loved the stars. Your Mommy loved the stars. Now she's gone to join them."

Cassandra would run to Jamie's house, and he would hold her while she cried. His mother would bring them chocolate chip cookies and warm milk, and Cassandra would cry herself to sleep. In the morning, she would wake up, and ask for her mom, and he still remembered the heartbroken look that would appear on her face when they told her that they were sorry, but she was still gone. Then she'd run.

Where she'd run, Jamie always knew. She liked to listen to the sound of silence.

He would find her there, under the tree, every day for a week, while she coped with the realization that her mom wouldn't be back in the morning.

She hadn't spilled tears again.

She had built a sort of barrier around herself, separating herself from the rest of the world. However, Jamie proved immune to those barriers. He seemed to be the only one who could tear them down so easily. With one look, he saw through the illusions to what was true.

Though Cassandra seemed chill, cool, and happy go lucky, he knew that deep down, in truth, she was scarred, hurt, cut up, bruised, and broken down. This was why she broke his heart.

So he forgave her. He forgave her for the cuts and burns he had acquired while handling her without caution. For that, she loved him alone. For he was like everyone else– human, and breakable, and because he reached out to mend her bruises, knowing that there might be consequences.

Now she sat in the tree's shade with him. She leaned her head back against the trunk of the tree and closed her eyes. Jamie watched her closely with his emerald eyes. The sun was shining brighter than ever and highlighted strands of his hair, which made them glow golden.

Then, she reached out. She reached out and took his hand. Her hand was warm and soft. Everything was good and well for that moment, all was right, and he was content. He leaned his head against hers and closed his eyes, and he whispered to her in the stillness and peace of the woods.

She smiled. *This is perfect. If everything could freeze right here, and we could be right here forever, that's all I could ever ask for*, he thought. Then, they heard a faint rustling. Cassandra and Jamie opened their eyes and looked up. They heard the swish of gossamer and silk, and then their eyes perceived the pure white of a wedding gown and the bright scarlet of fresh blood. Then, long, straight, and sweeping ink colored hair.

Jamie drew out his dagger, and Cassandra slipped out her blessed metal knife, but she didn't seem to notice them. She walked right past them, clutching a bouquet of withered roses. Then, she stopped. She turned and looked directly at them with wide, dark brown eyes. There was a trail of tears down her cheek, and her hands were bloodstained. But that was not what had caught Jamie's attention.

She was not transparent.

The woman smiled at them, and once it would have looked pleasant, but it didn't now. She looked feral, sick, and feverishly ecstatic.

"Oh, look, Joseph, I found two people! They can play hide and go seek with us! Joseph? I know you're just acting like you can't hear me, and I know that you're here somewhere! I'm going to find you!" She burst into a fit of giggles. "When I find you, Joseph, I'm going to tickle you!" She turned in a circle, looking for him. Then, she turned back to Jamie and Cassandra, who had now stood up. The hands that weren't clutching weapons were clasped. The young woman looked them in the eyes.

"Oh, dear. Love birds, aren't you two? Are you going to get may-reed? Like Joseph and me?" she asked. Quite frankly, she sounded like a seven-year-old. Their hands disconnected immediately. Jamie's cheeks burned, and Cassandra stared at her open-mouthed. Then, they heard another voice.

"Philomena? Philomena, where are you? Philomena! There you are! You made me so scared, running away like that." a voice intoned. However, it was a female's voice, so Cassandra figured it wasn't Joseph. Then, a seven-year-old girl with the same ink colored hair as Philomena, but it was put into two shoulder-length braids, made her way into the forest clearing. She had doll-like black eyes and smooth pale skin. She looked rather adorable and startling at the same time. "Philomena! You can't run away like that! Mommy and I got so scared."

The lady named Philomena giggled childishly and put her hand up to her mouth. "I was playing hide and go seek," she whispered.

"With who?"

Philomena gave her a secretive smile and whispered again. "I was playing hide and seek with Joseph." Then, she erupted into yet another fit of giggles. Her veil fell across her shoulders, and Jamie noticed a red stain on it that reminded him strangely of blood.

"Oh, Philomena," the little girl said sadly, shaking her head. Then, she turned to them. "Thank you for finding my sister." she thanked them.

"Actually, she found us," Jamie said. He turned to see Philomena climbing a tree. She was barefoot, and dirt was staining her pale white feet.

"Joseph? Are you up on the tree? I'm going to find you!" she called up to the branches.

"Did she bother you?" the little girl inquired.

"Not at all, no," Cassandra said kindly. "She just asked us if we wanted to play hide and go seek."

"Oh, good. I feel so bad for her. I don't know when she'll stop looking for him."

"Did he leave her?" Cassandra asked.

"Oh, no." the doll-like girl answered. "He's dead. It was very tragic. They had dated for four years, and then he proposed. She, of course, accepted. She was so fully in love with him. They were about to get married, but Joseph was killed in a car crash when he was driving to the church for the marriage." She shook her head sadly. "They couldn't save him. The doctors said that his last word was her name." She glanced up at Philomena, who was hanging on a branch overhead, giggling and waving. "She hasn't been quite right since. She was the sweetest and greatest big sister anyone could ever hope for. A shining star, the prettiest lily of them all. But now her heart has withered to dust, and her soul along with it."

"I'm so sorry," Jamie said.

"I am, too. I hope she gets better soon." Cassandra told her.

"Thank you." Then, she looked up at Philomena. "Philomena! Mommy wants us to come home. Climb down right now."

Philomena, who was now higher on the tree, shook her head rapidly, which made her flood of shock black hair scatter across her shoulders. "I'm not coming with you. I'm looking for Joseph."

The little girl looked so sad. Cassandra had previously never thought it was possible for such a small child to hold such sorrow. "Philomena, Mommy has candy for you."

"I'm not coming with you!" She stuck her tongue out.

"Philomena! Joseph called me. He says he's hiding at our house. Come on. We need to go."

"Okay!" The young woman squealed. She climbed down the tree and took her little sister's hand. She started to tug it in the direction that she had come.

"Thank you again for finding my sister." the girl said, and they walked away. Cassandra and Jamie sank back down under the shade of the tree.

"Your sister interrogated me today," he informed her with a smile.

"She did? About what?"

"She saw me kiss you in the dining room. She wanted to make sure I wouldn't break your heart." He smiled, and straight, pearly white teeth showed between his soft pink lips.

Cassandra smiled back.

Jamie laughed good-naturedly. He was a bit amused. "You know, most people would be annoyed at their sister for doing something like that."

"True. But I'm not like most people. It just feels so nice to have someone care about me enough to do that."

"I care about you enough to do that."

"I know. I meant in my family."

"I'm glad that you finally met your sister, and I'm glad that she cares about you so much. Even if that means she's going to inflict a new injury on me every time I kiss you."

Cassandra laughed. "You know you could just not kiss me in front of her."

"I know that. But I really don't want to do that."

Cassandra laughed. Then, she kissed his cheek.

* * *

As Roslyn walked back to her room, she was full of thoughts. Her mind was full of them. She had just been to the artifacts room and was researching the Barnes' family.

As a child, she had always known that she had been adopted. Her parents had tried to keep it from her, for ignorance is bliss, but she had worked it out on her own.

Most of the Pol Electi died young, and if you lived past 30, it was considered a big achievement. This was because the Pol Electi were constantly hunted. They had been trained to protect themselves and humans, more commonly known as normals. Her parents had died on patrol when they were defending a bunch of innocents normals from ten members of Diabolus. She had been two months old.

A family of norms adopted her after that, and she was brought up like a normal, but she knew that she wasn't normal. She had always known that she, in fact, was the very opposite of normal. Her adoptive parents told her that she had inherited the genes for the Pol Electi from an ancestor, but she knew better. She looked nothing like her adoptive parents. Her mother had brown hair and pure blue eyes, and her father had black hair and dark brown eyes. Roslyn had blonde hair and green eyes. It was quite obvious that she wasn't related to them. But if she had learned anything over the years, it was that family isn't those who are related to you, but rather those who care for you. The ones who would look for you if you went missing. The ones who'd follow you anywhere, just to be with you. That was family.

So, though she felt a great loss at losing the mother and father that she had never known, she knew that her real family was her adoptive parents and the members of the Sanctuary who were always there for her. Her mother, who always packed her jelly sandwiches for lunch because she knew that Roslyn hated peanut butter, loved her like her own, a fact that Roslyn was grateful for every day. Ana and Atticus, who always came with her on patrol duty regardless of whether she had asked them or not, regardless of whether they were busy or not, were her family as well, though they were not related. She knew well that they'd follow her through hell if she was determined to go there. It was simply what they did; no questions asked. Alana, who was as much as a big sister to her as her actual big sister might be if she had one, was also part of her family. She was always there for her, helping her up when she fell, coming to her soccer games and shouting words of praise loudly when she scored a goal and reading to her until she fell asleep when she was very young.

She looked up now, and pure sunlight filtered through the small and musty window of the attic. She hugged her knees to her chest and stayed that way for a little bit. She felt a fierce longing for something. She didn't know what, but she knew she needed it. She felt it was as essential to life as breathing. She wondered if he'd see the note.

Then, a faint noise. A flash of curly brown locks and a tall, lean boy hoisted himself into the attic using the ladder. When he saw her, he smiled. As he drew closer, the longing faded away. He looked as cute as ever with his dimples and mole. He sat right next to her, hugging his knees to his chest and turned to look at her.

"Say something," he whispered.

Roslyn was at a loss for words. She knew that she was supposed to say something deep- something long and sappy from a Shakespeare play or whatever, but she was never one with words. She liked to read, but words were more of Ana's thing than hers. She was a warrior, and though no one knew, she liked planting. A lot. She also liked to make things grow. She was interested in herbs, plants, and other earth-grown things. Her mother owned an apothecary, and she always collected jars from pasta sauce and planted random things in them. She wasn't afraid to get her hands dirty.

Atticus was looking at her now, and smiling at her, as if she were gold, awaiting her words. So Roslyn said the first thing that came upon her mind.

"You're so hot."

Atticus looked puzzled and shook his head, making curly dark hair fall into his eyes. This just made him look even hotter. Poor Atticus. It wasn't his fault that his face was aesthetically pleasing. "What is it with you girls and fevers? I'm not sick. I'm just not sick."

Roslyn rolled her eyes. "I meant that you look very handsome."

Atticus snorted. "Alright, then next time someone says that I'm going to perform black magic, resurrect my parents, and sue them." Roslyn laughed. "You do look beautiful, though. I like your green eyes," he said, then promptly turned red and turned away.

"Do you really?"

"Yes."

"Since when?"

"Since the day that I met you. I've always thought you had beautiful eyes."

"Well, I like that mole on your cheek and your amber eyes. And the dimples."

"Stop it."

"No. And now that you are officially my boyfriend, I finally get to say all the things that have been on my mind for the last ten years. And god, those curls. I want to run my fingers through your hair."

"Then do that."

"Really?"

"I'm not going to stop you. I belong to you. Every ounce of me, every cell in my body, every moment of my existence belongs to you and you only. Whether I knew it or not, I have belonged to you since the day that you held my hand and played with me at the playground. We were five."

"You still remember that?"

"Of course I do. It was the day that I met you. One of the most important days of my life."

"You're so sweet." She smiled at him, and he rested his head on her lap. They sat there in the darkness, Roslyn stroking his curly brown hair. His fingers found their way to her face, and he traced his fingers on her soft cheek, her silky blonde hair, and her high cheekbones. Then he traced her lips with his fingertips.

"You are beautiful. But that doesn't mean anything. You are you, and that is what I love you for." He whispered to her in the darkness.

* * *

As Alana stood in front of the burning blue hell's fire, she read from the spellbook. It was so ancient that if she wasn't careful enough, it would turn to powder. She murmured Latin words under her breath. Suddenly, she fell to her knees. She put the book down and picked up some herbs that had been arranged on the floor. Carefully, she put each herb into the fire, watching as they burned and turned to ashes. The fire was oddly quiet now, and one might not have noticed it until someone pointed it out. Alana reached over and unscrewed the lid to the angel's tears. Carefully, she poured them in and backed away, bracing herself. The fire grew brighter and larger and finally turned black. This was because this certain spell was classified as black magic. It was rather ironic that a few moments after Alana had accused Jamie of practicing black magic, she was practicing it herself. She frowned. She didn't like hypocrites, much less to be one herself. But it wasn't as if she could do anything else in this situation. She was willing to walk through hell if it meant finding Charlie. Even if that meant she had to be a hypocrite.

Once the fire turned black, it started to suck in energy. Dark magic was imperfect. You couldn't always get what you wanted. Everything had to have a price. Dark magic always drained energy from the person performing the incantation, and that was why Alana had chosen to do it in the morning when she had the most energy. This way she'd have more left over to actually interrogate Mitchell. Big spells needed a lot of energy, and this was a pretty large spell. She doubled over now, clutching her stomach and gasped. *Damn it. Now people are going to know that I performed the spell. I hope no one heard me.*

She didn't want anyone to know, because she knew they'd volunteer to do it themselves. They treated her like family, or more than that. She, as the leader of the Sanctuary, would not allow them to sacrifice a large sum of energy. The only reason she had told Jamie was because he was a normal and didn't know that dark magic had a price. Then, she heard the sound of footsteps.

Peter, redheaded and green-eyed, his hair was slightly tousled, eyes wide. He rushed into the room to where Alana was on her knees doubled over on the floor and put his arms around her, to keep her warm. It helped. She curled into him like a plant to sunlight and rested her head on his shoulder. She missed Charlie. He used to hold her just like this, with his arms around her protectively, caring and warm, as she placed her head on his shoulder.

Then, she lifted her head up off of his shoulders and looked into his eyes. He stood up and walked over to the bedside table, where he poured her some warm water from a thermos. He then slipped a bag of Egyptian chamomile tea into it. It was her favorite type of tea of all time. Peter, of course, knew this. Sometimes she felt as though he knew her better than she knew herself. He rushed back over to Alana and gave her the mug.

Alana took it gratefully and sipped the tea. It was soothing and good, and its sweet aroma and bitter taste warmed her up instantly. It wrapped her up like a blanket, and once Alana had taken a few sips and could speak, she said thank you to Peter.

"I was just walking to the library when I heard you gasp. I don't think anyone else heard you. You've got to be really brave and strong to be able to endure that and still have consciousness after a large spell like that." Peter told her admiringly.

"Thank you, Peter," she said.

"Alana, you shouldn't have done that. You often do kind-hearted and sweet things, like not letting any of us perform this spell, but every time you end up hurting yourself. I know you don't want to hear this, but you are reckless. You have to understand that you are mortal. You can die, too. And sometimes you do things to yourself without thinking about how it might affect the ones that love you."

Alana smiled. "Do you love me?" she asked.

"Yes. We all do. You've saved all of our lives more than once. Let us help you. Let us make the burden a little easier to bear. Please." He said this with a desperate tone in his voice.

Alana was speechless. She clutched the mug between her hands, which was slowly thawing her freezing fingers. "I'm so sorry," she finally said. "I had no idea that I was hurting all of you that much."

"It's alright. But please, no more. You break our hearts into smaller pieces every day when you take bullets for us. No more."

Alana looked into Peter's eyes. "Okay." Then, Peter hugged her again.

"Thank you. I know that you find it nearly impossible to let those that you love hurt when you can still help it, but please. Someday, you'll have to learn that you can't carry the weight of the world in your hands."

"Okay."

Peter looked into her gray eyes. A moment passed in silence, during which Peter looked into her eyes to see if she was lying or not. Then, Alana set her mug on the floor and took his hands.

"I promise. I promise I'll tell you before I do crazy reckless things again."

He shook his head, and straight red hair fell into his eyes. He impatiently pushed it out of his eyes and bit his lip as if he were contemplating whether or not he should do something. "You don't have to promise. I believe you."

Then, he turned her hands around so that the palms were facing upward. Slowly, he lowered his lips down to her palms and kissed them lightly. He promptly turned red, stood, and exited the room.

Alana was nothing short of flabbergasted. Her mouth was slightly open when she turned and looked into the black fire.

36

Upgrade

J amie and Cassandra were making their way back to the Sanctuary after they had received a text from Alana saying that the spell was set up and ready to be cast. They were curious and rather interested in spell casting and dark magic.

Twigs crunched underfoot as they trudged through the forest. Cassandra smelled the sweet scent of morning dew, pine cones, and trees. The sunlight filtered through the trees, which threw shade in some areas but not others. When they finally stepped out of the forest and onto a pathway, Cassandra looked down and saw that her hand was still encapsulated in his. He looked up at her and smiled.

Those dimples.

They walked up to the front door and rang the doorbell. Harley opened the door.

"Hey!"

"Hey." Cassandra and Jamie said at the same time.

"Come on in," Harley said and walked in. They entered, then locked the door behind them. "So I heard that you rap. Is that true?"

"Yes. I do Post Malone, Drake, Cardi B, Nicki Minaj, and occasionally Travis Scott."

"You do Cardi B? She's my favorite rapper of all time! You need to rap for me!"

"Sure. I memorized both "I Like It" and "Bodak Yellow.""

"Really?"

"Yeah. Here." She rapped a few lines while Harley whooped.

"Wow. That is so cool."

"Thank you."

"You're welcome." Now, she turned to Jamie. "So, how was your date?" she asked.

"What? That wasn't a date! We were just hanging out!" Jamie spluttered, his face going slightly red in the process.

Harley smiled. "Sure. You two go off on your own without telling anyone, holding hands, not to mention," Harley said, pointing down at their still clasped hands, which they quickly removed. Jamie coughed. Cassandra pulled out her phone and started to check Billboard's Top 100 spontaneously.

"So." Cassandra said hastily to break up the oppressive silence, "The remix for 'Girls Like You' by Maroon 5 with the rap part by Cardi B is at number 1 right now. I like it, but I wish it wasn't so overplayed. What do you think?"

"Um. I agree with you." Jamie said. His face was still scarlet, and he was staring down at his sneakers the same way a child might when caught doing something they weren't supposed to be doing. They found themselves in the living room then.

"She's in her room," Harley said, so they made their way up the stairs and down a hallway until they found an elegantly carved teakwood door with a golden plaque that said the following-

Alana Brooke Black

Head of the Sanctuary of New Jersey

They knocked and heard Alana's voice. "Come in."

So they did. When they entered, they faced some very strange sights. First of all, Cassandra was astonished to see that the fire was a new shade now. Pitch black. Cassandra wondered if this was the effect of the angel's tears. Secondly, there was blood on the floor, trailing from Alana's hand, which had a long gash in it. Fresh scarlet was on her hand, and she was clutching a short, sapphire studded knife. Thirdly, Alana was kneeling on the ground doubled over, as if she had just gotten a strong blow to the stomach and had the wind knocked out of her. It was odd because Alana was the very image of strength and determination. It had never occurred to her that her older sister could possibly get hurt. Cassandra rushed over to her, but the redheaded man she had seen at the interrogation named Peter was already at her side, kneeling on the ground near her, bandaging her cut.

"What did you do this time?" Peter was asking her.

"Actually, I don't remember, I was looking at the fire, and I sent Jamie and Cass a text, and then I was playing with a knife, when I thought of Charlie. I miss him so much."

Peter tensed imperceptibly. Alana didn't notice; she was staring into the black fire, but Cassandra did.

"We'll find him very soon," Peter reassured her. He finished with the bandage, and Alana stood up. She staggered for a moment, and nearly fell over, but Peter rushed to her side and held her up.

"Thank you, Peter, but I'm fine."

"No, you're not. I'm not going to let you do this. You're too weak right now. You need to rest. That was a high-level spell."

"What happened? Why are you weak?" Cassandra inquired.

"Dark magic takes tolls of energy. The amount of energy depends on the level. But I'm fine."

"How do you start the spell reaction anyway?" Cassandra asked.

"Easy. Just step into the fire. But don't even think about doing it. I gotta do this. For Charlie."

"I want to do it," Cassandra protested. "I've never interrogated anyone before. This seems fun."

"You don't have the experience," Alana said in a soft voice. Cassandra was suddenly struck by how pale she looked.

"You don't have the energy," she countered.

"I'll do it, Cass. It's too dangerous. I don't want anything to happen to you." Jamie volunteered.

"I'm not made of glass. Besides, you're not even Pol Electi. The spell will probably kill you."

"I'll do it," Peter offered. "I have the most experience and the most common sense out of all three of us who are Pol Electi. Both of you are so reckless that you aren't aware of your own mortality, and you," he pointed to Jamie, "You have plenty of common sense, but the spell will burn you. Sorry."

"It's cool," Jamie said easily.

"No. I'm not letting you do this," Alana said. "If Mitchell finds out who you really are, he will attempt to harm you physically. And Figura Mutante are very strong. He'll have a claw to your chest in a minute if you attempt combat without weapons and a lot of training."

"I'll bring a weapon then," Peter said.

"If you bring a weapon, he'll know you aren't Michael," Alana pointed out.

"Not if I hide it well."

"There's no argument. I'm going, and that's it." Alana said and attempted to walk to the fireplace. Then, there was a frozen moment, and she collapsed.

"Alana!" Cassandra shouted and darted forward to help her up, but Peter was already there. He had caught her, and she had fainted. In her unconscious state, with her eyes closed, Cassandra was struck by how young her elder sister looked. Without her calculating eyes closed and her usual scowl gone, she looked a bit like a child in Peter's loving arms. He picked her up and carried her in his arms to her bed, where he set her down. He tucked her in with her blanket and declared that he was going to get May to come to look at her. As soon as he left the room, Cassandra had that mischievous smile on her face.

Jamie knew that look.

"Oh god, what are you going to do this time?" he asked her. She said nothing, and in a split second, she ran to the fireplace and jumped into the fire.

* * *

Atticus looked into Roslyn's eyes. They were on the roof. They were sitting on the railing. It was both very dangerous and very tempting. The view was gorgeous. Atticus jumped off the railing and back onto the roof where he lay down with his arms folded behind his head. Roslyn watched him fondly.

"Have you ever been in a relationship before?"

Atticus snorted. "Twice. Both times I didn't even know they were into me."

"You're so pure and innocent," she said with a smirk.

Atticus frowned. "Ana said that too. I am not. I kill spirits and send them to hell. I play with weapons and see corpses three times a week. What about this makes you think I'm innocent? I'll never understand women." he said, shaking his head.

She sighed.

"Have you been in a relationship before?" Atticus asked her, curiously.

"Yeah. This guy called Denzel Williams. He was emo."

"Tell me about it."

"Chokers with spikes, large gold chains, and black leather jackets. And don't even get me started on the mohawk. He asked me out."

"You fell in love with an eboi?"

"No," Roslyn said as if it were obvious. "Of course not."

"Then why'd you go out with him?"

"To make you jealous. Duh."

Atticus took a deep breath. "Why didn't you just tell me that you liked me?"

"Because there was a chance that you didn't like me back."

"There was also a chance that I did!"

Roslyn rolled her eyes. "You're hot, you're sweet, you're hot, you're strong, you're hot, you're tall, you're hot, and you're funny. Oh. And you're hot, too."

"What are you doing?" Atticus asked in the monotone voice that he used when he was bored or confused about the topic.

"Reminding myself why I love you. You know, when I was younger, I really thought I'd fall for someone with just a bit more common sense than you."

"I have common sense!"

"Sure. And pigs can fly."

"Pigs *can* fly. Swine flu. Get it?"

Roslyn glared at him.

"Sorry. That was a bad pun," he apologized. "Fair point."

"All puns are bad puns." she countered.

"Fine. Well, if I don't have common sense, you don't either."

"Yes, I do! What have I ever done that shows that I have no common sense?"

"You dated someone you didn't like. You've loved me for ten years but never asked me out until now. You assumed that I'd become jealous of Denzel and fight him in a gladiator arena for your hand. You figured that I'd read your mind and find out that you liked me. You listen to Shawn Mendes. You–"

"Alright, I get it. I don't have common sense either. And by the way, Shawn Mendes is great. I was going to marry him, but I figured you'd do. You're pretty lucky."

"He's four years older than you!"

"He's an upgrade from you. Plus, he's Canadian."

"How do you think it works anyway? You find a boyfriend, then pay the boyfriend company ten dollars per month for an upgrade? Includes better hair, better breath, and a guitar. And besides, I'm half Cuban and half Greek. Plus, I've got better hair. And does Shawn have a mole on his cheek?"

"No. But he plays the guitar."

"I play the spear ended staff. And the long sword. I can kill spirits. Can Shawn Mendes kill spirits?"

"No. I suppose not. I guess you'll do."

Atticus frowned. "I feel underappreciated."

Roslyn smiled and walked over to him and sat down next to him. "I'm just messing with you. I love you. You're hotter than Shawn Mendes. And you do have better hair than him."

"I don't want you to love me because I'm hot," he said. For a moment, he had a very vulnerable expression on his chiseled features. "What will happen in forty years? Fifty? Eighty? Will you stop loving me when I'm not beautiful anymore?" he asked her.

"Of course not. I will always love you. I will love you, no matter what. I love you not for your face, but for your heart. You have a big heart, Atticus, and I have seen it. I love you for that. You are a kind and caring person, and if I searched the ends of this universe, I couldn't find a guy who cared about me more or a guy that I loved more than you."

He looked up at her with big, vulnerable eyes. "Not even Shawn Mendes?"

She smiled. "Not even Shawn Mendes."

Then, she muttered, "But he is pretty hot, though." She hadn't expected him to hear her, but he did. He looked at her with an expression that implied that he was thoroughly scandalized.

"What? He is!"

"But," he urged her.

"But you're hotter."

* * *

It felt rather ticklish. It didn't hurt at all as she had expected. Then, her beautiful and elegant features started to melt off of her, revealing a man in his mid-twenties underneath. Cassandra was astonished. This was so awesome.

When she stepped out of the flames, Jamie's expression of mixed apprehension and worry turned into one of utter disbelief and awe. Then, rather unexpectedly, he laughed.

Cassandra frowned. "What's so funny?"

"Look at yourself," Jamie said, and she did.

She guessed it was rather odd to see a man in his mid-twenties in a black tank top and ripped Hollister shorts. The man was a lot larger than her, lengthwise and widthwise, and the tank top rode up, exposing his belly button. Cassandra turned sunset red and held her arms around it to block it from sight.

"Relax. That's not even yours." Jamie said.

Cassandra walked out of the room. "I'm going to find something larger and more masculine to wear."

She walked into one of the spare rooms and found a man's shirt and jeans. She threw them on, then left the room. Jamie was looking into the fire, which was still black.

"Jamie. It's me."

He looked up at her then, and smiled.

"So. You should probably tell Peter that you used the spell so that he can tell you where they've kept Mitchell."

"I can't do that! He'll freak!"

"True. But he has the keys."

A mischievous smile came onto Michael's face.

"No. No way. I am not letting you steal the keys from Peter, let yourself into the dungeons, find Mitchell, and get Charlie's real location."

Damn it. How'd he figure out my secret plan?

"You can either help me or have nothing to do with it. Either way, I'm doing it."

"I can just tell Peter, you know."

"Not if you never make it out of here." Cassandra countered.

"You're willing to stab me for this?" Jamie asked with one eyebrow raised.

"No. But I might just kiss you to death."

"That seems a rather pleasant way to die. Even if I did like your idea, I would probably go against you just for that."

Cassandra smiled. "Will you please help me? I already know that I'll do something reckless and dumb without you to hold me back."

Jamie sighed. "Fine," he said. "But you should know that the only reason that I'm going along with this is that I love you and I don't want you to blow yourself up." he reminded her.

"I know," Cassandra responded, grinning. They were sitting on the floor, and Peter entered the room with May. May looked concerned, and she was carrying a wicker bin which held bandages, cleaning alcohol, cotton balls, a few elixirs, and throat drops. She walked over to where Alana was lying unconscious and laid a wet washcloth to her head. Cassandra could smell its tangy lemon scent from the other side of the world. Alana stirred slightly, and May removed the washcloth from her forehead and felt it with the back of her hand. Then, she went through her wicker bin and removed an elixir. She diluted a bit of it into hot water and tried to get Alana to drink it. She did all of this while Peter stood near her, looking worried.

Jamie walked up to him and started to engage him in a conversation. It was clear, however, that Peter's mind was elsewhere, because of his rather vacant expression when he spoke to him.

"So. Tell me about spells. How do you reverse them?"

"Oh yeah. You just have to step into the flames when you're done. By the way, Cassandra, I wanted to ask you," he turned around to see Michael's hand reaching toward the keys in his back pocket.

"You put the spell on yourself?!" Peter exclaimed, so full of thoughts that he did not even notice that Cassandra looked different when he entered the room.

"Maybe," Cassandra said.

"Why didn't you tell me?"

"Because I knew you'd freak."

"You should have told me anyway! You shouldn't have used that spell! You'll get yourself killed! Figura Mutante are strong and dangerous! Only trained people can deal with them."

"I've taken karate for twelve years!"

"That doesn't mean anything until you've been in a real-life situation."

"In case you haven't noticed, I have fought spirits before."

"If Alana found out that I let you cast the spell on yourself, she'd kill me."

"Tell her that I didn't ask for permission."

Peter sighed rather loudly and exaggeratedly. "I feel like everyone in the Black family is reckless to the point that they aren't aware that they are mortal too."

"You got that right." May looked up from Alana finally. "She'll be alright. But she needs the rest of today to rest."

"Thank you. Oh, good god, thank you so much."

"You like her, don't you?" Jamie asked, slyly.

"Yes, I do. We all like her. She's a great leader."

"I don't mean like that," he said.

"Alana is smart and kind, and beautiful, and if she were in trouble, I'd give my life for hers, because it would be worth it," Peter said truthfully.

"Okay," Cassandra said, with an amused expression on her face. "Let's go."

They walked down a hallway and three flights of stairs, and found themselves at the entrance of the dungeons. There was barely any light here, and it looked and smelled like a nightmare. Jamie shuddered inwardly.

"Before you go, make sure you remember a few things," Peter said. "If Mitchell finds out your true form and attempts to attack you, yell for me. I'll be right out here. But until then, remember that the Figura Mutante are a tricky sort. If you need to kill him, you'll need to cut him into three pieces to keep him from regenerating. Try not to kill him, though. We still need him for information. Are you ready?"

Cassandra nodded boldly. "Yes."

She started, then was immediately stopped by Jamie. "Wait," he said. He took her hands and looked into her eyes. "Be careful," he told her in a soft voice that he reserved just for her, and kissed her cheek.

"Okay," she assured him. "I will. For you."

Then, Peter unlocked the cell, and Cassandra was in.

37

Spicy Memes

Cassandra welcomed the darkness like an old friend. She sometimes hid in the shadows when she felt like she was drowning in sorrow and misery when she thought about her parents. The darkness often gave her comfort. She stepped forward, and slowly, her eyes became accustomed to the darkness.

Filthy brown hair. He was lying face down on the floor, and the flickering lantern that hung from the ceiling showed her a portly man in dark rags. She walked up to him and kicked him. Not too hard— just hard enough to wake him up.

He stirred, then opened one bleary red-tinged eye to consider her. Once he saw her, he smiled.

"Michael. You came back for me."

"Of course, I did," Cassandra said in Michael's deep voice. "You're my brother."

Michael sat up and scratched his head. His brown hair looked messy in the meager supply of yellow light that filtered out from behind the grimy glass enclosure of the lantern. He flashed him a grin and spoke. "Right then. Let's get out of here. Have you found a way out yet?"

Cassandra considered it for a moment. How was she going to get him to tell her where Charlie was without letting him escape? "Yes. But all in good time. I'm waiting for one of the guards to go on lunch break so we can sneak out. Let's talk for a few."

Mitchell looked noticeably disappointed. *It really must be terribly boring down here,* Cassandra thought. "Alright fine. So, have you gotten any news from Tara?"

Who's Tara?

"Nah, man. No news from Tara. Who's Tara, by the way?" she asked him curiously.

Mitchell laughed. "That's a funny joke. You can't seriously tell me that you don't know our leader? The leader of the Figura Mutante of New York?

"I was just messing with you. Of course, I know who that is."

"Well did Tara give you any new information from Fiona?" He looked around, checking for any cameras. "You know– about that…thing?"

Cassandra shook her head. "What thing?"

Mitchell looked at him incredulously. "You're kidding, right? This is not funny. She said she'd give…it…to us if we got the jewelry box.

"Why do they need the jewelry box, anyway?"

Mitchell rolled his eyes. "You've got to be kidding me. We've been over this a million times, Mike, how dumb can you get?" He took a deep breath as if to cool the flame of annoyance that could be heard in his voice. "She's got a Venificus, an old, strong one at that, and he knows a spell. One that can bring this world down in flames. But in order for us to survive, we'll need the Jewel of Protection."

"Why does she want to burn down the world so badly?"

Mitchell started to look very irritated now. "I don't know, do I? I ain't Fiona. Go ask her. Now," he said, "has Tara gotten it ready yet?"

"Gotten what ready?" Cassandra asked obliviously.

"The fake. If Fiona really wants the Jewel that badly, it's probably powerful. We can give her the fake, and exchange it for both the Gem and the Jewel. When the Veneficus brings the world tumbling down, we alone may survive, and return to our home realm. Has she got it ready yet?"

"Oh yeah. She has it ready."

Mitchell's expression became brighter, and his smile was easier. "Oh, good."

"So about Charlie."

Mitchell cackled. "That slimebag. When I went into the Artifacts Room to get the jewelry box, his good for nothing girlfriend showed up. And she asked for Charlie's location."

Cassandra adopted a worried expression. "You didn't give it to her, did you?"

Mitchell shook his head and cackled again. "Of course not. Guess which location I gave her? The Hellhound House." He laughed again. He evidently found this hilarious.

Cassandra forced a laugh, but she didn't think it was very believable, though. Mitchell apparently didn't notice.

"So, where is he, anyway?"

"Fiona's place, obviously. She caught him spying on them for the Pol Electi." He made a distasteful expression. "He's got him there, at their headquarters. Why are you asking me all of this? Did you get yourself amnesia again? I told you to stay away from that protection spell."

Cassandra nodded. "Yeah, I think that's what it is. I was probably playing around with the protection spell. I don't remember what I did. I have amnesia."

Mitchell didn't look convinced. "Right."

Cassandra didn't think it would be a good idea to ask him anymore, lest he find out her real identity.

"Well, I'm going to go check if the guard has left yet. If I don't come back in five, I've been found. Hopefully, that doesn't happen though."

"Okay. Make it quick. I want to get out of here. It's a hell hole."

Cassandra nodded. "I figured as much. It is a prison, you know. It's supposed to be a hell hole."

Mitchell rolled his eyes. "Very funny, Michael."

Cassandra made her way out of the dungeon and found Jamie and Peter looking at her anxiously. Jamie was biting his lip, his face pale in anxiety, and his cheeks turned crimson as soon as he saw her. Cassandra stepped forward into the light and opened her mouth to speak, but was cut off short when Jamie's arms encircled her and caught her in a big, warm embrace. He was tall and lean, and he buried his face into Cassandra's neck and breathed in her citrusy scent of limes, oranges, and the ocean.

When they disconnected, they found Peter with his eyes averted and arms cross across his chest, looking very embarrassed to even be there during a private moment. He hadn't yet noticed that they were done. "So. How much longer do you think we should stay here?" Cassandra asked.

Peter looked up. "Right," he said, reaching into his back pocket for the keys. "Let's get out of here."

They walked up the stairs and up to Alana's room. When they got there, Cassandra stepped forward into the black fire fearlessly. Jamie sucked in his breath and did his best to hold himself back from running forward and protecting her from the heat. When she stepped out, she was the same Cassandra he had always known. Cassandra, who as usual, couldn't tolerate the silence started to rap under her breath, and when they walked out into the hallway, they found Atticus, Roslyn, and Ana waiting for them with expressions that conveyed that they were very pissed.

Cassandra frowned. "'Sup?"

Roslyn spoke up. "What's up is that you had all that fun without us. You left us out!"

Ana nodded. "How dare you? We thought you were our friends!"

"How'd you figure out what we were doing anyway?" Jamie asked.

"Alana told us," Atticus said matter of factly.

"She's awake?!" Peter asked.

Atticus raised an eyebrow. "Yes. Why wouldn't she be?" But Peter had already run past him and down the hallway. Quite literally ran. Cassandra's lips twisted as if she had tasted something sour, and her eyes looked amused.

"Alana passed out while giving up some of her energy to the soul swapping spell," Jamie explained.

"Oh. I heard about the spell, but I didn't know she fainted. Well. That was rather interesting." Atticus said, indicating the direction in which Peter had just run. They began to walk to the infirmary to see Alana.

Ana was smiling. "Alana's got a secret admirer."

"I don't think it's a secret, by the way, he just ran to see her," Atticus remarked.

"True. And I know what you're thinking, and no, you can't interrogate Peter." Ana told him.

Atticus stopped smiling. "But that's not fair!" he whined. "He looks very suspicious. I think he's evil. I've even made a conspiracy theory. He's in cahoots with the Magister from The Infernal Devices, and plans to invade our Sanctuary with clockwork automatons." he said.

"First of all, no, he's not evil, you just think that because he likes Alana and you're super protective of her even though she isn't really your sister. Second of all, he's not suspicious. He's sweet. And he really cares about Alana. Lastly, the Magister dies in book three, Clockwork Princess, remember? Tessa kills him."

Atticus' eyes looked dark when he remarked nastily, "He deserved to die. He was a total creep."

Cassandra nodded. "I've read that book. He was in sicko mode. He need some MILK," she said. They all doubled over in laughter.

"You're obsessed with vines, aren't you?"

Cassandra nodded. "Only the iconic ones. And I like my hot and spicy memes."

Jamie nodded. "Man, she loves her spicy memes."

Then, Cassandra extended her arms outward in a T-pose. "Assert your dominance." Then, they all followed her lead and t-posed until they finally got back to the infirmary. Alana was lying on a bed with white sheets tangled around her. May was fussing around her and pressing a citrus-scented washcloth to her forehead, while Alana squirmed under all of the attention she was getting.

There was a comfy looking armchair near the bed, but it was pushed aside hastily, and Peter was kneeling beside her bed. His hands were clasped around one of Alana's hands, and his red head was bowed down. He pressed his lips to her hands and kept murmuring, "Thank god." Alana turned a deep shade of red.

"Stop it." she murmured, though it was clear by her expression that she liked the attention. Cassandra rushed to her side.

"Are you okay, Lana?"

Alana looked sad for a moment, bit her lip, and then immediately concealed her expression with a forced smile, though her eyes portrayed that she had someone on her mind.

"Yeah. I feel so much better now. Thanks, May." She looked up at May. May had light brown skin and kind caramel eyes. She gave her a kind smile and said, "I'm glad you feel better."

"Thank you." Then, she turned to Peter. Right, well, I feel like I've missed something important. Fill me in." she asked them. Jamie took Cassandra's hand and pulled her into the hallway as Peter started to recount the interrogation, which though he couldn't see, he and Jamie had been able to hear. They retreated to the shadows when he whispered to her in the flickering light.

Are you hurt in any way?

"No. Were you worried about me?" Cassandra asked him.

"Yes. I was very worried." Jamie murmured against her neck, as he trailed kisses up from her neck to her cheek, and then her forehead. Cassandra smiled for two reasons— one, because it felt nice to know someone was worried about your welfare, and two— because Jamie's kisses unlike anyone else's seemed to have a sort of chemical reaction in her, and made feel giddy and glow with happiness in a way she had never quite felt before.

Jamie, on the other hand, felt as though a butterfly apocalypse had taken over his stomach. He felt light-headed and dizzy. No one but Cassandra ever had this effect on him. The butterflies in his stomach were fluttering around, flying upward, and carrying him up above, and away from the stratosphere, away from what was familiar and taking him to where everything was uncertain.

"I can't wait for Saturday," he murmured into her hand, where his lips were placed.

Saturday was The Date. The Date had to be capitalized because it was going to be a major historical event that Jamie was sure would be recorded into the textbooks that future generations of school-aged children would be forced to read by the Teachers, because of the social hierarchy of school.

But he was lying.

This rarely ever happened. Jamie lying to Cassandra rarely ever happened. Jamie could totally wait for tomorrow.

In fact, the only reason he mentioned it was because he wondered if Cassandra even remembered that she had agreed to go on a date with him. If he mentioned it and she didn't ask why he couldn't wait, that meant she remembered, right?

Right?

Jamie was freaking out. He didn't know what to wear, what to say, how to act, what to do, if he should give her something, and if yes, what it should be.

So yes. Jamie was having a bit of a panic attack. What was funny was that Cassandra was the exact opposite of freaked out.

Our tall, funny, and lightly freckled main character had no clue what she was going to wear to The Date. She figured she might as well just go with whatever the first thing in her closet was. That was probably a Hollister sweatshirt and ripped jeans. The fanciest item of clothing she owned was a pair of jeans that weren't ripped. She didn't much pay attention to looks. That was why she never wore makeup or dresses. There were some girls at school who wore dresses and makeup and large droplet earrings to (and she quotes) "pick up a new boo." She never really cared much about boys—unless of course, that boy was Jamie. Jamie had been her best friend. Nothing less, nothing more. But they couldn't live without each other. It was impossible, unthinkable, unimaginable, and purely incorrect to think that Jamie would go anywhere without Cassandra tagging along, or the other way around.

Except for the men's bathroom. Cassandra wouldn't go in there.

Besides, she always thought, if she ever changed her mind and decided that she did want to "pick up a new boo" (which was probably as likely to happen as Atticus becoming ugly) she still wouldn't dress up or wear makeup. She decided that if the boy didn't like her without, he didn't deserve her.

In that case, Jamie totally deserved her.

That evening at dinner, when Teresa laid out the delicious looking lasagna, someone was staring at Jamie.

Or rather, four people.

Atticus, Ana, Roslyn, and Cassandra were looking at Jamie with amused expressions. More accurately, they had been looking at him with amused expressions for half an hour, during which he had played with his lasagna, stared at the wall with a dreamy, far off look, daydreamed, dropped his fork with a clang onto the floor, which drew him out of his very occupying thoughts, retrieved his fork, then looked up to see his friends looking at him as if they were trying not to laugh. Alana, who was sitting at the head of the table as usual, looked preoccupied. Cassandra had told her all of what she had learned from Mitchell and filled in the gaps that Peter was unsure about, and she had listened with great interest. She was strategizing today, and she planned to go with anyone who wished to go along to the place where Charlie was and rescue him tomorrow.

Atticus cleared his throat loudly, and his eyes looked back and forth between Jamie and Cassandra rather exaggeratedly and obviously. A flush appeared on Jamie's high cheekbones, and he looked down immediately. Atticus smirked. "Well. Are you high? On Cassandra, I mean." Atticus said. He rather enjoyed teasing people. Ana kicked his shin under the table, and he winced. "Ow. What! I'm just messing with him!"

"You're so freaking annoying!" Ana scolded him. Atticus grinned, that crooked half-smile that Roslyn lived for, that indicated that he was entirely pleased with the circumstances.

Jamie, who was now in the process of taking a sip of his raspberry lemonade, spit it back into the cup, made a choking noise, promptly turned red, coughed, hit the back of his own neck repetitively, took a deep breath, and looked down at his untouched lasagna.

Cassandra, however, had set her jaw in a stubborn line. "Maybe he is high on me. Must be easy, seeing at I'm this awesome," she responded.

"It's no fun teasing you," Atticus retorted, though he looked very pleased with Jamie's reaction.

Jamie was still bright red, looking down, and he was kept swinging his legs under the table. When they finished dessert, which was lava cake, the friends started to make their way to the living room. They were going to talk strategy on tomorrow's seek and rescue mission. "One must always be prepared for what's out there," Alana advised them. Cassandra, Roslyn, and Atticus were walking in the front, talking quickly and waving their hands around animatedly to illustrate their rather gory discussion about weapons and how to use them in the most effective way. Ana and Jamie were at the back, and Jamie was unusually quiet. He was consumed by thoughts, and his worries were dragging him down and under like a whirlpool.

"Hey. Are you alright?" Ana said in a quiet voice.

Jamie was pulled out from his thoughts by the sound of her voice so close to him, it was like a hand had reached in and pulled him out of the swirling whirlpool. Jamie looked up, startled, and his face must have mirrored his worry because she looked startled as well, once she saw his face. "Nothing. I'm fine."

Ana smiled a bit. She looked pretty when she smiled. Up close, Jamie could see her amber eyes that were so like Atticus', though on Atticus, they looked mischievous, and on Ana, they looked intelligent and all-knowing. Ana, though she was rather small, had the air of someone brilliant, sharp, and well versed. She also had a kind smile. "Oh, come on, Jamie, I know you're not. Something's on your mind. What's up?"

Jamie looked into her eyes. The depths of golden amber seemed to wear into his green emerald ones and light him on fire, forcing the truth and nothing but the truth out of him. "The day after tomorrow," he began, "is my date with Cassandra. And I'm totally freaking out."

Ana laughed. Jamie frowned. "I'm sorry! It's just, you guys are amateurs. Here. Let's talk for a little while."

Ten minutes later, Ana had excused them both from the planning party, and they had made their way to her room. Jamie walked in and looked around. It was rather pretty. The wall was painted a pale blue, there were a few lilies arranged in a glass vase near the window, and there were a lot of books. Books on the bookshelf, which was overflowing, books on the desk, books stacked on the floor, and books displayed on a nightstand. Jamie walked over to the bookshelf and marveled over the books. Then he turned around and gave Ana a pleading look. "May I?"

Ana smiled a big smile that quite plainly said, 'you are the one person in the world who understands me.' "Be my guest," she replied.

Jamie's eyes went very wide, and he pulled out books at random, reading their backs, tracing his fingertips down their spines, and exclaiming "Oh, I've read this!" and "This one was so good." Jamie had never known he and Ana had this simple adoration of books in common.

Ana walked over to the bookshelf and tugged a book out. It had the title "The Giver" on it. "Have you read this one? Ana asked, eagerly.

"No. I've heard of it, but I haven't read it yet. Is it good?"

"Oh, yes. It's an amazing read. A must have."

"I'm not surprised. Lois Lowry is a very talented author who never fails to please. I've read Number the Stars at least seventeen times."

Ana nodded. "I enjoyed Number the Stars. A work of art, if I do say so myself. Now, not to change the topic or anything, but would you like to tell me what it is exactly that is on your mind?"

Jamie nodded. They settled down in armchairs near the window, and Jamie rested his elbows on his knees. He dropped his chin into his palms and stared out the window for a moment. Then, he spoke. "The Date. We're going on two days. I don't know what to wear."

"Where are you going?"

"The Beacon Theatre for a Lorde concert. I think I should wear something formal. Like a suit or something."

Ana shook her head. "No way. You should wear casual clothes. You're going to a concert, not a restaurant."

"So...like a spotlessly clean white shirt and brand new, unripped jeans?"

"No. Remember, Cassandra agreed to go out with you because she likes you. Just be yourself. Wear what you'd usually wear."

Jamie took a deep breath. It was evident that he was stressing out. "What do I do? Should I give her a present? And if so, what? Should I hold her hand? And at what approximate time should I do this? Should I hold the door open for her, or not? Oh my god, I'm going to be a terrible boyfriend." He burrowed his face into his hands.

Ana smiled. "You're not going to be a terrible boyfriend. You're going to be a great one, and I know it."

Jamie looked up for a moment. He spoke, and his voice was slightly muffled by his hands, which were covering his mouth. "How do you know that?"

"Because," she told him, "if you were a terrible boyfriend, you wouldn't care what she would think."

Jamie looked up for a moment. "Oh."

"Also, you need an idea for a gift?"

"Yeah. Do you think I should give her a rose? He asked. His voice sounded thoughtful.

"Doesn't that seem a bit cliché?"

Jamie nodded. "Right. How about designing a mixtape for her? Grunge, Indie, and Rap."

Ana nodded. "Perfect. It's like a window to her soul."

"Do you have any pointers for me?"

"Just be yourself. That's all she ever wants. Trust me." Ana advised.

Jamie swallowed and nodded. "Thank you so much for your advice." He stood up and walked across the room to the door.

"Wait."

His fingertips just touching the doorknob, Jamie turned around and looked at Ana. Her hands clutched a white book under which a red font was slightly hidden. The Giver, by Lois Lowry. She walked across the room and pressed it into his hands. She looked up at him with those beautiful eyes that so resembled golden flames. They pierced into the green, peacock colored eyes and radiated intelligence. "Keep it."

"Are you sure? You said you liked it a lot."

Ana shook her head. "I've read it a million times. You haven't had the joy yet. There's nothing that I find more joyful and satisfying than that feeling you get after reading a good book. I want you to feel that once again. This work by Lois Lowry, it's beautiful. I want you to have it."

Jamie looked at her with wide eyes. He and Ana weren't too close—they had met about three months ago, but that Ana was doing something so sweet for him, such as this, was very kind of her. He was taken aback with her kindness. He took the book from her soft hands and nodded. "Thank you. That was very sweet of you to do."

Ana nodded and smiled. "Don't mention it." She had a tentative smile, and she looked so small and innocent, that one who saw her would want to wrap their arms around her and protect her like a child. One who saw her would never have guessed that this was the same girl who took out two spirits with one spear ended disc. One would never have guessed how her beautiful amber eyes could glow with a caged in fire. Jamie smiled, nodded, and walked down the hallway to the living room with Ana, with the book held between his hands.

"...and we can form this structure to take down Fiona's spirits if we're discovered. Three in the front, three in the back. There has to be an equal distribution of skill for this to work." Cassandra was saying. Jamie and Ana entered the room.

"Will there really only be six people going?" Roslyn inquired.

"I think it would work best if Alana and we went together. If they discover us, they will have the advantage of numbers." Cassandra answered.

"Okay. That makes sense. How many weapons are we bringing?" inquired Atticus.

"A million."

Atticus grinned. "Sound good."

38

Something Else

A lana looked up and chose the staff that was hanging on the wall of the weapons room. She leaned it against the wall while she pulled a bunch of blades from the cabinet and stuck them in the appropriate pockets in her jacket. She chose a few spear ended wheels as well, and a pair of sais. She had learned to use them when she was seven, and they were her weapon of choice. Though she was skilled in all weapons, she rather loved the sais especially. She stashed them in her jacket and walked out the door. She made her way to her room and found a red-headed man standing near it, knocking.

"Alana? Alana, may I come in?" Peter called as he knocked.

Alana smirked. "Sure."

Peter whirled around in surprise and flushed a deep red that traveled to his ears. "I didn't see you there."

"Obviously." She turned the doorknob and entered. Peter followed her and stopped near her desk. Alana removed her weapons jacket and placed it on her chair. She kneeled near the firelight and started to shine her favorite pair of sais. Atticus had given them to her for her 17th birthday, three years ago. They were made of blessed metal with a sapphire handle, and they worked like magic. She worked hard on it, shining and sharpening it, while Peter watched her with quiet fondness.

"Is there something you'd like to tell me, Peter?"

"Yes. I mean, no. I mean, I have something for you." One who was looking at his blazing cheeks might have been inspired to produce a movie named "50 Shades of Red".

"A present? That's very sweet, but it isn't my birthday yet," Alana replied, puzzled. She was still looking down and shining her sais, and her unbound, wavy dark hair cascaded down both sides of her head, hiding her expression.

"It isn't really much of a present. It's more of an…invitation." He flushed again and looked away. Alana was confused. She looked up. Then, understanding found its way onto her sharp, elegant features, and she gave him a smile.

"Are you having a party? And you're inviting me? That's so sweet, thank you! I'd love to come."

"Actually, no, I'm not having a party. This is something else. Something a bit more…private."

Alana was intrigued. "Okay." She stood up, rubbed her now grime streaked hands off on her ripped jeans, and walked over to where Peter was standing. He looked firmly down and forced his hand forward to give her a small box, wrapped in silver wrapping paper. "Thank you, Peter," she said. He nodded and quite literally ran out of the room.

Alana walked back to the fireplace and carefully unwrapped the box. She gasped when a little black jewelry box tumbled out. She flipped it open to find a shining locket with a large gray gemstone set into it. She unfastened the clasp and put it around her neck. She was overwhelmed with affection for Peter, but she was puzzled at how this had anything to do with an invitation.

She walked out of her room and shortly found Peter in the library. He was seated in an armchair near the Hell's fire, which crackled and sparked, radiating coldness and light. The torches on the wall were flaming, and they illuminated the room with a warm hue. Alana could have had someone come in and install lights in the ceiling, but she liked the antique look that the torches gave.

Peter was reading. He didn't notice when Alana entered the room and walked closer to the fireplace.

"Peter?"

Peter looked up from his book and saw Alana standing there. Immediately, as if she had some type of chemical reaction on him that he was unaware of, he flushed, and Alana noticed that his pupils dilated when he looked at her. "Yes?"

"Thank you so much for the necklace." she thanked him. Then, Alana leaned down and kissed his cheek. Peter instantly flushed and looked away sheepishly, as if he had just intruded on a private moment. "It was a very meaningful gift, but you really didn't have to."

Peter shook his head and muttered something under his breath that sounded mysteriously like *Iloveyouiloveyouiloveyouiloveyousomuchstaywith-meandnevereverleaveme*. Alana frowned. "Sorry, I didn't catch that." Peter couldn't even begin to say how thankful he was that she couldn't hear him.

"I just said you're welcome."

"Oh. I just thought it was a bit sudden. Is today a special day or something? Have I forgotten a holiday?"

"Oh, no, no, I just saw it and thought about how nicely it went with your eyes. It looks stunning on you. You have beautiful eyes."

"I didn't realize you were paying that much attention to my eyes." She went slightly red.

"I didn't notice I was paying that much attention to your eyes either. I thought that I paid attention to everyone's eyes that way, but I don't know the exact shade of May's eyes the way I know yours."

Alana shrugged. She was not catching onto Peter's very obvious flirting. "Maybe it's because we've known each other since we were six."

"Maybe. But I've known May since I was two, when I moved here. She's always been like a big sister to me."

"Hmm. It's a mystery." She smiled.

"I'm not sure it's much of a mystery rather than something else." He turned away to hide the fact that he had now turned redder than should be humanly possible. He couldn't believe that the words had fallen from his incontinent lips. They had tricked him and breached his borders, the way everything seemed to fly past quickly and dizzyingly when Alana was around.

"What is it, then?" Alana was intrigued.

"Something else."

"What is this mysterious something else?"

"I don't know. It's just something else."

Alana smiled. "I like this. This something else."

* * *

Atticus had manic energy around him. He was filled with the feverish ecstasy and the drunk, high feeling that he got when he was fighting. Roslyn stood across from him, grinning. One of her hands was wrapped around a long sword, and the other clenched into a fist. They were up in the training room. Atticus put both hands around the staff and made a diagonal line across his body just as Roslyn brought down her long sword on it. The strong wood did not give in, and Atticus whirled around and utilized an outer crescent kick flawlessly, just the way Alana had taught him. However, Roslyn was too quick for him. She leaped out of the way, and Atticus stabbed his staff forward. Roslyn caught it against her sword before it made contact with her skin. Atticus countered with a punch, and Roslyn blocked the blow with her a knife-hand block and proceeded to step forward. Then, she punched him in the gut.

Atticus didn't double over, the way most would. He had years of experience, and when you doubled over or showed weakness to your enemy, your enemy now had the confidence and the opportunity to strike back at you again. Instead, he distracted her with a knife-hand strike to the neck, then turned very quickly and used a butterfly kick.

Having trained since she was five, Roslyn knew all his moves by heart. She expected the kick; however, she did not act quickly enough. Atticus caught her hard on her side, and she fell backward. She threw her hand back to break her fall and attempted to bounce back, but Atticus had pounced on top of her.

"Oh, are we grappling now?"

"Yes. I'm good at it."

"Alright. But I'll warn you. I'm so freaking good at grappling too."

"I know. No weapons allowed in grappling." Atticus reminded her. She gave him a nasty look and threw her sword aside. Then, they both turned around and faced opposite directions. Atticus called out the start, and they began to wrestle each other to the death. Atticus was on top first and had her about five seconds. Roslyn utilized a well-aimed kick to escape him, then shortly threw herself on top. However, she forgot to fasten his hands with her own, because he punched her three times and got out from under her easily. He held her wrists behind her back while trying to get her in a headlock, which to those of you who aren't familiar with the rules of grappling, is how you win and end the game. Roslyn kicked out at him, got him off of her, and proceeded in sitting on top of his legs. He struggled and squirmed and punched out, but Roslyn caught both fists and held them down. Lastly, she got him in a headlock.

"Alright, alright, you win. Now can you please stop crushing my windpipe?" Atticus pleaded.

"Fine." Roslyn released him from the headlock. She released his hands but did not get up. Atticus raised an eyebrow.

"You can stop sitting on my rib cage, too. Any day now."

Roslyn grinned and looked down at him. "Maybe I don't want to."

Atticus used both hands to push her off, then leaped into the air. He landed on his feet. He had to have quick reflexes to escape Roslyn, who was about the fastest person on his training team. She somersaulted backward, leaped to her feet, and proceeded forward.

"Fistfight, maybe? We don't have our weapons." He indicated the staff and the long sword, which were abandoned on the floor nearby.

"Okay." Roslyn and Atticus went into a fighting stance, bodies facing sideways, so as to give the enemy less area of prone hits. Atticus started. He thrust his hand upward, the fingers curled in, and pushed Roslyn's face upward. He used her momentary distraction to aim a punch to her gut. Although Roslyn kicked ass at grappling, Atticus could beat anyone in a fistfight.

As Roslyn took deep breaths to recover from the punch, she swung her fist upward at Atticus' jaw, he whirled away and came around her. Roslyn turned, looking for him, and Atticus got her at the side of her face. Her eyebrows knit together as her hand yelped in agony. She wanted desperately to believe that it was because her hand wasn't in the right form. The only good thing about this situation was that she was distracted from her throbbing chin by the hurt in her fist.

He smirked now, and she scowled. Blood appeared at her lips and jawline. He aimed a hammerhead strike at her head, but she had already put out her hand to block it. Taking advantage of his momentary distraction, she kicked out her leg between his two legs and hooked it. Down he fell, astonishment, and a look of betrayal clear on his face. Roslyn smirked.

"Rosie! You cheated! We aren't sparring; we're in a fistfight! Sweeps aren't allowed!"

"I know." She was smiling, despite the constant throbbing pain in her jaw. Atticus was regrettably quick and strong with his fists. She offered her hand to him, and he took it and stood up.

"Again?" he asked her.

"Let's spar this time," she said.

"Okay." he agreed.

They started. She got the first kick in, at Atticus' side. He grimaced and whirled around with his special butterfly kick, the one he was known for executing perfectly. Roslyn stepped out of the way and elbowed him in the rib cage. Then, before he could even think, she whirled around an executed three inner crescent kicks. Atticus was gasping for air, even with his training. He doubled over and clutched his side.

"Hey. Hey, are you okay?"

"Yeah," he assured her. She took his hands and guided him to a room further into the training room, where training supplies were stored. She sat him down on the bench and walked over to the counter. She opened the freezer and pulled out two Gatorades. She tossed one to Atticus, and then pulled out two ice packs. She walked over to Atticus, who was grimacing in pain.

"May I see?" she asked him.

Atticus nodded, and she pulled the side of his shirt up slightly to reveal his side, which was swelling and red. She held the ice pack to it. "I'm sorry," she told him quietly. "I guess I don't know my own power."

Atticus flashed her a grin. "Don't worry about it. We were training. We're supposed to get hurt. It's part of the process." Atticus took a warm, lemon-scented washcloth from a white box, and wiped away at the blood in Roslyn's jawline and lips. "I'm sorry too. I didn't mean to put that much force in it…" he trailed off as he cleaned the red away and placed the washcloth down. His fingers traced her lip. She smiled and put the ice pack down. She took up the other one and held it to his side, which looked considerably less pink now.

Then, Ana walked in. She was wearing a tank top and shorts, her curly locks pulled up into a high ponytail, and a sweatband held her hair back away from her eyes. Beads of sweat were at her hairline, and she looked like she had been working out.

"The other training room ran out of Gatorade," she explained. "Teresa's refilling the fridge right now." Then, she looked up at Roslyn and Atticus and smiled her sweet smile. "Oh. I see. I fear that I have intruded on a rather private moment." Before either could say a word, Ana grabbed a bottle of Gatorade and ran out. Roslyn turned back to Atticus who was looking down. Blood had rushed up to his face.

Roslyn laughed.

39

With A Cherry On Top

ave you got all of your weapons?" Alana asked her little sister. "Yeah," Cassandra answered, and indicated her jacket and then her belt, both of which were indeed packed with a series of lethal-looking weapons. It was probably not what one expected to see when you thought of the typical seventeen-year-old girl.

"Alright, then, I think we're all set," Alana said to Atticus, Roslyn, Cassandra, Ana, and Jamie. "By the way, are you all sure that you want to come? You should know that it will be very dangerous- we're talking about a thousand ticked off spirits. That is, if they find us. We're going to be totally inconspicuous. If you want to step out now, there's no shame in that."

No one said a word. Alana turned to Cassandra and Jamie. "Are you two sure you want to go? You haven't gotten much training yet."

"Of course, I want to go! I can't just stay here, missing out on all the fun!" Cassandra told her.

"And I go everywhere she goes," Jamie said matter of factly. "That's just how we work."

"Oh. Okay."

The door to the library opened with a bang, and a startled looking Peter burst into the room.

"Alana, how dare you?"

"How dare I what?"

"How dare you try to leave without me?"

Alana looked slightly sheepish. "I thought you knew."

"I didn't. Anyway, I'm coming with you."

"Are you sure, Peter? It's going to be dangerous. I tried to convince them not to come along, but—" she indicated the group of teens standing next to her. "They wouldn't listen."

Peter shook his head. "No way. There is no possible way in hell that you're going to convince me not to come." Alana frowned. "You're reckless, Alana! You've been that way since you were six! I know you, and I know that you will take any and all opportunities to fight. I'm coming with you. You're brave, but you don't have a limit."

Alana stuck her tongue out at him. "Fine." she allowed. "But only because you insisted." But secretly, she was pleased that he cared about her that much.

They took a train to get to New York and then walked to the Infernum headquarters. They checked their surroundings and started into the building. It was locked, but after a few savage kicks courtesy of Cassandra, it gave in. They searched the place, but it was deserted. Alana looked astonished for a moment, then so angry that she looked dangerous, then contained her rage and showed a startlingly calm composure on her face. It was clear that she was anguished. She stared down at a patch of sunlight that traveled through the broken window and illuminated the splintering wood floor for a moment before speaking.

"Years ago, I led a massacre to this location. Where could Charlie be but here?" She reached into the pocket of her jacket and pulled out a map. However, this map looked quite different from a map you would find in an atlas anyone these days. Alana kept unfolding the map until it was about the size of a flat-screen TV. The map had our world, earth on it, with various locations pointed out with skulls, fires, and pentagrams. However, there were also other worlds, parallel to our own. The color of the sea was blue on earth, and the earth green. However, the other worlds had different colors, such as a blood-red ocean, and black earth. Cassandra wanted to look at it all day, every day, study this map, visit every place in our world and other worlds as well. She wanted to leave no stone unturned, see everything, and go everywhere. Her eyes lit up and searched the map hungrily, taking in everything of this hidden world she never knew existed for so long. Jamie loved it. It was in moments like these in which Jamie most wanted to kiss Cassandra.

Jamie laced his fingers through Cassandra's and held her hand tightly. She returned the pressure and squeezed his hand back. Then, a look of realization came onto Jamie's face. "I think I might know where they are."

Alana, who had set the map down on a broken-down table and used a few daggers as paperweights, looked up immediately. "Where?"

"So, when the spirits captured Cassandra and me, the spirits offered me freedom under the condition that I let them put a concealment enchantment on me that would prevent me from telling anyone the location of that building. I, of course, didn't agree. If that's where Fiona's location is, I wouldn't be surprised that they went out of their way to keep anyone from finding it out."

Alana's eyes lit up. "When they were taking you, into the building, did you see anyone? A man, looking around 20?"

Jamie squinted his eyes. "Yeah. I think I remember seeing a man. He had brown hair and hazel eyes. They were very hazel. He was coughing, and his hands were cuffed to the wall. He kept saying two names- Ariana and Alana. Then, he collapsed."

"Charlie has black hair. That's probably someone else. He probably knows someone else called Alana, because I only know one boy with very hazel eyes, and he died when I was five. Anyway, thank you so much, Jamie." Then, she turned the rest of the group, and she had a steely, fierce expression on her face. "Let's go."

They took a train back, and Jamie lead them through the forest towards the dreaded building, lurking ominously in the shadows. It was as though they were the victims in their own horror movie.

As they neared the building, they found that this building too looked deserted. Peter placed a hand on Alana's shoulder and murmured to her quietly. "I'm sure it's only an enchantment. You ready?" Half-heartedly, Alana nodded her head. "Let's do this."

They came closer to the door, and Alana pulled a small, shiny object from her pocket. "Gem of Incantations," Atticus explained after seeing Cassandra's inquisitive expression. "Removes spells from things." Alana pushed the gemstone to the door, and suddenly, it vibrated and shook in her clasping hand. Then, a sound, much like the type you'd hear after unlocking a lock, came from the door, and the vibrating stopped. Cassandra could now glimpse a light through one of the grimy windows. A fire. Alana smiled, and her rage and fury could be seen in the liquid fire that moving beneath her piercing gray eyes.

"Bingo."

Jamie led them down a corridor to where the dungeons were located. Cassandra couldn't remember it, because she had been unconscious at the time. They found a hallway lined with rooms, and they tried the first door. After Alana had a go at it with The Gem, and the lock enchantment burst with a bang. Peter winced- they had to be quiet, or Fiona and her spirits would find them. Alana took a deep breath and stepped inside. What she saw inside made her heart stop.

There, crouched on the floor of the entirely gray and red room say a young man, whose head was down. His long, chestnut hair fell forward and hid his expression. He started to look up when he heard the door burst open, and his expression was one of bewilderment, recognition, disbelief, and years of pent up sorrow. His eyes traveled slowly from Alana's face to Cassandra's. His mouth was slightly ajar, and he was wearing gray rags.

And the blood. It was everywhere, smeared on the floors, walls, and the boy's face and arms. It painted the puzzling scene like a morbid painting.

"This is him. The one I saw when they were taking Cassie and me down to the prison cell." Jamie said. No one answered him. Everyone seemed drawn and frozen at the center of the room where the boy was sitting. Even Cassandra was quiet as Alana stepped forward without a word. They all watched in silence as she got down on her knees and gently pushed his hair out of his eyes.

Nowhere else in the world could anyone have ever found a more pure hazel.

"Jules?" Alana whispered. The boy nodded at his name, and Alana fell into his arms.

"Lana." He whispered her name to her over and over again in the darkness.

Cassandra's eyes widened. *My big brother?* She, however, stayed right where she was and did not move. It was not that she didn't care for her brother; it was, in fact, quite the opposite. She just didn't think it would be right if she went and joined them. She felt as though the space of years distanced them, and that it wouldn't be right if she ruined this heart-wrenching moment, embracing her brother like an old friend when in truth, he still had yet to learn who she was.

After what felt like forever, Alana finally let go of Julian. She looked up, and Cassandra was appalled to see a trail of tears going down her cheek. Cassandra looked away hastily, and Alana wiped the tears off on her sleeve, determined not to let anyone else see her cry, as she was stubborn, just like her little sister.

"Lana?" Julian called.

"Yes?"

Julian looked up. "Who's that?" He pointed at Cassandra. "She has Mom's pretty eyes." He looked into her eyes, and his expression was one of a person remembering something pleasant in his childhood.

"That's Cass. Jules, Cass is our little sister." Alana told him. Cassandra smiled a bit and waved at him awkwardly. What did one do when one found that their long lost and legally dead brother was alive and imprisoned in a cell for eighteen years? Then, Julian did what she never expected.

He put his arms out for her, too.

Cassandra walked over to him and embraced him, and something about him seemed so familiar, though she had never seen him before. It felt as though deep down, she always knew he was there, but that she hadn't quite realized it until now. Jules. My big brother, Jules.

When they disconnected, Cassandra saw a look of contentment on Julian's chiseled features, that she mirrored. Julian also looked slightly lost. "I have two little sisters?"

Alana laughed, and playfully punched him. "I'm not that little."

Julian looked down at her and smiled. "You used to be so little. I used to push you on the swing. You liked that a lot."

Alana nodded. "And we used to paint together. On the walls. With Mom's paints. And when caught us, you'd take the blame. You were the best big brother ever."

Julian smiled and reached out to touch her hair. "I remember your hair. Black like a raven. And your smile. Brilliant as ever."

"Did you call my name?" Alana asked him. "Did you miss me?"

"Yes. I missed you so much."

"But then, who's Ariana?"

Julian flushed a bit, and then his eyes widened. "I can see her," he whispered. "I can see her for the first time."

"Who can you see, Julian? Who can you see for the first time?" asked Alana.

"Ariana," he answered. "My great, faceless love."

"Let's find her," Alana commanded the group. "Let's get her and Charlie and get the hell out of here." The steely, fiery expression had come back to her face, and Peter knew well that when she got like this, there was nothing that could keep her from getting what she wanted. Then, she turned back to Julian. "Can you stand?"

Julian smiled sadly. "I'm not sure. I'm sick. With a hell disease. I keep coughing up blood, and I get these hallucinations." A wave of realization passed over him, and he turned even paler than he was before. "This is a hallucination, isn't it?" His hazel eyes pierced through Alana's gray ones and pleaded with unspoken words.

This is too good to be true.

But I want it so badly.

"No. Jules, this isn't a hallucination. We're gonna get you out of here. Can you try to stand? I'll help you." She stood up and held out a hand. "Welcome to the club."

Julian grinned good-naturedly, then staggered to his feet. He turned paler, if that was even possible, and balanced most of his weight on Alana's shoulder. She winced. "Sorry, Lana."

"Don't mention it." Then, she turned to Peter. "Lead the way."

They walked to the next prison cell, in which Julian told them was were Ariana was. Cassandra asked Alana if she could try the Gem this time, and Alana allowed her. The Gem unlocked the door with a click, and Cassandra turned to her big brother, who limped over to the door and wrenched it open. The look on his face was one of admiration, love, and immense happiness. The girl was lying on the ground, unconscious. She looked rather attractive, Cassandra though, with her long lashes, high cheekbones, and full, red lips. She looked like the idol of some of the girls at her school if their idol had gone through a nightmare. She was tall and lanky, with curly dark hair with faded red highlights that went a bit past her shoulders. Julian half limped half-ran to her and fell to his knees. He held her carefully and whispered to her.

"Ari. Ari, wake up. Please wake up."

The girl stirred, then her eyes flew open. Those too were very beautiful. A perfect mix of caramel and hazel, they looked astonished for a moment. "Jules? Is that you?"

Julian nodded eagerly and immediately set to embracing her tightly and kissing every part of her that he could reach. "God, I imagined you in my dreams, and in my dreams, you were very pretty, but...god, you're so much more beautiful than that."

The girl called Ariana flushed. "No, I'm not."

Julian smiled. "Yes, you are." He pressed his lips to hers and continued kissing her until Alana cleared her throat. Julian flushed a deep red that brought some well-needed color into his face. It seemed that he just remembered that they weren't alone.

"If you don't mind, we need to get Charlie and leave, before Fiona finds us. There will be plenty of time for making out later."

Julian turned even redder, and Ariana frowned. "We weren't making out." She said defiantly.

"Right. And the earth is neither round nor flat, but rather shaped like a

270

celery stick." Alana responded. Ariana blushed furiously.

"Right. Let's go," said Julian when he and Ariana had contained themselves.

They started to walk down the corridor, but all the other rooms were empty. Alana looked anguished.

"Hey. It's okay. I'm sure he's here. He's probably just in the east wing. That's where they keep the top security cells, but I think we can get past them." Julian reassured her. Alana took a deep breath. She missed Charlie so much that every moment that wasn't spent in his presence, she broke a little more.

"Let's go."

Julian faintly remembered the path, as he had been there during the first few weeks of his stay. His volatile moods used to make him do crazy and impulsive things, so he had to be closely monitored to make sure he wouldn't kill himself. Later, he had learned that there was no escape, so he had given up and stopped. Then, they had moved him to a low-security cell. He knew where it was, because of that, and led the group to it. When they reached it, they found three spirits guarding it. Atticus and Cassandra made short work of two of them, and but the last one managed to get away from Ana. "Let's try to be quick. I wouldn't be surprised if he comes back with friends." Alana warned. The Gem did its job quickly, and they entered the room. The scene that awaited them was rather frightening.

A man with fine black hair and very red lips was kneeling on the ground, which was splattered with blood. Two long gashes could be found on his arm and leg, and his head was down. He was shirtless and wearing a pair of worn, dark jeans. Long red marks could be seen on his muscular back. His hands were shackled above him to the wall, and he looked unconscious. Alana ran forward and embraced him tightly. "Charlie," she called his name. "Charlie, wake up. It's me, Alana." He did not move. She put her ear to his chest and listened for a heartbeat. Cassandra saw the look of relief on her face when she heard one. She pulled out the Gem and unlocked his handcuffs, and his now released hands thumped down to the ground. He, however, did not awaken. He seemed to be in a deep slumber. Alana, who was clearly getting more anxious by the moment, roused him. "Charlie," she called to him, "Charlie, you need to get up. We've got to leave before they find us." Now, he stirred. His eyelids fluttered open to reveal two pure, beautiful, ocean eyes. Then, most vexing to Alana, he started to laugh.

"I don't get it. What's so funny?" Alana asked him, puzzled.

"I had a dream." Charlie said, in a rather childish voice, "There was a kitty in it. The kitty was driving a blue car. I said, 'Kitties don't drive cars!" Then, he continued to laugh.

"Charlie," Alana said in a quiet voice, "Come on. We need to leave."

Charlie pouted his lips and made puppy dog eyes. "But I don't wanna leave. I want to play hide and go seek with Fifi."

Alana stood up and dragged Charlie to his feet. "I've got candy."

Charlie's eyes widened, and he smiled. He started to jump up and down. "I want candy! Can I have candy? Pretty please with a cherry on top?" he pleaded.

Alana raised an eyebrow. "Sure. But you've gotta do something for me first."

"Anything." He looked up at her with big eyes. His hair started to fall into his eyes, but he didn't bother pushing it away. Alana did.

"You've gotta come with me."

"And then you'll give me candy?"

"Yes. And then I'll give you candy."

"Okay."

"Great." She started out the door, and everyone started to follow her out, but Charlie wasn't following them. "What now?" Alana asked him.

Charlie pouted his lips again. "You have to hold my hand."

"Oh, for god's sake." Alana rolled her eyes and walked over to Charlie. She took his hand and walked out the door, but stopped dead in her tracks. Cassandra, whose heart had fallen from her chest to her toes, turned around slowly, and the breath was stolen from her lungs immediately.

Spirits.

40

It's As If You're Sleeping

lana worked on reflex. Letting go of Charlie's hand, she reached both hands into her jacket, and when she pulled them out, two silver sais were revealed. She went to work immediately, slicing three spirits into shreds in seconds. Peter looked at her admiringly and went to help her without a moment of hesitation. Cassandra followed her big sister's lead and ran into the fight. Jamie fought bravely at her side, letting arrows fly around him and taking out three spirits at a time. Atticus had his staff out, and he was engaged in a battle with a spirit in black robes. Roslyn wielded her short sword, and Ana let her disc fly. Pretty soon, they stood in front of the collapsed figures of thirty spirits. Atticus, Ana, and Roslyn began to gather their energies and store them in arcas. When they were done, they began to leave.

"Not so fast." a voice warned her, and Fiona walked out of the shadows.

"Fifi!" Charlie shouted with glee.

Fiona smiled at him with a sort of evil admiration. "Charlie, my little ghostie! Come to me!" She held her arms out for him to run to, and he did. She embraced him and gave Alana a nasty look.

Blood rushed to Alana's face. Her cheeks were flushed with rage, and she felt her blood boil. "You did this to him. You drugged him to make him have amnesia, and you made him love you. You disgusting motherf—"

"That's a potty word." Charlie interrupted. "Potty words are bad."

Alana ignored him and tightened her grip on her sais. She stepped closer to the front of the group and looked Fiona in the eye, daring her. "Let go of him. Get your disgusting, slimy hands off of my boyfriend."

Charlie made a face. "I'm not your boyfriend. Girls have cooties," he explained in his childish voice.

"But I don't want to. And neither does he." Fiona replied nastily, ignoring Charlie's previous comment.

Alana looked at Charlie, and something clouded his pure, ocean eyes. He was smiling, but it wasn't the usual, beautiful, brilliant smile that he reserved for only her. This smile was empty and hollow, and more than anything, it made Alana sad.

"Charlie. Charlie, try to remember. Come on. She's not good. She hurt you."

Charlie looked pained for a moment as if remembering something that was better forgotten. "She hurt me because I was a bad boy."

"What?" Alana was puzzled.

"She hurt me because I was a bad boy," Charlie repeated. "I tried to go outside to play. So she punished me." He looked like a kicked puppy, with his big eyes and pout. "But I'm a good boy now. So Fifi won't hurt me anymore. I won't go outside to play. Then you won't lash me. Right, Fifi?"

Alana felt all of the blood that had rushed up to her face now drain out of it. "You lashed him?"

Fiona smiled evilly, and her destroyed teeth showed. "He deserved it. Didn't you now, Charlie?"

Charlie nodded obediently. "I was a bad boy."

"Why?" Alana spoke in a voice so low and full of sorrow, it was as though Fiona had grabbed her sais and stabbed her in the stomach, though Fiona had made no advances to her. "Why did you do this? Why take him, but not kill him and gain his power? What's the point?"

Fiona cackled with a knowing glint in her eyes. "Well, it worked, didn't it? It brought you here. And it brought her," she said, pointing to Cassandra. "No offense, but I don't care about you. Her, on the other hand," she grinned evilly. "She's something I could get something out of. Did you think I care much about hurting your precious Charlie?" She sneered. "I've got better things to do than to waste time killing off your kind for small bursts of energy. I want her. Give her to me, and I will give you mercy."

Cassandra paled. "How did you know I'd come along with her? How did you know—" she did not finish the sentence, for it was too much to bear. She must have known that Alana was her sister. She must have been tailing her, watching her every move, noting it down. She felt so sick so suddenly.

"It was me!" Fiona burst out. "It was all me. I'm the one who planned to have that nuisance of a girl kidnapped." She pointed to Ana. "I'm the one who arranged for those women to get you and your stubborn normie boyfriend! It was me, through and through, and I deserve this!" She exhaled for a moment before she repeated in a calmer voice, "Give her to me, and I will give you mercy."

Alana couldn't take it for another moment. "You know nothing of mercy! I won't let you touch my sister for as long as I live!" She slashed her blessed metal sais down at Fiona, who cried out in pain and surprise. She released Charlie and threw three fireballs at her. Alana blocked them with her blessed metal sais, and they seemed to absorb the power and shine a bit brighter than they had before. Peter rushed to help her, but she shook her head. "Just me. I want this fight all to myself."

Peter shook his head. "Please don't let your pride get the better of you, Alana. You know that you need my help. She's very powerful. She's killed thousands of our kind. Her elemental power is multiplied tenfold."

Alana shook her head dismissively. "No. I need this. She lashed Charlie. She lashed my Charlie! And now, she's going to try to take the little family that I still have."

She swore loudly, and Charlie cupped his hands around his ears. "Better count your seconds left in this dimension. Imma rip you to shreds. You lashed Charlie. You freaking lashed him. Imma make you pay. You better pray. You better pray to god up there. He ain't gonna help a freak like you, but it'd be entertaining to watch. I'll end you in the most painful and slow way possible," she said, while she circled Fiona the way a lion circles its prey before killing it. Then, action exploded. Alana stabbed forward with her sais, and Fiona dodged her. She turned around and threw five fireballs at her, one after the other, and Alana dodged each. Then, she kicked out at her and got her in the gut. Fiona doubled over, and Alana used this time to pierce a hole through her shoulder and neck. Black blood flooded from it, and she uprighted herself. Alana saw her wound stitch itself back together.

"This is what I'm talking about," Peter argued. "Please let me help you, Alana. She's too strong."

Charlie was now sitting on the floor, crying, "Don't hurt Fifi! She's my best friend!"

Alana shook her head. "No. I need to do this on my own." Fiona snarled and threw a fireball at her. Astonishingly, it almost got her shoulder, as Alana was distracted. She needed her full focus when she was slaying people or things, and Peter and Charlie were both distracting her.

"Alana, you know need my help."

"No, I don't! I can do this on my own!" she yelled, and Fiona utilized her momentary distraction to throw a fireball at her chest, and Alana wasn't quick enough to react. It was getting closer and closer, but Peter had already run and put himself between Fiona and Alana.

Down he fell, and broke, like a little china doll. Alana's eyes widened in shock. She went as pale as a sheet and looked as if her worst nightmare had come true. She knelt down near him and started to shake him. She called his name over and over again as tears cascaded down her cheeks. Cassandra rushed to her aid, fighting off Fiona. Fiona grinned a very nasty smile and set to throwing fireballs at her. Cassandra didn't even notice them hitting her. She walked closer and closer to her until she was only a foot away from her. The spirit cackled.

"So you're the Blessed one, aren't you? I'll make short work of you, and you can go join your parents in hell." she snarled.

Cassandra laughed. "Bitch, Imma put you back in your place. Speaking of which, do you have any brooms here? Someone seems to have left dirt on the floor." Cassandra shouted, indicating Fiona. Fiona snarled and held a pendant around her neck. It was a cat's eye jewel, in the shades of gray and green. It seemed to glow under her grip. Then, all of a sudden, there seemed to be a fire in her eyes. Black and dangerous, she raised her arms to make fireballs, and this time they were black.

"The Gem of Enchantments," Atticus breathed. "It multiplies an enchantment's power by 100. Very dangerous and lethal. Cass, step away from her."

Cassandra shook her head. "No. She's been hunting me for so long. I'm not going to run and hide anymore. I'm not going to play this morbid game of hide and go seek anymore. I'm going to stand here and fight."

Fiona cackled. "Brave, proud, and so incredibly stupid. Just like your sister." she hissed.

"Call my sister or me stupid again, and I'll break you into little tiny pieces," Cassandra warned.

Fiona laughed again. "I'd like to see you try."

Cassandra's eyes widened for a moment, and now there was a red fire burning in them as well. Cassandra put her palms up to face Fiona, and they lit up. The fire rushed up into a large and savage flame that lit everything up in a beautiful and dangerous type of illumination. Now, the fear was plain on Fiona's face for a moment before she smiled.

"I'll be back." Three words were hissed through her lips, and she vanished with a snap. Cassandra looked around with a vexed expression, then, satisfied that Fiona had indeed gone and was nowhere to be found, she rushed to her sister's said.

Alana was kneeling next to Peter, whose breathing was hurried and drawn in pants like he had been running miles. His evergreen eyes pierced through Alana's beautiful gray ones, as he struggled to keep his eyes open for a few moments later, so he could gaze into the beauty of the almond-shaped gray. He hungrily took in her face, studying it, one last time, before it was time to go. Alana was screaming his name now, tears flooding down her cheeks and leaving trails down her face. She put her head to his chest and embraced him tightly, refusing to let go. They had been best friends since they were very small, and she seemed unable to accept his mortality the way she never accepted her own. When she clutched onto him, her whole body shook. No one but Cassandra dared to come close to her, to try to comfort her, as

Alana never cried, and on the rare occasion that she did, it was likely that the world was ending. Peter took a last, shallow breath and breathed five last words into Alana's ear.

"You were my something else."

Peter's eyes widened for a moment, and then something seemed to disconnect behind them. Suddenly, Alana stopped crying and went deadly silent. Everyone in the group had an air of immeasurable terror, and Cassandra could see by the looks on their faces that they were absolutely terrified and uncertain of what happened next when Alana got like this.

Cassandra stood at her sister's side, unable to move. She took a deep breath and placed a hand on her sister's shoulder. Alana did not react. She sat there, in the deadly quietness and the only movements in the room were the tears drops that fell from Alana's cheeks and onto Peter's face. Alana reached out and closed his eyes. She leaned down and kissed his cheek and breathed a few words to him.

"Go with my blessing. Your memory shall not die in vain."

Alana continued to hold him as if he were a lifeline. She shook and buried her face in his neck. She stood numbly, and her eyes looked lost as she carried Peter's body gently in her arms. She carried him as they all used the transporter one by one.

When they all crawled through the hazy dizziness of transport through the transporter, they found themselves facing all of the members of the Sanctuary. Harley and Jessica were at the front of the group, and Alana barely noticed the movement and sound around her, as people gasped after seeing Peter's limp body in her arms. She barely noticed the crying, the despair, and the parting of the crowd as Jessica, Carter, and a tall man with sandy blond hair rushed to Julian's aid as he collapsed in a fit of coughing. She wasn't aware that Charlie was in the process of climbing a ladder and reaching for a priceless crystal ball because it looked fun to play with. She was completely oblivious to the fact that Harley's eyes had grown very large, that she had gone very pale, and that she had clutched both hands over her mouth, staring at her big brother, who was acting like a four-year-old. A young woman with long auburn hair was trying to convince him to come down from the ladder and let May have a look at him. Alana seemed to be disconnected from the rest of the world and trapped in a different space, where no one could find her.

Alana walked up two flights of stairs and kicked open the door to Peter's bedroom. It was scrupulously neat, and the bed was spotlessly clean. Alana set Peter down on his bed and tucked him in.

"Sweet dreams," she told him in a quiet voice. "Now, it's as if you're sleeping."

41

With Hope, Peter

She looked into the mirror. She looked like she acted in a horror movie. She spent hours scrubbing herself clean of blood and dirt. She had brushed her shoulder-length black hair out and was pleased to see that the red dye had stayed on the tips of her hair.

She put on a tank top and a pair of ripped jeans that Cassandra lent her. She partitioned her hair and then braided both sides. She looked like a doll, but a goth at the same time. When she was done, she walked out.

She was led to the dining room by Harley, and she chose the seat next to Julian. He smiled that beautiful, gorgeous smile that caught Ariana off guard and held her there. She smiled back and kissed his cheek. He reached for her hand and held it under the table. She noticed that he noticed his oldest sister looking considerably pale. Alana unenthusiastically chased a bit of sun-dried tomato around and around in her plate. Ariana remembered how the redheaded man fell down, and Alana's face when he did and felt a pang deep in her heart. Wanting to give her some space, she looked away and squeezed Julian's hand. She saw the corners of his eyes crinkle as he smiled. Now, a young boy considered her for a moment before speaking. "What's your name?" he demanded in a rather bossy voice.

"I'm Ariana Reeve," she answered him. He chuckled a bit, and Ariana frowned. "I don't get it. What's so funny?" She asked.

"Oh, I just thought it was rather ironic that you look Indian, but you have an American name." He told her.

"It's also rather ironic how Americans speak English, which was adopted from the British, although they hate the British and don't want anything to do them. It's ironic how you guys call yourself Americans when you're actually Europeans. The real Americans are the native Americans you stole this land from. It's also ironic how you tan yourselves to get this beautiful complexion- she indicated her face- but enslave and shun the ones who were born with it. That's ironic. Besides, I'm Canadian." She looked down and started to eat her dinner. Then, she noticed that all chatter had died out and looked up.

The boy's jaw had dropped. He had dropped his fork. Everyone was staring at her. "What? It's true!" she told them, but they weren't annoyed.

They were amused. They started laughing so hard that tears were coming out of their eyes. Their leader, Alana, was doubled over with laughter as well. Some boys were even yelling, "Okay, Ariana!" and "ayyy!" and "How'd you like it like that, Tyler?", which she assumed was the name of the rude boy.

A loud cacophony sounded beside her, and she turned immediately to see that Julian was coughing up blood into his napkin with one hand. Ariana let go of his hand and stroked his back repeatedly, praying desperately. Tears poured endlessly out the sides of her eyes as she looked around frantically for something to help her beloved. Everyone had now gone deadly quiet. Tyler looked repentant. Alana looked up in terrible horror. She rushed to Julian's chair, where Julian sat, still coughing hysterically.

"Somebody, do something!" cried Ariana. Something in the room suddenly broke, and there was an explosion of action. May rushed to the room, and Ariana sank to her knees.

* * *

"Will they be alright?" Cassandra asked May with an anxious expression on her face. She'd only been around these people for around a month, but they were already growing on her.

May gave her a kind smile. "Let's start with Charlie. Don't you worry. He'll be quite alright soon. The remedy will be ready in a week, and he'll be okay very soon."

"And Julian?"

May looked anxious, as if she didn't really want to talk about it. Then, she took a deep breath and spoke. "I'm afraid that Julian has been infected with a disease much greater and worse than we had earlier believed. If he had been brought to me a bit earlier, I suppose I could have cured it, but it's at its final stage right now. The symptoms have gotten severe enough that I am led to believe that he has, indeed, acquired this disease close to 18 years ago. It is a miracle that he has survived for this long. I am so very sorry," May said gravely. Cassandra shook her head sadly and buried her face into Jamie's neck. Jamie embraced her tightly and warmly.

"It'll be okay, we'll find a cure. I promise." He murmured into her ear. Cassandra sniffed and nodded.

"Thank you, May," she added.

"Of course," May answered, kindly. "Now, if you don't mind, your brother needs some rest." Cassandra nodded, and walked out the door with Jamie's hand in hers, keeping her strapped on to this world and preventing her from floating away into space.

Almost as soon as the door to the infirmary shut, it banged open again, and in stepped a tall girl with black hair and caramel eyes. "Dear, I told you, he needs his rest—" May began but stopped abruptly at the look in the girl's eyes.

"I'm sorry, but he's my Jules, and I need to see him. Now." Ariana said in a quiet voice. May nodded, and something in her intelligent brown eyes told her that she completely understood how Ariana felt and that she wished that she didn't.

"Go on then, dear. I won't stop you. He is currently unconscious, but you can try to talk to him and see if he wakes up."

Ariana nodded, looking astonished. "Thank you. Thank you so, so much."

May smiled. "Don't mention it." Then, she left the room, and Ariana was left alone in the infirmary. She walked slowly to Julian's bed, afraid of what she might find. She took a breath of relief when she saw Julian lying on the bed without any blood on his arms. He was breathing slowly, and Ariana sat at the foot of the bed. She held his hand and spoke to him quietly.

"I know you can't hear me, Jules, but I just wanted to say that…I love you so much, and even if the sun came down and lit everything on fire, I wouldn't stop looking until I found you and had you in my arms." Then, all of a sudden, Julian's hand returned the pressure. His eyes fluttered open, and he gave Ariana a brilliant smile, which Ariana returned.

"I thought you were asleep!" Ariana said.

"I was," Julian answered as Ariana helped him into a sitting position, "but I heard your voice and woke up."

"How do you feel?"

"Well," Julian considered the question for a moment, "honestly?"

"Honestly."

"I feel kind of dizzy, and excited, like the moment before you open a present. But I don't think that this has anything to do with the disease."

"Okay," Ariana grinned at Julian, "then, what's making you feel dizzy and excited?"

"Um…" Julian said and reddened. "…you?" He was looking down, but Ariana could see how flushed he was becoming because of her sheer presence. Knowing that she had this much of an effect on him, just sitting near him and holding his hand made her redden a bit, too. Then, he spoke.

"You told me that you loved me when we couldn't see each other. Now that you have seen me, …I guess I just wanted to know if you…you know…" he broke off.

"Still loved you?" Ariana finished.

Julian nodded quickly, still looking down at the white sheets of the infirmary bed. Ariana's eyes softened. "As long as the sun continues to rise in the morning and the stars twinkle in the sky at night, I shall love you, with all of my being, till one of us ceases to exist, for I care not what you appear like, but for what is inside of your being."

Julian's pure hazel eyes were large now. "Ari, that means everything to me."

Ariana's eyes got a bit dark. "You mean everything to me." Then, she leaned down and kissed him.

It was like swimming in the dark, but Julian was bringing her down and under. It didn't feel like drowning though- it felt like waking up.

* * *

Alana sat perched upon her clothing wardrobe. At her elbow was every glass cup she could gather. Her tongue traced the line of her lip as she picked one up, threw her arm back, and chucked it at the floor. It landed with a satisfying crash and broke into very small pieces. She had never once stopped to think about why she was doing this, and what the consequences of her actions might be. She supposed that she liked to hear the sound of the delicate glass shattering into pieces, but deep down, she knew exactly why she was doing this.

Each glass was delicate and ornately patterned, each perfectly identical to the others, and each as clear as crystal. She supposed that maybe that was why she was breaking them. Nothing perfect and good in the world could remain now that Peter was gone.

She remembered a different time, a different day, a different year. The sun was shining high up in the sky, bringing goodness, warmth, and light to everything in the world.

Except for Alana.

It was the day that she had escaped the Infernum, and found the Sanctuary of New Jersey, which, at the time was being led by Thomas Lancaster, who later moved to California to look into a spirit group that was causing trouble in Los Angeles. She was sitting all alone in her room, on top of this very wardrobe, and refused to come down.

That was, until Peter.

Peter knocked on the door, and she opened it, only because he kept knocking even after the first thirty minutes that she pretended not to hear him. In he came, with a large messenger bag slung across his shoulder.

"Pardon me, but you look like you need a friend," he told her.

Alana sniffed and hugged her knees closer to her chest. Peter then started to attempt to climb to the top of the wardrobe. To Alana, climbing things was as easy as tying your shoelaces, and after a few failed attempts, she pitied him and held out a hand. He took it and climbed onto the top of the clothing wardrobe. Panting a bit, he sat next to Alana.

They were rather peculiar. Both children were only five years old but had been exposed to many atrocities of the world that most five-year-olds didn't face. Alana fashioned her hair then the same way she did today- let it hang loose and short. It curtained around her face and hid her expression as she rested her forehead on her knees. The child form of Peter, hair redder than ever, freckles playing across his pale face, skinny and slight, hesitated before delicately taking one of Alana's shaking, pale hands. She did not react.

"Want to go somewhere that might take your mind off things for a bit?" A moment passed in silence before Alana nodded gratefully. She had been chained in a dark room full of spirits, had seen death for the first time, and

she missed her parents so very much. She very much needed to go somewhere to take her mind off of things.

"Okay. Where do you have in mind?" Alana asked in a quiet voice.

The small, scrawny and green-eyed little boy's eyes had widened so much that one might compare them to a beach ball. He clearly hadn't thought he had a chance. "You'll see. I think you'll love it." He told her, grinning.

Alana jumped down from the wardrobe as Peter watched in awe. He attempted to climb down from the top of the wardrobe in the safest way possible. When he finally successfully made it to the ground, he stood triumphantly and righted his oversized brown messenger bag. It looked a bit awkward on him- the shoulder strap had been adjusted to fit his short height, but the width of the bag was two times the size of his chest. Alana didn't question it. Then, she noticed that Peter was staring at her with big green eyes.

"What?"

"Can I hold your hand?"

Alana shrugged. "Sure, I guess." She held her hand out to him, and he took it eagerly.

They walked through the woods to a large, overgrown field. Alana supposed it might have been a part of a farm, but the house near it was completely deserted. She figured it wasn't trespassing if the people who own the property don't know or care that you were there. Peter led her through the undergrowth to a large peach tree. They climbed the tree. Peter was able to climb with Alana's help. They picked peaches and put them in Peter's messenger bag. When they were done, they climbed down sat in the shade of the wide tree. Alana bit into a peach, ate a few bites, then handed it to Peter, who did the same. She still remembered how it tasted-it was a perfect combination of sweet, sour, and tart. It smelled so citrusy and good, and she remembered watching the sunset, with Peter's fingers still entwined in hers. Peter had reached into his messenger bag, then and pulled out a daisy as pure and white as a dove. His big green eyes searched her gray ones for permission, and when she smiled at him, he reached up and put it in her dark, raven-colored hair. She remembered looking at the fiery tail of sparks that the sun left behind. Peter was looking at her as if she were the sun, if he could stare at the sun directly without damaging his eyesight. In his mind, she was just like the sun, shining brightly and lighting everything around it ablaze, such as his own, young heart.

He had felt as though if everything and everyone could freeze right here, if he could just be here, next to Alana, holding her hand and watching the sun set, that he wouldn't need anything else. For this girl's eyes, this curious, wild, spirited girl's beautiful gray eyes seemed to hold the key to every lock, the answer to every question, and the cure to every ailment. She was all he never knew he needed, and it seemed that if he had her, she'd be the last piece to his puzzle, and he'd finally be complete.

His parents went on patrol in Nevada, where there had been many reports of rogue spirits. As Peter was still very young, they had left him behind at the Sanctuary for his own safety.

They had never come back.

He had broken after that had happened, and so he tried to pick himself back up, and he had succeeded, for the most part. Alana seemed to be the last part of him left to be picked up and stitched back together.

But she had never known that.

In fact, now that she thought about it, it seemed quite obvious. He had always worried about Alana, because he loved her. He always had her back, and it seemed that no matter where she went, Peter would be there beside her, to help her, to guide her, and to protect her. That was why she was still in shock that he was gone forever. He even agreed to go along with her to save Charlie, because he didn't want her to get hurt, and because finding Charlie, though it would hurt him to see Alana with Charlie, would make her happy. He had covered up his pain and wounds to bring happiness to Alana.

How hadn't his feelings for her been obvious?

All of a sudden, something caught her eye. The weak sunlight that filtered through the window stopped to rest on a shiny piece of metal just below her neck.

It was the necklace that Peter gave her.

However, there seemed to be something else of interest in the glinting piece of metal. The specific area that was caught by the beam of afternoon sunshine was not the chain nor the border of the gray cat's eye gemstone. It was a screw, for this necklace was not a necklace, but a locket. Alana didn't have enough energy to be intrigued. Tiredly, her long, skilled fingers opened the locket with a click, and a piece of paper that had been folded many times into a very small square fell out and landed on the top of the wardrobe. Alana didn't notice that when the locker was opened, the two teardrop shapes fit together to make a heart. She picked up the piece of paper and unfolded it.

There, in the middle of the paper in golden ink was a note addressed to her in Peter's neat cursive. Her eyes scanned the page eagerly with newly gained energy.

Dear Alana,

It's been so long since I met you, but I can't seem to remember the time before I knew you. It simply seems gray, barren, and unimportant. I've known how I felt about you for fifteen years, and I've accepted that you might not feel the same way, but I just wanted to tell you that I love you. I love you more than you can ever know, for you are the sparks to my fire. You light me up, like nobody else. You've started a fire in my heart that I can't seem to put out. I just thought that after all this time, it was only fair that I told you the truth.

~With hope, Peter

42

It's Not Like You

A tticus and Roslyn stood in line to purchase tickets at the nearby AMC. The brilliant, bright lights made an already very nervous Atticus practically blind with worry. Roslyn, who stood beside him in a short black dress, was glowing brightly in comical contrast to her clothes. Her smile was so wide that Atticus found himself wondering more than once if her jaw hurt.

"What movie do you want to watch?" asked Roslyn.

Atticus turned to her as though it were the first time he had noticed that she was there. After a moment of pondering, he answered, "Anything you like."

Roslyn reached over and grabbed his hand. "That's sweet." She looked up at the screen over the counter, which projected a list of all of the movies that would be shown today. "How about a romance movie?"

"Sounds good," Atticus lied, sounding a bit far away as he looked out the window. Roslyn smiled, apparently not noticing. When it was their turn, Roslyn told the man at the counter the name of the movie they had chosen, and she chose their seats towards the back where they might be able to scavenge the tiniest amount of privacy. When it was time to pay, Atticus pulled out his wallet.

"No, let me pay," Roslyn protested, but Atticus shook his head, sliding a twenty dollar bill across the counter. When he had collected his change and their tickets, they headed over to the screening rooms.

Here, a rather short lady with an impish grin and short red hair ripped off a section of their tickets and permitted them across the gate. "The movie starts in fifteen minutes, if you don't mind waiting," she notified them.

Roslyn looked over at Atticus lovingly and tugged his arm. "We don't mind."

Atticus looked down at Roslyn and forced a smile onto his face. It wasn't that he didn't care for her much, but something was wrong.

However, Roslyn was far too high up in the clouds to notice, and she only beamed and led him into screening room five.

They found their seats at the back and were very pleased to find that they were recliner seats. Roslyn pulled her seat all the way out. They were quiet for a moment, and Atticus nervously played with his hair, a habit that originated from back when he was a small child and had to keep from showing his anxiety to Ana, an even smaller child, who would surely start crying if the only person she had left to look to for guidance couldn't take it anymore.

Roslyn took his hand from his hair and gently turned his face to face hers. Atticus gave her a tentative smile, though he didn't quite feel it.

"Tell me a secret," Roslyn prompted.

Atticus pondered his thoughts. None of them were coherent or made sense. He shook his head, frustrated.

"What's wrong?" Roslyn asked gently.

"Nothing," Atticus managed.

"You know you can tell me anything, right?"

Atticus nodded, his expression clearly giving away that something was terribly wrong, but his long hair hid his expression.

Something was wrong. Something that he couldn't quite put his finger on.

Atticus looked around, trying to find something to focus on to help bring his attention away from the throbbing pain in his head. He focused on Roslyn's dress. He saw Roslyn every single day, and had been over to her house plenty of times before, but he didn't remember seeing this dress before.

Moreover, it was very *un-Roslyn.*

She never wore dresses, not ever, not even to weddings. She was also characterized by positive thoughts, and never wore black. She liked to look on the bright side of things. Lastly, her clothes were mostly modest, like Ana, and preferred to wear jeans even during summer. The dress she had on was the exact opposite of that, small and lacy, with a low neckline and short skirt that barely reached the tops of her thighs. The color was a sort of black that made her look rather pale but brought out little specks of black luster in her dark green eyes.

"Shall I start?" asked Roslyn.

Atticus nodded again, only too eager not to say anything, for he was afraid that if he opened his mouth, bile might flood out.

Roslyn started to speak about something, but it all garbled into one big mess, for Atticus could not differentiate each word from the other. Something in the background buzzed loudly, and Atticus shook his head imperceptibly. Everything he saw crashed and collided and burned, and Atticus faintly felt his eyes tear up.

"You're staring at my dress," Roslyn said, breaking Atticus out of his thoughts with a start. "Do you like it?"

"No," Atticus said rather abruptly, and immediately regretted it. Roslyn's smile, as bright as a sunflower, had faded infinitesimally.

"Oh," she said. "I thought you would. I bought it for you."

Atticus looked down at his own clothes. He had thrown on a long-sleeved white t-shirt this morning and a pair of worn blue jeans. His hair was tousled, his black and white checkered Vans rather dirty. And though it was hard to see just how soiled they were in the dark of the theater, Atticus still felt his cheeks heat up when he saw how much trouble Roslyn had gone to for him and how much he hadn't for her.

"I'm sorry," Atticus said.

"That's alright," Roslyn said kindly. "This color just doesn't fit me."

"No," Atticus shook his head, looking up. "It's not that. It's not like you. Wait- is that lipstick?"

Roslyn nodded. "I borrowed it from my mother."

Atticus shook his head, not understanding. "Why?"

Roslyn smiled contentedly. "For you."

"Why me?"

Roslyn furrowed her eyebrows. "I don't know. I thought this was what boys liked."

Atticus felt faintly insulted, being taken with a population and being forced to a stereotype. He balled his hands into fists and pressed it into his abdomen. The feeling had come back. He was feeling sick, sick, sick. "What? Tiny, nonexistent dresses and redder than human lips?"

Roslyn blushed, bringing some much needed color into her face. "So you don't like it?"

He shook his head immediately, making Roslyn's smile fade ever so slightly, then nodded his head immediately.

Something is very wrong with me today.

"I like it," Atticus forced. "You look nice."

"No, you don't," Roslyn countered, seeing through it. Her excitement had faded, leaving a sort of unknowing sadness in its wake. "Tell me what's wrong, and I'll change it. Do you not like this color? Shall I change it? Is this dress not short enough?"

"No, stop it." Atticus shook his head. "Stop it, please."

"Tell me what's wrong," Roslyn pleaded. "I'll fix it for you."

Atticus shook his head, feeling more and more sick by the moment. "You look great."

Roslyn nodded, looking unconvinced. "Thank you."

The screen had lit up now, and ads were playing across the screen. Atticus focused on the large popcorn on the screen, but he could feel Roslyn's eyes on him.

The advertisements faded, and the movie started up. It was very dull, and Atticus rather hoped he had stayed home and declined Roslyn's invitation. The fact that he was feeling sick did not make the situation much better.

Halfway through, Roslyn said, "You look good tonight."

Atticus looked down at himself. His shirt had been filled out by his wide shoulders, but he had had to use a belt to keep his jeans from sagging, as he had a smaller waist than was usual for most seventeen-year-old boys. However, he was also rather lanky, and had to purchase his jeans in larger sizes in order for them to actually reach his ankle, which meant he almost always needed a belt set to the smallest hole. Still, it sagged ever so slightly, exposing an inch of skin between his jeans and the bottom of his shirt, where the skin indented slightly.

"Thank you," murmured Atticus, who didn't look up from the screen, still trying to hide his expression from his companion.

"You're welcome. I don't like your shirt, though."

Atticus examined his shirt, searching for any stains. There were none. "What's wrong with my shirt?"

"It's ugly. You should take it off."

Atticus frowned. He might have been wrong, but he was fairly certain that Roslyn was flirting with him. *Since when did Roslyn flirt?*

"I'll change it when I get home," Atticus said, hoping he was wrong.

"That's not what I meant," Roslyn contradicted, proving him to be correct.

Atticus stood immediately and excused himself to use the restroom. When he got past the hallway, he practically ran to the restroom and threw up in the toilet.

It wasn't the movie. Something had been very, very wrong, since before the movie had even started.

Heading over to the sink and splashing cool water onto his face, he looked into the mirror. He looked as he always had- curly, wild brown hair and amber eyes. His dark mole showed up in stark contrast against his newly pale face. His chest heaved, his head hurt. He wanted to bang his head against a wall repeatedly until he passed out.

Slowly, he sank to the floor, his head against the bathroom stall.

A knock on the door. Then, someone's voice from far away.

"Atticus? Are you alright in there?"

Atticus swallowed, not answering.

"Atticus?"

He took a deep breath. "I'm fine. You go on without me."

"Okay." Footsteps sounded, quieter and quieter each time. When they finally stopped, Atticus took another deep breath.

I'm so tired.

43

Blood and Roses

On Friday, Ana walked up to the roof with a heavy heart. She dressed in a very pretty semi-formal outfit- a bright red dress of soft satin, with black swirls decorating the hem. Wearing such a bright color was odd considering her usual dressing style- Her usual outfits consisted of a blouse, usually in a pale, pastel color, and jeans. Her clothing choices were almost always modest; her hair always worn up in her two elegant braids to keep them from frizzing up. However, she had taken the time to straighten it out today. Today, it lay across her shoulders in beautiful, elegant waves. She looked like a fairytale princess.

And in her patient, hopeful, nervous hand, she held a single rose. It was a nervous habit of hers- grabbing onto something small like a little toy for her fingers to play with. It often calmed her down and helped her with her anxiety. She wasn't always anxious; she had only newly gained it after her parents had died. She had been very young, and though Atticus did everything in his power to comfort her and hide his suffering from her eyes, she wasn't blind. She could understand, and she knew that her parents weren't coming back.

Now that she was older, she took her mind off of things by training. Hard. The training and the pain helped her get her mind off of things for a few, meager, ecstatic minutes. It also helped her reassure herself that the spirits would take no one else that she loved, for she would prevent that from happening. No longer would they take what was precious and loved and smash it into small pieces under their uncaring feet.

A sound of an old wooden door creaking drew Ana's eager eyes.

Carter, dressed casually in shorts and a t-shirt that advertised an old band, stepped out of the shadows. When he saw her in her dress, his eyes widened astronomically, his jaw dropped, and he flushed red. Ana's reaction, however, was its polar opposite. Her face paled, her smile dropped, and her eyes fell down.

She looked like a once beautiful but now faded flower.

Carter stammered at the sight of her. "Ana...I...I thought...I thought that...I thought we were hanging out as...you know...friends."

A spectator might have commented that everything turned stormy and gray. It was almost as if Ana's rose wilted.

Ana shook her head now, her eyes still on the ground. "That's...that's quite alright. I just thought...well, it was foolish of me."

"No, it wasn't." Carter sounded appalled. "I'm really sorry, Ana, I really am, but I like where we are right now. I'm not really looking for a relationship. I don't want love to ruin our friendship."

"I understand," Ana said in a choked voice.

"Maybe...maybe we could still hang out, but as friends?" Carter tried, but Ana had already fled.

Storming down the stairs, her red dress parading behind her like a mocking flower, Ana could feel the tears forming in her throat. Hot and slippery, the tears ran down her cheeks silently until she slammed the door to her bedroom shut. She was not angry at Carter, but only angry at herself. How could she ever hope, ever believe that he could love someone like her? She was so uninteresting, so plain, so modest and boring. Now that she was all alone, she let the rest of the tears come down through her in waves. It ran through her like a raging storm, forcing against her young heart and banging her chest, leaving her heaving on the ground. When all of the tears had finally left her, and when there were no more tears left in her body to shed, she took a panting stop. She picked the now bent rose up from the ground where she had thrown it in grief, and the thorns pricked her skin.

Blood stained her pale fingers, but she felt no pain. She rocked himself back
and forth then and waited while the warm and flowery smelling summer
breeze that entered the room through her open window blew her hair into
her eyes, and her heavy and broken heart longed to be light again.

* * *

A knock on the vast, mahogany door woke Alana out of her daydreams.
Alana answered it and gestured for Cassandra to come in and sit down.
Alana rarely ever daydreamed, she was usually too busy planning battles,
attacks, recoveries, strategizing, or studying the magical properties of
certain magical reactions to daydream, but the past few days had left her in
a haze. She felt as though the days that she had Peter by her side had gone
past quickly without her knowledge or her permission, and she was left
dizzy from the run, without no one to guide her. No, she couldn't turn to
Peter for help, support, and guidance anymore. Peter was gone, gone to
where no one could follow him.

Cassandra was staring intently at Alana now. "What?"

"I just asked you a question."

"Oh. I'm so sorry, could you repeat that?"

"Oh, that's fine. I can come back another time."

"No, it's alright. I need a distraction anyway."

"Are you sure?"

"Yeah."

"Okay. First of all, I'm so sorry for your loss. Peter was amazing, and
nothing I say is going to make up for him, so I'm sorry."

"Thank you."

"You're welcome. Also, the second thing was," she began and pulled out
the locket on which the ballerina was attached by a small metal link. Alana's
gray eyes widened when she saw the ballerina. Numbly, she reached out
but stopped before she did. She looked up at her sister.

"May I?"

"Of course. I just wanted to show you, because…this is going to sound crazy, but…I think it's showing me stuff."

Alana touched the ballerina's pink dress and delicate feet. Then, she looked up again.

"I need to show you something."

They went into the artifacts room, and Alana showed Cassandra the identical jewelry box.

"They both have the power to show you parts of your past, which are significant to your present and future. They were made by our ancestors, Clarissa and Ryan Black." Alana was telling her. "Don't worry; you're not going insane."

Cassandra looked at the jewelry box in wonder. She reached out and traced the line with her slim, pale fingers. Alana smiled. "What did happen to the rest of it?" she asked curiously.

"Oh, that," Cassandra said grimly as if remembering an unpleasant memory. "Helen broke it."

"Who's Helen?"

"My evil cousin."

"You know, you don't have to go back there, right? You could stay here, with us, at the Sanctuary. You have so much to learn about our world. You could even start your training."

Now Cassandra looked up. "Really?"

Alana shrugged and smiled. "I don't see why not,"

Cassandra looked happier than Alana had ever seen her. Cassandra leaped into her elder sister's open arms, and they stayed that way for some time.

44

Green Light

J amie was freaking out. He had changed his jeans close to 25 times, tucked and untucked his t-shirt, and practiced in the mirror. Plus, he made flashcards.

He feverishly checked the clock at his bedside table, and his eyes widened perceptibly. He went incredibly pale.

It was time to go.

Jamie walked as slowly as he could to Cassandra's room and knocked on the door. She answered it. There was loud rap music playing in the background, and Cassandra's hair was slightly mussed as if she had just gotten up. She was wearing a black camisole and gray sweatpants. Her hair had been tied up into a messy ponytail, and she was barefoot. She smiled when she saw Jamie.

"Hey, Jamie. What's up?" she murmured sleepily. Jamie's heart sunk. It seemed to show on his face, because Cassandra's eyes widened astronomically and she turned a bit red. "OH, SHIT! Today's our…you know what. I'll go change right away. Sorry, Jamie." She leaned in and gave him a quick kiss, which seemed to have a chemical reaction in him. Suddenly, he couldn't remember why he was here.

"That's fine." Jamie murmured. Cassandra shut the door, changed quickly into ripped jeans and a t-shirt, which amazingly, didn't advertise a band. She brushed her hair out as quickly as she could and fastened it on top of her head in a messy bun. After splashing some water onto her face so that she didn't look as if she just woke up, she walked over to the door and wrenched it open. She was very amused to see that Jamie was studying flashcards.

She smirked as Jamie attempted to play it cool and failed miserably. He started to stuff the flashcards into his pocket as quickly as he could and gave her what he hoped was a totally chill smile.

"Just studying for a biology test."

Cassandra cocked an eyebrow at him. "It's summer."

Jamie turned bright red. "Right. I'm anticipating a biology test when we start senior year."

Cassandra, who had bent over and picked up a flashcard that had fallen to the ground, asked, "Then, why does it have my name in it?"

"Oh, ...um...that's just an example. Like...Cassandra has two cups, one has a 0.5% solute, and the other has 0.2% solute. Which one does water travel easier from?" Jamie stammered while snatching the flashcard out of her hand and pushing it into his pocket.

"Cool," said Cassandra cluelessly. "Do you want me to quiz you?"

Jamie's eyes widened. "Nope. No, I'm good. You don't have to quiz me. I'm fine. I've got it."

Cassandra still had no idea what was going on. Her lips twisted slightly, and her eyes indicated that she was amused. "Okay."

"So, are you ready?" Jamie's flush traveled up to his ears the way it only did when he was extremely embarrassed. He was staring down at his shoes as if he were asking a question that was at the heights of impropriety, a question forbidden to all the world, but that hadn't stopped his lips from uttering the unholy words.

"Yeah. Are you?" Cassandra asked casually.

Jamie forced himself to look up. "Honestly, not really. I am not ready for this. Let's go back and try another time." Jamie turned to leave, but Cassandra caught his hand.

"No. Don't go."

Jamie looked back up at her with big green eyes. "Do you mean that?"

"Yes. Whatever this is, whatever this whole love thing is, I want it. Don't you?" she asked him earnestly.

He looked up, and she could see the desire in his eyes. "So much."

"Then, what are we waiting for?" She placed multiple kisses on his neck, then pulled him out the door and into the sunlight.

Jamie grinned, hands on the steering wheel, the road ahead of him dark and soaked with the pouring rain. It was highly unusual for it to rain quite this much in the summer. This weather would have been acceptable three months ago, in April. However, Jamie didn't mind much. He knew that one of Cassandra's most favorite things in the world were rain. Now, turning slightly, a very large feat for someone who had once campaigned against texting while driving and was a firm believer in safe driving, he saw Cassandra sitting just beside him, eyes open and mesmerized as she watched a raindrop draw its path down the window ahead. Jamie liked this, how he could watch Cassandra without her knowing that she was being watched. If she knew that he was watching her, admiring the way her lips tilted ever so slightly at the ends, watching the falling rain, if she knew that his heart raced faster and his chest felt a pang when he observed the beautiful, long, dark curves of her eyelashes, and how they fluttered when she blinked, if she knew that he loved the way her hair fell into her eyes and the perfect, impatient way she flicked it away from her face, as if it didn't matter, she probably wouldn't do it. All that she did, everything that was a part of her was purely there by accident. She was Cassandra, his own beautiful Cassie, and she was purely herself by accident. It was one of the things that he loved most about her.

If she knew that he was admiring and cherishing her for every little, minuscule piece of her being, she would try to better in her mind. She would try to appear cooler, smarter, funnier, better. It was another aspect of Cassandra that he had long past figured out. She had never thought she was good enough. She always tried to be what she thought was better in her mind, and always failed at being better than what she originally was. Jamie knew this, and he hoped that he could convince her to be herself in time.

Jamie didn't know that the corners of his eyes wrinkled, the way it always did when a guy really liked someone, when he looked at Cassandra. Jamie didn't know that he stared at Cassandra's lips as intently as he did, as though it were the one thing in the world that mattered. Jamie didn't know that he was about to run a red light.

"Jamie! Red light!" Cassandra said, turning away from the rain with a look of alarm and surprise at Jamie's sudden change of character.

Slamming his foot down savagely on the brake of his car, Jamie narrowly avoided being presented with a ticket. Jamie's cheeks pinked adorably as he considered whether or not Cassandra knew the reason for his blunder. She didn't seem to, and for that, he was thankful.

When they finally exited New Jersey and entered New York, Jamie resolved to drive with caution, as there was quite a cacophony of traffic ahead of them. Cassandra finger-picked an air guitar. Jamie knew that this was a nervous habit of hers. Butterflies fluttered around in Jamie's stomach when he saw that Cassandra was just as nervous as he was.

"Why are we nervous?" Jamie asked.

To his surprise, Cassandra flushed. "I'm not nervous."

"Yes, you are. You're strumming your air guitar."

Cassandra dropped her hands. "Well, shit."

Jamie laughed. "It's alright. I'm nervous, too."

Cassandra seemed truly bewildered now. "Why are you nervous?"

"Because I've been waiting for this moment my whole life."

Cassandra laughed, a sweet sound that Jamie wished he could get lost inside of. "No, you haven't. You're joking."

"I'm not," Jamie said truthfully. "This is on the top ten list of things I do before I die."

"What are the other nine?" Cassandra asked, curiously, smiling cleverly.

Jamie's cheeks pinked once again. "I'd rather not say."

Cassandra gasped playfully. "You're going to keep me guessing? No fair!"

"Oh, I think you'll find them out soon enough."

"I'm intrigued."

"I'm glad you're intrigued."

They were nearing Beacon Theater now, and Jamie started looking for a parking lot. After paying a rather round man with graying hair, who sat inside of a small hut with some rather ominous gang symbols, Jamie and Cassandra stepped out of the dented, black Ford and into the pouring rain. Jamie pulled out an umbrella and opened it up, holding it up above their heads. However, the umbrella was quite small, so they had to stand very close to each other.

When they neared the theater, they found that there were quite a few others who enjoyed Lorde's music. A very lengthy line fished out from the wide-open entrance of Beacon Theatre, security guards in flashy vests zooming around like little bumblebees in a garden full of flowers. Many people were exhibiting their indignation at having to wait out in the rain in some very obnoxious manners. However, Jamie didn't mind sharing his tiny space with Cassandra, cramped together under the puny black umbrella, watching raindrops puddling together in pools across the distressed streets of Manhattan, sleek, shiny cars sliding down the road like a hot knife through butter.

Jamie didn't want anything else. He cared not for kisses and lips, skin and heat, touch, and action. It was at moments like these at which he loved Cassandra most. Just watching her blink raindrops away from where they had been caught up in her eyelashes when water fell sideways onto their mortal skin was enough for him. Just living and existing and breathing the same air as her, watching her, being beside her, knowing her and all her quirks was enough for him. He didn't want or need anything else. Not gold nor glory could make him feel more purely *happy* than being here with Cassandra today, and sharing this one experience.

All everyone else saw was a sappy, lovesick puppy, but to be honest, he had approximately zero shits to give them on this issue.

Upon entering the extravagant and beautifully architectured building, the pair was admitted into a chain of security guards who took to putting their belongings through a scanner to avoid any fatalities caused by potential weapons. Cassandra had wanted to bring her dagger with her "in case" (she was very into sword fighting), but Jamie had advised her against it.

After they finally passed the security line, they made their way to the entrance to the theater hall and had their tickets checked by yet another security guard. When she gave them back and admitted them in, she wished them a terrific show. They walked in and found and took their seats. They were in the first row, courtesy of Jamie's excellent judgment. It was then that the excitement finally settlement and Cassandra started to squeal hysterically like a possessed fangirl. Jamie, now thoroughly entertained, watched on amusedly for ten minutes until the chaos finally subsided.

"What just happened?"

Cassandra took a deep breath before speaking. "I don't exactly know. I've seen other people do it. I thought that it was a socially acceptable thing to do."

Jamie nodded, a smile playing upon his soft lips.

"When faced with the social hierarchy of our very biased communities, one is often forced to choose between acting the way that they choose and acting the way everyone else deems correct in order to appear superior to the surrounding population. I guess that I'm so used to acting the first that I wanted to try out the latter to see how it feels."

"Who are you, and what have you done with my Cassie?" He promptly turned the shade of the setting sun after saying this, realizing his trip. My Cassie. Not Cassie. My Cassie.

Cassandra seemed to have noticed too, for she blushed as well, and blushed hard. It made Jamie blush even more to know that she was blushing at him. What she did next, however, baffled and surprised him.

She weaved her fingers through his.

"Your Cassie. After all these years, I'm just glad *somebody* wants me. I've been abandoned for twelve years. Now, I have a sister, a lover, a best friend, a *family*." She said this all looking down so as to shield her innermost hurt and pain from Jamie, where they had failed to be masked away after twelve years of hiding.

Jamie pushed her chin up and forced her to look him in the eye. "Don't you ever say that, do you hear me? You are loved. I have always wanted you, and I will always want you. No matter how badly you screw up, though I will tell you that you have, I will still want you. Your being," he added, "not your body. I would still love you if your face was ugly. If you were missing a leg, or two, or an arm, or all your limbs. Hell, I'd love you if you looked like a female version of The Hunchback of Notre Dame," he said truthfully, with an odd look of complete affection in his eyes.

"If?" Cassandra asked, puzzled. "My face is ugly."

Jamie laughed at how much she didn't understand. How did she not understand that she was so beautiful precisely because she didn't try? How could she possibly think that she was not beautiful? Didn't she know that she was the only reason he woke up in the morning? Didn't she know that whenever he saw her, he just wanted to kiss her, for true beauty is more than just looks, and that he saw the exact definition of beauty in her? Couldn't she see that he saw all that he ever needed in her eyes?

Cassandra frowned. "What's so funny?"

"You. You don't even know that you're so beautiful. And you know what? I've been wondering what made you so pretty for my whole life, and I think that the fact that you don't know that you are perfect is what is so beautiful about you."

Cassandra's eyes had widened, and she had flushed red. A few moments passed in silence before Cassandra interrupted it again. Jamie gazed at her dreamily without even knowing it.

"Jamie."

Jamie was abruptly pulled from his thoughts. "Yes, Cassie?"

"Why are you looking at me like that?"

"I'm not looking at you like anything."

Cassandra smiled amusedly. Jamie cleared his throat and hurriedly changed the subject before he lost his self-respect.

"So, why were you acting all weird?"

Cassandra grimaced. "I'm nervous," she finally confided after a while.

"What do we even have to be nervous about, anyway? We've known each other our whole life. We're just hanging out, the way we've done since we were little kids. Now isn't any different."

"Except for the fact that you have quite clearly added the Latin prefix of "boy" to the original title of "friend" that you used to hold. And that you can kiss me without making me think that you're on crack. And—"

305

"Hey. It's alright. I guess that it's easier for me, because the way that I feel about you hasn't changed. I guess it will change in time, but know that you don't need to be nervous when you're around me. Just know that I will love you either way. I will love you always." His eyes were wide and true and green, and Cassandra just knew that this was the sole truth, and whether he liked it or not, he could never change this.

Suddenly, the lights started to dim. When no one was able to see her, she took advantage of the masked haze and whispered into Jamie's ear.

"May I?"

Jamie didn't think twice. "Of course."

Slowly, she leaned into him, resting her head on his broad shoulders. His hair tickled her neck, and her face involuntarily broke into a grin.

"Is this alright with you? Is this okay? Is this—"

"Yes," Jamie said around a smile. "This is perfect."

The lights on the stage turned on. The waiting music dropped, shortly replaced by the background of Green Light from Melodrama. Jamie lined kisses across Cassandra's neck, and she gasped at the sudden amorous sensation. An elderly couple gave them nasty looks, but Jamie paid no heed.

An ear-shattering sound notified that Lorde had entered the scene. And indeed she had, standing in a stunning, short silver dress. There she stood, glamorous and knowing it, singing Green Light like there was no tomorrow. Cassandra promptly went insane.

As they crossed the street after the concert, Jamie marveled at Cassandra's gray-blue eyes as she watched the cascading rain. They were on the sidewalk outside of a large, abandoned building made almost entirely of brick with little windows that had been shattered in. Cassandra seemed to be utterly mesmerized with everything, and she watched the way the dark bricks seemed to get even darker with the rain. She admired the way the flower petals jumped up and down when large collections of rainwater fell down from the leaves of the small tree that hovered above when Jamie could no longer take it. He dropped the umbrella, took Cassandra into his arms, and gently touched his lips to hers. Cassandra gasped, then succumbed to his touch. He drew away suddenly, peering into her eyes to see if she wanted

306

it or not. All around them, New Yorkers walked around them, completely oblivious to the loud and fast pounding in the young pairs' chests. Cassandra gave him a look that said it all, and it was an expression of surprise and giddiness, consent and hope and joy and cheer. But mostly, it had love in it. Pure and unbound love, and Jamie could see that she saw everything that she needed in his eyes. He pushed her gently against the brick building and stepped so close to her that his breathing stirred her eyelashes, sparkling from each individual raindrop that had caught itself in its beautiful trap. Cassandra stared into Jamie's eyes as he eyed her lips. She stood on the tips of her feet, reaching up to put her arms around Jamie's neck, touching the sinfully silky locks of gold that grew softer around the softer, more vulnerable part of his neck. Jamie leaned down and kissed Cassandra the way he had wanted to for so long, their bodies pressed up against each other. It was like an explosion of color in a world of black and white. Jamie felt as

though he had sprouted wings and started to fly. He wondered if this was what being drunk felt like. He felt like he was high, high, high up above everything he had ever known to be true, flying unchained to the earth, happy, free.

Jamie's hands slid into Cassandra's hair marveling at its softness. Abruptly, he stopped, pulling away. Cassandra looked up at him with big questioning eyes, and Jamie stammered. She wanted another kiss.

"Are we sure we want to do this? If we do, there's no going back. If we do this, there will be no denying our feelings. We can never hide it away, the way we feel. This will make it feel so much more—real." Quite frankly, he looked as though someone just told him that his mother was found dead at the bottom of the sea. He was terrified. His young heart was racing, he was on a roller coaster, at that final moment before it goes down, and he'd never felt like this before.

"Okay, if you don't want to," Cassandra began, turning away to watch the falling rain.

"No! I mean, I do. So, so much. I just don't want to rush you into anything you aren't ready for," Jamie told her.

Cassandra smiled. "Okay." Something about the smile was so familiar and mischievous and perfect that Jamie could no longer hold himself back. All the self-control he had exerted over the years, holding himself back when he knew he loved her, seemed to fly out the window at that moment. He leaned in and kissed her, and everything else seemed to disappear. Everything disintegrated and turned into the air surrounding himself and this girl, to whom he had given all of his heart from the day that he took her hand and they walked away from the burning building. Cassandra seemed to have taken those very sparks and lit him on fire with it. Those sparks still existed, and they reignited every time she smiled at him the way she did.

Now the fire seemed to burn bigger and brighter than ever inside of him—the flame that she lit inside of him. Suddenly, he felt more alive, young, and happy than he had ever felt before. He knew that he needed nothing else but this and that he could die right now, and his life would be complete.

Acknowledgements

Imma try to keep this short so I don't bore you to death. I want to thank all of these people, without whom, I probably wouldn't have written this book (or even started it).

Mom and Dad, for pushing me to keep writing when I felt my book was a mess, and for telling me that my book was amazing when I was about to burn it.

Isabel Lindsay, who encouraged me to keep writing. You told me that my writing was amazing, even though we both know it wasn't. That meant a lot to me.

Shreya, my sister, who kept begging me to give her excerpts of the book while I was writing it, telling me that they were great, laughing at the funny parts, and begging for more. I love making people laugh, which was part of the reason why I wrote this book. Thank you for your encouragement.

Coach Bagley, Coach Mergner, and the cross country team for supporting me on my writing journey. You guys are the best.

Ashley Wyrick, my editor, for conveying exactly what needed to be changed in my book in the nicest and clearest way possible, why it needed to be changed, and for providing me with the resources to fix it.

And lastly, Anjana S. Gandavarapu, one of the greatest friends anyone could ever find in the world, for your encouragement.

~Shruthi